Also by Anne Girard

MADAME PICASSO

anne girard

platinum doll

MIRA

GIRARD, A.

MIRA®

ISBN-13: 978-0-7783-1866-8

Platinum Doll

Recycling programs
for this product may
not exist in your area.

For questions and comments about the quality of this book, please contact us at CustomerService@Harlequin.com.

www.MIRABooks.com

Printed in U.S.A.

First printing: February 2016
10 9 8 7 6 5 4 3 2 1

MAY - 9 2016

In memory of
Marlene Hanke
For more than words can express

platinum doll

"I wasn't born an actress, you know. Events made me one."

—Jean Harlow

CHAPTER ONE

April, 1928

"Slow down, Chuck, or you'll get us both killed!"

A giggle bubbled up through her as she clutched the scarf tied around her pillowy ash-blond hair. The ends of the floral silk flapped, billowing out like a sail in the warm sun.

In spite of her protest, she loved the speed. It brought the delicious sensation of being scared and excited at the same time. Giving in to the moment, she tipped her head back against the car seat of their convertible, tore off the scarf and let her hair fly away from her face.

Fresh air and sunshine could cleanse anything. Her mother always said it took the pockets of darkness away, and that seemed to be true in Hollywood especially. She said that very thing when they came here the last time, in 1923, when she was an impressionable child of twelve, and Harlean had never forgotten it. Mother still believed Hollywood was a magical place, even though she had been too old for that magic to turn her into a star.

Harlean felt the return of that old excitement as she entered this place again. Childhood memories flooded back as she and Chuck drove between endless orange groves beneath an arc of brilliant azure sky.

This impetuous trip was meant as an escape from the darker things they had left behind in the Midwest. The sudden way they had eloped last September, with Chuck twenty and she just sixteen, had only been the start of the turmoil. Then there were her grandfather Harlow's reproving words, and her mother's tearful charge that she had officially just ruined her life by marrying a spoiled boy, even though he had a trust fund. That had fomented Chuck's rabid desire to arrange their escape—and Harlean had agreed. After all, she had turned seventeen a month later, and so she, too, felt ready for a grown-up adventure.

She squeezed her summer-blue eyes closed and tipped her face up toward the sun, refusing to think about any of that anymore. When she opened her eyes again, she glanced over at her young husband, his nose dusted with a pale coppery spray of freckles, the waves of his wind-buffeted cinnamon-colored curls spilling onto his cheeks over stylish horn-rim sunglasses.

Men didn't have a right to be so appealing, she thought to herself. No matter who was angry with her back home for their impetuous trip to a justice of the peace six months earlier, she wasn't sorry she had gone against them to marry him. Really, was there anything more important than being in love with a man who took her breath away?

"I'm gonna do right by you, Harlean. See if I don't," he had earnestly promised her two days before they'd eloped, as they lay across the front seat of this same green roadster, wound together, bathed in perspiration. He didn't know it had not been her first time, but he had confessed it had been his. That had only made her love him more.

He gripped the steering wheel more tightly now as they

finally entered the vibrant city and then turned onto Sunset Boulevard.

Hollywood, she thought, her heart soaring. *I'm back!* Harlean hadn't a clue where they would sleep tonight, but she knew they were going to begin their married life here. They would work out the rest of the details later.

"So, does the place look any different to you, doll?"

"Oh, gosh, it hasn't changed a bit!" she replied excitedly as they passed Grauman's Chinese Theatre and a crowd of tourists milling outside looking for the footprints of their favorite motion picture stars. "Did I tell you we saw Miss Pola Negri there once before a picture show?"

"You've told me a few times," Chuck answered with a wink, followed by an indulgent grin.

"Most beautiful, exotic creature I ever saw." Harlean sighed wistfully at the memory of the dark-haired superstar, wrapped in ermine, waving and tossing kisses outside of the crowded theater.

"I've read everything about her in the movie magazines, you know. Mommie tried to get her autograph that day but it was too crowded. When the fans surged to close around her, Miss Negri ended up leaving without signing anything that day."

"Your mother was hoping a bit of Miss Negri's stardust would rub off on *her*, no doubt?"

Harlean heard the usual hint of sarcasm in his voice. It always showed up in discussions about her mother, who he knew perfectly well had tried everything to find her own stardom when they lived here last, but Harlean was determined to ignore it. Nothing in the world could ruin the excitement of today. "She tried to get the autograph *for me*. Mommie's idol was always Clara Bow."

"The 'It Girl,' hmm?"

"You knew people called her that?"

"Listen, doll, I'm not a complete dunce." He chuckled and took off extra fast from the intersection at Hollywood Boulevard and La Brea.

The drive soon took them onto a gracefully curving avenue lined with palm trees. She had only been this way once when she was here as a child. It was an up-and-coming residential area called Beverly Hills, dotted with chic, new homes. They had driven here the last time because her mother had wanted to show her the outside of the grand Beverly Hills Hotel.

"Everyone who is anyone stays here these days. All of the stars," Jean had told her daughter. "This is *the* place to be seen. If I catch a break, someday you and I won't be stuck down here on the street. We'll drive up and park beneath that big canvas awning, then sashay inside right along with the rest of them."

Harlean fought a wave of nostalgia as Chuck drove the roadster right up the long driveway, past the distinctive green hotel sign with the elegant scroll lettering.

"Where do you think you're going? We're sure to get caught," she gasped in a panic. "This is a private road, Chuck!"

"Yes it is, doll, only for the paying guests."

"My mother said this place costs a fortune!"

"Then it's a good thing I have one," he returned with a wink.

Chuck didn't like to talk about the accident that had left him wealthy, and he had only told her the story once. It was that night on this same car seat, with the top down, beneath a vast and sparkling canopy of stars.

"At least they died together," he had said quietly. "Father never could have gone on without Mother. She was his whole world. Like you are to me, Harlean. You're the best thing to happen to me, the only good thing since I lost them. Those were awful times and I never thought I'd be happy ever again until the night I met you."

Her heart wrenched. She couldn't imagine that sort of pain. "Oh, Chuck."

"No, I mean it, and I'm gonna marry you. I want what they had. I need it, and I'm going to do everything in my power to make you feel like a queen."

It was the sweetest thing anyone had ever said to her. It had felt like a fairy tale that night, like being swept up in one of the romantic novels she read.

And it brought out the longing for a relationship with her own father, a man who she saw so rarely after the divorce that he too might as well have been dead. Her gentle side came from him.

"You don't have to say that because of what we just did," she had said with a nervous laugh.

"I'm saying it because I love you, Harlean Carpenter. I'm crazy about you, and I *think* you feel the same about me."

"Of course I do, but I'm only sixteen, Chuck, and, jeez, you're just twenty."

"True, but I'm a rich twenty!" Pleased with the idea, he had smiled, his handsome face half in shadow from the moonlight. "Or I will be rich in November when I turn twenty-one and that trust fund is mine. Then I can take care of you in fine style. We can go anywhere in the world, do anything we want."

"You know Mommie said I can't get married before I'm eighteen."

"To hell with your *mommie*," he had snapped, but the vulnerable way he had just opened up to her about losing his parents in a horrific boating accident four years earlier, smoothed the harshest part of his tone.

"I'm sorry, doll. I shouldn't have said that." He gazed up at the sky for a long time and she knew he was considering what he was about to say. She could tell there was an internal struggle so she'd tried not to even move, fearing he would change his mind.

"It was the week after I turned sixteen. I was supposed to go out on the lake with my dad. He had it all planned. It was the thing we used to do together. He really loved that. 'Time with my boy,' he used to say. But I was being petulant that day, a real louse. I honestly don't even remember why, but I told him I wasn't going and that was that."

In spite of his achingly quiet monotone, Harlean could hear the tremble beneath it. "He had the trip planned so my mother went with him instead."

She watched a crystal tear fall from his eye onto the tip of his ear and disappear into a copper coil of hair. "She'd be alive today if I'd done what I was supposed to do."

She knew that meant he would have died in her place, but she couldn't bear to say what of course he already knew, and the guilt that must have been attached to that. Harlean touched his arm but he didn't react to it. The moment was extinguished when he sat up, composed again. His willingness to allow more of the recollection had vanished.

"I'm sorry for what I said about your mother earlier, but you can't let her run your life forever. Especially not once we're married. Then we will have each other to depend on, just the two of us."

It had never occurred to Harlean before that night beneath the stars that there might be a time she would want to avoid her mother's powerful sphere of influence and her deep, abiding love for her only child. The two of them had been a team since the divorce and that first trip they had made to Hollywood together, one underscored by their hopes and dreams.

What an adventure that had been!

The rooming house on Gramercy Place, with the tiny sagging beds and the paper-thin walls, her mother's auditions most days on the bustling Paramount and Fox studio lots, the parade of costumed actors that would pass by Harlean as she waited patiently outside on the curb with only a book to keep her company, and the promise of an ice-cream soda afterward... So many memories of that time would never leave her.

Harlean had known from an early age how much her mother relied on her as she tried to make it in the motion picture industry. They had become more like best friends than mother and daughter during those crazy, whirlwind days, and she had relished the sensation because it made her feel important to a mother she idolized.

Their bond became unbreakable, no matter what Chuck thought or felt about her. Harlean was determined to love them both, and have them both in her life, along with this exciting new chapter back in Hollywood. In time, she would convince him of that and they would learn to respect one another. The prospect of their future here was too thrilling for anything from the past to ruin it.

They pulled to a stop at the top of the incline before the monolithic white hotel. She nervously smoothed out the front of her skirt as she watched well-heeled guests coming and going through the main entrance. Women wore calf-length dresses, silk stockings, wide-brimmed hats or crocheted caps over stylishly bobbed hair set in tight finger waves. Men were turned out in expensive double-breasted camel-hair suit coats and fedoras. A bellman in a red uniform and white gloves rushed over to open her car door.

"We're really staying the night here?"

"We're paid up for the week. I wanted to surprise you," he said with pride.

Love really was like a whirlwind, she thought. It could catch you up and carry you along so that nothing else mattered.

They were shown to a large, terra-cotta roofed bungalow

overlooking an emerald-green lawn flanked by bougainvillea and hibiscus. The glistening new hotel swimming pool, surrounded by a ring of towering palm trees, lay beyond and gave everything a tropical feel. Harlean went to the patio door to take in the view past the painted wicker furniture while Chuck tipped the bellman and asked him to bring a bucket of ice. She knew it was for the bottle of bootleg gin he had buried in his suitcase. Never mind that Prohibition had made it illegal. Chuck always said that particular law didn't apply to people with money, or an ounce of ingenuity, anyway.

When she heard the door close, Harlean turned around, awestruck. "Everything is so beautiful."

"*You* are beautiful."

He came toward her, tall and sinewy, then drew her into an embrace. He always smelled like sandalwood cologne and Ivory soap. The combination was intoxicating. Sunlight streamed in behind them, making all of the silk, rose and gold-colored chintz in the room shimmer.

This was an enchanted place, just like all of Hollywood.

"Are you going in for a dip, to wash off a bit of that road dust?" he asked as he pressed a featherlight kiss onto her cheek, then another and another.

"I have a better idea," she said coyly.

"Oh?"

"Yes, much better," she said as she drew the draperies and luxuriated in the warmth of the sun. Then she wrapped her arms around his neck, closed her eyes and kissed him.

An hour later, Harlean dove gracefully beneath the surface of the sparkling turquoise water of the pool, then rose to the top with all of the finesse she had honed as an athletic tomboy not so long ago. After the way his parents had died, Chuck didn't like to swim, but he seemed perfectly content to sit on a padded chaise beside the pool on the patio and watch his young wife.

He was the first image that came into view when Harlean rose out from under the water, his face with a halo of sunlight behind him. She loved the way he looked at her, always with adoration and lust. The combination meant love to her. Most of the time, he really did seem like a character out of one of her favorite novels, a wealthy and handsome young man, who had come into her life and swept her away.

Energized by the swim, she smoothed her wet hair back from her face, then propped her elbows up onto the edge of the pool. Chuck, relaxing in his khaki shorts and white polo shirt, smiled down at her.

"How would you like to go to the pictures tonight after supper? *Lights of New York* is playing over at Grauman's."

"Oh, could we, Chuck? That's an actual talkie!"

"Your wish is my command," he said and made a gallant half bow from his waist.

"I love Grauman's. Mommie and I went there to see Lon Chaney in *The Hunchback of Notre Dame.* It's beautiful inside. That was the same night I saw Miss Pola Negri."

She came out of the pool and he wrapped her in the towel, then closed his arms around her.

After she dressed, they went to a cute little malt shop on Sunset Boulevard and sat in a red leather booth along the windows. Harlean loved the bustling city view.

She had changed into a conservative gray skirt, a short-sleeved rose-colored angora sweater, white socks and sneakers. He never liked the way men stared at her, even with her face freshly scrubbed, free of cosmetics, and her short blond hair brushed back from her face, yet they did anyway. She was as aware of their attention as he was, and she could feel Chuck bristle each time.

"Mommie always says it's just my hair that makes them look since there aren't many gals with my particular shade."

"More likely, it's the face and body that goes with it," he said, but he wasn't smiling.

She didn't like Chuck to feel jealous, but having been a bookish tomboy not so very long ago, secretly she reveled in the sensation she had when men acknowledged her. Mother had always been the beauty of the family, tall and shapely, with a dignified air. It had been difficult growing up in the shadow of what had seemed to her like a very bright light. But things were changing. She wasn't in that shadow at the moment. The sunshine belonged to her. Being back in an exciting city like Hollywood was only the beginning of a transformation that she could actually feel. It was exciting just to contemplate growing into her own version of womanhood here, and the things that might mean for her life with Chuck. She wished she could tell him about it, but she wouldn't dare. At least not yet.

The theater was packed since this first full-length talkie was the hottest ticket in town and people sat chattering excitedly and then cheering as the house lights were lowered. Harlean loved not having to read the dialogue and she found the new style of film, hearing what she was seeing, entirely captivating.

After it was over, and the audience had applauded, Harlean and Chuck walked outside beneath the bright theater lights and into the cool evening air. There were more handprints and signatures here now than when she was last here. It was exhilarating even to contemplate that stars like Mary Pickford, her husband, Douglas Fairbanks, Tom Mix and Harold Lloyd, true Hollywood royalty, had stood in these very spots and pressed their hands and shoes into wet cement to the cheers of adoring crowds.

She found Clara Bow's square and stood in those footprints for her mother's sake. She shivered at the feeling of being so close to the impression of someone so famous. She would tell her mother all about it when she phoned her on Sunday. Teenage fantasy spurred her on, and her heart beat very fast as she wondered what it must be like to be so adored by legions of fans, or to step before a camera knowing your hairstyle, your outfits and even your lipstick shade, would be copied around the world.

"Here's Pola Negri, doll!" Chuck called out. Then he held up his hands as if he were holding out a microphone. "Say a few words to your fans, Miss Negri," he playfully bid her.

Harlean smiled, then lowered her head and lifted her eyes as she'd seen the exotic actress do in the magazines. Then, with just a touch of embarrassment, she read what Negri had written in the cement.

"'Dear Sid, I love your theater. April 1928...' Oh, gosh, Chuck, she just did these! That's so exciting to think!"

"What is your favorite thing about being such a big star, Miss Negri, adored everywhere?"

Chuck's prompting made her giggle.

"Going to bed with my interviewers, most definitely."

"Why, you vamp." He smiled.

"How would you like to be my next conquest...what's your name again?" she asked, innocently batting her eyes and thoroughly enjoying the sudden silly role playing.

"McGrew's the name, Chuck McGrew. But I've got to warn you, I've got a very jealous wife."

"Is that so?"

"Oh, absolutely," he said with a devilish grin as he wrapped an arm around her shoulder. "But what she doesn't know won't hurt her."

"If I'm a vamp, you, sir, sure are a cad."

"Admit it, that's your favorite thing about me."

"Not my *absolute* favorite thing," she returned, happily playing along as they walked out onto Hollywood Boulevard toward their car.

"Time to get you to bed, doll."

"I thought you'd never ask," she teased. He held the door and she climbed into the shiny green roadster.

"I've got a surprise for you."

"For Miss Negri, or your wife?"

"Why don't *you* surprise *me* on that score?"

"A cad *and* a rake," she said as he slid onto the seat beside her and started the great rumbling engine.

Chapter Two

The next morning, Harlean couldn't help but feel excited when Chuck told her the surprise he had in store was waiting for her here in Beverly Hills. She hadn't seen much of this exclusive new residential area on her last trip to California, so that made the prospect even more enticing. It was still a relatively new neighborhood, one ornamented by curving lanes, vast stone or brick estates, a variety of charming Spanish-style bungalows and Tudor cottages—along with some still-empty wide, deep lots. Emerald lawns and rows of tall palm trees bordered lush parks and bridle trails. It was a true sanctuary from the bustling city nearby, and a world away from Kansas City.

"Now what do you think of this fine street?" Chuck asked her. "It's called Linden Drive."

"Very posh," she said, as they pulled over in front of a white stucco house with a terra-cotta roof. There was a small palm tree in the front yard and two bird of paradise plants framing the door. "Why are we stopping?"

"Because we're home. God, I hope you like it. If you don't, I'm in big trouble since I put a hefty down payment on the place, sight-unseen, a few weeks ago."

Her mouth fell open.

"You did *what*?"

"Married people need a proper home, doll. I wanted to give you that as a wedding gift. Since you liked it so much out here near Hollywood, it just seemed a good place for us to officially start our new life. The real estate agent told me this is one of the best streets in the area. Lots of stylish young couples, and movie types, are buying here right now."

In her mind, movie stars were like royalty. She and her mother had excitedly combed through all of the Hollywood magazines every month for as long as she could remember. They had read and knew every word of gossip about their exciting lives and careers. Like her mother, Harlean, too, had placed those glamorous icons on pedestals they could see but never quite reach. The prospect of actually living here among them was too spectacular to fully fathom.

He shoved his hands nervously into his trouser pockets. "So, do you like the place?"

"It's adorable on the outside, Chuck, but can I see the rest of it?"

Of course she would love it, but this was all so sudden. It was hard to know what to think, or even how to react, to his cascading generosity. Most new husbands bought their brides flowers or jewelry, not pretty houses in Beverly Hills. It seemed as if there was nothing he would not do to make her happy.

As they stood facing the house, he took the key from a pocket in his trousers. "Here, take it. It's yours."

"The key or the house?"

"Both. And all of my heart, too."

She kissed his cheek, and then he led her up the brick walkway. After he opened the front door, Chuck scooped her up and whisked her across the threshold.

Harlean found the house too charming for words. After he put her down, she first took in the beamed living room with a fireplace inset with indigo tiles. It was bright and sunny, and smelled new, like oil soap and fresh paint. Her heart was racing.

Next, they went into the dining room and on to the kitchen overlooking the back of the house. There was no furniture in the place yet, except in the bedroom, where a mattress was made up on the floor with pillows and a patchwork quilt. At the foot of the bed, Chuck had somehow placed a carved satinwood table that had belonged to his mother. A huge crystal vase sat on top, brimming with white orchids. They had always been Harlean's favorite flower for how delicate they appeared, but how hardy they were if tended to properly. Her hand went to her lips as she stifled a gasp of surprise.

"It's all just so perfect," she said in a whisper.

"Are you sure you like it?"

"Of course! I can't believe you did all of this for me."

"Who else is there, doll? You're everything to me, so you'd better get used to your husband spoiling the daylights out of you."

Harlean melted against him, then twined her arms around his neck and kissed him tenderly. Passion was never very far off after a kiss between them. "Touch has a memory. O say, love, say." The words of John Keats threaded themselves back through her mind. She had loved that poem since the first time she had read it and feeling Chuck's touch often brought it back to her.

"I'll never get tired of the way you taste," he murmured as their kiss deepened, and he pulled her more tightly against him. "I really am the luckiest man alive."

"What do you say we christen the place?" she asked.

"Right now?"

"Why not? I don't know how you did all of this without me finding out, and on top of everything you made sure we'd have a bed."

"I'm discovering there's not a lot money can't buy."

"I'm not sure if you're more handsome or more resourceful."

"As long as we christen this new bed right now, I don't care which one of those gets first place," he said in a low voice thickened by lust.

Afterward, Chuck fetched a hotel picnic basket from the trunk of the car and spread a red-and-white-checkered table-cloth on the living room floor in front of the fireplace. They feasted on ham sandwiches, a cluster of purple grapes and a wedge of cheese. Chuck had brought along a bottle of Champagne from his father's secret wine cellar in Chicago. Harlean flinched with surprise as the cork popped and he filled two teacups with the bubbly French nectar to celebrate the occasion. He stretched out, propped his head on an elbow and gazed over at her as she sat cross-legged in her bathrobe.

"A penny for your thoughts," he bid her.

"I just never thought life could be this good. If this is a dream, I never want to wake up. That's exactly what I'm thinking."

"Are you sure it's enough?"

"A husband I love *and* a home? Why wouldn't it be?"

"There must be something more. When you were a little girl, what did you want to be when you grew up?"

"Happy," she said truthfully. "That was it. And I am."

Harlean waited a moment to let that settle on him then, as it did, she watched his eyebrows knit together as his expression became a frown. "You don't want to be an actress or any-thing, since we're out here in Hollywood, do you?"

She could tell that the prospect was unsettling to him. They both knew that it was a difficult, demanding and largely disappointing dream for those determined to pursue it.

"Now, why would I want to go and do that? I saw how frustrating it was for my mother—the endless auditions and all those doors slammed in her face. That kind of rejection is for fools. No, thank you."

Harlean may have inherited that stubborn streak from her mother, and an absolute iron will for getting things she wanted, but better to savor her books, her new home and her marriage, and to enjoy the glitter and glamour of Hollywood from a distance.

Late in the afternoon two days later, a group of their neighbors organized a party to welcome them. The neighborhood was comprised of a wealthy young society crowd. Fit, tan men wearing monogrammed oxford shirts, linen trousers and bow ties bantered with each other as they carried bottles of bootleg gin up Chuck and Harlean's walkway. Beside them, their pretty wives and girlfriends wore a confectionary-colored array of cashmere sweaters and ropes of pearls. Each came bearing a casserole, a cake or martini glasses.

As the sun began to set behind the bristling palm trees outside, twenty people crowded into the living room, which was decorated so far with only a sofa, two folding chairs and a flea-market side table. Chuck whispered to her that he'd heard them talking, and two of the girls were heiresses, and one was the daughter of a studio boss.

Harlean herself had been raised in an upper-class group in Missouri and after her mother had remarried, she was educated at a posh private school outside of Chicago. But these people were a cut above that. There was a carefree air that surrounded them, and it was instantly intimidating. Harlean had a feeling that this party was actually designed more to size them up than welcome them.

Just when she was starting to think that this might've been a mistake, she saw someone she recognized. The mood lightened instantly as an old friend of hers came up the walkway carrying a bouquet of daisies. She wore a pretty floral dress cinched at the waist and a similar rope of pearls to the other girls.

"Rosalie McCray?" Harlean shrieked with surprise at the pretty, petite girl with the chestnut curls suddenly standing before her. "Gosh, what are *you* doing here? I remember you told us you lived near Hollywood, but I never imagined!"

"Who else do you think organized this little party?"

The girls embraced and Harlean took the flowers from her. "I wrote to your address in Chicago as soon as we all left the cruise, just like I promised I would," Rosalie explained. Her accent was sugary sweet, and pure Texas.

"I suppose you didn't receive it before you came out here? Anyway, Ivor heard that the two of you had moved in right down the street from us so we had to be the first to welcome you to our little corner of heaven."

Chuck and Harlean had met Rosalie and her husband, Ivor, on their honeymoon cruise through the Panama Canal in January, and the two couples had quickly become friends. Rosalie and Harlean found they had a great deal in common since both of them had been teenage brides with rich young husbands.

"Good to see you again, Rosie," Chuck said after he'd pressed a breezy kiss onto Rosalie's cheek. "Like a toddy, kids?"

Chuck had solemnly promised Harlean just that afternoon that he was only going to drink a little today while they entertained their neighbors, but she could tell that he had already knocked back a couple of stiff ones. His voice always grew just a little louder when he was drinking. Knowing that he used alcohol to bolster his confidence, she could see that he felt well out of his league with these people, trust fund or not. Secretly, his drinking frightened her because she suspected his reason for it was deeper than just wanting confidence. She believed, probably subconsciously, it was to keep from confronting his grief over the death of his parents, but for now she tried to put her mind on happier thoughts.

"Gosh, I'm happy to see you," Harlean exclaimed once Chuck had wandered off.

Rosalie glanced around the crowded bungalow. "Chuck sure got you a swell place here, honey. You know, last month Miss Clara Bow herself moved into the neighborhood, just a couple of blocks from here," she said in a gossipy tone.

"No! My mother would die of envy!" Harlean squealed, and then they both giggled. "Think she'd mind if we popped over for a cup of sugar?"

"So, how have things been between the two of you since the cruise?"

Rosalie asked the question so suddenly that Harlean was thrown off guard.

"Things are great," she answered, and she knew that it had been too quickly.

Harlean's friendship with Rosalie had been cemented when Chuck had gotten so drunk one night that he had passed out at the dinner table and had to be carried to his stateroom by two waiters. Rosalie had helped her outside as she'd wept, and the two had spent the rest of that evening up on deck watching the stars and talking about their childhoods.

She hated having to make excuses for Chuck but she couldn't bear to have anyone think poorly of him.

"Honestly, he's doing great now that we're here. That one

night with you guys was just a fluke. We'd had that quarrel after he'd had too much to drink. That's all it was."

Rosalie followed Harlean's gaze across the room to Chuck. At the moment, he was telling an animated story with great gesticulations.

"Of course that was it, honey. They're all like that once in a while. So what do you say to lunch tomorrow, just the two of us girls? I'll show you around town."

"Gosh, that'd be great."

"Can we take your car? Ivor has to take ours for an early tee off time with a few of the boys."

"Sure, but do you suppose Chuck can tag along to the golf course? I'm not sure what else he'd do around here all day while I'm gone."

She didn't want to say that she was nervous he'd sit alone and drink.

Rosalie's smile faded a degree. "Gee, honey, I'd really like to tell you yes, but since they play at the country club, there has to be an invite from one of the swells over there. Real obnoxious, blue-blooded, East Coast types control everything. Ivor only just got his invitation a couple of weeks ago so he's still on thin ice till they decide if he's all right or not." Rosalie lowered her voice and leaned nearer. "Between you and me, we both hate having to kiss everyone's posterior around here, but that's just the way it is when you're new in town."

"That's okay, I understand," Harlean forced herself to say.

She didn't really mean it, but she wasn't about to lose this chance with a girl who could show her the ropes. She would need determination in the coming days to get ahead with this tony group. Besides, she really did like Rosalie. She had an infectious laugh and a sweet, sincere disposition. She hadn't grown up with many girlfriends so this meant a great deal to her.

"Let's go see what you've got to wear to lunch. The Brown Derby is becoming pretty exclusive, so we've got to look the part if we don't want a table back near the kitchen."

"I thought you were an actress," Harlean said.

"For now I'm just an extra. If I'm lucky I get a walk-on here and there. But that sure as heck doesn't mean I can't act! You'll see what I mean tomorrow," she said conspiratorially.

Even though Harlean couldn't imagine what Rosalie meant, she was certain lunch was going to be interesting.

Harlean and Rosalie drove to lunch just before noon the next day. Chuck had washed the car until it gleamed because he knew how important it was that his wife had a friend in California and they were going off to do something together. Even though it was a warm day, she decided not to put the top down so she wouldn't ruin the careful wave she'd given to her usually fluffy blond hair.

The Brown Derby on Wilshire Boulevard looked just like its name: it was whimsically constructed in the shape of a huge hat. She had read all about the restaurant and the stars who dined there in *Photoplay* magazine, so she was almost as excited to see the building as to lunch there.

"Have you a reservation?" the maître d' asked, using a slightly snotty French accent. Harlean knew enough French from her school days to know that it was fake. The tag on this lapel read "Francois."

Rosalie met his gaze unflinchingly. "Lady Helen Crumley, table for two. My secretary phoned. As usual, we'll have a booth."

Harlean watched his reserve dissolve faced with Rosalie's hauteur and her believable English accent. "Yes, of course, your ladyship, here it is right here. Lovely to see you again. Please, follow me."

He fumbled nervously with the menus, and Harlean was relieved that he turned away to usher them inside, or her stunned expression would have given them away. They were shown to one of the coveted booths along the side of the restaurant. After he had bid them a "bon appétit," Harlean looked at Rosalie over the top of her menu.

"Where'd you learn to pull that off?"

"You know what they say about necessity being the mother of invention."

"Well, *I* certainly believed you, and so did he."

"People believe what they want to believe, Harlean. I've seen him at auditions, so I know his name is Frankie, not Francois. It mattered more to him that he might have seated some distant royalty that he could brag about than the fact that I might be the same kind of struggling, out-of-work actor he is."

Incredulous, Harlean shook her head and tried not to smile too broadly. "I can't believe the table, either. We can see everyone coming and going from here, and most everyone has to pass right by us."

"Speaking of that, you'll never believe who just came through the door." Trying not to show the awe she felt, Harlean lifted her menu again and carefully peered over the top of it. "Jimmy Cagney himself is coming our way."

"I may just die," Harlean said quietly.

"Indeed you will not. Lady Crumley and her sister are never cowed by lowly Hollywood *players*. We, after all, are from the land of Shakespeare and Milton."

Harlean glanced up just in time to see the matinee idol pass right beside them. The spicy scent of his cologne lingered. "Jeez, he's handsome! But not nearly as tall as he looks in the pictures."

"That's because directors have been known to stand him

on a crate. I saw it for myself when I was an extra last year in a picture with him."

Harlean wished she could order a drink with lunch to tame her open sense of awe and keep it from getting out of control. Her mother had taught her to have a love of gin, although hers was not Chuck's great passion for it, certainly.

"Don't look now," Rosalie said. "But that's William Powell sitting across from us. He was just in that picture called *The Last Command*. And I'm fairly sure that's Greta Garbo and Irving Thalberg with him. Thalberg is a huge producer over at MGM, even though he looks like a kid."

Harlean was certain that Powell was the most attractive man she had ever seen, far more so than on-screen. He had a thin, perfectly groomed mustache, a winning smile, and such strikingly bright blue eyes that she could not stop staring. There was something so debonair and sophisticated about him, not matched by any other Hollywood matinee idol.

When the waiter came to take their order, Harlean could only follow Rosalie by muttering, "I'll have the same." She had no idea what they had ordered, and she could not have cared less. She couldn't quite believe she was actually here.

A few minutes later, the striking ingenue Joan Crawford was shown to a table nearby. Harlean would have recognized her anywhere for all of the magazine covers she had graced this past year. She was dressed casually in loose-fitting trousers and a cardigan. It was an easy style Harlean longed to emulate. Casual elegance, her mother called it. If she were a star like Crawford, she would dress just exactly like that. Though the idea of comparing herself, even privately, to a girl like Joan Crawford was slightly absurd.

Before today, her movie idols had seemed only fantasy beings. Yet here they were, real and wonderful, eating steak and salad, chattering away at lunch tables that looked just like hers. She was a part of it all.

After lunch, they went down to the Bullocks Wilshire department store, a luxury art deco palace. The display windows along Wilshire Boulevard were full of the latest styles from New York and Paris. Inside, Harlean found a temple to fashion, complete with travertine floors and crystal chandeliers. There were as many fashionably dressed sales clerks as customers, and more attitude than ambiance. She could hardly quell what she knew was her awestruck expression.

Rosalie led the way straight through the vaulted first floor Perfume Hall as though she absolutely belonged. Harlean hurried behind her, trying in vain to match Rosalie's confident stride.

Upstairs in one of the showrooms, Rosalie selected two dresses from the mannequins and asked to see them modeled for her, as was the custom, since the store considered a clutter of hanging racks gauche.

She marveled at how Rosalie simply refused to be undone by the world, no matter the circumstance, and she understood now that her friend truly was the essence of an actress. She had promised yesterday that Harlean would see it, and she had delivered in spades.

"It would look great on you," Harlean said to Rosalie as the model paraded before them in a belted celery-colored dress with a lace collar and cuffs.

"That's an awfully expensive ensemble, my dear. Perhaps you would prefer to look at something a bit more...*practical*," the middle-aged store clerk suggested.

Rosalie lifted her chin a fraction as she turned around to face the clerk. "I'm the least practical person you'll ever meet. So, no, I don't think so. I'll take this one. And you can wrap up the other one, too."

The woman's mouth fell open. "My dear, have you any idea the cost of those two dresses?"

"Since I have a rich husband who loves to spoil me, no, actually I don't," Rosalie replied breezily. "You are all on commission here at this shop, I assume?"

Harlean watched the silver-haired woman's demeanor change abruptly and her expression soften. "Why, yes, we are, but of course—"

"Then today I'll be buying them from that sales clerk over there. And next time I decide to shop here, you would be wise to leave your attitude in the stockroom if you plan to wait on me, since I almost always buy something expensive, but not from someone with a chip on her shoulder." She met the woman's gaze unflinchingly as she tossed a business card onto the countertop. "Charge the dresses to my husband's account and have them sent to my home."

Both girls linked arms proudly once they had gotten a few feet away from the store outside. Harlean was fully realizing just how much she could learn from Rosalie, and she was duly impressed.

"You really are amazing," Harlean said with a zeal she could no longer contain.

"Aw, thanks, honey, but it's nothing you can't pick up. No telling where a little ingenuity can take someone like you, too. You've got that something extra inside of you, I can tell."

Harlean thought that it might just be true since she was quite adept at wrapping her mother and Grandpa Harlow around her finger with ease. In spite of their blustering threats, they both had eventually given in on the subject of Chuck. Her gaze, her pout and her ability to summon tears always won the day. Until now, Harlean hadn't fully considered the power potential in that. It reminded her of what her mother always said about star quality: it was as elusive as it was indefinable.

If you had it you had it, and if you didn't there was nothing in the world that could change that. Perhaps Rosalie was right.

"You need to try it," Rosalie said as they neared the car. "See what that smile of yours, and those brains, can bring you."

Men stared at them both as they passed. Some nodded and smiled, another tipped the brim of his fedora.

"I'm not sure why I'd ever want to find out, since I've already got everything I want—Chuck, the new house, certainly plenty of beautiful clothes."

"A little adventure, maybe? Nothing against my sweet Ivor, he's swell, but I just can't sit around the house all day baking cakes and waiting to have a baby. That's why I audition. When I get a walk-on or a part, I feel like I did something all on my own—that somehow for just a moment, I stood out."

Harlean looked over at her friend as they got in the car. "Chuck is enough adventure for me at the moment. Besides, I watched my mother try and try to get parts all over this town and all she ever got was rejection. You know the studios are absolutely crawling with gorgeous girls, one prettier than the next. For me, there wouldn't really be any point in an adventure like that."

"I see what you mean." Rosalie paused for a moment, and then she said, "But do you think tomorrow you could drive me over to Fox to check the casting-call roster? Ivor needs the car again."

"Sure. What else have I got to do?" But then she had an idea and suddenly she hopped out of the car.

"Where are you going?"

"I'm putting the top down. All of a sudden I feel like being a little crazy," Harlean exclaimed with a carefree laugh. "To heck with my hair!"

CHAPTER THREE

She had meant to stop and ask where to park but, to her shock that next day, with Rosalie beside her, the uniformed guard waved her car in past the imposing scrolled Fox Studios gates. He even had a smile for them as he tipped his navy blue cap.

"What the heck just happened?" Harlean gasped in amazement as she kept driving, afraid even to glance back.

"See what beauty and confidence will get you?"

"But that wasn't meant to happen! I've been here before and this place is like Fort Knox!"

"Well, honey, I'll go out on a limb and say he assumed you were someone else. Clearly, he thought two well-dressed knockouts belonged here. Or maybe you reminded him of someone's demanding girlfriend who he was afraid of offending," Rosalie opined on a tinkling little laugh. "Either way, we're in."

Nothing like this had ever happened when she had come here with her mother. Back then, extras had been herded onto the lot like cattle, lined up and made to wait.

"You can park right over there by the soundstage." Rosalie pointed with an authoritative air. "I won't be long so that'll be fine."

Harlean brought the car to a stop against the curb and raked her tousled hair back from her face with both hands.

"How do you do that?" Rosalie asked.

"Do what?"

"Get all wind-blown and still manage to look like a million bucks." She brought a comb and hand mirror out of her handbag and glanced at her own face. "I'm sure I'm an absolute wreck."

She thought Rosalie was a classic beauty, with her lustrous mahogany hair, round cocoa-brown eyes, perfectly arched eyebrows, small mouth and flawless olive skin.

In contrast, the white-blond hair of Harlean's childhood had deepened to a more muted shade of ash blond and her glass-blue eyes and a ruddy blush over porcelain cheeks gave her the look of a China doll.

"I'll be back in a flash," Rosalie declared as she strode, hips swaying, toward the door across the street marked Casting Office.

Suddenly, she stopped and pivoted back. Her brown eyes were shining as she stood there, holding her small, white gloves, and wearing one of the expensive new dresses she had bought the day before.

"How do I look now?"

Harlean cupped a hand around her mouth and happily called out, "A real stunner! I think today is gonna be your lucky day!"

Then she watched Rosalie join the long line of girls wrapped around the casting building. It was a sight she remembered all too well. She could never tell Rosalie, but after only a moment, she lost sight of her friend as she faded into the sea of other hopefuls.

She sat for a moment, taking in the activity of the back lot.

Huge props were being wheeled past groups of actors, and other workers were pushing stuffed racks of costumes. Harlean was fidgeting with her wedding band and finally growing restless, after almost thirty minutes of waiting, when a man in a gray three-piece business suit and a felt homburg walked briskly past the car, and then he did a double take.

Panic set in because surely he was going to ask her to leave. As he approached the car, she tried to think of something clever to say, a plausible reason why she was parked here so he wouldn't insist that she move along.

"Say, don't I know you?"

"I don't think so," she replied, and her voice broke as she looked up, shielding her eyes from the sun.

"No, honestly, whose wife are you?"

"No one you know," she returned with caution, but he was undeterred.

He looked down at her appraisingly. "You're in a new picture then, that's gotta be it."

He seemed to be taking her apart with his eyes as he waited for her to reply.

Harlean was surprised at his insistence. She could feel herself trembling like a leaf. "I'm not an actress. I'm waiting for a friend, Rosalie Roy. That's her stage name."

"Rosalie, yeah, I know her. She's a good kid. You sure you're not an actress?"

"I'm sure."

He glanced around, then back at her. He seemed hesitant suddenly. "Listen, could you, I mean, would you mind stepping out of the car just for a minute?"

Harlean looked at him as she tried to discern if he was flirting with her or about to call a security guard. But if he was flirting, he had a strange way of showing it. Not sure how to say no, she finally opened the car door and stepped out. His visual sweep of her went from head to foot and back again.

"Did you ever think of trying to break into pictures?"

Harlean softly chuckled as she shook her head at the absurdity of the question.

"I'm only here because Rosalie asked me to give her a lift, honest."

As an afterthought, he finally introduced himself and reached for her hand. "I'm Bud Ryan, a casting director here."

"Harlean McGrew," she said as they shook.

"Can you wait here a minute?"

"I'll be here till Rosalie comes out."

"Okay, good. Don't go anywhere!"

She watched him dash past the line of would-be actresses and inside the casting office, and then she sank against the car seat and slipped on her sunglasses, feeling entirely embarrassed by the encounter.

When she looked up again, the young man was hurrying back toward her car with Rosalie and two other men. They were older, serious looking, and they were staring at her with the most curious expressions, even Rosalie.

"See what I mean?" she heard the first one say to the others as they approached.

"So then, what *is* a dame who sparkles like you doing sitting here if you're *not* trying to break into pictures?" one of them asked.

She glanced over at Rosalie, whose usually cheery smile seemed hidden behind something that looked like a glimmer of envy.

"I was just waiting for her, that's all. Tell 'em, Rosie."

Rosalie was silent.

"Well, miss, whatever your story is, I want you to take this," the shorter of the two men said as he began to write something on his clipboard.

Harlean saw Rosalie look away.

"It's a letter of introduction to the Central Casting Bureau. All three of us are gonna sign it."

"That's awfully nice of you, but, honest, I'm not—"

"Listen, sweetheart, everyone has a story, so you don't need to sell us. Dave is definitely gonna want to see you."

"Dave Allen is the top guy over at Central Casting. It's at the corner of Hollywood and Western Avenue. Head over there right now and give his secretary this letter."

She didn't want to be *seen*. It was really the last thing she wanted but she had been raised always to be polite. "Thank you," she said as she took the letter and pressed it into her handbag. "Are you ready, Rosalie?" she asked, then stepped back into the car and started the engine.

As they drove off the Fox lot and back out onto Sunset Boulevard, she could feel Rosalie's reproving glare. "I've been trying to get that kind of attention in this town for over a year. All you do is sit there and they come to you like three foxes about to raid the henhouse."

"I didn't do a thing, Rosie, I swear."

"I know. And that's what makes it so damn frustrating! And where do you think you're going? This isn't the way to Central Casting."

"You're right, it isn't. I'm going home. I told them I don't want to be an actress, and that's the truth." It was certainly flattering to have been noticed like that, and to have had three studio executives see her as something unique. Secretly, it was even a bit enticing. However, the heartbreaking disappointment and struggle most actresses endured dampened any real enthusiasm she might have had.

"Well, what the hell *do* you want to do? Bake cakes and have babies?"

"Maybe write a novel."

Rosalie stared at her. "A *novel*? You?"

"I know it sounds silly but I've always wanted to try." She felt herself flush. "I love all kinds of books. I read everything, poetry, even some of the German philosophers—Hegel and a little bit of Nietzsche."

Rosalie's expression remained one of incredulity. "I've never even heard of those guys."

"I read them but I didn't really like it," she amended and blushed. "I really love poetry, Shelley especially."

"Now, him I've heard of," Rosalie said, sounding relieved.

"I read his poems over and over when I'm sad or when I'm lonely. And Keats, I just love Keats."

Rosalie shook her head. "Wow, who'd have guessed you were so well-read?"

Harlean had never told anyone about her love for Keats, her passion for reading in general, or about the novel she was starting to formulate in her mind. She wasn't sure why she had confessed it now to someone she didn't know all that well. Even Chuck did not fully understand the dear companions her books had become in the lonely hours of her childhood. They were both quiet for the next few blocks.

"So, a writer, hmm? Like Jane Austen or something?"

"More like George Sand. Now there was a gutsy woman."

"George Sand wasn't a man?" Rosalie asked, and Harlean could tell that she meant the question.

"No, Rosie, she wasn't a man. But she did have to figure out how to make her way in a man's world. Anyway, don't tell any of our neighbors about me wanting to write, okay? They would have a real good laugh at my expense."

"Now, why on earth would I tell those magpies anything,

honey? At least you *do* want to do something with your life. You've got goals, anyway," Rosalie said. "I don't think I could stand it if I thought there was nothing more than washing Ivor's dirty socks and cooking his dinner for me to look forward to."

"There's more to marriage than just that. Personally, I'm pretty fond of the more intimate parts."

"Is that a fact? I already find those pretty damn repetitive," Rosalie giggled.

"Then you sure aren't doing something right."

"Not everyone is as free-spirited as you, Harlean. You're this stunning young gal with an amazing head on your shoulders. No wonder Chuck's always all over you, and mad-jealous to boot. Especially after the awful way his parents died, he probably lives his life terrified he's gonna lose you."

Rosalie had been so kind to her on the cruise that night when she'd been so upset with Chuck's drunkenness. When Harlean had told her about the tragic death of his parents, she had offered sympathy and advice.

"Well, that isn't gonna happen," Harlean declared. "Whatever you think I am, first and foremost I'm Harlean McGrew, now and forever."

"What you are, honey, is a plain old-fashioned contradiction."

Harlean felt a smile begin to lengthen her lips at the sound of that. "I don't mind being a contradiction as long as *I* know my own mind. And I can write a book anytime as long as I have my husband with me. Chuck really is the only thing that matters to me when it comes right down to it."

After she dropped Rosalie off, Harlean rushed home. She burst through the door and called out for Chuck, eager suddenly for the assurance of his arms around her again, but the only sound that came in answer was from Duke Ellington's orchestra. Chuck had forgotten to turn off the radio before he'd gone out.

As she glanced around she saw that he hadn't even left her a note. There was only the *Saturday Evening Post* spread open on the sofa and a half-empty cup of coffee on the floor in front of it. She worked hard to press back her disappointment. She wondered what he would think if she told him about what had happened earlier at the Fox studio but of course she had no intention of telling him. He wouldn't be pleased, it might even make him angry because Rosalie was right, he did get jealous easily. He'd said more than once that he couldn't bear even the thought of losing her, which made sense to her after the traumatic way he had lost both parents, so she tried to be understanding about it.

After all, that was the deeper reason he drank so much, wasn't it? He hadn't yet fully grieved their loss, or accepted that he was not at risk of losing her to some sudden pull of fate, too. She had tried so many times to talk to him about it since that first night, but he always swiftly changed the subject. She wanted desperately to help him, but she just wasn't sure how to do it. Right now, the blissful calm between them seemed reason enough to leave it alone for now.

Since he wasn't home, Harlean went into the bedroom and stuffed the letter from the studio executives into a hatbox in her closet, then closed the door. When she turned back she saw their silver-framed photograph of the two of them taken on their honeymoon cruise displayed next to the orchids. He must have set that out before he left, and the assurance that seeing them gave her was enough to bring a smile back to her face.

Yes, the letter was certainly flattering but it was going to stay right there where she had hidden it. Her marriage meant more than the momentary whim of a collection of casting agents.

Chapter Four

"Breakfast in bed, milady," Chuck said with a gallant nod as he set the tray on her lap one morning after they had been out late the night before with Rosalie and Ivor.

He was barefoot and wearing only a pale blue pair of pajama bottoms.

Harlean struggled to sit up as she brushed the hair back from her face. "What's this for?" she sleepily asked.

"Just for being you. I brought all of your favorites—hard-boiled egg, orange juice, coffee and toast with marmalade. Look, doll, I know I'm not the easiest person sometimes, so I have to work that much harder at things." There was a single pink rose in a bud vase beside her coffee. She leaned in to smell its sweet fragrance before she looked up at him.

"You're perfect just as you are, Chuck."

He drew back the draperies and morning light flooded their bedroom. His expression was calm and she could see that he was totally at ease. "If only that were true."

Harlean pushed away all thought of the hidden note and pressed a happy kiss onto his cheek. "I'm starving."

"I knew you would be."

He sank onto the bed beside her and propped himself back against the headboard as she took a sip of coffee. "I have something for you," he said.

And with that, he drew from his end table a small leather volume and gave it to her. He was awkward with it, this humble offering, one he did not fully appreciate, but it was an offering nonetheless to the woman he loved—an early volume of Keats's poetry. Harlean gasped seeing it. Tears brightened her eyes.

"How did you know?"

"I've listened to every word you've ever spoken and I've heard them all. Read me one," he bid her.

"Are you sure?"

In response he very tenderly said, "I'm not going to pretend I understand any of those poems, but read me a bit of something and I promise to try."

And so she read him her favorite poem by John Keats, taking time with each exquisite line, because it was the one that had always reminded her of love, of marriages, and how they came apart sometimes, as her parents' marriage had. It also made her the more insistent that her own never would.

Afterward, she kissed him again but more deeply this time. Her heart was so full of love for this complicated, tender young man, and it made her worry for him. She so wanted him to be happy here. Then she asked him about his new world here, and how his golf game with the others was coming along.

Chuck had been disappearing from the house for hours at a time when she and Rosalie were off shopping for furniture. She knew he was working to be included in the group of young men in the neighborhood. But for now the saving grace in Harlean's mind was seeing him carefree, his demons hopefully put to rest. Winning them over was at least an ob-

jective and she decided that it was better for him to have some
sort of goal than none at all.

As she had predicted to him over dinner one evening a few
days earlier, he was eventually invited to the country club to
join them for a game of golf and then for tennis. Their days
of sporting routinely ended with drinks at the country club
bar in a private room where a blind eye was turned to the
dictates of Prohibition.

"I'm pretty pitiful at it really," he said of his golf game.
"But my aim at this point is to charm them sufficiently so
that they don't care."

She pressed another breezy kiss onto his cheek, rose from
the bed, then yawned and stretched in a long butter-yellow
ray of sunlight. "If you haven't won them over yet, you will
soon enough."

"You really do believe in me, don't you, doll?"

"One hundred percent. I just want you to be happy. And
thank you for the book."

"You really like it, then?"

She heard the familiar catch in his voice, just a note—but
it came from that fragile need for reassurance. "You knew
I would. It's incredible. It's a very rare volume, you know."

"I'd like to think I'll always know what you like."

"You sure don't have to win *me* over like that with things,
Chuck. You know I adore you already. I always will."

He searched her face for a moment and when she saw him
finally give away just a hint of a smile, she knew that he did.

Later that day they decided to go to the pictures. Harlean
was thrilled that Chuck was willing to sit through a romantic
comedy because she knew he disliked them. He didn't even
complain about this one, though, and he told her he actually enjoyed it as they walked back to their car. Marriage was
give-and-take, and it was so good to feel that they were both

doing their part. Harlean couldn't imagine anything that could be better than what the two of them had together right now. She loved decorating their home, and learning to cook. Even thoughts of writing a novel began to fade from her mind. The only thing lacking was that she missed her family more every day, her mother most especially, but she tried her best not to think too much of that.

Over the next few days, Harlean relished seeing how happy Chuck was here in their lovely hideaway, and how at ease he was when they were together, cooking together, or when she was trying to teach him about poetry. *Please let things stay just as they are*, she found herself thinking. She repeated that to herself daily until it became almost like a mantra. Coming to California had been good for him. He had left everything behind in the Midwest just as she had. She said it to herself even that evening a few days later, when his new set of friends delivered him back home, propped up between them after an afternoon of carousing.

"Ol' Chuck sure is the life of the party. He was dancing on tables over at Musso and Frank's an hour ago." Blake Kendrick who lived next door gave Harlean an apologetic shrug as he handed Chuck over to her.

Harlean did her best not to show her disappointment. Damn, why did he always have to drink so much?

She thanked them with a believable smile and, after they'd gone, she dutifully tucked him into bed, kissed his forehead and turned out the light.

An unsettling concern pressed in on her again as she leaned against the closed door and let out a heavy sigh. She needed for him to stay just as content as he had been at first. Everything for her depended on that. They were alone here after all, and with Chuck gone so often lately, she had begun secretly to feel the greater pull of homesickness every day. Of course, she couldn't tell Chuck that because he always said they were each other's family now. For his sake, she tried very hard to make that true.

A few moments later, she went to the telephone and quietly dialed the number, hoping he was too sound asleep to hear. It wasn't Sunday yet but, tonight especially, she just needed to hear her mother's reassuring voice on the other end of the line.

Once the house was fully furnished, Chuck insisted on organizing another party. He planned on inviting everyone they'd met so far in Beverly Hills. It seemed a huge undertaking, but helping him gave Harlean a way to keep busy as the shine of the housewives' world was fading by the day for her.

He planned to grill hot dogs, since he knew they were Harlean's favorite food, and he had a florist fill the house with orchids and fragrant roses.

"I've put out the rest of the hootch we brought with us from Chicago. I hope it will be enough," he said as he set clean glassware onto the kitchen counter next to bootleg bottles of gin and whiskey.

"Will you stop your worrying? Everything will be great."

"So many of them have houses that are so much larger than ours. Maybe we should have bought a bigger place."

Harlean went to him and twined her arms around his neck. She was wearing her favorite unstructured beige trousers, sneakers and a crisp white polo shirt, the way she had seen Joan Crawford do. Although, she didn't think she could look quite as chic as the young star it was certainly fun to try.

She pressed herself against Chuck's taut chest, and tenderly kissed him. In response to the gesture, he took her face in his hands.

"I love you like this, without makeup or anything. You have

such lovely skin," he said as he reached around and pressed his hands against her spine, drawing them closer together. "But I do wish you would wear a brassiere."

She turned her lip out in a pout. "You know how I hate them, and my breasts are so small no one notices anyway."

"Oh, they notice, all right."

"Just to make you happy, I'll put one on, then," she said with a seductive half grin. "And I was going to do up my face for the party."

"Then good thing that's not for a while, because I have plans for you first, Mrs. McGrew."

He pulled her more tightly, murmuring the words into her hair, and she felt a delicious shiver of anticipation. "Do you now, Mr. McGrew?"

"Oh, yes, indeed I do."

"Anything I should be warned about?"

His smile was fox-like and adorable to her. "Not a chance. That would ruin all the fun."

An hour later, the house pulsed with the sound of boisterous laughter. Music rolled and spilled out into the backyard where one of the guys was just lighting the BBQ. Harlean allowed herself a gin and soda with some of the girls. Then they wanted her to play the upbeat Louis Armstrong tune, "Weather Bird," on the gramophone so they could dance.

She went back inside to change the music and paused at the kitchen window. She glanced out, and was surprised and happy to see Chuck looking like the life of the party, a real part of the group as he told a story, and everyone looked rapt.

She turned back around and saw Rosalie and Louis B. Mayer's dignified and rail thin daughter Irene dancing the Charleston in the living room. Rosalie proudly explained earlier that she had met the MGM boss's daughter one afternoon after she had weaseled her way into the studio commissary after a casting call and they had become friends. Irene brought her boyfriend David Selznick with her tonight and was intent on showing him off since he was an up-and-comer in the industry.

The story of how Irene and Rosalie met hadn't surprised Harlean after their escapade at the Brown Derby. Clearly, Rosalie had perfected the art of looking like she belonged, and Harlean could stand to take chances like that, as well. Harlean had gone to school with Irene when she was in California the last time, but if Irene remembered her, she didn't show it.

"Come over and dance with us, Harlean!" Rosalie called out to her happily.

"Yes, come on!" Irene seconded, her face already glistening as they all did the animated steps of a flapper.

Harlean finally joined in and shimmied to the end of the tune, when they all collapsed back onto the sofa. Irene introduced her friend then, a dark-eyed and exotic-looking girl named Katie. Her father was a powerful director, Cecil B. DeMille. As they were introduced, Harlean tried hard not to gape at the two spirited girls whose fathers practically owned Hollywood.

"Well, there are certainly no dance stars among the lot of us!" Katie DeMille sighed as she dabbed her face with the back of her hand.

"Probably no stars at all," Irene added.

"I don't know if I'd say that's true," Rosalie countered. "Last week, Harlean here got a personal letter of introduction written to the head of Central Casting from two Fox executives, and she wasn't even trying. She was just sitting in the car waiting for me to check the rolls. They said she had 'the look.'"

"They did not!" Irene exclaimed.

"Dave Allen is the head of Central Casting, I know him quite well. He's a close friend of my father's," said Katie

DeMille as her smile gave way to a more measured expression. "Dave is not easily swayed. What'd he have to say when you got there?"

"I didn't go."

"What do you mean, you didn't go?" Irene Mayer gasped. She perked up and sat forward on the sofa. Her eyes grew wide. "That's absolutely crazy!"

"He wouldn't hire her right off the street like that anyway," Katie blandly countered.

"I bet you wouldn't have the nerve to go and see," Irene added. "Especially since you've waited all this time, it would just be awkward now."

"That's probably true," Rosalie chimed with a laugh. Harlean could tell she was trying to keep things light. "And casting offices are busy places. They've probably forgotten all about you by now."

Harlean huffed in response to being ganged up on. Faced with condescension, it ignited her fighting spirit. "What would you like to bet?" she asked Irene.

Katie and Rosalie exchanged a glance. "We were only teasing," Rosalie said.

"You mentioned a bet, let's bet."

Even though Harlean was smiling she could tell that they all felt the shift in her tone.

"All right," Irene cautiously replied. "What do you want if I'm wrong?"

She glanced up at the lovely pearl brooch attached to Irene's collar. "How 'bout that?"

Mayer's eyes widened just slightly. Beyond that, she hid her surprise well. "You'll never go through with it, so sure. But the brooch it is. And if I'm right and you don't find the nerve, one of those beautiful orchids, hand delivered by you to my doorstep once a month for a year."

Harlean fought a smile. Irene didn't know what a poor choice it was to bet against her. She wouldn't really take personal jewelry even after she had won the wager, she wasn't that cruel. But she might borrow it for a day or two just to make a point. One thing was sure, she reveled in the moment where Louis B. Mayer's daughter couldn't be quite sure.

After the evening was at an end, and the guests happily stumbled out to their cars, Ivor and Rosalie followed Chuck and Harlean back inside. Chuck had invited them to stay for a nightcap. At least that had been his proposal before he realized they were out of alcohol. As Harlean and Rosalie took stock in the kitchen, they found that every last morsel of food, and every drop of liquor, had been consumed.

"Man, those boys can drink," Chuck sighed, turning over a bottle of wine left on the kitchen counter to see if there was even a drop left inside.

"We held our own," Ivor returned with a snicker as he slung his arm fraternally over Chuck's shoulder.

"You sure did," Rosalie added. "You're both more than a little drunk."

"Aw, don't be a spoilsport, Rosie. We were all just havin' fun," Ivor replied with a smile as he smacked a breezy kiss onto her cheek. "Besides, Chuck and I can't have those boys thinking we can't keep up."

She frowned at him in response and pretended to wipe his kiss away but she did not try to conceal her real affection for him.

Harlean walked back into the living room to begin cleaning up, and Rosalie followed her. There were dirty dishes and glassware scattered everywhere. The pungent odor of cigarettes was strong.

"I can't believe you started that whole thing," Harlean said as she collected the plates and Rosalie gathered up the glasses.

"Started what?"

"The challenge."

Rosalie bit back a smile. "I didn't. Irene did. But obviously that was an opportunity not to be missed. Besides, it'd be worth it just to see the look on Katie DeMille's face if you went through with it, since she claims to know Dave Allen so well."

"You don't think I'll do it, do you?"

"I don't know. Will you?"

"Chuck wouldn't want me to, I know that. He always thought my mother had been foolish to try to break into Hollywood."

"Well, he wouldn't even have to know."

Harlean took the plates back into the kitchen and set them on the counter. When she glanced through the window over the sink, she saw Chuck and Ivor on the patio now. They were looking up at the sky and talking. "You think I should lie to my husband?"

"It's not like he always tells *you* the truth. Weren't you just telling me you have no idea what he does all day when he leaves the house?"

"I assumed he was with Ivor."

"Not all the time."

"Chuck wouldn't cheat on me."

"Of course not, honey. Any fool can see he's crazy about you. I only meant, even married people have their secrets. It keeps things fresh."

She turned on the tap, feeling a sudden flare of anger and doubt. She was trying to learn from Rosalie but Harlean, who was still only seventeen, wasn't as confident as she knew she could make herself appear, and she hated other people knowing it. Mother always said, *Look confident, Baby, and you will be confident.*

"What's the point, anyway? It's not like I actually want to *be* an actress."

"There's always a point to accepting a dare. Be bold, be daring!" Rosalie exclaimed, and her brown eyes glittered.

Outside, Chuck and Ivor laughed suddenly about something the girls couldn't hear.

"They have their little secrets, we should have ours," Rosalie declared.

"All right."

"You'll do it?"

"Why not?"

And that really was the point. Harlean couldn't think of any good reason not to do it. She certainly didn't have anything else interesting to do with her days. It was crazy, surely. But, who knew, maybe it would be fun. And it would be great to win a bet with Louis B. Mayer's slightly condescending daughter, and shock the daughter of Cecil B. DeMille, both at the same time. But more than that, this might just be an occasion to see if a bit of Rosalie's awe-inspiring self-confidence had rubbed off on her. Her proclaimed disdain for the Hollywood studio system was from her mother's experience, her fear of what it did to young women belonged to Chuck. Having a secret for a while might just afford her the ability to challenge herself and, for the first time, decide on her own how she actually felt about it all.

CHAPTER FIVE

What are you staring at?

Harlean felt a spark of indignation as she parked outside the Central Casting office at the corner of Hollywood Boulevard and Western Avenue. More than a few people passing by gave her a double take. So the car was a bit flashy, and her white silk suit looked expensive, but all of the attention was unnerving. She was already starting to second-guess coming here. She clutched the key in a death grip as she emerged from the car. Her knees were weak. She should never have stooped to a bet like this. What was she thinking? That was precisely what she got for having had a drink last night.

She should have asked Rosalie to come with her for moral support. But pride had gotten the better of her last night. And the same way Rosalie wanted to see Katie DeMille's face, Harlean now wanted to see Rosalie's expression when she announced that she had gone through with the dare when no one believed she would. She wanted to show them that no one should ever underestimate her. Oh, yes, Harlean McGrew could be downright daring. Those girls were about to see that!

And above all, she meant to prove it to herself.

All she had to do was present the letter and wait to be rejected. Then she would take a business card to prove she had actually been there, and be on her way, the wager handily won. She was meeting her old friend Bobbe Brown for lunch afterward which would soothe the rejection. Bobbe was a girl she'd met years ago when she and her mother had lived here the last time, and they had maintained a correspondence ever since.

Harlean thought it would be fun to see someone who had known her before she'd gotten married, someone who remembered, and liked, the slightly pudgy, sometimes awkward Harlean Carpenter even though, like Chuck, Bobbe teased her in her letters about still being called the Baby at the age of seventeen. She was eager now to spend some time with a girl her age, one who hadn't grown up so fast as the rest of her new crowd.

The secretary looked up from a notepad on her neatly arranged desk. Beside her was a row of chairs, each occupied by a very pretty girl. Many of them were blonde, though not as blonde as Harlean. Each had their long, slim legs crossed in the same direction.

On the wall behind them were posters for the hit films *The Sheik*, starring Rudolph Valentino, and Lon Chaney looking suitably frightening in character as *The Hunchback of Notre Dame*. She had seen both silent films with her mother in Kansas City, which reminded her, yet again, how far from home she really was.

"Yes?" the secretary said as she lifted her arched eyebrows a tick higher.

Harlean opened her mouth to reply but no words came out. She heard one of the girls in the row of chairs snicker in response to the sudden sound that came from the back of her throat. She drew the letter from her handbag and silently laid it down on the secretary's desk. Scowling, the woman gave the missive a cursory glance. Then Harlean watched her eyes widen as she actually read the letter of introduction.

"Wait here," she instructed as she went to knock on the door behind her desk and entered the office.

Harlean could feel the looks of contempt being shot at her as she stood waiting, her hands both tightly clutching her small handbag. It would be over soon enough, just a few more minutes, and she could be out the door and on the way to lunch where she and her old friend would have a good laugh about this.

"Mr. Allen will see you now. Go right in."

The secretary's expression had dramatically changed. For the first time, a glimmer of a smile turned up her carefully painted lips as she directed Harlean inside.

Dave Allen was surprisingly young, probably under thirty, with suntanned skin, bright hazel eyes and an engaging smile. He was not at all what Harlean had expected of the head of Central Casting. He stood and held out a hand to indicate a green leather chair opposite his desk. He was staring at her.

"Have a seat."

"Thank you, Mr. Allen."

"Dave, please. I'd feel ancient otherwise. And with whom do I have the pleasure of meeting?"

Harlean Carpenter, she nearly said but *Mrs. Charles McGrew* fought past it. Both names tangled in her mind then, dueling in that split second with the idea that she would have to explain being someone's wife at such a young age.

What if they contacted him? This was all just a silly lark anyway—her momentary adventure.

"Jean Harlow," she offhandedly replied, managing a smile. It completely surprised her that she had blurted it out, but her mother's name would suit for now.

"That gaze of yours alone is worth a million bucks. You *are* different, just like the letter says."

"Thank you…" she tipped her head to the side and held her smile "…I think."

"Just calling it like I see it, Miss Harlow. That's my job. We'll want to get you registered right away. Eleanor, my secretary, will get your information."

"Don't you need to know if I can act or anything?"

She was stunned that he was actually going to register her after less than a five-minute conversation.

"I have what I need. Just shine every time we send you out, like you have right now with me, and you'll be in business, believe me."

As she left the office ten minutes later, Harlean plucked a business card from the secretary's desk and gave it a victorious tap against her cheek. She was too stunned even to wonder what "in business" would actually mean in the coming days, but it didn't matter, she reminded herself. She had won the bet, and she couldn't wait to tell the girls, and see their faces when she did.

The next day, Harlean and Chuck took a picnic lunch into the bucolic grounds of Griffith Park. Chuck brought his camera, intent on taking photographs of his wife amid the lush surroundings. The rocky setting was like another world in the middle of a bustling city. There pine trees mingled with huge, glorious sycamores and a periwinkle-blue stream wound through it.

"The camera loves you." He smiled as he clicked away, instructing her to pose this way and that atop a huge boulder beneath the warm midday sun. "You take my breath away."

"I look like a schoolgirl in this outfit," she said as she gestured to the gingham dress, baggy cardigan and sensible white tennis shoes he had chosen for her that morning.

"Not to me, you don't."

"Well, gingham isn't very sexy."

"You are my wife, I don't want you to be sexy, at least not for anyone else but me. Besides vampy women are pretty loathsome. In my opinion, disgusting."

Harlean thought of Pola Negri, her dark eyes beneath a silk turban, the hypnotic stare. She could not have disagreed with Chuck more. She respected any woman who could have that kind of power through a camera lens. It didn't have to mean she was loose.

She had wanted to tell him about the dare all day, and about Dave Allen's reaction. But something stronger stopped her. She knew she should be able to tell her husband anything, especially something that was actually kind of exciting, but she certainly did not want to ruin such a lovely afternoon by setting off his jealous streak.

After he had taken a few pictures, they sat in the shade of a gnarled old oak tree and Harlean unpacked sandwiches and a thermos full of lemonade. It was quiet here, pristine. The only sounds were from the stream running nearby and birds trilling in the trees above.

Chuck propped himself on an elbow. For a moment, he just watched her sitting against a tree trunk, knees drawn up to her chest.

"What do you think?" he asked.

"Think about what?"

"About being back in California. Is it everything you hoped it would be?"

She leaned over and pressed a kiss onto his cheek. "Being married to you makes it all a hundred times better than that."

"Well, you're still the best thing ever to happen to me, that's for sure."

He said it matter-of-factly because he said it to her so often, but now there was a richness in his tone, like the sound of a pledge, and it touched her. She understood that it helped him believe in what they had together, and to remind her what was in his heart. Life had made him such a serious young man, and filled him with demons Harlean wasn't sure she could ever fully help him vanquish, no matter how fiercely she loved him—especially because he wouldn't acknowledge his feelings about the past with her.

But if she could continue making him happy, that would be a start and, she hoped, distraction enough.

"How about you, are *you* happy here?" she asked him.

"Why wouldn't I be?"

"I just thought maybe you missed home."

"*You* are my home."

He leaned over to kiss her as if to underscore the declaration.

"Sometimes I think I might like something to do."

He tipped his head, and she knew that he had heard the change in her tone. "Like what?"

"Oh, gosh, I don't know, just something to do with my days, that's all."

He ran a hand behind her neck and gently pulled her close so that he could kiss her again. It was so tender and sweet between them just then that she felt badly admitting to him that she could ever need anything else but his love and their marriage.

"Something more than keep our home and cook those wonderful meals you do?"

"I'm a horrible cook."

"You are not."

"Well, you are biased."

She smiled as he caressed her neck with skillful fingertips, but she pulled away from him suddenly, sat back up and busied herself with pouring a second cup of lemonade. This was not the place for them to get carried away with more than a few kisses.

"What do you do when you're gone from the house?" Harlean asked.

"I just knock around with the guys here and there, whatever they're doing. No big deal. Got to stay in their good graces, you know. What's with the third degree, doll?"

"I'm just curious."

But of course it was more than that. She didn't want to believe he had a serious problem with drinking, but his behavior with his new friends, and what happened on the cruise, had startled her enough to put the thought into her mind. She couldn't help but worry now every time he took a drink because she saw that it changed him.

After lunch Chuck took the picnic basket back to the car. Then they hiked along the trails up through the hills of the park where they talked about a bit of everything, and nothing, as young couples do. As they wandered, she told him the vision she had for decorating their house, and then he proposed the possibility of taking a trip up the coast to Santa Barbara. Later, she asked him whether he'd yet been convinced of the beauty of poetry through reading the Keats volume together in the evenings. Harlean loved how he could make her laugh one minute, and say something poignant the next. She liked to think they could talk about anything, yet she still could not make herself tell him about the dare. Besides, flattering as it was, it wasn't going to come to anything. Dave Allen had been polite but there really had been nothing more to it than that.

They held hands on the way back down to the car just as the afternoon air began to cool and the trees around them bristled.

"I need a long hot bath when we get home. I'm sore from all this walking," she said.

"I'll scrub your back."

"Chuck!" She gave him a slight smile.

"The privileged life of a happily married man," he declared, looking to her in that moment much older than he really was. Even when he smiled, there was always that deep sadness behind his eyes. Tragedy had a way of doing that to people, she thought, suddenly sorry she had never gotten to meet his parents. She had a feeling Chuck was a lot like them, and she found herself hoping they would have liked her.

Later that evening, after the dinner dishes were done, when Chuck himself surrendered to a bath she had drawn for him, Harlean had a moment to herself and picked up the telephone. While she had her mother's aunt Jetty nearby out in Long Beach, who she could telephone from time to time when she got lonely, she had longed for days to make a call home.

"Oh, Baby, it's so wonderful to hear your voice."

"Yours, too, Mommie. You'll never guess what happened, not in a million years!

"It really was the strangest thing." She lowered her voice and cupped her hand around the heavy black phone receiver as she explained about Dave Allen.

In response, her mother gasped. "You're joking! Why, that's absolutely wonderful!"

"No one will call me of course, but I had to tell you about it."

"Of course you did, my sweet baby girl. We tell each other everything. I'd have been hurt if you didn't!"

Harlean felt herself relax just hearing her mother's voice and the urge to confess further grew.

"I told them my name was Jean Harlow. I'm not sure why I did it. Maybe so Chuck wouldn't have to know for now."

"Sounds like you're dealing with the same jealous Charles," her mother said flatly. The dig at Chuck notwithstanding, Harlean still felt a familiar surge of longing for her mother's company. She never realized so fully until they spoke again after a few days' absence, just how much she missed their tender mother-and-daughter confidences.

Harlean could hear a sudden muffled exchange with a man on the other end of the line, her mother's hand over the receiver. "You know, as it happens, Baby, Marino and I have been talking about taking a trip out to California ourselves, maybe staying awhile."

She could hardly contain her joy at the prospect. Her dislike of her stepfather paled in comparison to her overpowering love for her mother.

Her father and slick Marino Bello were polar opposites. Mont Clair Carpenter, a prosperous dentist, had tried to give his beautiful blonde wife everything in order to keep her happy. As the marriage began to fall apart, he had worked hard just to keep her. In the end, no amount of money was able to do that. The fact that her mother had replaced her quiet, tenderhearted father with a huckster like Marino was as foul a thing as Harlean's romantic mind could conjure. But her mother loved him, so Harlean had resolved long ago to keep her silence about him.

"Well, that would be really wonderful. I mean, if it's no trouble for Marino."

"Don't be silly, Baby. Marino loves you as if you were his own daughter."

She didn't believe Marino really loved anyone other than himself, but as usual, she resisted saying it for her mother's sake.

"And while I'm there, I can go with you on auditions. After all, I do know my way around the studios, so things will go so much more smoothly for you, my darling Baby. Fear not," Jean Harlow Bello exclaimed, "Mother will be there soon."

CHAPTER SIX

Things were going so well between them that Harlean still hadn't found the courage to tell Chuck about the impending visit by her mother and Marino. She and Chuck sometimes spent long, lazy mornings reading the newspaper together with breakfast in bed, and wonderful afternoons—when he wasn't with the boys—ambling through quaint antiques shops in Santa Monica, hunting for special pieces to accent their home. She only wished it could be more often. In the evenings, they often played backgammon, or cards with Rosalie and Ivor. But her hesitation over revealing the visit sooner than she must was not without reason. Chuck found Jean Bello overbearing and controlling. And despite Harlean's best efforts, he could not be swayed to see what it was that she loved so much about her mother.

A yipping sound, a high-pitched bark, woke her very suddenly one morning, a few days after their hike through Griffith Park. Harlean struggled to see the clock on her bedside table. Half past eight. She could feel the bed was empty beside her. The heavy draperies on her bedroom windows blotted out most of the morning sunlight so she flipped on a Tiffany bedside lamp and sat up. On the floor beside her dressing table was a fluffy ginger-colored Pomeranian puppy, yelping at her for attention. A lover of animals, Harlean was delighted to see such a cute little dog mysteriously at her feet, however it had arrived there.

"Well, now, who might you be?"

She tossed back the covers, went across the room and saw a red bow and the note tied around the puppy's small neck.

Oscar will keep you company when I'm not here. He is the only other boy allowed access to your boudoir. Love, Chuck.

Entirely charmed by the cute and unexpected gift, she placed her hands on her hips. "Oscar, is it?" The dog stopped barking now that she was paying attention and his tail began to wag. "You're an awfully demanding fella, aren't you, Oscar?"

She bent down and scooped him up into her arms, which he quite happily tolerated with a whimper. Then he began to lick her cheek with his sandpaper tongue.

"Let's get one thing straight right from the start, Buster Brown. You might have access to my bedroom boudoir, but my husband is the only one allowed to kiss me in here, is that clear?"

It felt like ages since Harlean had had a pet of her own. Back in Missouri, she'd had quite a menagerie to care for and keep her company while her mother was out. When she was a little girl, Grandpa Harlow had spoiled her with kittens, a Labrador puppy and even a parrot—as many pets as she could convince him to let her have. She owed her grandfather a letter, she thought, and she would reread his last one to her for how much she missed him.

Her heart swelled with love that Chuck had thought to do

this. She'd been so horribly homesick lately, but this gift made everything seem so much better. Especially with the blindingly dull day of bridge and shopping which lay ahead for her today.

She stroked the puppy's head and, once again, he lunged for her face to lick her. "I can see we are going to have to work on your manners, Oscar," she joked as she took him into the kitchen to see if her very thoughtful husband's gesture had extended to the purchase of dog food.

It had to be done. Harlean knew she had already put off too long telling Chuck about her mother and Marino's visit, which was now only a few days away. In an attempt to divert an argument, she had decided to mention it just after Rosalie and Ivor arrived one evening for a game of cards. Earlier in the day, she had confided in Rosalie, who wasn't particularly thrilled to be caught up in another potential scene, like on the cruise ship, over the subject of Harlean's mother.

"I owe you," Harlean murmured to Rosalie in the kitchen as she stirred a pitcher of lemonade and set it on a tray.

"Damn right you do. Have you even told him yet about Dave Allen?"

"One battle at a time, Rosie, please."

They walked together back into the dining room where Chuck was dealing the cards. "Five card draw?" he asked of which game they would play first. Ivor nodded in accord.

"So, you know how much I've been missing my mother since we've been out here," Harlean began and, as she did, she felt her heart quicken.

She so desperately wanted this to go well and there were a dozen reasons that it wouldn't.

"The mother you talk to on the phone every week?"

Everyone exchanged a glance before they picked up their cards.

"Sorry, doll, yes, I know how much," he amended. "Why?"

"Well, she and Marino are coming out to California for a visit!" Harlean tried her best to make it sound like a wonderful announcement, but it took some effort with her heart racing as it was.

"Isn't that great, Chuck?" Rosalie asked cheerfully before he had a chance to react. "After all, we girls are never too old to spend time with our mothers."

"I'm really awfully happy about it," Harlean added, her glance shifting from Rosalie back to Chuck.

In the silence that followed, she reached across the table and put her hand over his. She was relieved when he didn't pull away, even though he kept looking at his cards. "If it's what'll make you happy, then I'll welcome them to California," he finally said. "How long are they staying?"

There was a note of humor in the way he had added the question, and how quickly. Or maybe it was just that the three of them were so relieved there wouldn't be a scene that Ivor started to laugh. Then they all did. When he gave Chuck a light brotherly clip on the shoulder, Harlean felt herself finally exhale.

Jean Harlow Bello always entered a room as if she were driven inside by the force of a strong wind. There was a confidence and attitude that came with her as well as a mighty swirl of her favorite Shalimar perfume. Today was no different. Chuck held the front door open as his mother-in-law strode past him, swirling onto the scene in a smart burgundy traveling suit, with a fox-fur collar, pearl earrings, fashionable black turban and neat black gloves. Having been a teenage bride herself, and a mother at the age of nineteen, Harlean's mother was still a beauty. But her overly strong personality made a far stronger impression.

Harlean watched Chuck roll his eyes as her mother was followed inside by her husband, Marino, with his oiled inky hair and waxed ebony mustache. He was wearing his customary tight-fitting pin-striped suit with white spats, and he was dutifully toting the luggage.

"Ahh, there's my baby, at last!" Jean cried out as she drew Harlean to her chest and squeezed her. The gesture was theatrical, but she loved being caught up in her mother's distinctive whirlwind embrace.

"Mommie is here now, Baby. All is right with the world when we Harlow women are back together."

Harlean heard the subtle challenge to Chuck in that, as she knew he was meant to, but she refused to react, and she hoped he wouldn't either to ruin their reunion. Besides, it had been cleverly worded as a compliment. Jean was an expert at that sort of thing. Harlean didn't love facing that, and the sensation was unsettling, even mixed with the joy of being reunited.

"Hello there, Charles," Jean said blandly as she tossed Chuck a cursory glance. "Provincial little place you've got here."

It hadn't been meant as a compliment but Chuck had been brought up well enough not to take the bait.

"Thank you, Mrs. Bello. We're happy here."

Harlean heard the unmistakable edge in his response. Jean had never forgiven Chuck for eloping with her precious only child and every look, every word, was meant to remind him of that. In particular, she had resisted inviting him to call her by her first name. But Harlean had gained such confidence these past months of their marriage, by taking chances and by watching Rosalie, that she had every intention now of finding clever ways to help the two of them reconcile their differences, and not allowing her mother to steamroller things this time.

If they spent enough time together, Jean would see what a wonderful young man she had chosen on her own. Going against her family to marry Chuck, when she knew that it was right for her, had only been a prelude to the bold choices she was beginning to make for her life, and she liked the way that felt. The independence she had begun to seek here in Hollywood was drawing her more strongly every day.

"Come on, Marino, let's find the guest room. You do have one, don't you?"

"Mommie, you and Marino take our room. It's larger and much more comfortable."

She didn't have to look in order to see Chuck's shocked stare. "You're staying *here*? Harlean, why didn't you tell me that?"

"Until we find our own place, where would you suggest your wife's mother stay? In a hotel, Charles?"

Knowing how close she was to her mother, Harlean thought he would have assumed the Bellos would stay with them. It was what families did, after all, wasn't it? But then again, as a young boy, before the death of his parents, perhaps they'd never had out-of-town family. How could she know that when he wouldn't talk about any of it? Whatever the circumstances, there had to be a way to make everyone happy. If there was, Harlean was determined to find it. Family and loyalty, after all, meant everything to her.

As the Bellos were settling into the master bedroom, Chuck came to Harlean as she was making up the bed in the guest room.

"Listen, doll, I completely forgot a tennis date I agreed to at the country club in half an hour. I can't miss it since I'm playing doubles. You understand, don't you?"

"I just thought maybe we'd take my mother and Marino out to lunch?"

In response, he pressed a halfhearted kiss onto her cheek

as he buttoned his tennis sweater. "Why don't you give Rosy a call? She can probably finagle another table for you all at the Brown Derby. Who knows, that might actually impress your mother."

Then, before she could object further, he chucked her under the chin and left the room.

When they heard his car engine begin to rumble out on the street, Jean came into the room, sank onto the edge of Harlean's bed and held up a hand to her daughter.

"Come sit with Mommie and tell me absolutely everything. Have you been well? You look terribly pale and thin. Is he even feeding you?"

"I'd rather hear about Grandpa. How is he doing? I try to call him once a week but you know how he hates the telephone."

Harlean sat down beside her, trying to press away her disappointment at Chuck's sudden leaving, as they embraced again. Her mother always smelled like that powdery citrus fragrance and for Harlean it was a comforting scent. Despite the way she had phrased it, Harlean understood the comment. While she encouraged her daughter to keep her figure, Jean would probably always worry about her daughter's health. The severe case of scarlet fever she'd endured as a girl had frightened them both. No one but the two of them truly understood how life-altering that episode had been. It was one of the many things that tightened the finely woven mother-daughter bond.

"Seriously, Baby, how are you?"

"I'm fit as a fiddle, I promise. And there really isn't anything to tell. I registered with Central Casting. Rosalie, that's the girl I was telling you about, didn't believe I'd do it, so it was fun to see her face after I did it."

"On the train here, after what you told me, I was thinking about getting you some elocution lessons, and a few ballet lessons couldn't hurt with bearing before you get a call. Believe me, the cameras see everything. I could never quite make the camera see what others tell me they see of me in person. You know how people have always referred to me as a beauty. But you, you're different, Baby."

"Mommie, there were more than fifty girls there that day, lined up around the office, and one was prettier than the next."

"The world is full of pretty girls, Harlean. You can't let that deter you."

"Deter me from what? It's not like I'm actually going to get an audition. It was a dare I took. Now it's over and done with."

"We shall see, won't we?"

Her mother smiled, and her flawless skin looked luminescent to Harlean in this light. She had always thought her mother was exquisitely beautiful, and she knew people thought they resembled one another. Harlean had always been so flattered by that, and she felt even more linked with her because of it.

"But in the meantime, it couldn't hurt to be prepared. We will get you those lessons. So tell me, how did Charles take the news?"

Harlean grimaced. "Now, Mommie, you know perfectly well Chuck hates to be called Charles since that was his father's name and it reminds him of his parents' loss."

"But *Chuck* just sounds so...pedestrian."

"Well, I'm ordinary, too, you know."

"There is nothing ordinary about you, Harlean Carpenter."

Harlean sighed. "It's McGrew now."

Then it was Jean's turn to roll her eyes. "Fine. What did your Chuck McGrew say about you going to Fox, then signing with Central Casting?"

"He doesn't know, and he's not going to right now, either, until I decide for myself what I think about it all. If he ever has to be told, I'll be the one to do it. Can we talk about something more pleasant, like finding you and Marino a house to rent?"

Jean lifted a shapely blond eyebrow. "Baby, what in heaven's name has gotten into you? This sort of contrary tone with me isn't at all like you. On top of that we've only just arrived, and you're putting us out?"

"I just thought you and Marino would want more privacy."

"And you and Chuck?"

Harlean was eager to change the subject. "Well, I certainly am glad you warned me about sex, I'll say that," she said with girlish delight and, by it, sounding more like the teenager she was than a married woman. "I mean, you really kept nothing back when you explained."

Jean put an arm around her daughter's shoulder and drew her closer. "What would've been the point of anything else, hmm? I always told you, your body is nothing to be ashamed of, nor is sex. It's actually quite splendid. Although I admit factoring you with Charles into that sentiment has somewhat dampened my zeal for it. And while we are on the subject of your husband, does he often go off like that so suddenly and just leave you alone?"

"He doesn't *leave* me, Mommie. He's making friends. It's good for him."

"Never entirely good to leave a beautiful young wife to her own devices."

"I trust my husband and he trusts me." She could hear a note of self-defense creeping into her own voice so she forced up a smile to mask it. But her heart was sinking further by the moment. It was certainly not how she had hoped this would go.

"Maybe he wouldn't be so confident if he knew about the casting office."

"I know you don't like Chuck, but I love him, and if there

is ever a reason to tell him I'll do it in my own time and in my own way. You wouldn't dare tell him about that!"

"Baby, it has nothing to do with liking him or not. You were too young and too impulsive when you married, and you have your whole life ahead of you."

Harlean had longed for this reunion with her mother. For days she had excitedly imagined these first tender moments back together, where she would have a chance to share all that had been happening in her life more easily than on long-distance telephone calls. But this was not at all the encounter she had hoped for. It felt like her mother was attacking Chuck—and therefore attacking her, in that artfully passive way she had mastered—and Harlean could feel her defenses flare.

She was certainly hurt by it, even if she wasn't ready to admit it to her mother. So far in her life, it had never been worth the price of Jean's days-long, stormy tirades if she felt even the least bit confronted or questioned.

"You were young when you married my daddy."

"And you see how that ended up."

"Well, that won't happen to us because *we* married for the right reasons."

"Time will tell, I suppose."

Anxious for a distraction, Harlean glanced down at her mother's lovely silk-faille-covered shoes, ornamented with large square, silver buckles.

"Gee, those are awfully keen."

She knew her mother well enough—better really than anyone else did—to know that this was the best way to divert a scene or end a problem. It was also far more clever than initiating a full-scale tirade so soon after her mother's arrival. Harlean might not always be as forceful as she would like to be, but she did take pride in her ingenuity. For now that would have to do.

Jean glanced down at her own feet, the tense moment between them extinguished in the face of sudden fashion talk, which they both adored.

"Oh, good, I'm glad you like them because, as it happens, I brought you a pair just like them, so we can be twins!"

"Gosh, that's great, thank you, Mommie. I just love them!"

Suddenly, Marino was standing in the doorway, leaning against the jamb, wearing his customary sly grin. He always reminded Harlean of a gangster, but that was another thing she would never tell her mother. Jean believed him to be the sophisticated savior of a floundering Midwest beauty. In reality, he was a smarmy, two-bit huckster.

"So what have you two gorgeous dames got in store for me today?"

As he posed the question, he touched his moustache. Harlean supressed a twinge of disgust in response. What her mother saw in him she would never know, and she certainly didn't care to. But they were here now, and Harlean fully intended to take advantage of the visit in order to bring her mother and her husband together at last. She certainly didn't want this turmoil, she didn't like it, so that was about to come to an end. She would figure out a way. Being in Hollywood again had given her a new confidence she never knew she had, and finally Harlean felt up to the heady challenge.

Over the next few days, Jean and Marino settled into the house as if they meant to remain there indefinitely. Clothing was steadily being strewn and piled everywhere in the bedroom and the bathroom. A few pieces even found their way into the living room. Jean's favorite tablecloth now covered the table in place of one Chuck and Harlean had bought on their honeymoon cruise, and the music on the radio was nearly always the Italian opera that Marino fancied.

As a clear response to their presence in his home, Chuck left early most mornings before Harlean awoke. When he returned at night, he was most often under the influence of more than a few drinks.

"I hate this damn guest room," he grumbled in the dark as he flopped onto the edge of the bed and tried to remove his own shoes and socks without falling over.

Harlean pressed a hand onto his shoulder in a soothing gesture. "You're only saying that because Mommie's in the other room."

"I'm saying it because I haven't made love to my wife since her mother installed herself in my bedroom!"

"Shh, pipe down, or she'll hear you!"

"This isn't normal, doll, us being separated. I miss the feel of you, the way you taste. Not having you is driving me crazy!"

He pivoted on the bed and pressed her back into the pillows, then arched above her before she had a moment to object.

"I need you, Harlean. I need us. Your mother is gonna ruin everything, I know she will."

"Don't say that. You don't know her like I do. She wants what's best for me."

"Not so long ago you told me that was *me*."

His thighs anchored hers to the bed, his hands were tightly cuffing her wrists. Harlean pressed her hips into his, wanting the connection with him every bit as much as he did. But the walls in this house were thin, the two rooms separated only by boards and stucco. The springs on the bed frame creaked.

She could hear the muffled sounds of Marino and her mother talking in the other room.

Chuck kissed her again, one breast then the other. They were straining to hold back from what they both wanted.

"If we're quiet..." he raggedly whispered.

"God, they'll know, for sure!"

Harlean was meeting his kisses with anticipation. He pressed up her silk nightgown straining over her. "So what if they know? I need you, Harlean, you're my wife!"

"Chuck! I *can't*!"

Their heavy breathing fought the silence, though Marino's muffled words still came through the thin walls. "I can't go on like this!" Chuck growled.

"They've only been here a few days."

He moved away from her and fell onto his back, his chest heaving. "Well, it feels like a goddamn eternity to me."

Harlean nestled against him, the sound of his heart slamming in her ear. He was being petulant and spoiled. She waited for him to calm beneath her tender touch. "I love you, Chuck, with all my heart. You know I do."

"Get them out of here, Harlean. I *want* my wife back."

It was the last thing he said before he rolled away from her and pulled the covers up to create a barrier between them.

Harlean rose early the next morning so she could let the dog outside in the backyard. There was a light mist covering the lawn and the sunrise sky was all rose and vermilion. She stood watching it for a while before she went back in to make a pot of coffee, then sank onto one of the new kitchen chairs. She'd been awake most of the night, wanting Chuck as much as he had wanted her and struggling with guilt over refusing him. As glad as she had been about her mother's arrival, it had changed things. The Bellos just needed their own house nearby and then everything would be fine.

Everything would get back to normal.

The ringing of the phone startled her. She lunged toward the dining room nook to answer it. She needed this bit of peace, time to herself. She certainly didn't want Chuck to wake in a fouler mood than the one in which he had gone to bed.

"Hello?"

"Jean Harlow, please."

"I'm sorry, my mother is still asleep and—"

Only then, as the words crossed her lips, did she remember the name she had given to Central Casting. *She* was Jean Harlow.

She cleared her throat. "Jean Harlow speaking."

"Bring your best evening gown to the Paramount Pictures lot. Get here by nine and be prepared to spend the day."

The voice was male, young and in a hurry. She heard the click on the other end before she had a chance to ask if she could bring her mother.

Stunned, Harlean set the phone back in the cradle, then sank against the wall. The spark of excitement she had felt faded quickly when she thought of her mother, asleep and unaware, in the next room. In spite of the enthusiasm she had initially shown, Harlean could not help wondering how the news would truly strike her. After all, Jean Harlow Bello was a beautiful woman who had struggled for years, then finally had given up on her dream only to have her young, pretty daughter called for work in a matter of days—and while using her mother's name.

Harlean fought against the disloyalty and worry she felt. Not only was her mother likely to feel envious, Chuck would doubtlessly feel threatened that a group of men might want to use her in a motion picture.

Hollywood is no place for a lady.

The echo of her grandfather's voice the last time they'd spoken moved through her mind now and added to what she knew would be a resounding chorus of discontent if she went through with this. A silly dare had very suddenly become something more. Harlean couldn't help but feel as if she were on the cusp of some monumental thing, but she still wasn't certain that finding out just what it might be was worth the risks with those she loved.

CHAPTER SEVEN

She decided to leave a note for Chuck saying that she was going off for the day with Rosalie and she was taking the car. Then she left before anyone was awake. She didn't trust herself with them about this yet—her mother would be pushing for one side and her husband would be dead set against it on the other. After all, she kept reminding herself, it was rare to actually be chosen for work from the huge pool of extras they called in. For luck, she had just pinned Irene Mayer's brooch squarely onto the collar of her dress and, before turning from the mirror's reflection, she had admired her ingenuity in obtaining it. Ah, Irene's face when she had presented the business card to her and demanded payment had made the entire adventure worthwhile. Of course she would return it in time, but for now the brooch was a symbol of her having set out to prove something to herself, setting a goal and then achieving it.

Always finish what you start. It was another thing her grandfather regularly said, and the maxim came to her as she walked across the studio lot with a renewed purpose. She wondered, with a spark of amusement, if he would think that applied to his only grandchild trying to wade into the turbulent, highly competitive waters of Hollywood. She already knew the answer to that, of course.

Skip Harlow would be livid.

Two men in silk top hats and tails, each carrying scripts, walked by her with bearded men in plaid shirts and cowboy boots. A group of actresses in dance-hall costumes stopped them to talk. Others wearing ponchos, sombreros and great false mustaches passed her by as she made her way through the bustling Paramount back lot. There was such energy to the atmosphere that she hadn't seen when she was younger, and there was a touch of mystery to it. Harlean hadn't expected to be drawn in by any of it today, but being in the center of everything, and on her own, suddenly felt exciting.

After she checked in at the casting office with a hundred other extras, the women were all shown to a huge room, the walls lined with mirrors, where they could change into the evening attire they had brought with them. Most of the women kept to themselves as they primped, straightened and pinned themselves together. They ranged from stout-looking matrons to slim ingenues. Her mother and Rosalie had both told her that if the hopefuls received a nod in the next few minutes it would mean a day's wages to actors who were more than a little down on their luck. She could hear several of them murmuring prayers and affirmations to themselves as they filed back outside to line up around the soundstage.

While they all waited together, Harlean began to feel as if she were trapped in a crushing jungle of competition and desperation. Most of it was costumed in stained, faded or mended satin, or taffeta and fake fur. The actresses around her gossiped, smoked cigarettes and cracked chewing gum to lessen the strain and pass the time.

Harlean fluffed the rose silk evening dress she had worn on the cruise. It was couture and had cost her grandfather a small fortune. She guessed that hers was the only dress that had actually come from a Paris designer as she compared it to the faded costumes around her.

A no-nonsense-looking woman and man, both in gray business attire, surveyed the long line. The man quickly assessed each hopeful extra and only occasionally said "you." The woman wrote down the person's name on the clipboard she carried, and they moved steadily on.

He had chosen at least thirty by the time he came to Harlean. To her surprise, she felt her heart begin to pound. Suddenly, she desperately did not want to be passed over. It was a curious sensation—one that felt unnervingly like a growing sense of ambition.

When he stopped in front of her, Harlean saw that he was a remarkably young and fresh-faced man for the job. However, his gaze held the critical stare of a professional who had been at this a while.

"You, what's your name?"

"Harl… Jean Harlow, sir."

"Quite a looker. The director will want you, for sure."

She was uncertain whether or not she was meant to respond.

"Follow the others," he said with no inflection in his voice. He moved along down the line and, just like that, her moment was over.

The chosen extras were herded inside a vast soundstage. Cloth-draped tables encircled a large dance floor and huge Georgian-style faux windows, covered with silk draperies tied back with claret-colored cords, gave the illusion of an elegant restaurant dining room.

There was a group of tuxedo-clad actors standing around joking as Harlean and the others came in. The extras were each told to take a seat, then wait for an assistant director to move them around in what felt to Harlean like a game of musical chairs. After everyone was settled, she found herself wedged tightly at a table beside a stout, white-haired woman wearing a rhinestone tiara and a long necklace of amber-colored glass beads.

"Any idea what the picture is called?" Harlean asked the older woman as she took out a cigarette and casually lit it with a gold lighter.

"Not a clue. But a paycheck is a paycheck. Lula Hanford," she said in a slightly graveled, no-nonsense tone.

Harlean was struck by the unique name. It was lovely.

"Jean Harlow."

"You're new around the lot, aren't you?"

"Does it show that much?"

She knew she probably sounded as green as grass, and looked it, as well.

Lula gave a raspy chuckle and exhaled a cloud of smoke as a production assistant began to fill water glasses on each of the tables, and another was shouting to the assistant director. "It only shows to an old broad like me. I've been around a long time, and I've worked with 'em all—Buster Keaton, Mary Pickford, John Barrymore..."

"No kidding?"

"Sure. They put their pants on one leg at a time just like you and me."

"Although I bet Miss Pickford wouldn't like her public to think of America's Sweetheart putting on her pants, just like all the boys," Harlean quipped in a low voice.

Lula Hanford chuckled. "You're sharper than you look."

"Thanks...I think." It was quickly becoming her standard response. She knew she could use more confidence, and she meant to work on that.

"Relax, it was a compliment. A talented girl who looks like you could go far in pictures."

"If one of *them* doesn't poison my water."

They both glanced at the next table where four sour-faced women were seated together. Each of them shot Harlean a foul glare before they looked away.

"Or trip you on your way to the toilet. That happened to me once when I was much younger, so you gotta watch out."

"I'll have to remember that."

"It can happen just as easily when you're older. I worked on a picture with Lillian Gish once and played the second lead. Beautiful girl, sweet, too, but she was always trying to steal my scenes, which I never understood since I was playing her mother."

Harlean found herself thinking that she could learn a thing or two from this woman as the work to set up the scene continued around them. Two of the actors in white dinner jackets were being instructed on how to hold the trays. Harlean hadn't realized before now about the details—every hat, every necktie—all needed to be in place. There was something fascinatingly meticulous about it.

"Still, that must have been so gratifying to see your name on a marquee."

"Not another feeling in the world like it, honey," Lula said.

"Places, everyone!" the assistant director called out. "Quiet on the set!"

Suddenly chatter, mimicking the sounds in a restaurant rose up naturally at the director's signal. Harlean leaned forward as though she were speaking to the other woman seated across the table. Her heart was still racing, even though she struggled to look exceedingly nonchalant. She tried to imagine being a worldly young woman, and conveying it, so that if the camera caught her it would pick that up.

Being in the middle of this was certainly more exhilarating than she had expected. The dare had become a surprising pleasure.

The scene took several hours to shoot. It was shot and reshot before the slim, gaunt-faced man sitting beside her injected himself into her conversation with Lula Hanford.

"Say, weren't we in that picture with Buck Jones a few years back?" he asked Lula.

"I love Buck Jones!" Harlean interrupted, sounding every bit seventeen, even if she didn't look it in her gown and makeup.

"Bit pompous for my taste, but handsome enough," said the man seated on Harlean's other side. His eyes were bloodshot and his hands were shaking. He looked like he could use a drink. Lula looked more closely at him.

"Lloyd Bradshaw, as I live and breathe."

"At your service," he said with a nod.

"My, my, well, it *has* been a while."

"Haven't won many roles lately. Honestly, I've been struggling a bit."

"Haven't we all, Lloyd, haven't we all. They're saying *talkies* are about to change everything. They seem to be looking for different types now than they were when you and I were working a lot."

"Change would be good, if there is a paycheck to be had. When I audition now, though, they keep saying my accent is too distinctive and isn't right for the part. My voice, my accent...all we ever cared for even a couple years ago was our facial expressions and how that came across on-screen. Don't get me wrong, though, work is work."

Harlean thought how Lula's dignified tone matched the image she projected, Lloyd Bradshaw's high-pitched Bronx tenor did not. That could not bode well for his future in talking pictures.

They shot the scene again and then someone shouted out, "Take ten, everybody."

Harlean stood to stretch her legs. She had a cramp in one of her calves. Lula stood beside her. "Not a fan of brassieres?" Lula asked as she glanced at Harlean's chest.

"I loathe them, actually. Anything constricting makes me want to run the other way," she admitted, and then she felt herself blush. "I was ill with scarlet fever when I was a child, and confined to my bed. After a while, it began to feel like a cage, the bedding felt like prison bars. It made me panic. Ever since then, I've been kind of a free spirit, I guess you could say."

"Good thing you've got a small bosom, then, beauty that you are. I'd cause a riot if I tried that."

They had a chuckle together at that. It was easy speaking with her. There was something about Lula that reminded her of her mother. Not her looks, it wasn't that. Rather, it was seeing a gutsy woman's more human side, a hint of vulnerability. The monotony of sitting there for all those hours had created a bond, as well. Women could talk of just about anything when that happened. This surely was not the glamorous side of Hollywood.

Harlean's gaze then landed back on Lloyd Bradshaw who was cautiously swilling from a silver flask, then stuffing it back in his coat pocket.

"Poor Lloyd. I knew who he was the moment I saw him. We go way back. You might have guessed he's a bit overly fond of the drink."

As Harlean sat back down, waiting for them to call an end to the break, she noticed an extra across from them whose auburn hairpiece had slipped just slightly, revealing coils of gray beneath. He quickly adjusted it and then pridefully tipped up his chin. She had been struck by others in the group of extras, too, but to her he symbolized the struggling young actors, hopefuls and has-beens that permeated the movie industry. Perhaps she could relate more to these people than she had initially thought—they had their own insecurities, just like she did. There was weakness and pride, such dimension to all of them, once she really looked.

Filled with the newfound realization, Harlean sank against the chair as, once again, crew members began adjusting the lighting. Lloyd's hands had stopped shaking, no doubt courtesy of the contents of his flask.

"Since it looks they're going to be a while, tell me about the picture you did together," Harlean asked Lula and Lloyd with genuine interest.

"It was *Hearts and Spurs* with that cute young Carole Lombard, if memory serves."

"Why, yes, that was it!"

"I played a gambler. You ran the saloon," he recalled with a broadening smile.

"We shot it in the Santa Monica Mountains. I had my own trailer on that picture."

"We both did." He let out a nostalgic sigh. "I thought I was really on my way to being somebody back then."

"All right, everybody, places!" the assistant director finally called out on his bullhorn again.

For Harlean the tedium of the process was balanced by the entertaining company surrounding her. She was fascinated by the stories they began to tell, and she felt relaxed with them both. No one here knew who she was, that she had been so sheltered her whole life—or that, until she met Chuck, she had considered herself a loner and a bookworm. Nor did they care. They seemed to be taking her at face value. Today, she was just "Jean," a new girl in the business, one who could use some advice, and camaraderie, from two seasoned professionals.

During the lunch break, as they ate bologna and cheese sandwiches and drank lukewarm coffee, she could hear a murmured conversation between the two assistant directors as they looked at her then looked away. She could see that Lula heard it, as well.

"Now, see that one, Harry, the blonde over there? I'm tellin' you, the camera loves *her*. She jumps at you right through the lens. I saw it for myself when we were setting up the last shot."

Even though they spoke in low tones, Harlean did not miss a word of their conversation. She drank it in, savored it and thought of how she might use it to her advantage. Touch the line without crossing over it—she was learning for herself that was the key.

"No fooling. Who is she?"

"How the hell should I know? She's some extra, for now, anyway. But if she's got an ounce of ambition, we'll be seeing her again."

Lula took a swallow of the cold coffee. "They're talking about you."

Harlean felt a sly grin turn up the corners of her mouth. Their compliment was flattering to her.

"I didn't think I'd like this whole picture business, but I actually kind of do. Around here, no one is judging me."

"My dear, everyone is judging you. It's just that, for the moment, it's in a good way."

"How can I do what he said, come around again, get more work?"

"For that, you'll need to be smart, and stand out for more than your looks."

"But how can I do that?"

"To begin with, make sure your shoes are clean. Assistant directors always look at your feet first. And another thing, if

you really want my advice, invest in a few smart-looking hats.
You can fake clothes, but you can never fake a stylish hat."

She thought for a moment. Those things would be easy.
Her mother had given her a strong sense of fashion and her
grandfather had long funded it. "Sure, I can do that."

Lula reflected for a moment on her own advice as extras
began to stand up and toss the remains of their lunch boxes
into a garbage can at the end of the table. "And watch your
makeup. You'll never get a close-up if your skin isn't flawless."

"A close-up?"

"I *assume* you aren't going to want to do extra work forever.
That dress of yours alone is worth more than a lot of these
folks earn in a month."

"I hadn't thought…"

"Well, you've got to think ahead. Believe me, your competition does."

She hadn't fully considered that it was a competition—but
Lula Hanford was right, that's just what Hollywood was—one
great, big, tumultuous competition. But suddenly, the prospect
actually seemed more exciting than frightening.

It had been a long day and Harlean was dragging by the
time she arrived back at the house, toting her evening dress
in a garment bag. Marino was making pasta and her mother
was sitting at the kitchen table filing her fingernails. A lively
Duke Ellington tune blared from the radio, threading through
a conversation between Jean and her husband. Finally, at least
it wasn't opera she had to listen to.

Chuck came in a moment later and stood in the doorway.

"Where the devil have you been all day? I talked to Ivor
and he said Rosalie hadn't seen you."

"No, I wasn't with Rosalie," she confessed.

The nail file stilled in her mother's hand as she glanced up.

"Well, at least you're not planning to lie now," he grumbled.

"Oh, for heaven's sake, Chuck, is that really necessary?" Jean sighed as she rolled her eyes. "Sit down, Baby, and tell us about your adventure today."

"How the hell do *you* know what my wife was doing?"

"Best to watch your tone, my boy," Marino interjected matter-of-factly as he stood stirring marinara sauce at the stove.

"A mother's intuition, is how I know, and a mother is always right," Jean replied in a curt tone.

Harlean sat down beside her mother as Chuck sulked around the kitchen. "It *was* an adventure, Mommie, an amazing one."

"There, you see, Chuck? So, Baby, you got a casting call?"

"I went to Paramount. They called me in when you were all still asleep, and then I was chosen from a huge herd of people. Gosh, you wouldn't believe the size of the crowd, people were everywhere and it took the whole day to shoot the one scene. It was for a picture they're going to call *Moran of the Marines*. Richard Dix is the star. I saw him, Mommie, I was as close to him as I am to Marino! I made seven dollars all on my own, and they gave us a box lunch."

"Insipid title. Sounds like *Moron of the Marines*."

"Don't be rude, Charles. Clearly, the directors could see how exceptional your wife is, the way I have seen it all along. She was picked from an enormous crowd," Jean boasted with an overabundance of maternal pride.

"I can't believe you went behind my back."

"It was early, Chuck, and I just didn't want to wake any of you, that was the only reason, honest."

"Well, seven dollars won't even buy a pair of those fancy buckle shoes you insist on wearing, so I sure as hell don't see what all the fuss is about," Chuck grumbled.

Marino set down the wooden spoon and pivoted away from

the stove. His blue-black hair shimmered in the light from the milk-glass ceiling fixture. "Good gracious, boy, can't you be happy for the Baby? She had herself an adventure. Why would you begrudge her that?"

"She's *not* a baby, she's my wife, goddammit, and I don't see why either of you would want to get her hopes up. Particularly not you, Mrs. Bello, since you know how tough rejection is in Hollywood. You sure got enough of it yourself during your failed attempt at becoming a star."

Jean shot to her feet. "Impertinent prig."

"That's enough, both of you," Harlean said, trying in vain to run interference. "Come on, Chuck, take a walk with me till dinner's ready."

"Tell me this first, did you get another job?" Her mother interjected as Harlean walked over to Chuck and clutched his hand.

Harlean saw Chuck's deep frown. His face had flushed crimson with pent-up frustration. She wanted to tell him first, and privately, once they'd gotten some fresh air and he had calmed down a bit. She knew he was already tolerating so much by having her mother and Marino here, and with her mother still needling him at every turn. Harlean was disappointed she had yet to take command of that, although she was trying.

"Well, did you?" Jean repeated anxiously.

"The assistant director took a liking to me and introduced me to a casting director before I left. Joe Egli."

Jean gasped. "You actually *met* Joe Egli?"

"That's how I got the next job. He called over to Fox where he knew they were hiring. I have a call tomorrow. It's a prison picture called *Honor Bound*. It's just another crowd scene, but it's more work!"

"Oh!" Jean exclaimed as she drew her daughter to her chest

and wrapped her into a tight embrace. "That's my Baby! I knew if they could just see you this would happen!"

Harlean and Chuck walked outside after that and stood beneath a bright quarter moon in a breeze that was balmy and soothing. Chuck had tried to pull his hand away from hers, but Harlean had only clamped onto it more tightly, her determination overpowering his strength in the moment. She reached up and cupped his chin in the palm of her other hand. His jaw quivered at her touch.

"They'll be gone soon. Mommie said she had an appointment lined up tomorrow to look at a house for rent."

"God, how I hate when you call her that," he groaned as he looked away.

"Listen, Chuck, you know how sorry I am about your mother but you don't have to take it out on me because I still have mine."

Harlean heard her own harsh tone the moment the words left her lips, and she was instantly sorry that she had allowed her frustration to lead her.

"I'm sorry, that was cruel of me," she said. "There's just so much inside you that you won't share with me. Sometimes it's difficult to know how to reach you, especially when it comes to that subject."

"I don't like you talking about her, or my father, either. I think I've made that pretty easy to understand." She heard the sharp defensiveness in his tone, and she was even more ashamed of herself. She willed her next words to be spoken slowly and tenderly.

"But it might do you some good. People need to grieve, Chuck, or it'll be like poison. It'll tear your heart up inside."

"How the hell would *you* know?" he snapped at her.

"I lost my daddy."

"Mont Clair Carpenter is still breathing, doll," he shot back.

His tone was still harsh but now it was fragile, too. She hated how easily she could imagine him shattering. "You have no idea at all what my grief feels like."

She put a hand on his shoulder. "I'd like to, though. I want to share everything with you, even that."

"Well, you can't. No one can."

"I can't because you won't let me."

"Because I *can't* let you! I refuse to feel that pain, or even think about it, because there's not a damn thing I can do to change it!"

Harlean saw tears suddenly shining in his eyes. "Do you think maybe that's why you lash out sometimes, though?" she asked very gently.

She hoped he wouldn't lash out at her even more for suggesting it.

Chuck ran a hand behind his neck and took a deep breath. "I just don't have a good feeling, Harlean, that's all. It feels like a premonition and I can't shake it."

"About the jobs? I won't do it if it makes you unhappy," she said still very tenderly, but not certain even as she spoke if she actually meant it.

Harlean had really liked the experience she'd had as an extra and secretly she couldn't wait to do it again. There was a bold new sense of adventure beginning to ripen and strengthen inside of her since the day she'd watched Rosalie at that Brown Derby when a world of possibilities felt opened up to her. That sense was increasing little by little every day. It was a powerful thing that had begun to shape her into what felt like two distinct people. One was an ambitious young woman with a new zest for adventure, a girl who wanted to take chances. The other was a teenage bride, still content in the comfort and security of a great first love. Despite what she had told

Chuck after they'd first arrived in Hollywood, Harlean had begun now to want both.

She just wasn't sure about how to have one without risking the loss of the other.

"It just seemed fun, that's all, and to tell you the truth, I was already bored to death going to lunch every day with the girls, and endlessly shopping. It's not enough for me."

She could see him fighting a smile hearing that. "That would be pretty dull, especially with Irene Mayer leading the pack. God, she's a raving bore."

"There, you see? Now, how can you consign your wife to the company of dull women while you're having a grand time around town with the guys?"

His smile broadened just before he pulled her against his chest and wrapped her so tightly up in his arms she almost couldn't breathe. But, God, how she loved the sensation of being so close to him, and the anticipation of what she knew would follow. She had missed every other sensation he made her feel when they were alone like this.

Chuck kissed her then, pressing the lean length of himself tightly against her. She knew how desperate he was for her, as they stood together like that beneath the moon, and she thought again how desperate she was for him, too.

"You know..." she said seductively as his mouth found her throat and then the lobe of her ear. A shiver worked its way down her spine. "It's amazing how many uses there are for the seat of a car, when you put your mind to it. You taught me that."

He stopped kissing her for a moment as he realized what she was proposing. "Marino is making dinner, you know."

"So he is. But that's the great thing about spaghetti. It tastes just as good cold. I'm sure that moon looks even brighter right now from Griffith Park. Shall we take a quick drive and see?"

Harlean held his hand tightly as they headed toward the car. Suddenly everything seemed a bit brighter to her. She was so glad they had cleared the air, and worked things out. It was awful when they quarreled, but they were moving forward now, and doing it together. He held the car door for her and she felt a spark of delight when she realized that her optimism and determination might actually be paying off, if only she stuck with it. Suddenly now, she could hardly wait to see what tomorrow would bring.

Chapter Eight

A background scene in *Honor Bound* did come next, and then a two-reel comedy called *Chasing Husbands*. As spring fell fully into the summer of 1928, each job brought another, and over the next few weeks, Harlean was ever more drawn to the bustling atmosphere around the studios, and the interesting collection of people she found there. She was gaining confidence that she did have something distinctive to offer in this competitive business, so long as she was patient and very smart.

For a time things were less volatile at home between her mother and Chuck. Harlean placated and satisfied him in every way she could in order to keep him from flying off the handle. But his greatest reward came a month after their arrival when Jean and Marino Bello announced they had finally found their own house to rent nearby on Maple Drive.

When Harlean came home after a full and exhausting day of work on a film called *Why Be Good?*, Chuck was waiting for her at the door in a stylish black suit and crisp red necktie. He was holding a huge bouquet of white orchids. In that moment, he looked every bit the matinee idol Harlean had seen around the studio lots. She felt an overwhelming rush of tenderness and love.

"What's this for?" she asked as he pressed a kiss onto her cheek.

"Can't a fella dress up now and then for his doll? I'm taking you out," he said.

"Oh, Chuck." She was exhausted and all she wanted to do was soak in a hot bath and go to bed. But seeing the look in his eyes, Harlean didn't dare admit that. "So, where are we going?"

"How does the Del Monte strike you?"

"The speakeasy over near the boardwalk at Venice Beach?"

"That's the one."

"I thought that place was impossible to get into."

"Ivor's got a pal who knows the bartender. He's gonna let us all in."

He seemed genuinely excited by the adventure he had planned for them.

She decided, as Chuck kissed her again, that they could do with a night of fun together, even if they would have to be with Rosalie and Ivor. Harlean was not a great fan of Ivor's monosyllabic responses when he spoke, and his general disdain for literature as "pointless." But the prospect of something daring, like an evening at a speakeasy, suddenly filled her with renewed energy and brought the color swiftly back to her cheeks. She wrapped her arms around his neck and let him kiss her more wantonly.

"Where are Mommie and Marino?"

"Out buying a bed for their new place."

"Who needs one of those when you've got a car?" she giggled.

"Beds *do* come in handy, though."

"So how was your day? What did you do while I was away?" she asked him, intent on changing the subject, and because she truly did want to know.

They walked together into the kitchen so that she could put the flowers in water.

"What I did was I missed you—and I went downtown to buy you flowers." The playful evasion of anything more did not concern her because she could see that he was happy.

"Anything else?"

"I phoned my grandparents in Chicago, actually."

Harlean set the flowers down and leaned against the kitchen counter. She pressed her curiosity down so that she wouldn't ruin the moment by saying the wrong thing. She was still ashamed of herself for what she'd said the last time the subject of his family had come up.

"Oh? How are they?" she cautiously asked.

"My grandma had a nasty fall a few days ago, but Grand-dad is taking care of her himself, and spoiling her rotten apparently. Just what I'd do for you."

She heard the slight shift in his tone with the last few words. She knew it was the reference to family, and the tie from there back to his parents that had brought the change. Harlean needed to be careful with this sudden and fragile first step she hoped he was finally taking with her. So she would put it away for now, and keep it safe for him. Hopefully one day soon he would bring it up again, and when he did she would give it all the tender care he so needed.

"How was it to speak with them? I mean, are you okay?"

"Why wouldn't I be?" he sharply asked, playing it off and shifting things quickly between them. "It was just a phone call after all. Now come on, we need to get changed. We're running late as it is."

Rosalie and Ivor rode with them out to the Venice board-walk and parked right in front of Menotti's, a grocery store that was the front for the basement speakeasy. It was a lovely warm late-summer evening.

Harlean was wearing a calf-length powder-blue satin halter dress and strappy heels, and she had dabbed a bit of Shalimar perfume behind her ears. It had always been her mother's favorite scent but it was hers now, too. Rosalie wore a red beaded dress with sparkly fringe at the knee and a matching plumed headband.

She found it a curious sight to see so many couples in evening attire filing into a grocery store, but the sly grins all around made the prospect of the night ahead all that much more exciting.

Chuck squeezed her hand as they followed Ivor through a back workroom door. Two swarthy-looking male employees of the "market," both wearing long white aprons, nodded as they passed. One of them winked at Harlean.

As they trooped together down the steep and narrow staircase into the basement, Harlean forgot entirely about the long and tedious day of endless takes, lighting adjustments and wardrobe changes to wait through.

This was pure fun.

After giving the password to a gruff sounding man on the other side of a closed steel door, they waited for what seemed an eternity beneath a single bare lightbulb. Finally, the heavy door was drawn back and laughter and loud, inviting music spilled out around them.

They were ushered inside, and the door was locked behind them by a massive bald man in a dark, pin-striped suit. Harlean felt a shiver when their eyes met for a moment. She wasn't sure if he would have liked to kiss her or kill her.

She and Chuck were quickly engulfed in the frenzy of the trendy, illegal nightclub, already in full swing. Scantily dressed "flappers," in fringe with bobbed hair and headbands, were shimmying and shaking in time to the music. Nearby, couples stood chatting with friends, all holding cocktails or glasses of Champagne.

Thick cigarette smoke cast everything in a deep blue haze.

"Come on, y'all, let's grab that table by the dance floor," Rosalie called to them over the din of music as she pulled Ivor more deeply into the mix. Chuck and Harlean exchanged a quick glance, then dutifully followed.

The music was so loud—horns, strings and a throbbing base—that all any of them could do was smile and laugh as they wound their way past the bar and through a tangle of waiters and patrons. They went past two men who looked like gangsters, then a couple locked in a passionate, unashamed kiss as they stood and swayed to the music, making a halfhearted attempt at dancing.

There was nothing about this place, Harlean thought, that made her feel the slightest bit comfortable, yet she was loving every moment. All of the tension from the constant friction between her mother and Chuck, for the moment, was forgotten. Seeing him so happy here was blissful to her.

By the time they reached the free table, a Charleston contest was beginning. The flappers were happily pushing their way onto the dance floor beside them as Ivor ordered highballs all around and a bottle of Champagne. The beat of the music was hitting Harlean deep in her chest, making her dizzy, but she savored the wild sensation.

Ivor lit two cigarettes and handed one to his wife in the cliché style of a leading man. Chuck tapped in time to the music on the tabletop and drank his cocktail in one swallow as soon as it arrived. "Come on, doll, let's dance!" he exclaimed, as he pushed back his chair and stood.

"I still can't do the Charleston, Chuck," Harlean yelled

back, leaning in and hoping he could hear her over the loud music. "I'm awful at it!"

"Then we'll just move around and have fun," he shouted with a wide smile. "That's why we're here, isn't it?"

Because she couldn't argue with that, she let him lead her into the mix of couples. This was so much fun, and she did so adore him.

After they were predictably eliminated from the competition, they rejoined Ivor and Rosalie, who were kissing almost too passionately for Chuck's liking, at the table. Harlean knew it because she saw his brief scowl but she was determined that nothing was going to ruin this evening for them, so she reached over, grabbed his necktie just beneath the knot and playfully drew him to her.

God, but he could kiss like nobody's business, she thought with dizzying delight. She was blindly, so wonderfully in love.

"Let's have some of that Champagne now, shall we?" Harlean suggested lightly.

Chuck poured four glasses of the glistening, bubbly liquid, and Rosalie and Ivor leaned back into the center of the small table, rejoining the conversation.

"What'll we drink to?" Harlean asked over the blare of a rousing horn solo.

She lifted her glass and everyone followed.

"Since she says we can finally tell you, Rosy landed a walk-on part in a picture!" Ivor proudly announced. "So that's why we're celebrating tonight."

Harlean smiled joyfully and lunged across the table to hug Rosalie. "You minx, why didn't you tell me?"

"Because you, my beautiful little rival, are stealing all the work!"

"I'm not, either," Harlean laughed and shook her head as they all clinked Champagne glasses and the music flared.

"If we weren't suited for entirely different roles, Harlean, I'd absolutely hate you."

Rosalie grabbed her hand then and dragged Harlean back onto the dance floor with a quickly growing group. The song had changed to the jazzy tune "Black Bottom Stomp," which everyone in the place seemed to want to dance to.

Their moves were a joyful shimmy and bounce to the heavy drumbeat and the wild blare of trumpets. Now and then, they all raucously tossed their arms in the air, reveling in the freedom of the moment, until Harlean felt a man's firm hand cup her bottom.

For an instant, it shocked her, but of course it was Chuck, she thought. This evening was proving to be far more fun than she ever could have guessed. But when she glanced over, she saw it was one of the men in the pin-striped suits dancing beside her. He tossed her a suggestive grin and grabbed her again as a tangle of arms and hands, and skirt fringe, moved around them.

It only took a blink after that to feel Chuck's hand tighten like a manacle on her upper arm just before he yanked her back to the table.

"Get your purse. We're leaving, before I kill the son of a bitch!"

Harlean's carefree smile fell as she tried to catch her breath and process the swift change in everything around them, beneath the loud, suddenly grating music. A new crowd of revelers surged past them and onto the dance floor as Rosalie came skittering back to the table. Taking one look at Chuck's furious expression, his body coiled like a spring, Rosalie pressed herself in between them.

"Now, kids, what's all the fuss? Everyone's just having fun."

"No one touches my wife's ass! No one!"

"Good gracious, is *that* all?" Rosalie laughed blithely and took a sip of her Champagne. "Come on, everyone is smashed in so close over there. I'm sure it was an honest mistake."

"I *said*, get your purse, Harlean."

"Jesus, Chuck, don't be such a hothead. The girls were just having some fun," Ivor interjected.

"Stay out of this or I swear to God I'll coldcock you right here!"

"It's all right," Harlean said, putting a hand on Rosalie's arm.

She knew it was anything but all right, yet Chuck's cold stare drove her to do what she could to placate him.

Ivor said they would take a cab home later, and Harlean and Chuck jostled through the crowds to leave. Harlean was glad Rosalie and Ivor stayed behind because she knew the tension in the car would have been unbearable. Besides, the McCrays were their dearest friends in California, and Harlean could not bear the thought that, while tempers flared, Chuck might endanger the close tie the four of them had.

She would get him to calm down once they were alone. She always could.

But when they pulled up in front of the house, she could see the red rage still alive on his face. She hadn't expected that. His hands were gripping the steering wheel so tightly he looked like he could actually rip it out. He was staring straight ahead, his jaw a rigid line of tension.

Chuck turned off the engine and the headlights, and they were plunged into darkness and shadows from the glow of the moon. The light from the living room lamp they had left on spilled out onto the front lawn.

"Tell me you didn't say something to encourage that," he finally said.

"How can you even ask me that?"

"I told you to wear a damn brassiere—at least tonight in that slinky dress, but you wouldn't do it, would you?"

"So I brought it on myself?" she asked with an incredulous gasp.

He was pushing the line with her and now she was the one struggling to keep calm. Harlean could be an understanding wife but she refused to be a doormat.

"That's not what I'm saying."

"Then what *are* you saying, Chuck?"

"I see the way men look at you!"

"Grandpa Harlow always says you shouldn't try to tame a horse by breaking its spirit."

He looked at her, incredulous.

"What the hell do you need spirit for when you've already got a man who loves you?"

"I love you, too, you know I do." Harlean tried to speak as tenderly as possible even though she was getting angry and frustrated. "But that's the movie business, men are probably gonna look at me sometimes, Chuck. I just don't want to stay cooped up here all the time. I actually like working. It makes me feel like I'm accomplishing something all on my own."

"Standing in a crowd and getting seven dollars a day is accomplishing something?"

"They just paid me ten for the last picture!"

It was a defensive retort too swiftly spoken. She knew it the moment she said it, but she had been trying to convey that, though the progress might be slow, she was getting ahead, and Harlean was proud of that. She watched his eyes narrow. A short silence followed and she knew what he was going to say next even before he said it. "What'd you have to do for the raise, Harlean?"

"Damn you to hell, Chuck McGrew!"

Having known he would say it hadn't made it easier to

bear. Instead, it intensified the hurt. She bolted from the car, slammed the door and stomped across the front lawn.

"Don't you dare walk away from me!" he shouted, quickly catching up with her.

She stopped and reeled back around, her face full of fury. "Or what? What'll you do, Chuck?"

"Don't make me show you!"

"Ivor's right, you are a hothead, but you won't hit me so don't even act like you would!"

When they got to the front door he barred her from opening it. She knew her mother and Marino would be inside. She had seen them through the front window. She didn't want Mother to see Chuck in a state like this—it would just give her a reason to start up her tirade against him again.

"Stand aside, Chuck. I'm exhausted."

When he didn't budge, she looked at him squarely with her own confrontational expression. His anger was not subsiding, and she was furious as well now that he had dared to even hint at using violence with her.

"Why didn't you tell me you got a raise? Were you ashamed of what you had to do for it?"

"Did it ever occur to you that I got a raise because I'm damn good? That maybe, just maybe, I earned it? That I have *talent*?"

"You're an extra, for Christ's sake! You stand in the background! At least I hope that's all you did for the raise."

"Go to hell!" she growled at him as Marino opened the front door and Harlean dashed inside.

"What's going on?" he asked Chuck as he stood with a drink in one hand and a lit cigarette in the other.

"Get out of my way!" Chuck snarled and pushed past him.

Before both men were fully inside of the house, Jean came out from the kitchen, carrying her own drink from the private stash of alcohol they had brought with them from Chicago.

Her blond hair was pulled back into its usual elegant chignon and she wore a lace apron over a beige dress.

"Marino, what's happened?"

"The kids appear to be having a spat, dear," he answered as he closed the door.

Chuck began to shout and pushed two living room chairs out of his path which tumbled to the floor. "Harlean, don't you walk away from this! We aren't nearly finished!"

"Well, I say we are!" she hollered from the bedroom. "You're behaving like a barbarian, and that is definitely *not* the kind of man I married!"

It frightened her to see him so out of control like this but if she gave in to her fear, Mother would step in and that would make matters that much worse. She was a woman now, a married one at that, and she needed to handle her own problems.

She heard Chuck upend the telephone table in the dining room alcove and everything clattered onto the hardwood floor.

"Marino, for heaven's sake, do something!" her mother cried.

"Come, my dear, let's take our cocktails out to the backyard and survey the night sky, shall we?" Marino replied calmly.

"I can't abandon the Baby when he's like this!"

"Now, now, *cara*, you know perfectly well Charles won't hurt her. Perhaps it is best to give them a moment's privacy."

Harlean didn't hear them after that so she knew her mother must have complied just as Chuck came into the room and slammed the door. He collapsed onto the guest bed beside her, hunched his shoulders and surrendered his face to his hands.

She waited a moment before she touched him. Then she draped an arm tentatively around his neck. His shoulders sagged at her touch. The rage faded away.

"I'm sorry, doll. I don't know what gets into me sometimes.

Just the thought of how other men see you, your body so perfect, and with a face like an angel."

"That's quite a compliment."

"It's only the truth… I always wondered what you saw in me, honestly, why you chose me. You could've had any guy that summer we met. You're a knockout. No one looks like you. No one ever *will* look like you."

"I didn't want any guy. I wanted you," she said, feeling her tenderness for him swell up again and take the place of her anger. "I still do."

"I'd do anything for you, Harlean, you know I would. I just get scared sometimes…your mother, Marino—Hollywood. I feel like I'm always racing against this great big wind that one of these days is just gonna rise up and carry you away from me."

She kissed his cheek. "Only if you let it."

"And I just can't stand the thought of you being hurt or rejected by a whole lot of second-rate hacks who don't know how special you are."

"I have to try. I'm going to do this, Chuck—with or without your support. But I love you, so I'd sure rather have it than not."

"It's just that you're everything to me, Harlean. I can't lose you. I don't think I'd make it if I did."

"You're right, you *can't* lose me. Unless you are the one to chase me away," she said as she took his hand. "Come on, I want to take you somewhere. This feels like the perfect time."

A quarter of an hour later, Chuck helped her out of the car with a gallant hand and they stood together on a dirt-covered plot of ground at the top of a very steep hill. It had a majestic view over the city lights.

"So, then, what do you think?" she asked cautiously. She was steepling her hands, resting them beneath her chin.

"As bare lots go, it's mighty fine."

"Not as a lot, silly, as the site of a home." She could see that he still didn't understand. "I bought this land for us, Chuck, as a surprise. I was planning to bring you and Ivor and Rosalie up here and make a real celebration of it after we were finished at the speakeasy. I even got Marino to give me one of his precious bottles of Muscatel, which is still in the trunk."

He looked around again and sank, stunned, against the car's front hood, suddenly appreciating the spectacular view more fully. "But how…? I mean, with what?"

"You know my grandpa gave me a bit of money after we got married. He wanted me to have something to fall back on."

"Besides me?"

"Yes, sadly. No one thinks we're going to work out but the two of us. Anyway, for now, even with adding what I've made here and there as an extra, all I could afford on it was the down payment. But I wanted this to be like my wedding gift to you, at least something in return for all you've done for me—for us. Are you surprised?"

"You always surprise me, doll."

"But do you like it? I mean, can you see us building a home here one day?"

"It's pretty breathtaking," he finally replied. She could see that he was stunned by the commitment she was offering to their marriage.

She hugged him as they looked out at the twinkling city lights, in the darkening night. "Can't you just see us here, chasing a couple of our kids around?"

He drew her against himself and they kissed. "Only a couple?"

"For starters. A boy and a girl. Then we'll see."

"Let's start trying right now, what do you say, doll?" he asked as he pressed her back against the hood of the car. She knew he would not take no for an answer and tonight she was glad of it.

★ ★ ★

The phone was ringing out in the dining room alcove.

Oscar was barking at the foot of their bed. Harlean rolled over to check the time on her clock the next morning. Half past seven. She tried to focus, remembering only then how they'd drunk the last drop of Muscatel up on that hilltop.

They had come home after midnight, having made love in the car, steaming up the windows so that Harlean drew little hearts on them. Then they just sat for a while, holding one another until all of the anger from the evening had faded away.

She did so adore him. His power and sheer need always took her somewhere so far beyond herself that she never wanted to come back. Chuck was perfect, she thought. Perfect for her. She believed that she was perfect for him.

She hoped with all of her heart, he was reassured about her devotion.

"Hello?" she said into the receiver. Harlean struggled to push away the slight hangover she felt as she held the phone. This was a daily ritual for a working extra, the prayed for, yet jarring, early morning phone call. She, too, had begun to hope for it in spite of the repetition.

"Jean Harlow, please."

"This is she."

"Miss Harlow, this is Eleanor, secretary to Mr. Allen over at Central Casting. They have a walk-on role for you the day after tomorrow. It will be brief but you'll be highlighted on-screen in a frame or two. It's a comedy with Maurice Chevalier and a new actress, Jeanette MacDonald."

Harlean slumped against the dining room wall. She couldn't believe what she was hearing. It was definitely an improvement from a background scene, and with Jeanette McDonald, who she had read all about. "What time?"

"You'll need to be on set by eight."

She scrambled to keep her voice sounding calm. "Sure, I can do that."

"Perfect. I'll let Mr. Allen know."

Dazed, and still only half-awake, Harlean hurried back to the guest room. She couldn't wait to tell Chuck. Perhaps from now on they could share these small victories, and finally, he could be happy for her. She wanted so badly to have his support in this new adventure. They were a team, after all.

"Chuck!" she excitedly cried as she burst back into the bedroom.

Only then did she notice that Chuck's side of the bed was untouched. She felt the stirring of a new panic and that protectiveness for him flare.

"Chuck?"

Her heart began to race as she dashed back down the hall, calling his name. She found him in the backyard, asleep in a camellia plant. There was an empty bottle of gin still in his hand.

Disappointment flooded her. But instead of feeling defeated, her spirit soared.

"Damn you, Chuck McGrew. You won't ruin this for me! I won't let you!"

Jean's unfailing belief in her, especially in the face of Chuck's reticence, only spurred Harlean's ambition now. She thought with pride of the bare plot of land she had taken it upon herself to buy and only just shown him—a place she could envision a fabulous grand home once they had conquered this town together. She wanted that for herself one day now more and more. Anger and disappointment redoubled her determination. Oh, yes, she was going to show up for that walk-on role and she was going to find a way to make something of it. She fully intended to surprise everyone—with or without his support.

With that thought like the punctuation mark at the end of a bittersweet sentence, Harlean turned and walked alone back into the house to let him sleep it off.

Chapter Nine

"Hurry up, will ya, this stuff smells like poison!"

"It *is* poison, honey," Rosalie said in her Texas drawl. "But you want it blonder, don't you?"

Harlean leaned farther over Rosalie's sink and squeezed her eyes against the burn of ammonia. Noxious fumes filled the kitchen and burned their eyes. It had been a while since she had bleached her hair and now, as her scalp began to burn, she remembered why. The complex process, a combination of peroxide and ammonia, was slightly barbaric, and certainly painful.

With each role as an extra, she had become ever-more fascinated by the complex process involved in movie making: timing, lighting and staging. There was also definitely an art to being noticed on film—to seducing the camera, winning viewers with just a look, a tip of the head. She tried to learn from everything.

Last week, on one of the sets, she had seen a young actress with almost white-blond hair who stood out noticeably from the crowd. It was closer to the shade with which Harlean had been born. The ash-blond shade she had grown into was pretty but it was not striking. The only way to stand out from the hordes of beautiful competition she faced every day was to look striking.

"Well, you want it light, so you've got to be patient," Rosalie instructed. "By the look of it, I'm pretty happy to stay a redhead!"

"I can't say I blame you. I know it's a risk but I've got to stand out somehow where the beautiful girls are just all over the place. This isn't easy, though, a minute too long and all of my hair would fall out. I'm gonna need to find a real hair salon one of these days." Finally, she stood and wound her hair in a towel. "Thanks, Rosie."

"What are friends for? My sink is your sink," she joked as Harlean blotted the tears from her eyes with the corner of the towel. "But, man, it does look painful."

"That it is. But you know my mother. When I was growing up she always used to say a woman has to suffer for her beauty. I guess I took that to heart."

"And it looks to me like you are proving her right. Like a drink?"

"What've you got?"

"A new bottle of whiskey. We could make highballs. Ivor got it from a guy he knows at another speakeasy under the Rosslyn Hotel."

"You and Ivor sure know all the joints around town, that's for sure."

"The other night was a kick. Well, in the beginning it was, anyway. How are things with you and Chuck since then? He was pretty steamed."

"He just drank too much, that's all," she lied and she felt uneasy about it even as the words left her lips. "We're fine, honest."

"He really can be a hothead. Good thing for you he's so damned in love with you."

Harlean smiled even though she was growing increasingly uncomfortable with the conversation. It felt disloyal to Chuck, first and foremost. And she didn't like thinking about their quarrels. She had always wanted to fix the problems around her, not create them, or make them worse. But lately, it seemed the harder she tried to avoid conflict the more complicated things became.

Suddenly she very much wanted that highball.

"You know the ironic thing? About my hair I mean," Harlean said as they walked toward the living room. "When I was a little girl, I hated my white-blond hair so much, you can't imagine. Girls in school called me cotton top and my daddy always said, 'don't worry, sweetheart, you won't have that hair forever. And maybe, just maybe, someday, you'll wish you had it almost white like that again.'"

"Wise man, your daddy. Too bad your mama didn't think so."

Rosalie mixed their cocktails as Harlean unwound the towel and began to blot her freshly blond hair. Her scalp still burned.

"They never got along. Mommie always thought she could have done better."

"Your daddy loved her, though?"

"He would've done anything for her."

"Kind of the way Chuck is with you. Good thing you appreciate your man, right?"

"Yeah," Harlean said carefully as she took a sip of the cocktail and felt the warmth calm her. "Good thing."

She knew it was a tepid response but she certainly didn't want to find herself confessing to Rosalie the condition in which she had found Chuck that morning, and how angry with him she still was over it.

"He wants babies, right?"

"Yep." It was becoming a challenge to retain a tone of nonchalance, so best, she thought, to keep her answers brief.

"Ivor, too. I do what I can to put that off," Rosalie said. "I want a career first, otherwise what's the point of me being *me* at all?"

Not so long ago, Harlean would've had no idea what Rosalie meant. Today, she understood it completely and felt the same way. She was experiencing so many new things about the world of movie making, and about herself. She was using her wits, spirit and a substantial dose of her newly kindled determination and, to her surprise, she really liked how it felt to challenge herself.

Harlean would have confided in her mother about her recent change of heart involving a career, but Jean would have held that over Chuck's head in their rivalry for her loyalty. It still broke her heart that the two people she loved most had to be at such odds. At the moment, it felt to her like Rosalie was the only one who understood this bright flare of ambition she was feeling and the price she was beginning to pay for it.

"So, what was the rush with your hair today anyway?"

Since they were confessing, she might as well keep sharing, Harlean thought. And talking about their careers would keep the conversation away from her personal life. "I've got a walk-on tomorrow. The picture is with that pretty Broadway singer, Jeanette MacDonald. It's only one scene, a moment really, but I'll be one of just a handful of girls in an opera box, and I get to stand and applaud. For that moment, I'll only share the camera with them, not a big group."

She couldn't keep the excitement from her voice. Jeanette MacDonald was about to be a huge star, everyone was talking about her, so it was a picture a lot of people would see. If she didn't plan to remain an extra forever, it was time for a gamble, not just with her hair, but with her entire career—the career she suddenly intended to have. Fully admitting that to herself now came as a revelation.

"Gee, that's really great, Harlean. Why didn't you tell me before now? Don't say it's because I'm an actress, too."

"I don't know, actually," she said, but her tone was not convincing. She reflected for a moment before she added, "For so long, I said I didn't need a career. It was what I told Chuck, and I honestly didn't think I wanted one. But something has changed inside of me since I've been back. I've found that I really like all of the activity, and the challenge of trying to figure out how to stand out from the crowd."

"You knew I was joking the other day about being mad at you, right? Any director who would hire you wouldn't give me a second look, and vice versa. Sure I'm envious of you, who wouldn't be? You're a knockout. But I'm not jealous. There is a difference."

A reluctant smile broke slowly across her face. "You're sure?"

Rosalie laughed. "We're friends, honey. That just wouldn't be right. Have you told Chuck?"

"He doesn't care about that stuff, Rosie. As long as he has his friends in the afternoon, and his supper on the table when he gets home, and a drink or two, he's happy."

"You mean he's not angry."

They were both finishing their drinks and Harlean's short wavy hair was quickly drying a feather-white blond. She was not going to get back into a discussion about Chuck and his temper so she chose for the moment not to respond.

"Wow, go look at your hair in the mirror!" Rosalie exclaimed, the former subject suddenly, thankfully, forgotten. "It's striking, honey, it really is."

"Striking good or striking bad?" Harlean asked warily as they trooped toward Rosalie's bathroom.

"In your case, it's more than good. It makes you stand out."

"Exactly the result I was hoping for."

"With that figure of yours, you look like a goddess now."

"You're exaggerating."

"I wish I were. If Ivor had a thing for blondes, I'd sure be in trouble."

"You know how tough competition is in this town. All that matters is that, for one instant tomorrow, the camera sees me as alluring, or I may not get another shot."

"Oh, you'll be plenty alluring, no doubt about that, honey. The camera doesn't lie, and your best friend doesn't, either," Rosalie said with a wink that made Harlean smile.

The next morning while she was dressing to leave for the studio, Chuck brought her a cup of coffee, then watched as she sat on the edge of the bed and pulled up her stockings. She slipped on a pair of low-heeled calfskin Mary Janes because she knew she would be standing around a lot today and her feet wouldn't be on-screen anyway.

She had taken to heart the advice Lula Hanford had given her, and her face, in morning light, had the dewy, pearlescent quality of something almost angelic. She had worked on her makeup for almost an hour in case there wasn't anyone available for the extras once she got to the studio. It was a perfect complement to the sleek, willowy body she had sheathed in a new ivory-colored, knee-length crepe de chine dress with a band of lace at her hips. Ivory and white had always been her favorite colors so she wore them often. Today Harlean felt pretty and ready to make an impression.

Chuck leaned against the doorjamb with one hand behind his back. He was holding his own cup of coffee in his other hand. He had just come from a bath so his hair was wet. He was barefoot, shirtless and wearing khaki trousers.

"You nervous?" he asked.

"Nervous as a cat, if you want to know the truth."

"Well, you look gorgeous as usual, doll."

She glanced up from her shoes and gave him a fleeting grin. "You're biased, I think."

"Guilty as charged. Love does that to a fella."

"Do you have plans for today?" she asked.

"I'll find something to do, don't you worry about me."

It was these days when she knew he was bored and aimless that Harlean worried about the most. Afternoons at the club or with the boys already weren't enough to entertain him. But she didn't want to upset things between them by starting another argument now that her mother and Marino had moved out and things were beginning to calm down. "I don't know how late I'll be."

"That's okay, you just do what you gotta do. I bought you a little something to wear in your big scene," he said as he held up an exquisite orchid corsage that he had been holding behind his back. Harlean gasped at the surprise, and how delicate and lovely her favorite flower was.

It looked like a work of art.

"For good luck, doll. I hope they let you wear it with your dress."

She rose from the edge of the bed and went to him. "Oh, Chuck, it's beautiful."

"Nothing but the best for my doll."

He could be so wonderful when he wanted to be, she thought.

"I need all the luck I can get today so I'm wearing it, no matter what," she declared and let him kiss her cheek.

She had no idea why he was being so nice to her right now

about today when he had been so set against this endeavor of hers in the beginning. But Harlean wasn't going to question it—she didn't want anything to get in the way of the day she had ahead of her. The only thing she wanted to think about now, what she must focus completely on, was making a spectacular impression on film somehow, since she would have only a brief moment to do it.

She tried not to stare too obviously at Jeanette MacDonald's handsome costar but the crystal-blue eyes and French accent made that almost impossible. He seemed to Harlean the quintessential example of *dashing*. As if he could feel her eyes on him, Maurice Chevalier glanced up from his chair on the set and lowered the script into his lap.

"Well, *bonjour, cherie*, who might you be?" he asked flirtatiously.

"Jean Harlow, sir," she sputtered in reply, embarrassed that he had clearly caught her staring.

He was wearing a white military uniform with huge epaulets and a wide sash. The costume also had red cuffs above his white gloves. Together, all of it made quite a statement on such a handsome man.

"Do call me Maurice."

"Oh, for heaven's sake," Jeanette MacDonald groaned. She sat next to him in her own costume: a gown, white gloves and a large feather boa. She was playing a queen opposite his role as a count. "She's an extra, Maurice. Put your eyes back in your head before I tell your girlfriend."

"Haven't got one just now," he said with a wink directed at Harlean.

This moment seemed surreal. To have an opportunity to meet, even for a moment, an actress, and soprano, she'd read about who had actually been on Broadway, and to do so now while the gorgeous leading man flirted with her, was almost too good to be true.

She glanced down at the gown she had been given to wear for the scene. Unlike the one she'd brought from home for her first film, this one, a pretty cobalt-blue satin, had come from the studio's costume department. She loved how it set off her blue eyes and complimented her newly lightened white-blond hair. Even though that element wouldn't register on black-and-white film she felt beautiful, and unique, in it. Harlean's heart was pounding so furiously that, for a moment, she thought she might faint. The lights were bright and hot. They felt like the sun, and she could feel beads of perspiration beginning to collect and drip onto her cleavage.

She knew this was her moment to seize, a chance to shine, but she knew also that it would be over in a blink. As she prepared for her scene, Harlean took the corsage from her bag and pinned it onto the jacket with which they had accessorized her gown. She wanted Chuck with her now, for luck. Her complex emotions about him lately returned just then to pure love.

Finally, the young actress herself hurried onto the set—a makeshift opera box. She stepped between Harlean and the other girl, her irritation showing.

"God, this thing is itchy," she murmured. "I'd kill for a cigarette but they're afraid I'll set the damn thing on fire."

She seemed nice enough but she slipped ever so slightly in Harlean's esteem. The way she spoke didn't quite match her regal costume, or the reputation she had built. But then she reminded herself that this was a musical with high comedy and everyone was on edge with the unknown commodity of sound, so surely there was leeway for that.

"Quiet on the set! Places, everybody!"

Harlean was starting to grow accustomed to that particular

cry, and even to like it. She found it as exciting as everything else about the process of movie making.

Suddenly a production assistant rushed forward.

"Miss MacDonald, you won't need the boa in this scene. And we need to change your necklace."

"Why the devil didn't you do that in Wardrobe?" she snapped.

The young assistant looked absolutely stricken. Harlean watched his hands tremble as he unfastened the necklace. He was new at his job. She knew the look because she was sure she'd had it not that long ago, so she offered up a smile and a compassionate shrug.

"All right, everybody quiet!"

The assistant backed away with a grateful half smile in return. Harlean's moment was coming. She could feel it sizzling, growing, making her heart race. Ideas swam wildly in her mind. She just wasn't certain she would have the nerve to do anything, especially when she knew what the director expected.

Show them your sparkle! she thought frantically, remembering the word and repeating it in her mind until it was like a silent chant. *You've only got a blink to sparkle!* It certainly was now or never.

"Scene five, take one."

The clapboard snapped and her heart skipped a beat. She heard the camera begin to roll. She was glad this wasn't a speaking part, since her throat was suddenly dry as desert sand.

Gradually, the crowd of extras just off camera began to applaud, creating an audience sound, which would be enhanced later in editing. There was no turning back. The girls were meant to give a standing ovation. It was then that something powerful took her completely over. That quiet spark of ambition reared up inside of her again and in spite of her fear it was beyond her power to ignore it.

As she stood in her satiny gown and newly distinctive white-blond hair, Harlean shifted her gaze. It was just a tick— but enough, for an instant, to meet the camera lens head-on. It was like making eye contact, ever so briefly but distinctively with someone across a crowded room.

Her heart was still racing when the director yelled, "Cut!"

As the three actresses filed off the makeshift opera box set, the same production assistant approached her. "Mr. Lubitsch wants a word with you, Miss Harlow," he said.

Dammit. She had overplayed her hand. A director like Ernst Lubitsch would not take kindly to having to repeat a scene because of the audacity of an extra with stars in her eyes. She had gambled and lost.

Harlean walked slowly over to the director's chair. There was a collection of assistants gathered around him, and another man in a gray suit and tie who she had not seen before. He was a stocky, middle-aged man with a dark receding hairline and heavy, black-beetle eyebrows.

Harlean steeled herself for the lashing that was about to come. Hopefully, he would excuse these people and do it privately. Under the circumstances, that was probably the best she could hope for. Lubitsch was not known as a director with an overabundance of tact.

"Miss Harlow, this is Hal Roach," Lubitsch said.

The Hal Roach? she thought. Everyone across the country had heard the name. He was the director of the wildly popular *Our Gang* comedy series of films. She had loved them so much and they always made her peal with laughter.

"You've got quite a presence, young lady," Roach genially remarked as he extended his hand. "I watched your scene just now and you didn't need to say a word. You just stand out."

She felt her cheeks warm with shock as she met his handshake with a firm grip of her own.

Roach had a deep voice, and a thick New York accent, but there was a kindness in his eyes, and that helped her racing heart slow. She could feel her expression soften.

"Mr. Lubitsch warned me that my face would only be in a couple of frames."

"But what a face it is, little lady. Are you funny?"

"Hysterical," she replied without missing a beat.

She saw a smile touch his lips then disappear. He seemed pleased with her response. "I actually believe you could be."

"Thank you," she replied, with only a slight crack in her voice.

"How old are you?"

"Seventeen, sir."

"Underage. That's a complication," he said with a frown. "Got anyone who can cosign a deal with you? A mother, or maybe a father here in town? I'd like to hire you for a couple of shorts we're shooting next week out at my studio in Culver City, see how you do in those."

This was going so much differently than Harlean had expected.

"That would be wonderful, sir. I'd be grateful for the opportunity."

"Don't get too excited yet. These are just bit parts. That way we can see what you've got."

"Of course, but I'm just excited for the opportunity to come out to Culver City to work with you."

Culver City seemed so far away, out in that vast, bare area of Los Angeles. But this picture with Jeanette MacDonald had whetted her appetite to see how real comedies were made and to take on more challenges wherever she had to go to find them.

"You can take the Red Car line all the way out there, you know."

"Oh, thank you, Mr. Roach, but I have my own car."

He arched a brow now in surprise. "Do you? Not usual for starlets."

"Well, my husband has a car. I mean, we do. We have one. What I mean is, he bought it but that makes it ours and—" She was babbling and she knew it.

He smiled indulgently as he held up a hand. "Less is more, my dear, even sometimes in comedy."

Of course he didn't care about her source of transportation, or her marriage. Embarrassment colored her cheeks, and she could feel them burn.

"Glad to see you're a quick study," he said of her sudden silence. "Are you done with her here, Ernst?"

"Yes, all finished."

"Splendid. You start first thing Monday morning on *The Unkissed Man*. Sound okay to you?"

"Thank you, Mr. Roach," she said as they shook hands again. "You won't be sorry."

"Oh, I never am, my dear. What was that name again?"

"Jean, Mr. Roach. It's Jean Harlow."

Since the next day was Saturday, Harlean and Chuck decided to hike up into the Hollywood Hills. They had not spent enough time alone together lately and that, among the other things, was taking its toll on them both. The thoughtfulness of the corsage had helped mend the worst of the tension, and she allowed herself to admit that she had missed him. It had been difficult to forgive him entirely for ending up passed out in the bushes, however, or for making such a scene at the speakeasy.

Those images were still proving difficult to shake off.

But this was a new day, she told herself, the late-summer air was warm and inviting. They had always adored being outdoors, just taking long walks and talking. Harlean had long marveled at the way the two of them could talk for hours, even about little things: what books she was reading, perhaps a new recipe she wanted to try, or what they thought of the world. That sense of being truly heard was one of the first things that had attracted her to him.

How much richness they found in one another's company, beyond physical attraction, was a thing they seemed to have forgotten these past few whirlwind weeks. They were both guilty of letting it slip away, particularly since her mother and Marino had arrived in town.

"Come on, slowpoke," she teased, a few feet ahead of him on the inclining dirt trail.

"Hey, slow down, will you? It's not a damn race."

"If it were, I'd win," she lightly taunted him, unable to keep the sharp tone from her voice because a part of her was angry with him. "That's what you get for drinking so much lately."

"Don't you worry about me, doll!" he exclaimed, bursting forward in a sprint until he caught up to her at the top of the ridge. "I'll always be able to keep up with you."

He pulled her to his chest, kissed her and then brushed her hair back from her face with both of his hands.

"Don't be so sure about that. I'm a challenge, remember?" she asked.

"It was the first thing I liked about you, actually. Nobody ever challenged me like you. Right from the first I knew you were different."

"Nobody gives you a rougher time, either, I suppose, right?" she asked as she twined her arms around his neck for a moment and then let him kiss her.

"Well, that's true. So, you ever gonna tell me how your

big scene with Jeanette MacDonald turned out, or will I be doomed to wonder forever?"

"I thought you wouldn't be interested."

"I'm interested in every single thing about you, doll. If it's important to you, then it's important to me. Look, I'm trying here, I really am."

"Well, it wasn't a big scene, Chuck. I'm sure if folks blink when they watch the movie they'll miss it."

"I'd still like to hear about it anyway." They began to walk more slowly together, holding hands as they spoke back and forth. "For instance, how did it feel when the camera was on you?"

His tone held a sincerity that suddenly made her want to risk being truthful with him about it. "Exhilarating, terrifying and wonderful, all at the same time. Kind of like being touched with a magic wand or something, I'm not really sure how to explain it, but it all happened so fast, when it was over I felt like I had imagined it."

"Sounds great. And kind of unsettling, truthfully."

"It is both of those things. I mean, it was. I have no idea if I'll ever get a chance like that again, though."

"Sure you will. Hal Roach hired you, didn't he?"

"I wouldn't make too much of that. He's only trying me out in a couple of small comedies, like an audition. Who knows if I can even be funny on film."

"I don't suppose there's much of anything you can't do when you set your mind to it, doll."

"Thanks, Chuck," she said as they walked on, and birds trilled in the trees around them. "And thank you for being interested, at least for pretending really well."

He gave her hand a squeeze. "No pretending at all. I promise."

"Since we're being truthful, tell me what you think of living in California now that we've been here awhile."

"It's not bad."

"No?" she pressed.

"All right, honestly I miss the Midwest sometimes, I do, and I miss my grandparents. But there's always the telephone, right?"

Harlean thought how phone calls had been such a poor replacement for being with her mother and spending time with her when they were apart. Chuck kept everything so deeply inside himself but she knew it must feel something like that for him. She wanted his honesty, but she didn't want to bring up things that would hurt him, either. At least not too much all at once.

"How 'bout the rest of it? Do you have enough to do with Ivor and the boys?"

She couldn't bear thinking that he was drinking so much lately because he was bored here, or unhappy.

He gave a little grunt and a shrug. "Sure, they're swell. Don't worry about me, doll, that's my job—to worry about my gorgeous wife, and see that you're happy."

She pressed a kiss onto his cheek. "Well, I'm happy. And right now, all this walking has given me an appetite, I'm starved."

"Me, too. What do you say, shall we cook something or would you rather go out?" he asked as they finally reached the car. "Whatever your heart desires."

"Let's make that pot roast you like. We have the house to ourselves now so we can do it together."

"Music to my ears, Mrs. McGrew," he said as he closed her car door for her.

After they'd had dinner, with music and candlelight, and read together on the sofa before the fireplace, they lay in their bed in the bedroom reclaimed after Mother and Marino, three days earlier, had moved a few blocks away.

"So, tell me what you're thinking," she bid him as she touched his cheek. She was eager to keep the tender connection from earlier that day and this romantic evening between them.

"I'm thinking we just found one of those ways to set our hearts racing."

"Be serious, Chuck."

"All right, seriously then, in a few weeks your ole man here will be turning twenty-two. What I'm thinking is I'd like to take that trip we keep talking about, up the coast for an early celebration, just the two of us—get away from everything and everyone for a while. Unless, of course, you forgot my birthday."

She had forgotten, completely, and it wasn't actually all that soon. She knew he was just looking for a reason to take a trip. There had just been so much happening lately with her parents, and the increasing number of jobs. "Of course I didn't forget," she fibbed. "And I'd love to do that with you, but I have work."

"You have your hobby, you mean."

"It's not just a hobby, Chuck, it's real work, you said you understood."

"I do understand. When we got to California, away from everything, I just thought I—not some part-time job—would be your first priority."

"Of course you are, you always will be my priority," she said in an urgent tone. "But I'm proud of myself, and you know that right now I have this commitment to Mr. Roach. I'm earning enough to put a bit of money aside for our plot of land and help out Mommie and Marino with their rent and not come to you for it. At least that's something, isn't it?"

Chuck rolled away from her and swung his legs over the side of the bed, then sat up. The tenderness between them was suddenly extinguished.

"That lazy creep could get his own job and not take your money, Harlean. It really burns me the way he boasts about being a man of leisure when he's perfectly fit to work."

"Oh, now," she countered as she sat up beside him. He really could become petulant so quickly, and she had wanted to savor the newly rekindled calm of their wonderful day after that upsetting night at the speakeasy. "I don't really *need* most of my checks, and if it helps them until Marino can find a job out here that he's qualified for, I feel good about that."

"What makes you think Marino Bello has even the slightest desire to get back to work?"

"They're family, Chuck. I don't mind helping them."

"And Bello sure as hell knows it!"

"We were having such a nice evening," she said, showing a half pout of disappointment as he strutted across the bedroom in search of his trousers.

Part of her knew—and had always known—that he was right about Marino. Still, she couldn't be swayed to side against her mother.

Back when she had contracted scarlet fever at summer camp, without a thought for her own health, her mother had raced to her aid, and refused to leave her side while she nursed her daughter back to health, amid the angry protests of the camp director.

Harlean didn't like to talk about it but she had been weakened by that illness and still sometimes she did not feel as robust as she knew that she should. It always reminded her then of what her mother had done for her, her devotion to her only child. It was an event they rarely spoke of but one of the many things that had so tightly bonded them.

"I just hate him, I really do, and I'm not overly fond of your mother, either. Why do they always have to get in the way of what's between us?"

"Stop it, Chuck, please. Why the hell do you always have to ruin a good thing?"

She stood and wrapped herself in her silk dressing gown. It shocked her how quickly her heart could take her from adoration to pure disdain of him, especially when the topic was her mother. Harlean certainly didn't feel that his level of contempt was justified. It made her feel that something else must be at play tonight. Whether he was feeling more threatened than usual by her working, or whether it was those suppressed feelings of loss and grief over his own mother rearing up, she couldn't know. And clearly he was not about to tell her. The frustration she had begun to feel over that was overwhelming.

Chuck shoved his arms through his shirtsleeves as she took two steps nearer to him. "You knew how I felt about Jean when we got married," he said hotly. "She didn't like me or trust me. And the feeling is mutual."

Her mother would never be able to forgive the fact that he had run off with her sixteen-year-old daughter, her only child, and Chuck was not going to let go of the animosity, either. It appeared to her right now that none of them were ever going to get past that and move on.

"*You* knew how much I love her. That is never gonna change!"

She did not even try to keep the warning tone from her voice now. Harlean was too disappointed in him even to try. She might like to be agreeable when she could, but she was fiercely devoted to those she loved. Mother, Daddy and Grandpa Harlow topped the list. For a while, in the glow of a new love and marriage, she had lost sight of that. She would never abandon her mother for Chuck, or the other way around. Sooner or later, they were both simply going to have to learn to share.

He sat on the edge of the bed and shoved his shoes over his bare feet as she watched.

"Where are you going?"

"Out," he grunted. "We're done here, aren't we?"

"Chuck, that was crude!" She gasped at his icy tone when only moments before they were so intimate with one another.

"Your mother brings out the best in me."

"She's not even here."

"Oh, she's here, all right, every day, every night, in our kitchen, and in our bed with us, because she's in your head!"

She tried desperately to think of a retort, but she was so upset by his cruel comments that the words simply would not come to her.

"Please, let's not fight. Stay and we can read together and talk about the poems, like we always do."

He glanced at himself in the mirror over the bureau, as he raked a hand through his hair. Then he paused to look at her. "I've lost my interest in poetry, doll. Why don't you call your mother? I'm sure she'll be happy to come over and keep you company."

"Where are you going?"

"Does it matter?"

She followed him, padding barefoot, to the front door with the question hanging unanswered between them, and her fury growing with each footstep. Once, she would have wanted to answer him. She would have meant to answer—to say something that would make him stay because that was what she had always done. But she was growing up finally and ridiculing her mother had been too much on top of everything else that was happening. This was infuriating, and so was he.

"All right, then go, damn you! And go to hell, too, while you're at it!" she declared as he walked away.

He hadn't heard her, but it didn't matter. Harlean simply could not find any more compassion for him at the moment, no matter what dark demons, or insecurities, might be driving him. Even as he slid into the car, slammed the door, started the engine and drove away she shook with indignation and she could not press away the feeling that she was glad for now that he was gone.

CHAPTER TEN

To Harlean's delight, even by her third day on the set, the cast and crew at the Hal Roach Studios showed a strong camaraderie, behaved almost like a family and welcomed her into it. She enjoyed being around them immediately, and they genuinely embraced her, treating her like part of the team even though she was just a bit player. Everyone referred to the studio as The Fun Factory, and that's exactly what it was. The long drive out to Culver City didn't bother her a bit and she sang to herself all the way to work in the morning.

Oliver Hardy, who everyone called Babe, and Stan Laurel—known as the comedy duo Laurel and Hardy—quickly became her favorite fellow actors. It was guaranteed that they could reduce her, and everyone else, to fits of happy laughter after every take.

Portly, cherubic Hardy took particular joy in making Harlean giggle, and between scenes they began to chat endlessly about their lives. The things they shared cemented the bond between them. His wife, Myrtle, was battling alcoholism, so Harlean felt safe talking to him, as she did to no one else, about Chuck.

"How go the wars today, Sunshine?" he asked her in his

charming way, a way that made her want to tell him every-thing by Friday of her first week.

"I think it's a war I'm losing, Babe," Harlean said sadly as she glanced up from the book she was reading. She sighed and closed it.

She hadn't heard him approach but she was glad to see him. He was just so endearing with his cherry cheeks, shoe-black hair and thin mustache which he colored in with a grease pencil. Around them, production assistants moved some of the scenery as Stan Laurel spoke with the director. Babe had insisted she use his nickname from the first day and now he had given her a nickname of her own. Sunshine was a term that had fit her since that day she and Chuck had first drove down Hollywood Boulevard.

"Another argument?" he asked.

"One seems to run into the next, I'm afraid."

He shrugged his shoulders in empathy, and then exhaled a great breath. "When Myrtle drinks, she can be damn vicious. She's always sorry in the morning, but the insults still sting. I'm a fat bull one night, a clumsy ox the next. Sometimes I wish she would be a bit more creative with her disdain."

She turned her lip out in a pout, not knowing how else to react. "I'm sorry, Babe. You deserve a lot better."

"We both do, Sunshine."

The truth was, she and Chuck had argued every night that week. It was difficult to admit that, even to Hardy who would have understood. The fights felt so raw and futile, since they always seemed to revolve around Mother. Harlean pled with Chuck to agree to disagree. In spite of her warnings against ever putting her in that position, increasingly, he insisted on making her feel as if she must choose between them, and that had begun to fray the one thing that had always tethered her to Chuck—her passion for him.

"Mr. Roach offered me a contract," she finally admitted to Babe as he sat down beside her and she put away her book. "Five years. A hundred dollars a week."

Hardy looked at her. His eyes were wide.

"He said I register well on film."

"You don't need film for that, Sunshine. You're a beautiful dame, wherever you are."

She felt herself relaxing and letting go of her anxiety over her marriage. Her new friend always seemed to have that effect on her. "Thanks, Babe."

"Is that what you fought about with Chuck last night, whether to sign a contract or not?"

"He didn't object. He's just so jealous sometimes."

"I'd be jealous, too, if you were my wife."

"I love him so much, but things are just so difficult right now. I'm not eighteen yet so he's required to cosign the contract, and that just stirred things up between us all over again last night. I resent having to run everything past him like I'm looking for permission."

"His permission…or his approval?"

"I don't know, both, maybe."

When the assistant director called for "places," he reached over and gave Harlean's knee a supportive pat. "Come on, Sunshine, let's go give 'em their money's worth."

"Make 'em laugh, you mean?"

"Yep, loud as possible. That way you'll never feel your own tears. Words to live by these days."

Harlean knew he was talking about his wife but he could as easily have meant Chuck. Unfortunately, the motto fit them both.

By Friday evening of that first week of her working for Hal Roach, Chuck insisted that he was proud of her and, to her surprise, he willingly cosigned the contract. To celebrate her success, and because she wasn't needed back at the studio until the following Wednesday, he proposed a trip to San Francisco for a few days.

She had always wanted to see the famous city by the bay. She knew perfectly well that spending time alone together—particularly away from the Bellos, was something that really mattered to him, and something they both needed so she eagerly agreed.

His mood lightened the moment the train pulled away from the station in Los Angeles. Perhaps this getaway would be really good for them. Perhaps it would help to get them past the tumult of the past few weeks and back on a solid, loving footing with each other. And maybe, just maybe, she could convince him at last that there was enough love in her heart for both of the people she held most dear.

The St. Francis Hotel on Union Square was elegant and so full of history that Harlean had been eager to stay there. Former president Woodrow Wilson had once been a guest, along with numerous celebrities. But the most delicious story was of the ingenue companion of silent film star Fatty Arbuckle, who had died in his suite there after a party. People still gossiped about that.

There was a vase filled with cut orchids and an iced bottle of bootleg Champagne waiting in their room when they arrived. Despite Prohibition, Chuck always managed to find people who knew people to arrange getting alcohol. She adored Champagne, but after everything that had recently happened, her heart sank seeing it there.

As he opened the bottle, she went to the window and gazed down at the crowd of people in their heavy coats and hats milling around the square, going this way and that. She could hear the distinctive clanging of the cable cars.

"Like the suite, doll?" he asked as he poured two glasses.

"It's beautiful."

She was reluctant to take the glass from him, but it was delicious. It was definitely her weakness. Champagne and Chuck McGrew.

She watched him drink the whole glass in one swallow and she said nothing about it. Then she let him wrap her up in his arms as another cable car clanged in the square below.

He kissed her tenderly, taking her chin in his hands. She felt the defenses she had built up over the tumultuous past few weeks very slowly begin to fall away as she gazed up into his eyes. They were beautiful green eyes that were bright and happy in this moment, mirroring her love for him back at her.

She felt new hope flare brightly.

"I'm proud of you, doll, getting the contract and all," he said tenderly after they had kissed. "Ivor says Rosalie always tells him how much competition there is to get one of those."

"That's sure true. Most days on the lot there are pretty girls as far as the eye can see."

He let go of her and she felt the shift in him as he walked back to the Champagne bottle, poured another glass and drank that in one swallow, as well. His biceps flexed as he held the glass and, for a moment, she was afraid it might shatter beneath the force of his grip. She had no idea what the devil she had said this time. Her heart was fluttering like bird's wings in her chest.

"Makes a fellow wonder."

"Wonder what?" She suddenly wasn't sure she wanted to know.

"What might happen if you turned the head of some handsome actor. You even told your mother that French guy, Maurice Chevalier, flirted with you."

"Damn you, Chuck. Not again!"

"Don't say it's not a possibility."

He poured a third glass of Champagne for himself and drank it swiftly. She wrapped her arms around herself and tried to wait a moment so that she didn't speak from the place of anger that she felt. The fury had returned so swiftly that it almost made her dizzy.

"You said you were happy for me and I guess I was a fool to believe you, hmm? Acting is the first thing I've ever been good at and you want to ruin that for me."

"Technically, not the first thing, doll. Hence, the root of my concern. After all, you do know how to use your charms when you want to. You could have any man in the world if you put your mind to it."

He might be trying to bait her to get her reassurance but still she was going to stop herself from striking back at him, which would just keep this going. Harlean tried yet again to see past his insecurities—beyond those defenses that could even make him say something cruel or rude, and through to his fragile core, even though that was becoming more difficult by the day. Summoning her love for him and wrapping it up tightly inside of her compassion, she went back to him, determined to be as gentle as she could. They might be young but they could both do with as much understanding for each other as they could manage these days.

She reached out and touched his arm. He did not look at her at first, but she saw his jaw tighten. Another streetcar passed by below, and the clanging was loud in the silence between them. Yes, Chuck was too volatile, she thought, but then she hadn't exactly given him the consistency she had promised, which could have calmed these insecurities. She bore some responsibility for assuring him that she had no real ambition outside the home, only to have had a rather abrupt change of heart. That much suddenly was becoming very clear.

Harlean had understood from the day they married what a stable home life meant to him after his earlier loss. Even so, she had been evasive about Dave Allen, and about her first few casting calls. From the start he'd had a right to know about how she was changing inside. The truth was that she simply hadn't been brave enough to share it because she didn't want anyone to be angry, or disappointed, with her—Chuck or her mother most especially.

"There is no other man but you, Chuck. Whether I work or not, that can't happen because you are all I see, all that I love," she said with all the reassurance she could gather.

Finally, he looked at her and his eyes were wide with sincerity. "I'm sorry, doll, that was a low blow earlier about your charms. It's just a lot for a fella sometimes when things are changing so fast, knowing full well what it feels like to lose someone you love and having no control over it."

"You won't lose me. I want—I need a partner to go through all of this crazy stuff with… I want you. I'm depending on *you*."

"Do I have your word on that?" he asked.

Her heart melted again and the pressure of this raging whirlwind between them made her want to weep with him. They were both so young, naive to the world, and there was so much unknown in life ahead of them. Still, she nodded.

"You will take my soul with you, if you go," he warned.

"Then always come with me?"

"I'm trying, Harlean. I really am. I'm glad we finally are having some time together, just the two of us," he said. "We really need that."

They ate at a restaurant down on Fisherman's Wharf as a cold October rain buffeted the window glass beside their table. But it was cozy inside, all varnished wood and red leather.

They were warmed by steaming bowls of clam chowder and hunks of crusty sourdough bread, as Celtic music played by a duo nearby drifted melodically around them.

Chuck sat across from her in a cable-knit turtleneck sweater, his curly copper hair untamed tonight, and his green Irish eyes twinkled as he dabbed a bit of soup from her top lip. They spoke of the things they wanted to see while they were in San Francisco and about how happy they both were to be there.

After dinner, they huddled together beneath a single black umbrella and took a walk through the rain out to the end of the pier nearby. A thick layer of fog swirled at their knees and Harlean was glad for the heavy coat Chuck had bought for her earlier in the day. She clutched his arm tightly as a seagull cried out plaintively as it flew past.

"So, what do you think of San Francisco so far, doll?"

"I love everything about it. It's amazing."

"Well, *you* make it amazing." He kissed the top of her head and drew her closer against him. "I want a child with you, Harlean. I really do."

"I want a couple of them, too, you know that."

"But I mean now. If we had a child we'd be tied together for life. Bonded. Nobody could tear us apart."

She understood that this was still coming from a need for reassurance about her career, and their argument earlier, so she lay her head tenderly on his shoulder as they walked. "We already are bonded, silly, it's called matrimony."

"That didn't bond your parents," he reminded her. "Look at them. Your mother loathes your father."

"True, and they had a child. Me. Even that couldn't save them."

The thought stopped him.

His cheeks were ruddy from the cold and she could feel his

mind working. "But a baby, Harlean, something that would be just ours. God, she'd be gorgeous because she'd look like you."

She gripped his arm more tightly as they gazed out past the harbor into the dark water. She could never replace his mother, or the trauma of losing his parents so horrifically, but just maybe if she gave him a baby all of this insecurity of his would stop.

"And what if it was a boy?" she asked.

"Then my son could say, for the rest of his life, that the most beautiful woman in the world was his mother."

She felt a shy smile turn up the corners of her mouth. How did he always manage to do that? They were the epitome of tumultuous together. Their marriage had begun to feel like they were living out a performance of *The Taming of the Shrew*. They could be furious with one another one moment and then crave each other the next. That truly was a thing beyond her understanding. But there was no doubt in her mind how much in love they both were.

Feeling his obsession with her was a powerful draw.

"At least, can we go back to the hotel and practice?"

"Mommie always says practice makes perfect."

She watched his smile fall like icing on a cake, and her heart sank along with it. "Always her, isn't it, Harlean? Even when we're hundreds of miles away, she's here with us. Why don't you tell me what Marino always says, too, while you're at it."

He pivoted away and began to walk back up the pier.

"I really thought we were getting to a better place of understanding with each other!" She could hear the disappointment in her own voice as she caught up to him.

"I thought so, too. But then, like a bad dream, no matter where we are, no matter how many hundreds of miles I have to drive, there's your mother wedged right in between us.

Forget it, doll. The mood is gone. I'm not angry with you, I just need to go back to the hotel for a drink."

"Then if you're going to drink, I'm drinking with you. What did you bring?"

"Gin. Lots of it."

"Good."

"Stop it, Harlean. You can't compete."

"Does it have to be a competition? I just want to be in your world, Chuck, whatever that means."

"My world is lots of heartbreak, over ice, easy on the introspection."

"Then let's go drink. But only after you make love to me again and we practice for that baby of ours, hmm?"

She was surprised that he flashed a hint of a smile at the suggestion before it crawled back beneath his frown. He seemed to be only half listening to her, as if thoughts and memories had taken the rest of him away. A child meant the stability of family to him, yet his history had made family as much about grief as it was about longing. She wondered again now, as she had so many times, what Chuck saw—what he felt—when he remembered his parents. He needed to get to the other side of all this stored up pain, she thought, and she so badly wanted to be with him when he did. But he certainly wasn't making it easy for her.

Two hours after they had returned from dinner, and with the moonlight glinting in through the uncurtained windows, they lay together sprawled across the sofa. Clothes and shoes were strewn around the suite, his white pair of socks dripping like melted ice cream from the edge of the coffee table. The scent of alcohol and damp wool from his wet sweater moved through the air.

Harlean watched him as he reached over, tipped back his head and drank directly from a bottle of the gin, not bothering to use a glass. When she rose from the sofa and reached over for her dress, he playfully swatted her bare bottom.

"Mine, all mine. Every glorious inch of it," he slurred.

I belong to myself, first and always, she nearly said, but she held her tongue. She reached for the empty Champagne bottle and glasses to tidy up the table instead.

"Leave that for the maid, doll. That's why people come to a hotel, after all. One of the reasons, anyway," he said and chuckled at himself. "I'll bet that fella Roach would love to be in my place in a hotel room with you. He hasn't, has he?"

"Hasn't what?"

"Been in a hotel room with you. That's not why you were suddenly getting all these parts, is it, a fringe benefit from the big-time director?"

He leaned forward and dangled the bottle from one hand. She knew he thought he was teasing but it wasn't funny to her in the slightest after their earlier argument. Lately they seemed to go from one to the next with hardly any breaks in between, and it felt as if his jealous insecurity was starting to choke the life out of her.

The husband she adored was physically present in the room right now, yet every time the alcohol took him away like this, Harlean felt herself missing him less and less. Even though she tried to deny it, it was true.

"You know perfectly well I wouldn't do that," she said flatly.

She walked into the bedroom and he followed her. Harlean fought the queasy feeling that was growing inside her over what she knew was about to happen.

"Why not? He's a powerful man."

"He makes two-reel comedies in Culver City. Hardly President Hoover or King George," she shot back, outraged at the ridiculousness of his charge.

"Well, I'm just a nobody with a trust fund. Maybe that's why we don't have a baby yet. Maybe you'd rather have a little Roach tyke."

She busied herself with slipping on a bathrobe. This was madness. "Please stop it, Chuck. We had such a lovely evening. You're tired. You wouldn't be talking like this if—"

"If what? Say it, Harlean, you think I'm a drunk."

"I think you're tired. I know I am. I'm going to bed."

"Are you *dismissing* me? Just like you do every day when you leave me to go see your hoi polloi studio friends?"

She glared at him then, unable any longer to hold her tongue, or her frustration, for the pure venom she heard in his voice. Something in her shifted. The realization was painful. She would not take this abuse. Nothing was worth that, not even love. "All right, I do think you're drunk, quite drunk, which is becoming all too frequent, if you ask me."

He tripped on the leg of the dressing table chair, stumbled, then grabbed it and tossed it toward the bed. "Well, I'm a grown man and I can do whatever the hell I want when I want to, do you hear?"

"Well, same goes for me!"

"Yeah, you and Roach—foul, fat, greasy bastard!"

"At least Mr. Roach respects me too much to scare me!" she declared in a shattering cry.

"Because he wants to get into your damn drawers, if he hasn't already!"

"This isn't you, Chuck, it's not! It's the grief that's taking control of you!"

"You don't know what you're talking about!" he brayed.

"Well, I know that if you don't deal with the horrible death of your parents, and how insecure it's making you feel, it might well be the death of *us*!"

"You're not changing the subject. You're not clever enough

for it!" he yelled, then picked up her slip from the edge of the bed, balled it up and pitched it at her. "You wear this for him, doll, did you?"

"You are being crude!"

"Maybe if you wore a damn brassiere I wouldn't have to be half out of my mind with worry!" He picked up a tube of her lipstick and tossed that next. She held up her hands to him but he continued. "And this war paint, maybe if you wore less of this, men wouldn't think you were a damned floozy!"

Harlean's hands were trembling so badly that she struggled to tie the sash as he began tearing up things, bedding, pillows, pulling drawers out of the dresser and casting them aside. He was like a different person when he got like this. He was a person she didn't even know.

As she headed for retreat in the safety of the bathroom, Chuck put the bottle to his mouth and tipped his head back, intent on draining the contents, but it was already empty. "I warned you last time, don't you dare walk away from me!"

Then, in a motion that seemed as terrifying as it was fluid, he hurled the empty gin bottle at her. Harlean gasped, ducked, and it hit the wall, then tumbled onto the carpet.

The moment seemed to sober him and the crimson fury on his face quickly paled to parchment white. There was a long silence as they stared at one another, both shocked. She wrapped her arms around herself again, trying to rein in the desolation she felt.

"I am *so* sorry, Harlean," he murmured.

"Please leave, Chuck. If you don't, I will."

He held up his hands in total surrender to her warning. "No, I'll go. You're right, I drank too much, I admit it... Everything will be all right in the morning."

She didn't respond as he took his jacket, then went toward

the door to their suite. She could say nothing because she knew then that it would never be all right between them again.

Right now, all she wanted was to sleep, and to escape everything.

In the morning, she would see if she still wanted a divorce as badly as she did at this moment. Until now, when she thought of divorce, she still saw her father's face. The absolute despair in her father's eyes when her mother had walked out on him remained a vivid, haunting image. It was one she could never quite forget and one of the reasons she had given Chuck so many chances—that and her sympathy for the death of his parents.

She needed to take her time, think it through. She still loved him with her young and open heart. She just wasn't certain any longer if the love they shared could ever be enough.

Early Wednesday morning, she was back at work on the set of a picture called *Thundering Toupees*. As much as she adored the comic duo, Harlean was relieved that this first one did not feature Laurel and Hardy. She wasn't certain she could confess to Babe the details of what had happened in San Francisco without completely breaking down.

She had not told Rosalie about it, either. No one knew the pain she was enduring.

After a tense train ride home, where she kept her nose in a book to avoid conversation, she and Chuck had tiptoed around each other. They'd met Mother and Marino for dinner at the popular Paris Inn on Market Street. Mother liked it there because she had seen the handsome actor John Barrymore there once. Harlean had forced herself to be believably cheerful, telling them all about Fisherman's Wharf, the cable cars and Union Square.

Chuck as well seemed to want to pretend that the incident

had never happened. He was sweet to her, contrite, and even solicitous to Marino and mother. He filled the house with flowers, not gin. But it had loomed between them the entire time—the great, silent giant in the room, his unresolved grief, the insecurity, the outbursts of anger and the way he suppressed it all with alcohol.

When they returned home that evening after dinner, Harlean told him she had a dreadful headache. He offered to sleep in the guest room, as he had since their return, so she wouldn't be disturbed and she had not objected. She rose, dressed and left the house for Culver City before he was awake the next morning.

A week later, when Hal Roach temporarily suspended productions so the studio could be modernized to shoot talkies, Jean interceded. Rather than allow Harlean to remain idle, she took it upon herself to obtain permission from Roach for Harlean to take a role in a movie at Paramount called *Close Harmony*. The star was Buddy Rogers, her first crush as a girl. His film three years earlier with Thelma Todd and Clara Bow had been her favorite movie.

She had always marveled at her mother's steadfast determination when there was something she wanted. Jean Harlow Bello was not a woman who could be dissuaded once she had made up her mind. Heaven help anyone, or anything, that stood in the way.

"I'm so glad you got me that role, Mommie," she said as they shopped for new dresses at Robertson's Department Store on Hollywood Boulevard. It wasn't quite as chic as the Bullock Wilshire near downtown, but the fashions were not inexpensive by any means.

"You leave all of that nasty business dealing to me and you just worry about seducing the camera, hmm?"

Harlean nodded. "Don't tell Chuck I said this but Buddy Rogers is dreamy."

"Tell that jealous brute anything? Believe me, Baby, your secrets are safe with me."

"He just loves me so desperately, that's all. Wasn't Daddy ever like that?"

"Far from it. Although, if he had been, if he'd shown even just a bit of passion..." She stopped herself from finishing the sentence.

The day she married Marino, Jean had told Harlean that real passion mixed with love was life's blood. It was something Harlean had hungered for without knowing what it was. The day she met Chuck, she felt she understood what her mother had meant. Now she was trying to hold on to that very powerful feeling in the face of a toxic brew of confusion and doubt.

A model stepped out of the dressing room in a striking dove-gray belted dress and began to pose in front of them. "How do you think I would look in that one?" Jean asked her daughter as they watched the model pivot and turn.

"Gee, that looks expensive. How much is it?" Harlean asked the clerk.

Jean held up her hand to stop the clerk from responding. "Whatever it is, Chuck can afford it. We're all doing well enough for a few frocks."

"Chuck thinks Marino should maybe look for a job."

"Does he now?"

"You know it wasn't that much money his parents left him. Not compared to the fortunes our friends here have. He worries a lot, and I think that's part of what's been wrong lately, the pressure to keep up with that group."

Jean laughed dismissively. "Don't let him fill your head with that 'poor me' nonsense. An inheritance of a quarter million dollars is a fortune and if it's not enough for him, maybe *he* should look for a job since he's a hell of a lot younger than poor Marino." She waved over the clerk. "We will take that one, and the dress before it, we'll take two. One in my daughter's size, one in mine."

She looked over at Harlean and added her favorite line. "Then we will look just like twins! Won't that be fun?"

CHAPTER ELEVEN

After what had happened in San Francisco, Harlean appreciated even more the camaraderie of The Fun Factory that existed at the Hal Roach Studios. Although she had gone through the motions of being a contented wife, and keeping the truth of her doubts from her mother, Chuck's twenty-second birthday celebration in November and the holidays that followed felt brutally tense. New Year's Eve with Rosalie and Ivor hadn't been much better, since the whole evening she feared a repeat of what had happened at the speakeasy.

By the second week of January, with the news that the renovations at the studio were complete, Harlean was back at work on another film. Enough time had passed that she was thrilled to be assigned to another picture with Laurel and Hardy, even if it was entitled *Double Whoopee*, which sounded completely risqué to Chuck. But to Harlean's surprise, he said nothing more than, "Good luck today. I'm sure you'll be great," as he kissed her forehead at the front door and tenderly tucked a wisp of hair back behind her ear.

"Welcome back, Sunshine. We've missed you around here," Babe Hardy declared in greeting.

Harlean gave him a warm hug as she walked into the makeup room and set down the satchel of books she always brought along. "Hi, Babe."

He smiled at her and rocked back and forth on his heels, then tickled the tips of his fingers placing them beneath his chin. She found his signature comedic move as endearing as the rest of him. Stan Laurel was more reserved. Between takes, he sat and wrote letters or smoked, so she was glad she and Babe connected so well, and she appreciated how patient he had been with her.

"I just read the script. You lose your dress in this one. You ready for that?"

"I'm ready to make it memorable."

"That's a girl. Make 'em laugh?"

"Till you can't feel your tears."

He gave her a compassionate smile. "Gorgeous *and* a quick learner—one with a great memory. What more could we ask for?"

Harlean was set to appear in only one scene later on in the film, so as the other extras talked, she sat in the shadows and watched Laurel and Hardy work together. She found their chemistry both brilliant and fascinating. Their sense of timing was perfect. She marveled at how much skill was involved to make slapstick look spontaneous and funny. She would have to do what she could in order to stand out and keep up with their pure comic genius.

"Harlow," Lewis Foster called out to her from his director's chair.

She rose and, in a silk dressing gown that covered a black lace teddy, went to where he sat, arms crossed over his V-neck sweater and with his face scrunched into a frown. "Yes, sir, Mr. Foster?"

"Are you properly underdressed beneath that for your scene, young lady?"

He indicated her body with his eyes.

Harlean was surprised by his unexpected sense of humor. It would make filming her scene at least a little less awkward. He was making sure she wasn't wearing a brassiere or panties which, under such a skimpy costume, might show up awkwardly through the camera lens. That was a relief.

"Not sure how properly," she tried to joke. "But yes, sir."

She then let the production assistant lead her into the backseat of the prop taxicab that had been brought onto the soundstage. She sank comfortably against the leather seat as the lighting was adjusted and the cast moved into position.

Babe was doing most of the scene with her so she sat forward in the seat and watched him as the scene opened. Harlean struggled not to laugh at their skilled antics. Choreographed or not, they were hilarious, and she so respected them for their talent. The first time on film she was going to have a real chance to show Foster, and Mr. Roach, too, when he saw the dailies, what she could do. She was terrified and thrilled at the same time and her heart raced with the anticipation.

With cameras rolling, the car was drawn forward by a pulley and she was helped out by Stan and Babe. Both were in full slapstick mode. It was not at all easy to keep a straight face. From here on out, just as she had in her fleeting scene with Jeanette MacDonald, Harlean meant to make her moment count. It was the only way to build a real career.

The first bit was that Stan would close the car door on the length of her skirt, thereby ripping it off without her knowing as the two of them moved forward toward the hotel entrance. Then she was to strut into the hotel on Babe's arm without realizing what the audience was seeing of her from behind. Harlean did her best vampy stride.

"Cut!"

She knew the bark had come from George Stevens, the cinematographer, because he had such a deep, forboding tone. Harlean and Babe both stopped cold, and turned slowly back around. Stevens and Foster were charging toward them and chaos erupted as the rest of the cast and crew fell into fits of murmurs and laughter.

"For Christ's sake, Lewis, her bare ass comes straight through the camera lens! What the hell were you thinking, Harlow?"

Harlean's heart sank. She didn't understand—and she was horrified.

"Someone go get Roach, will ya. He'll probably want us to reshoot the entire damn scene," Foster groaned.

Harlean glanced at Babe. Tears pricked her eyes.

"No one told me she'd be naked under that flimsy thing," she heard the actor who played the desk clerk say. "I could see her tits and everything else. I know my mouth fell wide-open when I saw her. They won't want *that* on film," he chuckled.

"Where the hell is your underdress?" Stevens angrily asked her.

She fought back the tears but they came anyway, running in ribbons down her cheeks. Her voice was shallow and she could barely force herself to speak. "Mr. Foster asked me if I was underdressed and so I thought...well, I mean... I told him yes, because I don't wear undergarments as a rule."

Lewis Foster's tone went lower. He was visibly irritated. "Miss Harlow, *underdressed* is a term for the nude undergarment that goes beneath a revealing costume in this business. How on earth could you not be aware of that?"

She glanced helplessly at Babe, who could only offer her a grim hint of a smile and a shrug as Hal Roach himself now approached. An assistant director was speaking to him, presumably explaining the situation.

When she looked at Roach, however, her sense of panic turned to confusion. She saw that, unlike everyone else, he was actually smiling.

"Someone take Miss Harlow to Wardrobe and get her some undergarments. You boys all right to do the scene again, same way?" he asked Laurel and Hardy.

"No problem," Babe replied.

"Sure," Stan seconded.

As Harlean was escorted to the wardrobe department by a production assistant, she was not certain if she felt more foolish for misunderstanding or more grateful for Roach's apparent sense of humor. This was a complicated industry, and an even more complicated world for a seventeen-year-old girl from Missouri. But this setback only made her more determined than ever to learn from each experience, especially the bad ones, and to thrive.

She would not be the second Jean Harlow to return to Kansas City in defeat.

Ten minutes later, her spirit renewed, she returned to the set in her black teddy, the pull-away skirt and the fancy black buckle shoes that her mother had brought out to California for her. She had wiped away her tears, pinched her cheeks and painted a cheerful smile back on. The actors took their places and Harlean slipped back into the prop cab.

"Quiet on the set!"

The camera began rolling. She glanced heavenward and said a silent prayer. Once again Stan Laurel helped her from the backseat, mugging and hamming it up with Babe, as they brought her into their routine.

To her surprise, Harlean could see, from the corner of her

eye, the broad smiles from the crew who stood gathered just off camera.

With her confidence newly bolstered, she hammed it up even more expertly in this take, waiting for Stan to take off his coat to cover her. When the scene ended, the cast and crew broke into applause.

"That was great, honey," Stan quietly said. "Even better than the first time."

"Do you really think so?"

"Trust us, you're a natural, Sunshine." Babe smiled. "I hear we'll see you back at work here with us on Monday. We are starting *Bacon Grabbers*. Heck of a title. That one should be a kick."

She giggled at the silly title, too, but she loved the idea of how these comic pictures made people laugh and forget their troubles for a while, and she was happy now to be even a small part of their genius. Harlean wasn't certain she could be any happier than she was at this moment, doing something she loved, with people she so admired. Life's road was certainly full of twists and turns but she had really begun to enjoy the ride. There was no part of any of it she was ready to give up on just yet.

"Cover your eyes, and *no* peeking!" Chuck said as he led her out the front door of their house and across the lawn Sunday morning.

He seemed so happy that it lightened Harlean's mood, and she pushed everything else to the back of her mind. "Where are we going?"

"You'll see."

When they reached the curb, he gently pulled her hand away from her eyes. The sun was shining brightly down on them. There, before her, was a glistening maroon LaSalle convertible coupe, the hood tied up with a giant red bow. She looked at Chuck quizzically.

"What's this?"

"Your new car, silly. I can't bum rides from Ivor every day." He offered up the key. "I hope the color is okay. There weren't a lot of choices this time of year," he said with the charming grin of his.

"It's too extravagant, Chuck."

"Not for my doll."

Harlean let him kiss her deeply then, which was the first time in a very long time, after what had happened in San Francisco and the tension between them that had followed. She understood why he had really bought the car for her. It was more peace offering than practical gift because he felt the estrangement between them just as much as she did. She had considered leaving him a dozen times just since Christmas but the words *For better or for worse* still pressed heavily on her heart. If she had enough stubborn resolve to make a career out of nothing, she told herself that she was foolish not to try a little longer to save her marriage.

"The car is beautiful," she finally said.

"It's okay, then?"

"It's way too grand, but it's perfect, Chuck, it really is."

He kissed her so tenderly again that it made her remember what she had felt in those lovely first days here. It was followed by a rush of sadness that it simply wasn't the same now.

"I wanted you to have your own transportation so you could come and go as you please. But I also needed to try to begin to make amends for what happened in that hotel. The hold on your heart your mother has just scares me sometimes. It makes me a little crazy, it really does."

At least he was admitting what she had already known, which helped a little. "I can love two people, Chuck."

He shook his head. "I don't know what got into me, Har-lean, I swear I don't. Sometimes I just love you so much that I can't tell where I end and you begin, and it scares me to death. You're in my blood, doll, in my soul, and every other part of me."

He reached up and anchored his palms on her chin. "Things are gonna be different from now on, I promise."

She offered up a tepid smile since it was still all she could enlist, and she wondered if that was a promise he had any possible way of keeping.

That afternoon, they decided to test the new car with a tour out to Long Beach to at last introduce Chuck to her aunt Jetty. Jetta Belle Chadsey was actually her mother's aunt but her connection with her niece's daughter was no less enduring.

Harlean remained so plagued with conflicting feelings about her marriage—and frustration over her fear of speaking about it with her mother—that a test drive seemed as good an excuse as any to spend time, at last, with a woman whose opinion she greatly valued—a woman in whom she had confided already and who would keep her confidence.

Harlean adored the boisterous, spirited woman who she hadn't seen since the last time she had lived in Hollywood but with whom she spoke often by phone. She really didn't have a good excuse, other than the distractions of a young marriage and life in the city, for not having visited sooner but she knew Jetty wouldn't require one.

Tall, thickly-set and silver-haired, Aunt Jetty met them on the front porch of her shingled beachside bungalow with a warm smile as Harlean climbed the porch steps first, holding Oscar under one arm. Jetta was the family renegade who'd had a baby and been divorced by the age of eighteen, then gone on to live with another man.

"Oh, let me look at you!" she exclaimed after they had embraced and she then held Harlean out at arm's length. "Lord, if you aren't a grown woman now, and a gorgeous one, too!"

"She does take your breath away, doesn't she?" Chuck said with a proud smile as he stood on the porch step below Harlean. He then took Oscar from her so the two women could have their reunion.

"So you're Chuck," Aunt Jetty said a moment later as she gave Oscar's head a little pat. "Good to finally meet you, my boy. The Baby here has told me an awful lot about you over the phone."

"Then it's good to know I'm still welcome here," he quipped.

"Just mind your p's and q's and you always will be," she quickly returned, and added a firm nod before she led them into her quaint living room. It was a mix of lacy curtains, tattered furniture and hurricane-style lamps painted with flowers. She left the front door open to let in the unseasonably warm winter ocean breeze.

Just as they sat down, a sleek Persian cat with bright blue eyes came seemingly out of nowhere, hopped onto Harlean's lap, nestled in and began to purr.

"Well, now, will you look at that," Jetty chuckled. "That sweet ol' boy doesn't come around for just anybody."

"My wife has a way with all the boys," Chuck mused as he stroked Oscar, who was contented in the crook of his arm, and Harlean was relieved when she realized he meant the comment in a lighthearted manner.

Jetty poured them each a glass of lemonade from a glass pitcher.

"So, now, tell me everything about the picture business. How exciting that all is!"

"She's just an extra," Chuck interjected. "It can't be all that exciting."

"But Mommie and Marino think it's going to become a lot more if I keep at it. I've gotten to work with that new young actress people are talking about, Jeanette MacDonald so far, and my second short with Laurel and Hardy comes out tomorrow. It's just a little part, but I think it's really funny."

"It's going to play out here, right over at the Regal. I'll be there with my bells on. Looking forward to it, sweetie."

"I've learned so much already about timing from Mr. Hardy. He's so generous with his advice."

"Good thing that Hardy is so damn fat or a man could get pretty jealous of how often you go on about him."

"Good gracious, Chuck." Jetty gave him a heavy nicotine chuckle. "I know you're a young fella and all, but take a word of advice from old Aunt Jetty, any colt like this pretty one here is gonna bolt if you pull the reins too tight."

He shot Harlean a sheepish glance. "I believe my wife used a similar phrase not so long ago. Guess I should take your advice."

"Guess you should," Jetty said before she turned to Harlean. "So, child, how is your mother?"

"And we were having such a nice visit," Chuck deadpanned.

Harlean glowered. "Not here, too, Chuck, please."

Aunt Jetty looked at each of them in turn. "All right, you kids, out with it."

"I am not saying anything unkind about your niece, Miss Jetty," Chuck replied.

"For a change you're not," Harlean muttered.

"Well, now, I know my niece can be difficult sometimes..."

"Isn't *that* just an understatement."

"So much for promises."

"I'm sorry. Change of subject."

"Look, you two, you kids are crazy in love. Any fool could see that a mile away, so I'm going to tell you a story. I loved a man like that once. More passion between us than common sense, that was for damn sure. We broke all the rules. We argued, we battled, we loved... He wasn't my husband. Wasn't anyone my mother, or anybody else, approved of since he was an Osage Indian. Can you just imagine, in our little bitty town? Everyone was against us right from the start."

Harlean knew the story and that it had not ended well but she let Jetty tell it anyway. After leaving her husband for him, Jetty had borne her lover twins. She had endured the ruthless small-town scrutiny, and the cruel rejection by her family, but the babies had died anyway. Her love affair died with them.

When she looked at Harlean and Chuck, there were tears shining in her eyes.

"Don't let anybody steal your dream, you two. Not anybody. You fight for it, both of you—learn from your mistakes. And, for goodness sake, be kind to one another."

Later, as Chuck took Oscar for a walk before the car ride back to the city, Jetty and Harlean stood alone in the kitchen.

"How are things really, sweetie?"

"Oh, Aunt Jetty, if I only knew," Harlean sighed. "One day I think we're going to make it through this and then he goes and says something to stir it all up again. I know we're young, and that we made a vow. That means something to me, it really does, and I'm trying so hard to honor it. But sometimes I get scared that we won't grow beyond this phase, that I'll have to live the rest of my life never knowing when he's gonna explode next. He's been walking on eggshells with me since San Francisco but he's so jealous all the time and he's got so much anger inside of him."

"Because of his parents?"

"I don't know, probably. He won't talk about them."

She shook her head. "Oh, child, that sadness has got to go somewhere..."

"I've tried to get him to face it, Jetty, but it only makes him more angry."

"And it makes him drink more," she said knowingly. "Well, you're not his savior, all you can be is the best partner to him you know how."

"But what if that's not enough?" Harlean asked desperately as she pressed her face into her hands for a moment.

But Jetty didn't answer that, she didn't need to, because they both knew the answer.

Harlean carried that exchange in her heart on the long, silent car ride back to Beverly Hills. In one arm she held her sleeping dog, and the other hand she rested on Chuck's knee as they sat in the shiny new car that, for a moment earlier today, had symbolized a new chapter between them.

Yet her touch, a desperate one, felt to her like their only connection just now and she had no idea at all how to change that.

CHAPTER TWELVE

The gilded movie theater, with its burgundy velvet draperies framing the stage, was crowded for a weeknight in February. Harlean insisted they sit downstairs in the back near the exit and enter only after the lights had already been lowered for the first showing of the short she had made with Laurel and Hardy. As the music began, her heart started to race. She had never seen herself on-screen for more than an instant, here or there. She squirmed against her velvet seat cushion as the curtains parted. Then she slithered down farther into the seat, unable to stop herself.

Her mother, sitting with Marino in the row behind her and Chuck, swatted her shoulder. Harlean quickly perked back up as Babe Hardy began the on-screen routine. Stan Laurel joined him in one of their delightfully slapstick romps. Harlean remembered every moment of the filming, what they'd said, the murmured jokes they made back and forth, and how hard she had struggled not to laugh.

She vacillated between pressing her hand over her eyes, and peeking through parted fingers, and then she squirmed again. She was reassured by the laughter around her. Chuck clutched her hand, then ran his thumb soothingly over hers. This was going to be all right, she told herself. It was just a short, after all.

And then she watched more closely as the car pulled forward into the shot. She saw herself in the backseat which made her cringe. She bit down onto her knuckle. Why had she slumped like that? A gust of self-criticism rushed at her. She resolved to watch that next time.

She held her breath as she watched Stan help her out of the prop car. Chuck squeezed her hand again. Stan slammed the car door, and her dress tore away. The crowd pealed with laughter at a damsel's predicament. Then, as the camera focused in on their backsides, with Harlean wearing only her black teddy, black stockings and high heels, two women in front of her gasped. They weren't laughing. She heard murmurs around her and felt the blossom of a shiver. The laughter that lingered was fully male, which made it seem more tawdry to her.

She felt Chuck's hand slacken in hers. When she glanced over, she saw the muscles tightening in his jaw. She had warned him about the farcical skit, and yet she could see that he was not amused.

"It was delightful, Baby," Marino said from the backseat as Chuck drove them home from the theater afterward. "You really were very funny."

"Thanks, Marino," Harlean said quietly.

For every step forward she took in life these days, Harlean felt herself fall backward by two. A shining moment in her career was followed by an argument with Chuck. The thrill of a new job was a prelude to the gritty reality of Hollywood, reminding her that she was just another pretty extra—one who was not sought out for her ability to do comedy but to show her alluring backside.

It was all so confusing since, thanks to Stan and Babe, she had truly connected with the art of comedy and she wanted desperately to be good at it. She believed, if she studied more, practiced more—if people looked beyond her beauty and gave her a real chance, she could absolutely shine. But the predicament remained; she couldn't get work without being alluring, but she would have to fight to be taken seriously because she was beautiful. She had to use her assets, whether she liked it or not.

One thing was certain to her now, Harlean was more determined than ever to fight. She wanted the challenge. She needed it.

When they all walked in the front door, Oscar was barking and the phone was ringing. "Get that will you, Baby?" her mother directed, as though she still lived there.

Harlean dashed for the receiver. It was her grandfather Harlow, the one whose love and money had supported them in Hollywood the first time. He was also the one who had primarily funded the plot of land on which she still fully intended to build their dream home. She loved him dearly, and was so excited to hear from him, until she heard that his tone was not a happy one.

"I'm as ashamed as I can be of you, Harlean Harlow Carpenter."

She squeezed the receiver as her heart sank. He, too, refused to acknowledge her married name, which didn't help.

"Grandpa, I—"

"I'll tell you one thing, young lady. Neither Miss Clara Bow nor Miss Mary Pickford would ever be seen in a picture in their goddamn knickers!"

Marino opened a bottle of Champagne. The cork popped and Harlean jumped with a start at the sound. Her mother sidled up beside her in the dining room. "What's he saying, Baby?" she whispered.

Stricken, Harlean looked at her mother. She finished the conversation that had been little more than a tongue-lashing in which Grandpa Harlow vowed not to send her another penny as long as she intended to be an actress. As she hung up the phone her eyes flooded with tears. The day had been too long for her to feel otherwise. Chuck came up beside her a moment later. He handed her a glass of Champagne and held one for himself in his other hand.

"Look at you. You're white as a sheet. Your mother might be right, doll. I think it's time for you to give up on the picture business. We all know that I'm a full-time job, as it is."

He quirked a condescending look. In response, she shot her mother a desperate glance. Surely Mother, of all people, had not suggested something like that.

This career was her mother's dream as much as her own.

"Mommie?"

Jean Bello's tone was surprisingly calm and measured. "I just think perhaps the Roach Studios might not be the best place for you in your life right now."

"But you're the one who was there when I signed the contract!"

"Yes, I know I was, Baby, but I feel that things have changed."

Harlean's mouth went dry. This couldn't possibly be her mother talking. She didn't know how to react to this.

"What things have changed exactly?" She glanced at each of them in turn, her confidence rocked in the face of what could only be their collusion. "You both decided this *for* me?"

"The thing is, I've tried to support you, Harlean, but we have never fought so much as we have since you started working, and your mother thinks maybe it is best for you to bow out," Chuck carefully said.

"But there is a contract."

"Dear girl, contracts are made to be broken," Marino blithely interjected as he joined them in the dining room, bearing his own glass of Champagne. "Your mother will find a way, that's for certain."

"Leave it to me, Baby," Jean concurred with a self-confidence that suddenly made her shiver.

For the first time in a long time, her mother and Chuck exchanged a smile.

Marino slung his arm affably over Chuck's shoulder then, which was almost too much for her to bear for all of the underlying tension that regularly existed between them. "Come, my boy, let's the two of us leave our ladies to it, shall we?"

None of this made a bit of sense to her. She gulped her Champagne and headed toward the kitchen, intent on finding more. The two people she loved most in the world, trusted most, seemed suddenly to want something very different for her than what she wanted for herself.

Her mother followed her. She could smell her Shalimar perfume swirl around them. In the moment, for the first time, she despised the scent of it.

"I don't understand at all. I've been working so hard. I thought you, of all people, believed I had potential to make something of myself."

Jean lowered her voice. "And so I do, Baby. More than you will ever know."

"Then why would you encourage Chuck to push me out of the business?"

Jean lowered her voice again and leaned closer. "Surely you know me better than that. I simply suggested he encourage you out of your Hal Roach contract."

"But, why? They've been so good to me there and *Double Whoopee* was my biggest part yet."

"A walk-on, Baby. You were the joke *and* the punchline. There is far more out there for you, I know it. And Mother is going to help you get it."

Jean held her daughter's shoulders and filled her gaze with conviction. "I have it all figured out. You turn eighteen next month and, after that, you won't need Charles McGrew to cosign anything for you. *We* can make all of the decisions about your career, just the two of us." Her mother was still gripping her shoulders, still locking her gaze. "There are five much more important studios who would clamor to have you now if they knew you were available. You've begun to create something of a buzz, and we need to keep that momentum going, not have you languishing in slapstick two-reel silent pictures when talkies are about to become all the rage."

"You know Mr. Roach is going to start doing talkies."

"Well, *you* will not be a part of those," Jean said dismissively. "Tomorrow morning, you will march into his office, call up the appropriate quantity of tears and tell him that you need to retire from acting because it is ruining your marriage. Most men can't bear to see a girl cry. I've done a bit of checking on Mr. Roach and, as it turns out, he is happily married with two small children. Unless I miss my educated guess, he will offer to tear up your contract to honor marriage and family."

Despite her efforts to grow up and begin taking some responsibility for her life, Harlean felt like a child who had just fallen off the merry-go-round, one that had been spinning very fast. She was trying to understand this fully formed plan her mother had in mind, and she was trying to decide if it would be a good thing for her career, or for a marriage she was struggling to preserve.

"So, you want me to tell my husband that I'm quitting, only to turn around and sign on with a new studio after I turn eighteen?"

"Something like that."

Jean looked around to make certain they were not being overheard. Then she continued. "A docile Charles is a far more manageable one. When the next contract from a studio comes our way, we simply tell Charles that things have changed, and that the offer was too good to pass up. Once you are of age, he can't complain, or stand in our way," Jean further explained.

"Marino and I talked it all through this morning and we are going to act as your management team temporarily, so you needn't worry a thing about any of that. Your job, Baby, is to stay beautiful. Which reminds me, it's time to do those roots again. You must always put your best foot forward since you only have one chance to make that first impression."

Harlean thought suddenly of the faded actress, Lula Hanford, who had befriended her on the day of her first extra work, and the similar advice she had offered.

"This *is* what you want, isn't it? What we both wanted so dearly for you?"

Harlean thought of Chuck and her mother's question lingered like smoke, wrapping itself around her heart. It was what a part of her wanted, even craved. She loved making her mother happy and she knew in her heart that she could be good at comedy, or really meaty dramatic roles, if she were ever given a chance to play them.

"If you and Marino find me a new contract, do you think you could help me tell Chuck?"

The sedate grin Jean had worn lengthened then. "You just leave everything to me, Baby," she said.

That night, Harlean lay awake long after Chuck had fallen asleep, nestling close against his chest just to hear him breathing—and she silently tried to call up the feelings of great passion this nearness once had stirred within her.

He loved her, frightened her, surprised her and over-whelmed her. She could not imagine anything more pow-erful than that combination. But the strength of it, and the volatility behind it, was still wearing her down and making her question everything she thought she believed when they married. It was a doubt she was still tenaciously trying to con-quer and to get past.

Perhaps she would take her mother's suggestion and go to Hal Roach in the morning to plead with him for the sake of her marriage. At the moment, she felt she could make that a believably earnest request.

She knew how happy it would make Chuck to believe that she was going to stop working. If another contract with a more powerful studio came her way, then that would be fate. But she would deal with that when, and if, it happened. For now, one battle at a time seemed more than enough to manage.

CHAPTER THIRTEEN

On March second of 1929, Hal Roach released Harlean from her contract. The stated reason was in order to save her marriage. Before she left his office, he pulled her into a great, paternal bear hug and wished her the best.

"Now then, if circumstances change and you decide you'd like to start working again, you have only to phone my secretary, all right?"

She felt guilty tears pricking her eyes. "Thank you so much, sir. You've been very kind."

"I don't mind saying that I hate to lose you around here, Miss Harlow, you're a real asset. But there's nothing more important in the world than family. You take care of that young man of yours, hmm? And give him my regards."

Roach was such a gentleman with her that Harlean cried in the car all the way back to Linden Drive. The tears she had shed in his office had not needed to be conjured. She had taken a risk, done the right thing. That was what her mother had said. So she wasn't sure why every part of her felt regret. The next day, she turned eighteen.

She had never even had a chance to tell Babe goodbye.

In the weeks that followed her birthday, and with nothing to do all day, a restlessness settled back in on her. Harlean purchased a typewriter at a secondhand store. That idea for a novel had been rattling around in her head for a while, and if she wasn't going to be an actress, she decided that the creativity inside her might be expressed in a different way. Books were such friends to her that she was suddenly determined to craft one of her own.

She set the typewriter up on the table, along with a stack of paper and cup full of freshly sharpened pencils for editing. The view of their charming little backyard through the kitchen window would inspire her. Oscar sat at her feet looking up and wagging his tail.

"All right, little man, you behave yourself now so I can concentrate," she instructed him. "I intend to write two full chapters before Chuck gets home and I need to make his dinner. Is that clear?"

She did write the first chapter, after wadding up a number of pages and tossing them in the trash. She wanted to write a novel about what she knew. It would be the story of a young and glamorous Hollywood couple in the 1920s. She could draw on her mother's experiences as well as what she knew from Rosalie and also their new group of friends. The next day, she wrote a second chapter before deciding that it was drivel and surrendering those pages to the garbage, as well. She had read enough books to know that something was missing from the writing. She could feel it.

"This is harder than I thought, Oscar," she said on the third day.

The truth was that she hadn't experienced Hollywood fully enough yet to tell a believable tale. But she couldn't just sit at home and become a homemaker, or continue enduring the obligatory and endless shopping trips enjoyed by women of leisure, now that she had faced the challenges and tasted the rewards of a career. She wouldn't dare admit it to Chuck, who seemed happier than ever, but she was already going a little stir-crazy at home alone all day.

After several additional weeks poised at her typewriter during every free moment, and with more crumpled up pages in the wastebasket than not, she accepted Rosalie's invitation to lunch. "Now, what has you in such a stew, honey?" Rosalie asked as they sat in the same booth at the Brown Derby amid the noonday rush. "If you keep frowning like that you're bound to get wrinkles!"

Since the termination of her contract with Hal Roach she had managed to find only one job as an extra at Fox. Chuck agreed to let her take it because there was no contract involved, and he was still surprised that he had gotten what he thought of as "his way" regarding her career. But now she was reduced, once again, to those dreaded shopping excursions and endless games of bridge over cocktails in the afternoon, since her novel, like her acting career, was at a full standstill.

"It's just that my mother's plan isn't working. No studio has come up with an offer like she thought they would, I'm out of inspiration for my novel, and I'm going a little stir-crazy trapped home most of the day with the dog."

"I'm sure Chuck is happy, though."

"Deliriously," Harlean groaned.

Rosalie's eyes widened with surprise then as she glanced across to the table on the other side of the aisle. "Oh, my stars! Don't look now too obviously at that man staring right at you, but do you know who that is?"

Harlean lowered her menu just enough to slide a careful glance in the direction of a balding, diminutive man in a business suit and horn-rimmed eyeglasses. He was sitting with two women. One was middle-aged and stout, the other was a brunette and clearly a starlet, or a girl who hoped to be.

"That's Edwin Bower Hesser. I recognize him from the magazines."

When Harlean did not react to the name, Rosalie leaned in closer. "He's famous for taking artistic photographs of women that help them become stars."

"By artistic, do you mean nude photographs?"

"Not always, no, but when he does they are like works of art. Very tasteful, honest. His photographs are really all the rage."

Before she had finished her sentence, Hesser excused himself from his table, came across the aisle and addressed Harlean.

"Do pardon me please for interrupting your lunch, my dear, but I am a photographer and my wife and I noticed you immediately after you sat down. I wonder perhaps if you would consider speaking with us about the possibility of posing for me."

The man extended his business card to her and made a dignified bow. "I am Edwin Hesser."

"Harlean McGrew," she said, too stunned at the moment to remember the professional name she'd given herself.

She glanced down at the business card, then across at his luncheon table. His wife smiled and nodded. Chuck would be livid if she posed in anything less than a full ensemble. On the other hand, if what Rosalie said about him was true, it would be an incredible opportunity to pose for a photographer whose work was thought by Hollywood to be upscale and artistic. If his photographs had advanced the careers of other actresses this could be a turning point for her, as well.

And of course, her mother would be thrilled.

"Do you require all of your models to pose nude?" she asked, and then she felt her cheeks flush.

In response, he gave her a measured look. "I leave that up to the moment and the theme of the shoot."

"Could my mother come with me?"

"Why, of course, my dear. While I make no excuses for being artistically drawn to the female form, my wife is always with me while I work. It's all quite aboveboard, I assure you."

Harlean tried to smile as he focused his gaze in on her more tightly, his eyes assessing her head, face, neck and chest. "My, you do have absolutely luminescent skin. And your hair is the precise shade of eiderdown."

He didn't speak flirtatiously. Rather, he seemed transfixed, even as waiters and new customers moved back and forth behind him. He was such an unassuming, serious little man with a gentle tenor voice. His eyes never left the study of her.

"When would you like her to call on you, Mr. Hesser?" Rosalie asked cheerfully, and Harlean knew she was only trying to help move things along.

She wasn't certain what she would have done without Rosalie's friendly intervention. The scramble of thoughts running through her mind was overwhelming. But an adventure did sound enticing, there was no denying that after these past dreary weeks.

"Nancy over there with my wife is my subject this afternoon, so we are free as soon as tomorrow. Why don't you speak with your mother and, if she's amenable, come by my office tomorrow at eleven. I would like to shoot you up in Griffith Park. There is an exquisite spot there that your look would suit perfectly."

After she had agreed, he nodded to them both and said, "Good day, ladies," before returning to his table.

Rosalie lowered her voice. "Well, don't you just have all the luck. It seems like fate means for the world to know who you are, no matter what you or Chuck do to the contrary."

★ ★ ★

Jean was indeed amenable. In fact, she was overjoyed at the prospect.

They headed to Hesser's studio the next morning, chatting about what potential costume, setting and style of portrait the photographer might choose to employ for her. Neither of them were able to contain their excitement. Harlean had not told Chuck of her plans for the day. She wanted to be honest with him, but Jean countered with conviction.

"Now, Baby, you know perfectly well that Charles is incapable of appreciating artistic photographs in spite of the boost they might give to your career. He will never see them anyway, unless of course you put them next to a glass of gin."

They pulled up at the curb in Harlean's car.

"I just don't understand why you hate him so much."

"I don't hate him, but he is certainly not good enough for you. He is holding you back and I won't stand for that."

"We love each other, Mommie."

"But love will never be enough. You already know it isn't."

As indelibly bound as she felt to her mother, and as full of conflict as she had been for months, Harlean could not yet force herself to agree to that. Nor did she feel safe admitting to her the tenuous state of her marriage. She was still clinging to the tether of her wedding vow, and doing so as if it were for dear life.

After the terms were agreed to, they rode with Hesser and his wife, in a car stuffed with camera equipment and props, up to a vacant place in the vast, bucolic Griffith Park. The isolated spot to which he led them—tall pine trees, open sky and a small crystalline lake framed by craggy rocks—was an immediately familiar one. It was the very spot where Chuck had photographed her last autumn wearing her conservative little dress, cardigan, socks and respectable shoes. She shivered at the coincidence and tried to forget the vision that seemed very far away now.

Hesser's vision for the shoot was simple. As he prepared the scene and readied his equipment, his wife, Rhea, explained that he intended it to be reminiscent of ethereal Isadora Duncan studies with Harlean draped only in a flowing chiffon scarf, staged in various dramatic poses among the rocks. As her mother urged her with a firm nod to begin disrobing, Hesser's wife detailed the soft focus lens her husband intended to use so that the final images would make her appear more like a wood nymph than a model, which sounded wonderfully creative.

Harlean wanted to do it—or she had believed she did when she agreed to it, but as she removed her shoes and then began to unbutton her top, her mind flooded with misgivings. She suddenly felt shy. This was not a prelude to lovemaking with Chuck, where she could freely acknowledge her lack of modesty. Rather, this was the broad light of day in the company of strangers. Artistic photos or not, it suddenly felt rather risqué, even a little tawdry. That diaphanous scarf was going to leave very little to the imagination.

"Do get on with it, Baby. They aren't going to wait all day," her mother urged her in a low voice.

Slowly, Harlean stepped out of her skirt, and then she began to peel away her blouse, wishing she'd had more layers beneath.

"I really don't know about this, Mommie," she whispered with desperation as Jean took her blouse and skirt and she tried to cover herself with the scarf. "Maybe it's a mistake."

"Ready when you are!" Hesser called out.

Jean moved a step nearer to her daughter and lowered her voice further. "Don't be ridiculous. We need this job. Mr. Hesser is an important artist, one who has the power to jump-start your career. Everyone who is anyone in Hollywood follows his work, so he may well be our ticket to stardom!"

"But maybe there's another way—*with* my clothes on."

"If there is, I sure haven't seen it these past weeks. Now for heaven's sake, let's act like professionals here. You're eighteen years old. Don't make Mr. Hesser sorry he hired you."

Then, with a sigh of resignation, Harlean padded barefoot toward the boulder, and reclined on top of it as Hesser directed. "Gorgeous. That's it. Tip your head back just a bit more..." She could hear the *click* of his camera begin and she tried to focus on the sound as a way to steady her nerves. *Click. Click. Click.* She wanted nothing so much as for this to be over. "Yes, that's it...utter perfection."

She shifted awkwardly then, as he continued to direct her movements. The chiffon slipped away from her breast and when she grabbed for it, a stray giggle slipped out. She touched her lips and caught her mother's sharp stare, but Hesser only smiled before he continued. She so badly wanted for this to be at an end.

"Young lady, your love affair with this camera cannot be denied. That is something to be enormously proud of," Hesser declared as he worked. "It certainly places you far above your competition. Young Gloria Swanson tried these same poses here for me a month ago and it just didn't work. Joan Crawford was all wrong for them, too. You absolutely sparkle."

That word again. How could Hesser have known? Perhaps it was an omen—a sign that she was meant to do this after all. From that moment on, she tried her best to breathe, to relax— to be the professional her mother wanted.

As the small handheld Graflex camera clicked away, Harlean caught another glimpse of Jean standing behind Hesser, hands suddenly now poised prayerfully beneath her chin. She was biting her bottom lip and her expression was filled with so much pride that Harlean was suddenly just as proud of herself as her mother was. Work, determination and triumph further strengthened the bond between them. She felt her self-confidence begin to grow as she moved, smiled and posed.

The odd sensation with which she had begun the photo shoot steadily slipped away in the face of Hesser's thoroughly professional demeanor, and the businesslike presence of his wife. Since there had been little way out of it, Harlean resolved to learn from it. After all, she had read that the ability to seduce the camera was the key to success with all great movie stars. This was work. It was business, and she meant to become, not only an actress, but a businesswoman.

After the photo shoot was at an end, Rhea Hesser asked her where she would like her copy of the photos sent. Thinking of Chuck, she said, "Could I come by and pick them up at your office instead?"

"Certainly." Mrs. Hesser offered her a polite nod. "We shall phone you when they are ready."

Harlean gave her the phone number for the Bello residence rather than her own.

Late that afternoon back at home, in the private sanctuary of a locked bathroom, she vigorously scrubbed the makeup off and watched her bare face gradually reappear in the mirror's reflection. It reminded her of what she'd once read about a sculptor's process, how the form beneath the marble gradually revealed itself.

This was the young her revealing itself again in the mirror—the guileless naive self staring back at her. But she was so many more things now. She gazed for a long time at her reflection, the raccoon eyes, which warm water, soap and tears gave her—and she wondered in that private moment who she was really.

Chuck pulled at her. Mother pulled the other way. She so wanted them both to be happy. *She* wanted to be happy, and she felt at the moment as if no one really was.

Chapter Fourteen

In June, everything in Harlean's life changed. This, however, was a thing she could not hide from Chuck. She was pregnant. Since there were still no new acting jobs, she decided that fate had given an answer to her question; her future held motherhood, not a career.

"Will you *finally* stop thinking of working now, and make our family your dream?" he asked her with tear-brightened eyes after she had told him.

Part of her wanted to be a smart businesswoman and sparkling actress, one whose success made her capable of helping her mother and Marino, of building that dream home on a hill, and being known around the world. She still longed to be that girl who had posed for Hesser, feeling as if she was about to take Hollywood by storm. But another part of her wanted the child she was carrying and the domestic experience of motherhood that went with that. Inconvenient though the timing might be, this child had been conceived in love, and would live its life engulfed in it. She hadn't so much chosen which of those two directions her life would take, it seemed to have chosen her.

"Our family means everything to me, Chuck," Harlean replied, and she so dearly wanted to feel every syllable of her declaration, in spite of their problems and her hesitation about their marriage.

Things had been better lately, they both were trying. She just hoped and prayed now that it would continue, especially for the baby's sake.

That afternoon, he insisted on taking a picnic lunch up to Griffith Park because it was nearby, and they both loved it for how pristine and secluded a place it was right in the middle of the city. It was one of their favorite spots. Harlean felt a little shiver of guilt as they passed the spot where she had posed for Hesser, but she shook it off. Everything was different now, or it soon would be.

They sat down in a field of wildflowers, framed by enormous trees. He just gazed at Harlean silently for a while as she plucked a flower and absently twirled it between her fingers. Together then they watched the mazy path of a butterfly fluttering beside them.

"I really hope it's a girl. And I just know she will look exactly like you," Chuck said.

"And what shall we name this daughter of ours?"

"I would like to name her after my mother, if you wouldn't mind."

She moved over to him and matched the length of his body with her own. Then she kissed him gently. "I think that's a lovely idea."

"But I wouldn't want a son to be called Charles, too daunting to be Charles Fremont McGrew III. I would rather name him Mont Clair, for your daddy, because I know how much you miss him. We could call him Monty for short." He smiled and brushed back a wisp of hair that the wind had pushed across her cheek. "I know we've had our problems, doll, but those are all over now. You believe me, don't you?"

She wanted so desperately to do just that. "I want to, and I do love you, Chuck McGrew."

"Likewise, doll."

Afterward, they went to a shop on Sunset Boulevard that carried baby clothes. Harlean chose a white silk and lace christening gown and Chuck picked out two yellow pairs of booties.

"These will work for whatever we have," he said happily.

The next morning, Jean and Marino stood at Harlean's front door like two stone pillars. Neither of them were smiling. Jean wore a black turban, sedate black suit and pearl earrings. Marino was in a dark suit and tie. They looked like they were on their way to a funeral.

Harlean smiled anyway as she held the damp dish towel she'd been using.

"Is Chuck in?" her mother asked in a clipped tone.

"He left for a tennis date about an hour ago. Why?"

"Get your handbag."

Her smile began to fade as she looked back and forth at each of their faces, and an uneasy feeling took the place of her calm. Their demeanor frightened her. "Where are we going?"

"Marino made you an appointment. I will *not* have all of our hard work and sacrifice ruined now when we are one role away from stardom."

Her words came with more cold calculation than Harlean had ever heard, and a chill tore through her. "Mommie, my career is over."

"Like *hell* it is. I said, get your handbag."

Harlean did not move. "Where are we going?" she asked again, feeling a sudden rush of fear warm her face.

"It's all arranged. At eleven, you are having a miscarriage."

* * *

Her mother and Marino had needed to force her into the car as she shouted in protest, resisting Marino's firm forward press at the small of her back. She had struggled against them both at first, urging them to listen to reason, but Jean had barked at her not to make a scene for the neighbors before they each took an arm and drew her down the brick walkway.

"This is insanity! I really *want* my child, Mommie! I won't do it, I tell you!"

"You *are* a child, you have no idea what is good for you yet. Thank heavens I do."

As Marino drove, Jean sat with her in the backseat and held her hand.

"Let me out of the car this minute!" Harlean angrily cried as she began to struggle against the grip her mother had on her.

"You should know by now that there is no use arguing with your mother," Marino tepidly offered without turning around as he drove. "Besides, there will be other children. Now just isn't the right time."

It hadn't been the right time when she was conceived, either, but her mother had made that work, and now here she was—something different, a girl who was told she sparkled. But a child changed everything, and hers was threatened by her inability to know how to fight fully for it because she had always trusted her mother's advice. Career or not, approval or not, the ramifications of the act they were proposing were as horrendous to her as the procedure itself seemed. From this day forward, the knowledge that she had not lost this life inside of her, but that she had allowed it to be taken, would be a thing she could never escape.

Harlean reached down and pressed her free hand against her abdomen in a vain attempt at protecting the life within. When the car door opened, she would bolt. Yes, she would dash away from the car and give her mother time to come to her senses. This plan of theirs was madness. In time, her mother would see that. Harlean darted an anxious glance up at the front seat, then back at her mother.

"Please, let's just talk about it. This is your own grandchild."

"It isn't anything of the sort. You mustn't think of it that way, Harlean. I certainly won't." Jean Bello stared unflinchingly ahead, her gaze fixed on the road.

"God, let me out of this car!" Harlean cried out in vain, but her mother remained focused and unyielding.

"Turn left here, Marino. The route is faster," Jean directed him.

Harlean struggled again, and again her mother restrained her with that one firm hand. How could she fight this and win? A kaleidoscope of competing thoughts whirled through her mind. If she ran away from the hospital once the car door was open, and later she told Chuck about this, the already tumultuous fissure between her husband and her mother would be permanent. She wasn't certain she could live without either of them—her child and its father—or her mother. There was no one in the world whose opinion she valued more than her mother, no one who calmed her more surely, or made her laugh more quickly. Jean knew what she was thinking before she said it, and Harlean trusted their bond implicitly.

She whimpered and laid her head against the window glass.

"I am well aware that you are a fine actress but do stop with the dramatics for the moment, Baby. You really are making this much worse than need be. It's a simple procedure on something that hasn't had time yet to become anything at all."

She tried to lean forward, hoping to reason with Marino. Her heart was in her throat and a new wave of nausea was rising inside of her. "Marino, please, you understand, don't you? You like Chuck, I know you do! This is our child, conceived in love!"

He forced a grim sigh, and she watched him shake his balding head. "Well, I hate to say it, my dear, but lately the two of you have fought more like cats and dogs than like anyone in love. I'm not certain it would be right to bring a life into the world only to become a child of divorce. You should know that better than anyone."

She felt herself crumble against the car door. This wasn't happening. It couldn't be happening.

Her mind spun now with a new barrage of questions as the car slowly approached the hospital driveway then began the slow incline. What if she did find the strength to run, to keep the child she carried, and her marriage did fail as her mother predicted? Or worse yet, what if Chuck's drinking worsened, along with the violence and she was forced to leave, what then? She had not been willing to consider that before San Francisco.

At least the McGrew Trust would still be required to support the child, wouldn't it? *Oh, God…wouldn't it?*

Perhaps it wouldn't be if she was the one to walk away from the marriage seemingly in order to return to a career. She could only imagine how a high-powered law firm could spin that fact against her. If they did, at eighteen years old, was she equipped to support herself, and a baby?

Tears welled in her eyes. *Just run!* a voice inside her urged. *What then?* another voice challenged. It sounded more like her mother. As much as she hated to admit it, there were some circumstances in life just too complex to outrun. Perhaps this was one of them.

Challenging Jean Bello would have been like trying to thwart the power of a great wave. The magnitude of what was happening did not fully hit Harlean at first. But later, as she lay at home alone in her bed, her guilt was overwhelming. She wept, lying curled up and alone, arms wrapped around herself, until there were no more tears, and the trembling ceased from sheer exhaustion.

In the end, shame overcame her for how easy it had been to make Chuck believe the lie of a miscarriage. She had summoned up her best acting skills to convince him, for both of their sakes. She could not lose him now, too, when they had both been trying so hard to make things better between them.

Chuck doted on her for a week afterward, insisting that she rest while he did all of the cooking and cleaning without complaint. It went on like that until Mother stopped by unexpectedly while Harlean and Chuck were napping. She left a note on the dining room table indicating that she hadn't wanted to disturb them. Along with it, she placed a folio containing Harlean's set of prints of the Hesser photographs. It was propped against a vase of flowers so it would be impossible to miss.

It had been eight days since the procedure at Good Samaritan Hospital when the photographs arrived—eight days in which Harlean had tried in vain to fill the emptiness she felt, even though nothing really helped.

She saw the folio, emblazoned with the words *Hesser Photography*, on the table as they came together out of the bedroom. Instantly her heart crashed against her chest and her mind surged with panic. *No*, she thought, *not now. We are not ready for this.*

"What's this?" Chuck asked her. His voice was piqued by suspicion. It always began like that.

Harlean could feel the hot rush of blood, pushed forward by guilt, as it blossomed on her face. Oscar was nipping at her heels, barking. She swatted him away as a dozen thoughts and possible responses to yet unasked questions crowded her mind and tangled there. She had been so proud of that daring photo shoot with a man of Hesser's caliber, and she was eager to see the results, but now felt like the worst possible time for that to happen.

She moved behind him as he shuffled through the prints, certain at that moment he could actually hear the slamming of her panicked heart. But as she looked over his shoulder, Harlean was stunned by what she saw. Each print was an exquisite black-and-white piece of art. Hesser had captured the scene, and the mood, exactly as he had explained it to her beforehand. They were beautiful, not tawdry at all, for all the difference that would make now.

When she glanced over at Chuck, his face was a hardened mask.

"You posed for naked pictures without consulting me?"

"I am eighteen, Chuck. I didn't need to ask for your permission this time!"

He stepped back as if her sharp response had struck him. Harlean knew he was trying to hold on to something they could both feel slipping away.

"Jesus, Harlean. Were you carrying our child when you whored yourself out for this?"

He pressed his hands against his forehead and turned away from her in a futile attempt to push away what they both knew he was about to say. The words moved into his mouth, driven by too many deep wounds, and already she felt herself drowning in the turbulent sea of everyone's expectations of her. Chuck's, most especially.

Once upon a time, she thought, he had called her perfect. Now he raged at her, and it broke her heart.

"My wife the whore."

"Chuck, please, I'm begging you, don't do this again."

"Do what? How could you strip bear like that for some pornographer?"

He began to stalk the length of the dining room, and she felt the opening of old wounds that had not healed since San Francisco.

"Mr. Hesser is an artist, I swear to God. Mommie was there, his wife, too!"

He slammed his hands against his head, pressed on them tightly. She could see that he was painfully struck. But this time she could not stop him from hurting because she did not regret it. She was not sorry she had posed for Hesser. And there were other things she wasn't certain she regretted.

She had wanted the child, truly mourned the loss of it, but reflected in his rage now, Harlean saw the sad truth that perhaps her mother had been right after all. A child would have complicated a situation that was already frighteningly volatile between them. Realizing it surprised her. She was not justifying what she had done, she could never do that. Yet still… She could not save him. She knew that she could not save *them*.

He flashed her an angry glare. "Your body is for my eyes only! I'm your husband, for God's sake!"

Even though he had a point and he was justified in his anger, she couldn't make herself do this again—the back and forth of his rage and her pleading in these charged encounters.

"I'm going to take a bath."

Suddenly he grabbed her wrist and spun her back to face him. It was a violent movement and, in it, all of their previous arguments, the many scenes, flashed back hotly into her mind.

"Oh, no, *not* again! Let go of me!" she yelled.

Harlean could see that her defiant tone startled him because his hand quickly fell away and he freed her. It was a small thing and yet a final straw—an accumulation of months that happens in an instant. It certainly had for her.

Harlean turned, and yet she felt in that motion of her body, the pivoting away, that she was leaving far more than just this moment between them. As she closed the door then turned on the faucet, she realized her hand was shaking. She sank onto the edge of the bathtub and poured soap into the rushing water until it bubbled. She thought then how she wanted to escape beneath them into the calm, dark quiet of the water, hidden, so she did not have to face what lay ahead. This was a crossroads. She was afraid of taking the wrong path, and so she had refused before this moment to see how inevitable their end was.

I do so love him, she thought as Chuck began to pound on the locked bathroom door. Her mind was whirling, her heart breaking. *But if I remain, will I not only lose the love I have for him, but begin to lose myself more and more?*

She submerged herself fully in the bath water then, so she could no longer hear his pleas. She had been a good wife, done everything that she could. She would still grieve the loss of something so precious to her as a marriage, but she would not, could not, allow the regret to consume her.

Hesser might have rekindled her ambition, but it had been there inside of her all along.

She had to survive.

Harlean stayed awake all that night as Chuck slept in the guest room. Too angry with her to confront her again, he had gone off and slammed the door, but she knew he would be back at it in the morning. For her part, she felt too drained from her many conflicting emotions to seek him out and try to mend things just now. Part of her knew that she owed him an apology for having posed for Hesser without telling him. She would have owed him another apology if he had known about the abortion. She would never forgive herself for that.

It was only one of the many things that could not be changed for wishing it were so.

Early the next morning, with eyes blurred by tears, Harlean quietly packed a suitcase, picked up Oscar and tucked him into the car. It was wrong to leave without saying goodbye, but she simply couldn't face a final confrontation since there was nothing he could have done to convince her to stay, and she was afraid of what he might do if she gave him the chance to try. They both needed to cool down and find a bit of perspective.

Neither of them would get that chance if she didn't leave. Considering the months of turmoil, she knew in her heart this was the only way.

Then, with more sadness in her heart than she had ever felt in her life, and a quiet anguished cry, she drove the short distance to the house her mother shared with Marino and asked if she could stay with them for a while.

CHAPTER FIFTEEN

"Line up over there, ladies. Have your information handy. We'll call each of you when it's time."

Ten days after she left Chuck, Harlean attended another casting call at Paramount Pictures. She had lost out at an audition with Joel McCrea last week and she was certain she had only gotten this because her mother had relentlessly peppered Dave Allen's secretary with phone calls. Ordinarily, it would have embarrassed Harlean to know that, but she felt rudderless without working.

The call was for a small part in a picture starring Clara Bow, and the number of actresses going for the role was daunting. While it was a small part, even Betty Grable was auditioning, and she had just done a movie called *Happy Days* that everyone was talking about.

Harlean tried to relax and remember that she had done this before, but she was so far down the snaking line of girls that she was certain they would cast someone before they got to her.

"Jean Harlow."

She heard her name and her heart vaulted into her throat.

Maybe she wasn't ready for this yet after all, with everything that had happened, and all she was still going through. She certainly wasn't eating or sleeping well.

Reluctantly, she followed the casting assistant through a set of heavy metal doors and onto a soundstage. Ahead of her was a set designed to look like a bedroom. Beside it was an empty director's chair, lights and two cameras. A tall, dark-haired young man was reviewing a script with a production assistant. This was about to be a repeat of her audition last week, a part she did not get in spite of their enthusiasm for her. Harlean needed to steel herself against the inevitable rejection and just get through this.

"Jean, this is Jimmy. He will be doing your test with you."

He had such a genuinely kind smile when he looked up at her that some of her hesitation faded right then. Harlean extended her hand. *James Hall*, she thought, recognizing him. She had loved him in *The Fifty-Fifty Girl*, with Bebe Daniels. As intimidating as it was to meet someone famous, he had an easygoing air. She had no idea what she would do if she got to meet Clara Bow herself. Bow was one of the biggest silent film stars in the world.

A moment later, the director and assistant director sank into their canvas-back chairs as Harlean took the script from the casting agent.

"You and Jimmy will be reading from here down to here." She motioned to the page where a passage had been highlighted.

Since Harlean was such a voracious reader she scanned the page quickly and saw that it was a romantic comedy, so she adjusted the way she planned to deliver the lines.

"Think you've got it?" Hall asked her.

"I better have it."

He smiled and she could sense that he was charmed. *Good,* she thought. Now, if she could just charm the director.

"Okay, Mr. Sutherland. We're ready when you are," Hall called out.

It was over with quickly, and she felt good about her performance. She had even heard the assistant director chuckle at one of her lines. But then there was the murmuring and waiting while the two directors conferred. Harlean could see the next girl waiting with the casting assistant in the shadows back by the door. Her heart was racing. She needed the work so badly. The weight of expectation, supporting herself, Mother and Marino before she was even nineteen, felt crushing. Her pride would not allow her to ask anything of Chuck anymore.

"That's it, Alice. You can send the other girls home," the director called out. "We've got our Hazel."

"Does he mean *me?*" she whispered to Hall.

He nodded. "Yep. Jean, wasn't it?"

"Well, Harlean actually, but I'm trying to be Jean Harlow. My mother thinks it sounds more professional. Although that might have something to do with it being her name," she said, chattering out the explanation as she often did when she was nervous.

"Well, now, *that* sounds complicated."

"We're just close, that's all."

The assistant director called out to her. "All right, Miss Harlow. Show up in Wardrobe tomorrow morning at eight. Alice over there will see that you get the script before you leave. It'll be a day's work, maybe two tops."

"Thank you, sir," she called back.

"Congratulations," Hall whispered. "And you'll like Clara. She's a kick. A little insecure about this being a talkie, though, since she doesn't like the sound of her own voice. She's got a

New Jersey accent thick enough to knock your socks off, but anyway, I'm sure you gals will get along just fine."

"I hope so," Harlean said.

She certainly didn't need any more complications in her life.

Harlean and the Bellos celebrated that evening with dinner in the ballroom of the Miramar Hotel because they had an orchestra there, and mother said she felt like dancing. Harlean wore her favorite white silk sheath dress and the way it clung to her body gave her a sense of daring. It was nice suddenly to feel that she was breaking free without fear for the repercussions.

They were shown to a linen-draped table near the bandstand, which was flanked by several massive potted palms. As the maître d' held her chair, Harlean saw a few of the young men in the orchestra look at her and smile. She liked their attention, particularly since there was no guilt attached to it any longer.

The hotel was in Santa Monica, on the side of town where police turned a blind eye to the liquor laws, so Marino ordered highballs for all three of them as the orchestra struck up a new tune.

"I'm telling you, Baby, this is finally it. Clara Bow! There aren't bigger stars than her. If you get on her good side there is no telling what might happen."

"It's a small part," Harlean reminded her mother.

Secretly, she had never been more thrilled at the prospect of anything in her life.

After another round of drinks, she realized that the dark-haired bandleader was staring at her. He had deep, expressive eyes, a long, square jaw, and he looked to be in his early thirties, which made him the antithesis of Chuck. And even though she sometimes missed him, she was growing angry.

Yes, she had been the one to leave but why had he not even tried to phone? In spite of having said he couldn't live without her, he was making no attempt at all to fight for her.

Chuck... Damn him. She had gone against her family to marry him. She had gone against her better judgment to remain with him after San Francisco. While she, too, had made mistakes in the marriage—yes, withholding things had been wrong—she had given him more than a few chances to right their course. His erratic bursts of anger had sealed their fate.

Harlean had no intention of being a fool for love any longer. In that, her resolve surprised her. She was eighteen now and apparently that chapter of her life really was over.

She settled back in her chair then and watched the bandleader more closely. Fortunately, her mother and Marino were so engrossed in their own conversation that she knew they didn't see him smile and nod in acknowledgment of her, or that she returned his gesture with a smile of her own. Tonight she was allowing herself to be a bit rebellious. She felt a growing sense of deliverance at the absence of Chuck's constant volatility.

She finished her second cocktail and took a long sip from her mother's glass.

After the set concluded, Harlean excused herself to go and find the ladies' room. Her mother nodded to her, and then turned back to Marino, who was ordering yet more cocktails.

When Harlean came back out a few minutes later, she found the bandleader waiting for her in the softly lit corridor that smelled of the gardenias that were floating in a glass bowl beside her. There was no one else coming or going around them. He was leaning against the wall, one leg crossed in front of the other, hands shoved into the pockets of his black tuxedo trousers.

"I do believe you are the loveliest creature I have ever seen grace my audience. I had to meet you. I'm Roy."

"Harlean."

"Can I see you later, after we finish up here?"

"I'm married. Separated, actually, but still."

He offered her a crooked smile. "I wasn't asking for your hand. At least not yet, anyway. I'll be finished here at midnight. Would you consider waiting for me so we could get acquainted?"

She felt the attraction flare between them. Only one time before she'd met Chuck had she felt anything like it. But flirtation this powerful was a little frightening to her for where she knew it could so easily lead.

"I'm here with my mother and her husband tonight."

"Tell them you have a ride home."

"I'm staying at their house for a while, Roy."

"Then we won't go to your place. I'll think of something. *If* you want to spend some time together, that is."

An image of Chuck flared in her mind. She closed her eyes to it. It was too late for that, too late for them. Was there any real reason not to ease the pain from the tear across her heart?

The element of control was a thing she had never possessed, and she knew she had paid a heavy price for the lack of it in her life. There was always either Mother or Chuck to make every decision for her. But curiosity, circumstance and growing up were steadily transforming her from an uncertain girl into a confident woman. She would only be dipping a tentative toe into the water of independence but, just now, the lure of that was too strong to turn away from.

"Sure, I'd like that, Roy," Harlean said.

Chapter Sixteen

The next morning, Harlean selected one of her favorite dresses to wear to the studio. After the time she had spent with Roy the night before, she felt more sensual and beautiful than she had in a long time, and her clingy black crochet dress seemed perfect for the day.

She paired the dress with her favorite black strap high-heeled sandals, fluffed her freshly bleached hair and grabbed her handbag. She was eager to work with James Hall but she was beyond excited to meet Clara Bow. That alone seemed like a dream come true.

She only hoped she didn't trip over her own feet, or her tongue, when she did.

Rosalie, who hadn't been getting parts lately, offered to go with her as moral support but Harlean didn't trust herself on the subject of Roy if it came up. While their friendship was strong, she and Rosalie were both still married women and she wasn't sure she was willing to risk the potential of Rosalie judging her. Especially since Harlean fully intended to see Roy again in the face of yet another day of continued silence from Chuck.

She felt collective eyes on her the moment she walked onto the set. Someone whistled.

"Check out the tomato," one young technician said beneath his breath. "Yeah, and take a look at those gams," another chuckled.

She saw Arthur Jacobson, the assistant director, look up at the sound. "What in the Sam Hill is she wearing?" he asked his assistant, who was sporting horn-rimmed glasses and a smug smile.

"I'd say it's more what she *isn't* wearing, sir."

The sound of muffled laughter followed. It occurred to Harlean that perhaps her favorite dress was more revealing than she had intended it to be for the occasion. True, she was feeling liberated, and she had planned to wear it for Roy after the shoot today, but she might have pushed it too far for work.

"Show Miss Harlow to Wardrobe, Sam," Jacobson said with an exaggerated scowl.

As she passed by the set, she heard a woman with a strong New Jersey accent call out. "Are you kiddin' me? Oh, not a chance that girl's gonna be in this picture! I want her out, Arthur. Fire her!"

Harlean didn't need to turn around to see that the angry voice belonged to the star, her mother's idol—sassy redheaded It Girl, Clara Bow.

Her confidence was shaken by the time she walked into the costume department with the assistant, who continued to grin the entire time they walked.

"This is Jean Harlow, Miss Head. She's playing Hazel in the picture."

A plain-faced woman of about thirty, with short, jet-black hair and a sharp fringe of bangs, looked up from her needle and thread. To Harlean's relief, her smile seemed genuine. "Call me Edith." She set the costume down onto her worktable. As she stood, she extended her hand and offered an affable shake. "Now, let's see what we've got here for you."

She went to a costume rack marked *The Saturday Night Kid*, the movie's title. Each hanger bore a character name pinned to the front of it. She glanced back at Harlean, gauging her size.

"I'd *like* to put you in this one," she said in a low voice, pulling out a slinky, gray, bias cut dress with a shawl collar. "I designed it for Miss Bow, but she's gotten too fat to wear it."

Harlean could already tell that Edith Head was a clever and savvy woman competing in a man's world here at the studio, and she seemed to be doing it with flair. That was something to respect. The dress she'd designed was striking.

After Harlean had donned her own costume, she returned to find the set in an uproar. Bow was still irate, stalking back and forth in front of the director, who had his hands out in a pleading gesture. James Hall, who everyone called Jimmy, appeared to be explaining things to the other woman in the cast, whose name was Jean Arthur.

"Be reasonable, Clara. We start shooting this morning. I don't have the time or the budget to recast."

"To hell with reasonable, Arthur! I'm askin' ya who'll see me next to *her*?"

The fragile tone of the question, even though spoken in anger, struck Harlean. It had never occurred to her that a legitimate star could feel an ounce of insecurity when faced with a bit player. She lingered near Jimmy, trying not to move or make things worse.

"I'm sorry, Clara. I called up to the offices. It's a no-go. The girl stays."

Bow huffed in response. She finally turned and met Harlean's shocked gaze. "What are *you* staring at? You look like a goddamn China doll, and I'll bet you know it, too, doncha?"

Harlean pushed away a sarcastic retort and summoned up

a sunny smile instead. The next moments were critical. She knew they could change the entire path of her career.

"It's a real honor to meet you, Miss Bow. I've seen every one of your pictures. Most of them I've seen twice. You really are the best actress around."

The silence was a palpable thing as Bow eyed her suspiciously. "Is that so?"

"Oh, it is! You were really swell in *Get Your Man,* and in *Wings.* I thought you were downright brilliant."

Everyone knew that the war epic *Wings* had won the first Academy Award ever for Best Picture three years ago.

Harlean could see the anger slowly slipping from her face. Still, no one dared to speak a word as the two young women confronted one another like rivals—one, the ultimate actress, the other an unparalleled beauty. Thankfully, her mother had taught Harlean the art of flattery.

Bow softened her expression in the face of Harlean's fawning. "That was a man's picture and I was nothin' but whipped cream on top of the pie." The crew cautiously began taking their places. Bow moved a step nearer. "I'm Paramount's biggest star, ya know, so they rewrote that whole damn script to accommodate me."

"They knew what they were doing," Harlean remarked.

"So…how do you get your hair that color? It looks just like a cotton ball."

"It's pretty painful, honestly. And the smell could chase away the devil."

Bow laughed at that.

The commotion around them increased as the crew, sensing a lessening of the tension, slowly returned to normal. James passed by and winked at Harlean in support. She drew in a small breath and continued to smile back sweetly at the star.

"You ever been in a motion picture?" Bow asked.

"Nothing like you, Miss Bow. And never a talkie."

"Me, either. Pretty damn terrifying. Don't tell anyone though, hmm?"

Harlean crossed her heart. "I promise."

After they shot the first few scenes, Bow invited Harlean to sit beside her on set as the crew set up for the next shot. Clara Bow's chair had her name embroidered on the back. Harlean could not begin to imagine what that kind of acclaim would feel like.

"I'm sorry I gave you such a rough time earlier," Clara said as she gazed out past the cameras. "I got myself into such a state over being in a talkie that I've been consoling myself with a little too much spaghetti lately. Couldn't even fit into my costume yesterday. How's *that* for a bucket of cold water poured over the big-time *movie star*?" she said with surprising self-deprecation.

"Miss Bow, you're beautiful!"

"Well, thanks, kid. But even ten pounds lighter I sure as hell couldn't hold a candle to you in the looks department. You're goin' places, I can feel it."

"You're a star, Miss Bow, and I'm a bit player. Girls like me are a dime a dozen around this town."

She smiled as she settled her gaze on Harlean. "Call me Clara, first of all, and let's see if we can change that, because there ain't nothin' ordinary about you. In fact, come with me, I have an idea. We have a little time before they're ready for us."

With that, she stood and took Harlean's hand in a firm grip.

Bow then led her across the lot and into the costume department where Edith and several male designers were working with seamstresses on an array of ensembles for different films.

"Edith, where's my dress? The one you have to pour me into."

Edith, who was wearing thick black eyeglasses now, pushed down onto the tip of her nose, glanced up. Seeing the star, she shoved her chair back and shot to her feet.

"Over there on the rack, Miss Bow, I'll get it for you. I haven't started working on it yet, though, since they said they wouldn't be shooting you in it this whole first week."

"Good, since Jean is going to wear it in the picture, not me, and she can fit into it just as you designed it."

Harlean saw the widened expression of surprise in Edith's eyes even behind the thick eyeglasses and a small grin passed between the two of them.

"All right, well, put it on already. Let's all see what that gorgeous thing is meant to look like on somebody. And call down to Publicity, will ya, Edith? Have someone send a photographer up to the set. I want him to take a picture of the two of us together and send it out to the papers. Tell 'em down there I want to see if we can help her out."

Harlean was stunned by the stroke of good fortune. She had no idea how the circumstances had changed so completely, but she was enormously grateful that they had.

Later that afternoon, when Clara had gone back to her dressing room during a scene change, Jimmy approached Harlean. "Cup o' joe?" he asked, offering her one of two cups of coffee he had brought from the catering table. After she took it he said, "You certainly have charmed our star. Feel like sharing your secret?"

"I have no idea, honestly. I was just being myself."

"Well, that must be the magic. Beautiful, funny *and* sincere. The whole package. Clara is right, you *are* going to go places."

Harlean felt herself blush and she averted her gaze. In response, he drew her chin up by his index finger. "Be proud of the effect you have on people. Say, listen, how 'bout you get all dolled up tonight after work and I'll take you to dinner. The Cocoanut Grove sound good?"

"I've never been there," she replied, trying to keep the excitement at the prospect from her voice.

It was the nightclub in the Ambassador Hotel where all the celebrities dined and danced. The problem was that she had agreed to see Roy again later that night.

She was enormously attracted to Roy, but an evening of being wined and dined at the famous nightclub was too enticing to decline.

"I'd love to join you, Jimmy."

"Swell. I'll bring the hooch to add to our drinks since it has gotten harder there on mid-Wilshire to get anything that's drinkable."

"That sounds swell," she replied, feeling excited about the evening ahead already.

"Pick you up at seven thirty?"

Harlean was so looking forward to finally being at the Cocoanut Grove that, as she dashed into the house to change and grabbed her stack of mail her mother left near the door, she almost didn't open the letter she saw was from Chuck's attorney.

Once she did, she paused for a moment, set down her handbag and picked up Oscar. Her heart started to race. She wasn't sure she even wanted to know what was inside. The lawyers were involved now. From some things, there was no turning back. How well she had learned that already.

She trembled as she read that he was moving out and giving her the house on Linden Drive. Chuck was moving forward with the divorce. She closed her eyes, trying not to remember his face as he presented it to her that first day.

It was a good thing that she couldn't see it now. He had done too much to chase that image away.

Harlean wore the same slinky white silk dress she had worn with her mother and Marino the night she met Roy. She was even more confident in it now, though; she could feel it with each step.

"So tell me about yourself," she bid Jimmy as they settled in at a table for two in the center of the busy ballroom.

He smiled in response. "I don't believe anyone has ever asked me that before."

"Well, I guess there's a first for everything."

"I'm from Texas. Dallas, to be exact. Been at this game and gettin' work from it for about six years now."

"That's impressive."

"Don't let me kid you. If they'd been big hits, you'd know all about me."

Harlean laughed. "Actually, you were in the first talkie I saw. *The Canary Murder Case*."

"First one I was ever in. This will be my second. I've actually been working on a silent film, too, since last year, but it seems like decades. Thing just doesn't seem to want to fly, which was why I had to take this job. Big war epic Mr. Hughes is calling *Hell's Angels*. Now, in the middle of everything, he has decided he wants to make it a talkie, too, so we're having to shoot everything over again."

"Howard Hughes, the millionaire aviator?"

"Yep, that's the one. He owns Caddo Productions and, if you don't mind my saying, he's damned eccentric for such a young fella. I don't think he's even twenty-five yet. Everything's gotta be just so with him all the time."

Harlean felt a giggle bubble up. She was having such an unexpectedly nice time already.

"I tell ya, it's been one crisis after another with that picture. He also decided to dabble in multicolor when he turned it into a talkie, and that just set us back even further. I have serious doubts it's ever gonna get made at all."

"I'm so sorry," she said as he drew a silver flask from a pocket in his dinner jacket for a second time and splashed another liberal dose of gin into her water glass.

"And on top of that, Hughes hired this Swedish dame to play the lead when it was a silent film. Don't get me wrong, she's a real looker, but we're all supposed to be from England and her accent is so thick none of us can even understand her, much less believe she's from ol' London town."

They both dissolved into a fit of laughter at the prospect of such an absurd circumstance. The warming effects of the alcohol took over from there and mixed with the upbeat tune that the orchestra was playing.

In that moment, once again in her life Harlean felt like a part of two worlds: this one in which she was young, happy and free to explore the woman she felt on the verge of becoming; yet in the other she was an old soul where obligation and duty heavily bound her. Chuck was still there in that mix. Even after her dalliance with Roy, Harlean remained unsure if she was meant to fully let Chuck go from her life. Divorce was such a final thing when she had loved him as she had.

She was brought back from her thoughts when Jimmy smiled and raised his hand, beckoning someone across the room over to their table. "I didn't know Ben would be here tonight! He's suffering through that picture with me. We're playing the two leads. You've gotta meet him. Do you mind?"

Jimmy stood as the handsome man, with a beautiful dark-haired girl on his arm, approached. The two shook hands heartily before Hall kissed his friend's companion on the cheek.

"Guys, this is Jean, we're working on a picture together. Jean, Ben Lyon and his very lovely girlfriend, Bebe Daniels."

Harlean resisted the urge to say she had seen all of Bebe's movies or to gush at the sweet-faced starlet. She had done quite enough of that fawning over Clara Bow earlier in the day.

"May we join you?" Ben asked, even as he summoned two extra chairs from a waiter and then held one out for his girlfriend.

He seemed affable, with lovely hazel eyes and such a winning smile, and it was clear that the three of them were good friends.

"I was just telling Jean all about the *Hell's Angels* disaster we're both tangled up in."

Ben laughed at that. "Probably never to be free of it, at the rate Hughes is going. Did you tell her about Greta?"

All three of them started to chuckle since it was clearly a subject they had discussed before.

"The movie is a war epic that seems to be turning into farcical comedy," Bebe explained, and she did so in such a believable Swedish accent that Harlean started to laugh with them.

Later, as Jimmy drove her home, he put a casual hand on Harlean's knee. He let it linger there for a moment at a stop sign before he took it off to shift the gears. Along Beverly Boulevard, he pulled over to the curb and kissed her. The Gershwin tune, "Fascinating Rhythm" was playing softly on the car radio he'd just had installed.

"What do you say we take a drive out to the beach in Santa Monica? Look at the waves, maybe make some waves of our own?" he asked.

Harlean smiled before he kissed her again. He was attractive, and she liked him. But even after this evening, and the fun she'd had with him, and his friends, she still didn't feel what she had felt with Roy, and certainly not the consuming passion she once had felt with Chuck. Letting this go any further with a fellow actor would be a mistake.

"Can I take a rain check? It's been a long day and we both have an early call at the studio again tomorrow."

The grip he had on her thigh steadily eased.

"Sure thing, doll face. Sweetest brush off I've ever gotten."

She reached up to touch his cheek. "It's not that, Jimmy. Honest. You're swell, really you are. I've just got a lot on my mind right now with the separation from my husband, and trying to support my mother and her husband, and with not a lot of work coming in to do it."

"Your husband isn't helping you while you guys figure things out?"

"He and my mother don't get along. He doesn't want his money going to her."

"Grandparents, aunts, uncles, anybody who can help tide you over?"

Harlean sighed and stared straight ahead for a moment into the lamp-lit night of the busy boulevard. "My grandpa Harlow got angry over a little short I did with Laurel and Hardy. He told me that if I was strong enough to make it in Hollywood, I need to do it without his money since he doesn't approve of the pictures I've been in."

"He thinks you're that resourceful?"

"No, he thinks I'm gonna quit. He's just trying to make me come to my senses sooner than later, but I'm damn sure gonna try to prove to him that I'm stronger than he thinks."

He exhaled, sank back in his seat, then shook his head. "Tough break. Say, I could loan you some suds until you get back on your feet? No strings."

"There would be strings, Jimmy," she said as she wiped her lipstick from his mouth with her thumb.

"I like you a lot, Jean."

"I like you, too, Jimmy. So, I'd rather have your friendship than your money."

"Don't think I won't try things again with us," he warned.

"I'd be offended if you didn't," she said as she flashed him her best version of a breezy smile she didn't fully feel. But then again, she thought, that was acting.

Her mother and Marino were asleep by the time Jimmy dropped her off in front of the house. Harlean waved goodbye and then, after he drove off, she got into her own car and let out a deep sigh. She was feeling nostalgic tonight, missing parts of the life she had shared with Chuck more than ever, especially after spending the evening with a man she did not know well, or love. She missed so many things that were part of the comfort of married life: the ease of being with one particular human being, the private jokes, intimacy, a growing history, even difficult times that knit them together as they faced them.

Chuck had surely laid down the gauntlet by sending her word through his attorney this afternoon. He had declared that it was officially over. Separation was one level, divorce was quite another. The finality of it shook her.

He had his problems, they had their history, there were those things he could never take back having done…but if only they could talk, just the two of them, to make absolutely certain that the final step of divorce was what they both wanted… If they both did, then perhaps saying so in person was a more mature way of parting than through attorneys and cold legal jargon.

She had no idea at all what she would say to begin a conversation. Harlean only knew that she needed to be the bigger person and find out.

Knowing Chuck would be there packing since he would

be moving out in two days, she drove back to Linden Drive for the first time in weeks. She turned the engine and head-lamps off next door and let the car coast to a stop in front of the home they had shared, not quite ready to be seen until she steadied herself.

Suddenly, a young woman who Harlean did not recognize passed before the window. It was almost as if she had come on-screen in a film for the deliberate way she moved, paused, turned toward Chuck. Then she stopped, lingering beside him. She was speaking to him and he did not move away from her. An imagined conversation filled Harlean's mind. She let out a heavy sigh. There would be no final conversation, no resolve. But suddenly it didn't seem so important after all.

She drove back to the Maple Drive house after that and fell exhausted into bed. Tomorrow was another day, she told herself, and who knew what lay ahead, but now she was more excited than ever to find out. Tonight she would allow her-self a bit of melancholy over the death of her marriage. That much seemed deserved. Then tomorrow it would be onward, and with a renewed zest for the future which she was more determined than ever now to make bright.

After the shoot for *The Saturday Night Kid* had concluded, true to her word, Clara Bow posed for a publicity photo with the female cast members, one that would be released to the press. Clara made certain Harlean was prominently positioned beside her and she even put an arm around her. Clara's one note to her own vanity was making sure that Edith Head put Harlean in a sedate black dress with a demure white lace collar.

"I'm a good friend, but I'm no fool," Clara chuckled as she glanced at the lace collar. "You hafta make it the rest of the way on your own talent. But I know that's gonna happen."

Mother had taught Harlean to value smart women and to study and emulate their ladder to success. She couldn't feel anything for Clara Bow but enormous respect, and a growing desire to make a place for herself, one just like Clara's, in the motion picture industry.

Chapter Seventeen

For all of her hope that *The Saturday Night Kid* might have finally signaled a career change, provide more substantial work and lead to her big break, the jobs her mother promised would come still eluded her.

As the days wore on, Harlean began once again to doubt everything she believed was meant to be. She felt increasingly adrift, and as if the decisions she and her mother had made were one mistake after the next—insisting that a career take prominence in her life, walking away from her marriage to a boy she so loved, and then how she had handled her pregnancy.

She kept people around her all of the time in order to avoid thinking about any of it. There was dinner with Ivor and Rosalie, a tennis date with Irene Mayer and shopping with her mother. She meant all of the activity as a cushion for her wounded heart, and yet she had never felt more alone.

Harlean saw Roy two more times and then she simply could not continue.

He was a complete gentleman about it, embracing her before he pressed a kiss onto her cheek. "Chin up, kid," he said with a smile. "It'll all work out for the best."

The only problem was, Harlean had no idea anymore what "the best" for her actually was or how to get it.

"Where do you want this box, hon?" Ivor asked, as he and Rosalie trooped in the front door at the Linden Drive house.

Their arms were laden with Harlean's things that they were bringing back for her.

She had gone in first an hour ago, half thinking she would find Chuck there and that they would finally be forced to talk. Her heart squeezed at how vacant the house felt now. All of the furniture was still there, but no essence of the two of them lingered.

The only reminder came from a large bouquet of cut orchids left on the dining room table that stunned her. There was no note, but that was not needed. She knew what it symbolized, and who had left them. For a moment, Harlean surrendered her face to her hands to catch her breath, allowing the flowers to speak for him where words could not. There was still love between them but it just wasn't enough for either of them just now. Despite misgivings, she had decided to move back in because Chuck was giving her the house and also, after all of his volatility with her, a defiant side of her felt she deserved it, as well as this opportunity to begin living on her own and making her way as an adult. Once again, though, with the symbolic flowers, he had managed to make her feel a spark of tenderness for him.

"Oh, that lout makes you sad even when he's not here! I'd clock him if he walked in that door right now!"

"Hush!" Rosalie snapped at Ivor.

"He's not coming back," Harlean said as Rosalie wrapped an arm around her shoulder. She hadn't realized her expression had conveyed to them the dolefulness she felt today.

"Do you want me to dump those things in the trash for you, honey?"

"Thanks, Rosie, but I want to keep them for just a little while longer. I know it's odd, but it helps me remember the good things."

"Tough break," Ivor weakly offered, not knowing what else to say as he paused and stood awkwardly between the two women. "But there'll be someone else."

Harlean simply could not imagine that.

For now, Chuck's grandfather, the relative who oversaw his inheritance, had grudgingly agreed to temporary alimony payments to Harlean while he pushed details of a divorce forward. Unfortunately, Mother and Marino quickly spent the first $375 installment. She had tried many times to steel herself enough to confront her mother on her free spending ways. The indignant reaction and flares of temper she got in response, however, were never worth the stand. Harlean had faced more than enough volatility during her marriage, and even if it meant she saw little of the money she earned, for now at least, it felt worth it to her.

In the face of that, she was relieved to have gotten another bit part in a film that began shooting tomorrow. She not only needed the money, she welcomed the distraction—she was going to summon her courage yet again and keep on trying to make a real and lucrative career of this, no matter what.

Weak But Willing was another comedy being shot at Metropolitan Studios on Las Palmas Drive in Hollywood. Harlean had found work only as an extra in it but she was more determined than ever to let her spirit shine through. Her part took place in a ballroom, the irony of which was not lost on her after the setting for her first extra role. She may not have found her big break yet, but Harlean believed she had already learned a great deal about the movie business, just by watching and listening, and when a chance came her way she knew she would be ready for it. As she sat now, waiting for her part, Harlean heard the cast and crew talking about the war epic *Hell's Angels* being filmed across the lot by a man they called the young "hayseed" multimillionaire. It was the picture James Hall had told her about.

She hadn't spoken with Jimmy since their evening at the Cocoanut Grove, but she remembered his story about the trouble they'd had shooting the film because of Hughes. She was happy to hear, for Jimmy's sake, that apparently the picture was back on track. She only wished she could say the same for her own career, and for her swiftly dwindling finances.

The electric company and the phone company were barraging her with letters of nonpayment because most of the money she'd earned, or gotten grudgingly from Chuck's family, only went so far each month. With herself, her mother and Marino to support, it seemed to go more quickly than she could earn it. Harlean tried not to feel resentful about being the only one working because she knew it would have changed nothing anyway. Besides, her mother made regular declarations that helping her daughter find suitable roles to audition for was a full-time job that took the effort of both her and Marino. While she didn't know if that was true, Harlean knew that she could trust them to support and encourage her career and, to her mind, that at least was something.

To make ends meet, she had recently sold two fox stoles Chuck had bought for her and decided her engagement ring had to go, as well. In spite of her pride, and the belief that she deserved it, the house would be the next thing to go if things didn't improve.

She wore sunglasses and a big hat onto Sunset Boulevard to a pawnshop there. Not that anyone in Hollywood would recognize her without them, nor was the ring anything of particular value, yet still Harlean was ashamed of what she felt driven to do.

"Seventy-five dollars."

"But it's worth twice that," Harlean argued.

"Sorry, lady, but this ain't a jewelry store, you know?"

Someone else entered the shop behind her and ushered in the traffic noise from the busy street beyond. Harlean watched the owner, in his torn cardigan, finger her ring, the white-gold band and tiny diamond chip as if it meant nothing. She hated having to do this.

But going back to Missouri was not an option.

Pride pushed her shoulders back a tick for her. She thought of how good Rosalie was at this sort of thing. "Eighty, sir, please."

"Push me, doll, and I'll make it sixty."

"Don't ever call me that," she growled.

"Look, sweetheart, whatever you want to be called, that ring is basically junk. I'm doing you a favor buying it, as it is."

She was no longer anyone's doll, and she certainly didn't feel like the Baby at the moment—even if people still called her that. There was no one to take care of her, like a baby or a doll, both precious fragile things. She needed to be stronger than that, tougher, and she believed she was becoming both.

"All right, seventy-five," she said and turned away from him.

She couldn't look at the ring, or him, a moment longer.

"Hey there, good-lookin', remember me?"

She was startled from her thoughts as she sat outside of the soundstage with the other extras all in evening wear, all of them intent on getting a breath of fresh air between scenes.

Her own costume was a figure-hugging, black satin gown with tiny rhinestones.

She closed the novel she was trying to read while everyone else drank coffee and chatted around her, and glanced up into the smooth-skinned face of Ben Lyon, Jimmy Hall's co-star and friend. He was standing with another, slightly older, man right in front of her.

"Of course I remember you, Ben," Harlean replied as she tucked the volume onto her lap and offered up a smile.

"Oh, sorry, this is my agent. Arthur Landau, I'd like you to meet Jean Harlow."

"You're not an extra. Not a gal who looks like you," Landau declared.

His long nose, heavy chin, slicked-back hair, wire-rimmed glasses and two days' growth of beard gave him a somewhat unkempt appearance.

"Afraid so." Harlean shrugged, comforted in the moment by the compliment. "So, how's the picture coming along? Has Mr. Hughes got all the wrinkles ironed out?"

"Afraid not by a long shot. We're all left to cool our heels a lot of the time, and shoot out of sequence, while he searches for a new dame for the lead. I think he's tested every actress in Hollywood and then some." There was a short pause before his eyes suddenly lit. "Say listen, how would *you* feel about playing the lead in *Hell's Angels*?"

Harlean gave him a scowl. "Don't kid around, Ben. I'm not really in the mood for a joke like that."

"No, seriously. What time is your lunch break?"

"Twelve thirty, why?"

"Hughes can't use Greta anymore because of her accent. Now he wants a beautiful unknown and he's at his wit's end over it. How 'bout I get you an interview with the boss man?"

Harlean was too stunned to reply. The papers were full of

what an epic picture it was shaping up to be. It was the buzz all over Hollywood. In the silence, Arthur Landau gave Ben a nod of approval which convinced her suddenly that this was not a joke.

"All right, well, I've gotta get back to the set or Mr. Hughes will have my head on a platter! Why don't you get to know Arthur a little better and I'll see you back here at twelve thirty sharp."

"Have you got an agent, kid?" Arthur asked once they were alone.

"I have my mother, which is kind of the same thing, if you knew my mother."

"Not if the best she can get you is work as an extra."

Harlean had to agree as he sat down on the bench beside her and they both gazed out at the group of actors trooping back and forth in front of them. "You really should have actual representation if you're going up before a studio boss."

"I suppose you're right," she conceded, shrugging again, and she knew her tone was wary. Her mother was so much a part of her life and work.

"Look, kiddo, I'll be honest with you. I could use another client, and if Ben is right about you having some earning potential, you'll need an agent who knows his way around this crazy town. I'd like to be that man."

"I can't afford a real agent, Mr. Landau. I'm barely scraping by as it is."

"Another reason you could use me. You need someone to teach you how this business works. I only get paid when my clients get paid. I'd like an opportunity to help you get a real pay day, Jean, and not just a couple of nickels to rub together from work as an extra."

She liked the way that sounded and she felt herself softening to the prospect. "Do you think Ben was serious about actually getting an interview from Mr. Hughes?"

"I know he was. You need a job and Hughes needs a star. Listen, could you use a couple of bucks to help tide you over? A loan, mind you, not a handout. I have a good feeling about you and this war picture so I'd like to help out a nice kid like you if I can."

"I couldn't possibly..."

"It was Ben's idea so he'd be in on it, all strictly legit. I loaned him a few bucks last year so he'd vouch for the kind of man I am."

"I don't know..." She was mulling it over.

"Look, it's not all noble on my part. Clients with star potential are hard to come by. I agree with Ben that you have it, so a temporary loan of a few bucks would start a working relationship between us, and help me out as much as you."

Harlean wanted to say no. She meant to. The words were on her lips. But so many bills were past due and, after *Double Whoopee*, her grandfather had made it clear that she could no longer come to him for money if she meant to remain in Hollywood. She hadn't pleaded with him or with Chuck, and she wasn't going to. She was going to make her own way in this town somehow, or she would die trying.

Borrowing money was different, however.

"Okay, thanks, Mr. Landau, I'll think about it. But if I do, I'm gonna pay you back, with interest."

He smiled at her. "I know you will, kiddo," he said. "I only gamble when it's a sure thing."

Jimmy was waiting for them outside the door of Howard Hughes's office when she and Ben arrived on the other side of the lot. Seeing her, Jimmy gave a happy hoot before he drew her into a hug.

"Wow, when ol' Benjie here said he found a girl, I had no idea he meant you! He's right, though. You'd be perfect for the part. Come on, we'll introduce you to the boss."

It was ten minutes before one when Harlean was shown into a bungalow that was the private office of Howard Hughes. The tall, dark-haired and intimidatingly handsome Hughes sat hunched over behind the desk, shuffling papers as she stood shifting awkwardly back and forth, waiting for him to look up and acknowledge her. He appeared quite uninterested in being disturbed. An oiled forelock of ebony hair fell forward. He didn't seem to notice. His brow was furrowed far too much for his age. He was clearly a no-nonsense sort of man.

"Give us some privacy," Hughes finally grumbled.

Jimmy indicated with a toss of his head that he would be just outside as he and Ben walked out and closed the door.

The office was enormously cluttered. There were precarious piles of books and manuscripts stacked on the floor around his desk. There were several coffee cups and a full ashtray on the desk. Harlean lingered near the door, nervously twisting the handles of her small handbag. She was uncertain if she was meant to sit or simply stand there waiting to be acknowledged.

At last, Hughes glanced up in an entirely perfunctory manner, looked at her for only a moment, and called out to his secretary in the next room. "Phone Tony. Tell him to make a test of her tonight," he instructed, speaking past Harlean as if she weren't even in the room. Then almost as an afterthought, he said, "You don't have an accent, do you?"

"I don't think so. I'm from Missouri, sir."

She watched the thick furrows over his eyebrows deepen as he eyed her more closely. "That's an accent you've got, all right, pure Midwestern, but nothing as impossible as Greta Nissen. The director I've got could work with it. You got any experience?"

"Mainly extra work, but a couple of two-reelers with Laurel and Hardy, and a scene in Clara Bow's last picture—the one Jimmy told you about."

"So you're an unknown."

"I suppose so," she conceded, feeling the sting of how sharply he'd said it.

"Good. I like you better that way. We'll see how you test." He was clearly about to dismiss her before he added, "Be on the *Hell's Angels* set tonight at seven. They'll be done shooting by then. Ask for Tony Gaudio. That's the cameraman who will do your test."

With that, Hughes looked back down at his papers.

Their brief meeting was over.

"I don't think he liked me very much," she said to Jimmy and Ben once she was back outside.

"I wouldn't be so sure. He's hard to read," Jimmy acknowledged as both actors walked her back to the other soundstage so she could finish out the day.

"Do you think you can manage an English accent?" Ben asked as they strolled past the dressing rooms building and then a row of offices.

"I'm not sure. I've never tried. But I'm a quick learner."

"Well, you're fast on your feet and real smart, that's for sure," Jimmy acknowledged as he wrapped an arm over her shoulder. "The camera will pick that up in no time."

"I guess there was a reason this picture has been such a bomb all this time. *Hell's Angels* was just waiting for *you*," Ben said.

Harlean had no idea what anyone on set thought of her screen test. Tony Gaudio, an intense man with graying hair and round wire-rimmed eyeglasses, used two different cameras as the screenwriter sat nearby with his chin propped in his hand. A prominent scowl marked his expression as she went through the lines.

The phone rang early the next morning, waking Harlean, who lay with Oscar wrapped into the curve of her neck. The sound startled her because she had quite expected the phone company to have cut her service off by now, and she'd had no time to send in the money from Arthur Landau which she had received yesterday.

"Miss Harlow, this is Mr. Hughes's office calling. Can you get here by nine?"

Harlean glanced over at her bedside clock. She ran a hand through her tangled hair and tried to focus on the time. "That's in half an hour!"

"Yes, it is. But Mr. Hughes has a very tight schedule today. If it can't be nine o'clock, I'm afraid it will have to wait until another day."

"No, no, I'll be there," Harlean quickly replied. Her curiosity would kill her if she had to wait.

Once again Hughes barely looked up from his cluttered desk when she entered the office. She was not asked to take a seat. Five minutes later, Harlean walked back to her mother's car with tears in her eyes, happy she'd asked her to drive her over as moral support for whatever she was about to hear.

"He gave me the part, Mommie. I got the part!"

Hughes had told her that she would be the first actress Caddo was going to put under contract. Howard Hughes and his team would be taking full control of her image from this day forward. He had a vision to promote her as an unknown "society girl" that would make her perfect for the role of Helen.

Jean hugged her daughter tightly, then pulled her out at arm's length. "What's the bottom line? How much are we getting paid, Baby?"

"It's $150 a week to start, but he says he fully intends to make me a star."

"Oh, I *knew* it! We'll be rich, then, soon enough! My, this is so exciting."

Harlean noticed that her mother said "we," but after so many months of disappointment, she was determined to overlook that and feel nothing but the thrill of victory at having won a role that half of the girls in Hollywood had coveted.

Chapter Eighteen

The next few days were a whirlwind of costume fittings, script consultations and test shots. Harlean rose at dawn and fell into bed exhausted at night. She hardly had a moment to think about anything other than what Howard Hughes and his team wanted from her. She did not even have time to worry, like the rest of the country, over the devastating stock market crash or what that might mean to her grandfather Harlow or to the McGrew estate. She certainly hadn't any money to lose and for now she was living life one day at a time.

"What is it, Baby?"

Her mother stood behind her, wringing her hands, as Harlean closed the front door and turned back around. She was holding a special delivery envelope, proffering it to her daughter.

"Something from Mr. Hughes?"

Jean followed Harlean from the front door back into the kitchen with Oscar nipping at her heels. "No, Mommie, it's not from Mr. Hughes."

"Gracious, it's not about our money, is it? The McGrews haven't lost our alimony in the crash!" Then a worse thought came to her. "Oh, tell me it isn't your grandpa, losing everything! After all that frightening stock market business the last week I don't know how much I could take!"

It wasn't about the stock market crash, or about her grandfather, but it might as well have been for the devastation she felt when she opened the envelope. The heading on the stationary read, "McGrew Family Trust." Harlean sank onto a kitchen chair to read the rest of it.

"What in heaven's name has happened? You're white as a sheet, Baby."

A rush of tears clouded her eyes. *Oh, Chuck*, she thought.

"The McGrews didn't lose all of their money but they are stopping us from getting any more of it, Mommie. They are terminating my temporary alimony. Without that I can't possibly make the house payments on my own, and help you and Marino out, too. Not on what Mr. Hughes is going to pay me."

"I thought Charles told you he was giving you the house."

"I guess his grandfather didn't agree."

"Well, we will just sue them for abandonment then, since the divorce was his idea. Take them for all they've got, and then some!"

"Stop it, please! I need to think!"

This was not how she wanted it to be—legal dealings between lawyers, all of it loaded with acrimony chipping away slowly at everything good that had once been between them. But there seemed no other way to remain in Hollywood and pursue this dream on what Mr. Hughes was offering to pay her for now. If she didn't agree to sue Chuck for divorce—thus requiring the court to award her at least a few more temporary funds to live on while she finished making the picture, and then perhaps a settlement, she would need to return to Missouri. That would mean utter failure. She could not go back now as her mother had once been forced to do. She simply couldn't allow herself to repeat that bit of history—nor, for that matter, ask her mother to do it with her a second time, now that she was here absolutely dedicated to helping Harlean find roles that would advance her career.

But it would be cruel to charge him with abandonment. She knew how much that would hurt him. Did he deserve that—from her, most especially when he had allowed her inside the shelter of his guarded heart? This all felt as if it had gotten so far out of hand. Thoughts twined with the emotion of it all, weaving a blanket of confusion across her heart so that she wasn't certain what to feel or to think.

Yet Chuck was letting this happen, wasn't he? It was his inheritance, after all, and he was permitting his grandfather to dictate what became of it after he had given her his word that the house was hers. At first, she thought he had bid her to move back into the Linden Drive house as a way to keep them tethered—to keep a spark of hope alive for them once some of the anger had faded. He knew damn well that this latest move would force her to sell their home. *Here, take it. It's yours... The key, or the house? Both. And all my heart, too...* Clearly Chuck himself bore some responsibility in forcing her hand if she went ahead with this countermeasure.

As she grew each day in confidence, and a sense of independence, Harlean was realizing that she still fought back only in fits and starts, asserted her desires randomly and not always fully, but one must always begin somewhere with everything, and she was really beginning to grow up. *Damn you, Chuck, for even making this an option. Damn you for not fighting harder for me when you had the chance...*

"What grounds do you suggest suing them on if I don't declare abandonment?" she found herself carefully asking.

Jean straightened her spine. Her eyes narrowed. "Why,

cruelty, of course. I wasn't the only one to have seen it, Baby. He was awful to you!"

Awful one moment, achingly tender the next.

But if she agreed to sue Chuck, and he still didn't come after her, didn't put a stop to this, there might be no turning back for either of them.

"Ouch! Watch it, will ya?"

"Well, hold still," Rosalie laughed as she poured the bleaching solution over Harlean's head yet again in what had become a weekly ritual to keep her unique color. "You wanna look gorgeous for your first day tomorrow, don't you? Can't have those roots showing!"

While Harlean enjoyed the distinctive white-blond look of her hair, the burning of the process to achieve it was still brutal.

"We've got to find you a real hair salon soon, so I don't need to keep being your torturer. I don't think it's helping our friendship," Rosalie chirped. "I'm green with envy, you know. Things are really starting to happen for you."

It had been a whirlwind few weeks since Harlean had signed the contract with Howard Hughes. While his publicity team had begun an all-out media blitz announcing that a "Chicago society girl" had won the coveted role of Helen in *Hell's Angels*, her personal life continued to disintegrate.

As she had predicted, Harlean's marriage, and any idea of reconciliation was rolling away from her faster than a freight train going downhill. Their divorce case was now headed to court, Harlean having charged cruelty, and Chuck was countersuing. She had been forced to sell their Linden Drive home, and at a loss. She wasn't thrilled to be moving back in with her mother in the interim and living by her rules in that little rental cottage, especially after she had been on her own as a married young woman, but she didn't entirely mind the change because Harlean hated the loneliness. The silence in that house with so many reminders, like looming ghosts, had become deafening.

She needed to work and to focus on it to the exclusion of all else.

"So, have you memorized your lines?" Rosalie asked as Harlean raised her head from the kitchen sink and wiped the dripping solution from her neck and ears with a towel.

"Mainly. I'm just not sure I understand the character. She's kind of a tramp, honestly," Harlean revealed with a sheepish grin. "She goes from man to man, and doesn't seem to care. She's the exact opposite of me."

"A bit cheeky, is she?" Rosalie giggled, doing her best British accent.

"I tell you, I think I'm gonna die of a nervous collapse before tomorrow ever gets here. This is a real film, a talkie."

"Yes, I know. Everyone in Hollywood knows all about it," Rosalie laughed.

"I'm just relieved that Mr. Hughes said the director he hired understands the character because he's British."

"See there? I'm sure he'll give you plenty of good advice. Nothin' to worry about. So, have ya heard from Chuck?"

"Just from his lawyer," Harlean said sadly. "They are countersuing."

"I knew that was a gamble, a way for you to knock some sense into him. Gee, honey, I'm sure sorry. You two had your problems, but I know he loved you. Ivor always talked about how Chuck went on and on about you, how good you were together. He was so happy you were starting a family and all. Well, until your miscarriage."

Harlean had not told anyone what had really happened. Now there seemed no point in it anyway.

She glanced up at the clock to see how much time was left before she could rinse. She couldn't bear to think or talk about any of it any longer. Not Chuck, nor even her first day of shooting tomorrow. It was all making her quite ill. After all, this was not another walk-on role, or a slaptick short, this was a huge gamble for her name, her face and her distinctive platinum-blond hair.

"You know what I want to do when we get this stuff out of my hair? Let's go out to Santa Monica and walk on the beach," Harlean proposed.

The beach suddenly sounded so freeing to her: the sea air cooling her burning scalp, their toes slipping into the wet sand as the gulls screeched overhead. "Believe it or not, I haven't been to the beach even once since I've been back in California because of how much Chuck hates water now. But it feels like it's about time for me."

"Sure, honey, sounds great, and I agree with you, it really is about time you try a whole lot of new things. You're young, beautiful and soon-to-be single. But before that, do you have anything to eat around here, I'm starved! And I wouldn't mind an early toddy or two if you've got any of that around, either," Rosalie said with her usual breezy laugh.

The set was humming with activity all that first day of shooting.

Hughes's dogged insistence on altering the project from a silent movie to a talkie had breathed new life into the cast and crew. Everyone seemed excited—all but James Whale. The stiff-spined, slim-lipped British director intimidated Harlean from the first introduction early that morning. He had a volcanic personality so she did her best to stay out of his way during the long, monotonous hours required to set up shots and position the actors in various scenes.

Even so, Harlean was still hungry to learn every element she could of the motion picture business, so as always she watched intently from the shadows. Only when there was a complete break in the activity did she open the satchel she always brought and allow herself a few minutes of welcome diversion among the pages of her books.

As the next few days of shooting progressed, she made friends quickly and easily with everyone—except Whale. It was apparent very quickly that he was an unabashed perfectionist, one who ruled the set like a sour-faced boarding school headmaster. Whale made it abundantly clear from the start that this was not a family environment. It was not to be a "Fun Factory" like the one she had known working with Laurel and Hardy.

This was, he sniped in his clipped British accent, "the big leagues."

By the fourth take on her first awkward love scene with Ben, Harlean's optimism for her place among the cast began swiftly to fade. When Whale's tyrannical raging at Harlean made her knees go weak, she found it difficult to speak her lines. She was trying as best she could to give him what he wanted—although she had no earthly idea what that was.

Hooded eyes with a critical stare, and a shock of thick silver hair, intensified his intimidating presence. "Cut! What the bloody hell was that?"

He bolted from his director's chair and charged at her. "Are you aware, young woman, how truly irritating your Midwest accent is to the civilized ear?"

Stricken by the tone he used in front of the cast and crew, she glanced helplessly over at Ben who could only offer a silent shrug. Her throat tightened and her words came out in a tone just above a whisper.

"I didn't know I had an offensive accent, Mr. Whale."

"Well, you bloody well do, and if you don't abandon it, this picture is doomed before it starts, and *you* will be the chief laughingstock among us!"

As he strutted back to his chair, Harlean bit her lower lip hard to stop the tears that had forced their way into her eyes. Running eye makeup would only infuriate him more.

Ben reached over and gave her arm a squeeze with the director's back to them. "Come on, give it another try. We can do this. Let's show him," he said in a low voice that only she could hear.

Harlean assumed that Whale deemed that take acceptable since he finally moved on to another scene. She allowed herself a single breath of relief as she walked back to the chair where she had left her satchel of books. It was Jimmy who found her there and sat down beside her.

"Need a pep talk, kiddo?" he gently asked.

"Will a pep talk make me speak like a proper English girl?"

He gave her a lopsided half smile. "He's a brilliant director, but he's also a pain in the ass."

"Seems more ass than brilliant, if you ask me."

"Oh, now, come on. Remember, Hughes chose you over every other girl in Hollywood. And everyone says this is going to be a major motion picture."

"He only chose me because he had already looked everywhere else. He was just out of time and out of girls, Jimmy, we both know that."

"Listen to me. You *are* Helen. Believe it and everyone else will, too."

"I don't understand her, Jimmy. She's a tramp and not a very nice one."

"If you want my take on it, here's what I think—Helen needs to exude sexuality, but there needs to be some vulnerability from her, too, and you've certainly got those bases covered," he patiently told her. "Thing is, we need to like her, and root for her—just like I root for you to do well in the role."

"I'm just nothing like her," Harlean said. "I loved *my* man. He was my one and only."

"It's called acting, kiddo," he said and gave her a gentle, good-natured sock in the arm.

"Some of these lines are just so corny," she softly complained. "How am I supposed to say, 'Would you be shocked if I put on something more comfortable?' and do it without laughing? Helen is a caricature to me."

"Only if that's what you bring to her. I'd make her a tender-hearted seductress instead, if I were you. Lord knows it would have been easy enough for you to seduce *me*," he cracked.

Harlean couldn't help but laugh. Jimmy was becoming a real friend. At this moment, for Ben and Jimmy's belief in her alone, she was stubbornly determined to succeed in her role. If Whale thought he could chase her from this picture with his browbeating, then he had another think coming.

By late afternoon, she ached to be home and surrender herself to a hot bath, and drink a cocktail, yet Whale insisted there was another scene to shoot. He was not allowing anyone to leave until it was finished. It was another love scene, and his mood had turned even more foul with the lateness of the hour.

Harlean and Ben shot the scene once, twice, then three times.

"You are an absolute disaster! I have no earthly idea why Hughes hired you!" Whale seethed, toppling his director's chair and clutching his head in dramatic fashion.

Emotionally drained, and more than a little confused, Harlean could fight the valiant press of tears no longer. He had been badgering her continually all day. Now, anger and frustration took her over entirely and she held her hands out to him in an open plea as tears slid down her cheeks.

"Tell me then! Tell me exactly how you want me to do it, Mr. Whale!"

"My dear girl, I can tell you how to be an actress, but I cannot tell you *how to be a woman!*" he cruelly sniped in front of the still-assembled cast and crew.

Harlean was so horrified that she couldn't think of what to say that wouldn't involve such a vulgar retort that it would likely cost her this job. She forced herself not to respond. Arrogant prig! He had underestimated her. Everyone had.

"We are finished here." He snapped his fingers in dismissal. "I cannot stand the sight of you anymore for one day."

Back home, her dress shoes, dress and all the pretense of the day cast off, her fought-for composure dissolved the moment her mother hugged her. Harlean burst into tears, collapsed into her mother's arms and openly wept.

"You can do this, Baby! I know you can," Jean soothed as she gently stroked her daughter's hair. "Don't let them knock you out. You have the strength I never had to survive this. All of my hopes and dreams, and yours, too, rest in this role!"

Her mother's words, and the passionate way she spoke them, were a balm on Harlean's weary spirit. She brushed back her tears and sniffled.

"I'm just so drained, Mommie. Not telling that bastard where he can shove his precious attitude is exhausting."

"I can only imagine."

"Everyone expects so much of me."

"Then expect it of yourself, too. We've come too far to go backward now. We want this. *You* want this for yourself!"

"He is just so frustrating that it makes me angry."

"Then use that anger, Baby. Channel it into Helen. She's a strong girl. *Be* her."

That advice bolstered her determination more than anyone else's could because she believed, with a daughter's devotion, her mother was her greatest champion. Harlean did want this, and she wanted to make the character come alive. She began to see that she and Helen really weren't so different. Helen found it easy to seduce two men just as it was for Harlean to entice Roy, and even Jimmy, all the while still desperately loving Chuck. It was circumstance—decisions of the moment.

But even so, Helen had a vulnerable sweet core. They both did.

She knew then that she could breathe life into Helen, and tomorrow she was about to do just that.

Chapter Nineteen

"Dazzle 'em!"

Howard Hughes's dramatic mantra was the thing he imparted to the cast and crew every time he left the set. It gradually began to pervade the attitude of everyone involved in *Hell's Angels*. They all knew that this young, upstart Texan had invested a fortune and that he fully meant to make the film a hit, no matter the cost. To that end, the sky was the limit and it was exciting to them all to imagine what he had in mind to promote it.

But after viewing the dailies, Whale, and now Hughes, too, were unhappy with Harlean's performance. Whale cruelly declared that she was the problem and she could well threaten the success of the entire picture.

As the first scene for the day was being set up, she didn't hear her agent, Arthur Landau, approach her for how lost she was in the novel she was reading. She jumped when she realized he was looming over her. She snapped the book shut when she saw by his expression that whatever news he had come to deliver, it wasn't good.

"Hughes is going to try to direct you today and see if that helps things," he told her.

"Mr. Hughes wants to do it himself?" she gasped. She could feel the panic settling in.

Hughes was so tall, handsome and so damnably mysterious-looking—always slipping onto the set in his expensive suits, then lingering in the shadows, never smiling—that the prospect of rehearsing a love scene with him seemed quite horrifying.

"He feels that they've got to get this right."

"But Mr. Hughes isn't an actor!"

"Neither are you, yet. Not an experienced one anyway," he countered. "Think of that personal kind of attention as him doing you a favor to get you where we all want you to be."

It felt to her like there was so much against her all of the time as she tried to make something of this career—something that would make the loss of Chuck worth the price she had already paid. The feeling was made particularly worse now when her light blue eyes were bloodshot and painful from the eighteen-hour days she had endured standing beneath hot lights. Nothing helped to soothe or lighten them. Reading beneath the softened light of soundstage corners was one thing, but the harsh glare was excruciating.

To make matters worse, none of the rest of the cast was equally plagued. It set her apart from everyone else even further, and she did not believe it was in a positive way. The studio doctor had diagnosed her with a condition called "klieg eyes" where the membrane covering her eyes had actually been burned. But Harlean was absolutely determined not to complain or let it deter her. She had come too far to let that happen. If Howard Hughes wanted to run her lines with her, then dammit, she would do it and she would learn how to make Helen better.

She planned to surprise everyone with just how determined she could be.

Hughes came onto the set with Lincoln Quarberg, the publicity director, just after nine o'clock. She heard Hughes had been playing with the aerial combat scenes for weeks and he was frustrated with those, as well. His mood did not seem greatly improved by needing to be here today to work directly with her. His scowl was quite pronounced beneath his slick, dark hair. As tall and slim as Hughes, Quarberg had a prominent forehead and a mop of curly hair that reminded Harlean of the top of a chrysanthemum. Between scenes, the two men stood at a distance, looking at her and conferring.

"Easy, kid, don't panic now," Arthur said. "They're only talking."

"Talking about me."

"Here's the concept—we need a gimmick to make you into a star," Quarberg announced as the duo approached her. "You need a tagline. Clara Bow is the 'It Girl,' and Mary Pickford, well of course she is 'America's Sweetheart.'"

"Lincoln has come up with quite a few of those gems here," said Hughes as he studied Harlean.

"Okay then, I started with, 'The Passion Girl.' That took me to, 'The Joy Girl'…"

"Both awful," Hughes grumbled as he shook his head.

"From there I decided to highlight your most obvious feature, so I came up with, 'Blonde Landslide' then 'Blonde Sunshine'…"

Oliver Hardy would have approved of that one, she thought with affection.

Harlean watched Hughes roll his eyes. "Get to the point, Lincoln."

The publicist straightened his spine, cleared his throat and paused for a beat, as if it was to be an announcement of some magnitude. He held up his hands like a banner, something already in lights. "'Platinum Blonde,'" he announced with an eager smile. "It ties your hair in with something expensive and classic. We're gonna sell your sex appeal until the public doesn't know what hit 'em!"

Harlean disliked it enormously and instantly. It didn't sound at all like the catchy taglines given to Bow or Pickford.

"Yep, that's the one," Hughes decreed, but he did so with neither smile nor excitement.

"We're going to make every girl in America want to look like Jean Harlow. I'm telling you, when this gets rolling, people aren't going to care that you can't act worth a damn," Quarberg added with enough enthusiasm in his voice for both men.

"This will be the start of a blitz, a full media campaign that's gonna send Jean Harlow straight to stardom and, if I have my way, *Hell's Angels* is gonna be a smash hit before it ever even hits theaters," said Hughes.

Harlean's eyes still burned and her mind was spinning.

In spite of the challenges, success suddenly felt nearer because of the commitment Hughes and his company were making to her. If she had to be exploited initially in order for people to take notice of her, then she would keep her head high and accept that as one of the many steps toward fame. And no matter what Hughes or Whale—or anyone else for that matter—thought, by damn, she was going to show the world that she could act!

"All right—little miss Platinum Blonde, shall we take it from the top?" Hughes asked her and, in that moment, he seemed slightly less irritated than he had been when they first had come onto the set. Maybe she had a chance to convince him yet that she was good enough to play Helen. At least—at last—this felt like a start.

"Yes, sir," she said. "Ready when you are."

★ ★ ★

In spite of the excitement over her Platinum Blonde appellation, and demand for Jean Harlow throughout the industry they expected it to generate, after shooting on *Hell's Angels* finally wrapped there were no other projects Hughes would approve of for her. Once again Harlean began to worry about all the bills needing to be paid. The paltry $150 a week income, and with the divorce still tied up with attorneys, barely paid the rent and bought groceries. It certainly didn't cover her mother's extravagant shopping trips that Jean Bello firmly declared she had earned for helping her daughter come this far.

Harlean eventually felt forced to surrender her pride and attack head-on the distasteful business of pleading with Howard Hughes. She urged him to loan her out to another studio while the film was in postproduction, and she felt the sting of it more sharply when he stubbornly refused to do it. She was property, his property, he declared and he kept that stance until suddenly, one day, when he summoned her back to his bungalow office.

There, he gruffly grunted that he had changed his mind.

The right-hand man to the powerful Irving Thalberg at MGM wanted her to come in and interview for a picture they were doing at their studio out in Culver City.

Hughes told her to see someone named Paul Bern.

Harlean wore a sedate white-and-navy-blue nautical-style dress and white low-heeled Mary Janes. She had dressed intentionally, hoping to tamp down the sexually charged image that the publicity machine at Caddo was actively creating. Quarberg's team had been so good at it that she had begun receiving fan mail at the studio even though the movie premiere was months away.

After her experiences with Whale and Hughes, Harlean was

more wary than ever of ill-tempered studio executives. The idea that this man, Paul Bern, had most likely seen one of her sexualized publicity photos made her even more hesitant as she was shown into his large office. While she still believed that she needed her looks in order to stand out from the crowd, she did not want it to be the only thing people saw in her.

Legs crossed, handbag gripped tightly and held on her lap, she sat across from him at his desk and tried not to make her hesitation obvious. Unlike Howard Hughes's cluttered office, Bern's was sleek and impressive. A burl-wood desk, commanding leather chair and a wall of leather-bound books made it distinctive.

Bern himself, however, was a surprisingly diminutive, curious-looking man in a pin-striped suit and stiff purple necktie. He was twice Harlean's age, at least, with a receding chin, bulging dark eyes, and a patchy mustache. But his smile, as he introduced himself, was so sincere that it took her completely aback.

He gazed at her with kindness and genuine human interest, to which she was wholly unaccustomed—particularly in Hollywood.

"Tell me about yourself, Miss Harlow," he said as he began the interview.

He leaned forward over his desk. In the sunlight through the window behind him, his eyes reminded her of melted chocolate, and he had the longest black eyelashes she had ever seen. They really were such extraordinarily kind eyes.

"Well, I've had a few walk-on roles, nothing much to speak of until Mr. Hughes found me. I was in a couple of shorts with Laurel and Hardy last year, and I had a scene with Clara Bow in one of her pictures, but I'm just an extra."

He steepled his fingers. "I meant, tell me about *you*. Where are you from? After all, no one is really *from* Hollywood," he said with a patient smile.

"I'm from Missouri."

"Which accounts for the lovely natural quality about you. Most ingenues come to my office dressed to the nines and wearing so much makeup that it appears to have been applied by trowel."

"I wasn't honestly sure what sort of interview this was meant to be, Mr. Bern, and I've suffered an eye injury lately that prevents me from wearing eyelashes or mascara anyway."

"Ah, so I see. Your eyes, lovely though they are, look quite painful at the moment."

"Excruciating, if you wanna know the truth."

"Oh, always, Miss Harlow. I don't make time for anything but the truth. May I offer you a cup of coffee? I was just about to order one for myself and I hate to drink alone."

Her smile widened at the way he had said it. He seemed to have an attractively understated sense of humor which somewhat balanced out his lack of physical appeal.

"All right, then. Thanks, Mr. Bern."

"I'd really rather you call me Paul. A man does what he can to hold on to the vestiges of youth."

Harlean laughed as he picked up his telephone receiver and ordered two coffees from his secretary in the next room.

"So, do you have any hobbies? What do you like to do in your spare time?"

He had propped his chin in his hand and was leaning on his elbow, appearing to actually be interested in her response.

"I'm really quite dull, I'm afraid. I'm a bookworm. People make fun of me, saying I've always got my nose in something."

He lifted his eyebrows. "Is that a fact? What do you like to read?"

"Oh, everything. Poetry, history, and I love how novels let

me escape…and the classics, too. I just finally finished reading *The Odyssey* last night which certainly took me a while."

"You read Homer?"

She sat back at the tone in his voice. "That surprises you?"

"Perhaps it shouldn't, but it does. My own volume of *The
Iliad* is as worn, and well loved, as a child's blanket."

He was becoming an increasingly interesting man to her.
Not at all what she had guessed when she was shown into his
office moments before. He had such a natural way about himself that she felt herself begin to relax just a bit. She certainly
felt less defensive about being seen for only her looks with him.

"And I'm trying to write a novel," she found herself revealing.

The only other people who knew about that were Chuck
and Rosalie.

"The story is still really only in my mind so far, but I like
the idea of creating characters. There's a feeling of magic in
that."

His smile broadened. "You really are quite an extraordinary being, Miss Harlow," he said as the secretary brought the
two cups of coffee, placed them on the desk and left again.
"Since honesty is my policy, I'm going to tell you that the role
I called you in to speak about isn't right for you. It's a period
piece, and it's clear to me now that you are meant for different challenges in the industry. For one thing, I see that you
could shine in a comedy."

That was what she secretly wanted to do but he was the
first important person to recognize it in her, or to confirm
that she might have a chance with it. The acknowledgment,
coupled with his sincerity, struck her. He was speaking with
her as if she were something far more than a sexual commodity to be marketed and sold.

As she tried to decide how to respond, Bern stood. "Rest

assured, I will be looking for the right vehicle for you. It may take some time, but it's a hobby of mine once I have a vision for someone. I've done all right by Joan Crawford, so far," he said.

Crawford was certainly an actress on her way up. Harlean had seen her picture *Our Dancing Daughters* last year. Photographs of her recent wedding to Douglas Fairbanks Jr. had been in all the magazines and newspapers since that had made her stepdaughter to Mary Pickford, and there was great gossip about how the two actresses got along.

"Miss Crawford is a star."

"As you will be soon enough. I'll see to that."

"But I work for Mr. Hughes."

"For now," he said as he came around the desk and extended his hand. "As it happens, I have a bit of pull in this town myself. I'll be in touch, Miss Harlow," he said politely as he walked her to the door. "And take care of those eyes. They're really quite beautiful."

After she left the studio, Harlean went home to find her mother on the telephone, speaking in that sweet, breathy voice she used when she wished to impress a man. Harlean knew the tone well since Jean had used it on a number of men before she had met her current husband.

"It's Mr. Bern from MGM," Jean said in an eager whisper as she handed her the receiver.

He seemed powerful enough based on his corner office with a view alone but it was surprising that he had already found her a role. "Hello?"

"Jean, Paul here. I've asked your mother's permission to take you out this Friday night."

Her heart sank a little. She hadn't expected that. "I see."

"She informs me that you are married, but that it's just a matter of time before that is no longer the case."

Harlean glanced up as Jean Bello began to flit happily around the living room where the phone was connected.

"Did she?"

Mother had no right to say that because Harlean hadn't fully made any sort of peace with it. When she did, that much needed to be up to her, she believed.

"Anyway, as it happens, I have two tickets to a poetry reading at a little bookstore over on Sunset. I'd be honored if you would join me."

She certainly hadn't expected him to propose a date, or that somehow he could make it sound innocent and quite proper. In spite of how homely she found him, the prospect of that sort of evening was enticing, especially since it involved something she loved.

"All right, sure. It sounds like fun," she said, hoping she wouldn't regret it.

They laughed and laughed. There was a great deal that surprised Harlean about Paul, not the least of which was his sense of humor. What surprised her most however was that, throughout the evening, he behaved like a complete gentleman. The respect he showed made her feel special in a way she never had before.

Chuck had loved her, but Paul seemed to respect her.

After the poetry reading, he took her to Schwab's Pharmacy for an ice-cream soda, instead of out for cocktails. The gesture charmed her all the more.

"I was looking through scripts for you all day today," he said as they sat atop two chrome and red leather stools as if they were teenagers, both of them sipping their sodas.

"I doubt Mr. Hughes would ever actually loan me out to

work on anything really good. He's already turned down so many offers."

"You leave that to me," he replied. "His publicity machine is working hard to make you a star even before his movie premiere. If he can't find a follow-up for you himself, he will have to let someone else try eventually since you're already a valuable commodity to him."

Harlean laughed. "He only offered me my usual $150 a week, if you had hired me for your picture."

"He was going to charge MGM $1,500 a week if we hired you."

She was stunned. "And keep the rest for himself?"

"Of course."

"That rat."

"He's a businessman, but then so am I. He might be filthy rich but I've been at this game a while longer than he has and, in the end, I always win."

"I like the way you think, Paul."

"Thalberg always says that same thing. He's powerful, more so than Hughes actually, but he doesn't have a stomach for the fight. I know they call Irv 'The Boy Wonder' around town, but he's rather sickly for his age, which is why he made me his right-hand man. I face the slings and arrows for him."

Everyone who worked in the film industry knew who Irving Thalberg was. Just thirty years old, he was a handsome wunderkind, the genius behind the movie hit *The Hunchback of Notre Dame*. He and his wife, the actress Norma Shearer, were one of Hollywood's golden couples, along with Douglas Fairbanks and Mary Pickford, and Marion Davies and William Randolph Hearst.

"So tell me about your marriage," he asked suddenly, changing the subject. "Is your mother correct, that it's over between you?"

Paul was kind and also direct. She gave it more thought about how she wanted to respond because she liked him. It was such a complicated issue in her mind, and until now that hadn't felt to her like anyone's business.

"I wish I knew," she said, and she heard the sadness in her own voice.

"It's gone that far?"

"Like a runaway train." She sighed.

"Do you still love him?"

"Yes. I think I always will."

"Perhaps you should fight for it, then."

She absently twirled her straw. "I wish it were that simple. The lawyers are handling everything now."

"It's as simple as you want it to be, really. Talk to him. It wouldn't seem like either of you can move on in your lives until you do that."

Unable to free her mind of his advice, the next morning, she drove alone out to Long Beach to see Aunt Jetty again. After a sustained embrace that brought her to tears, Harlean sank into the same overstuffed chair she had the last time. Being reminded of that day only made things heavier on her heart.

"Well, that *is* a fine mess," Jetty sighed after Harlean detailed things. "Your mama didn't exactly explain it in the same way. She made that boy sound like a tyrant."

"He has an awful temper, Aunt Jetty, and he can be as peevish as a little boy sometimes but this honestly wasn't all his fault. There were things I did, too, and shouldn't have, that I regret."

"Most things rarely are one-sided, child."

"Mommie thinks he will hold me back. She hates him for it, she always has," she said softly.

"*Hate* is a strong word. But then your mama is one strong woman when she sets her mind to something."

"I just don't see why I had to choose between a career and my marriage, but that's really what they both made me do."

"Well, now, that's curious because when I spoke to him last, Chuck told me how proud he was of you and your career. I mean, you have to do what's right for you, Baby, and you know I'll support you in it, but you deserve to know the facts."

Harlean looked up from her hands. A chill of surprise ran through her. "You've spoken with him?"

"About two weeks ago. Must've been before the lawyers got all mixed up in everything. He asked if he could come out to speak with me and I didn't think it'd be right not to give him a hearing."

"That was my fault, I'm the one who charged him with cruelty to get the judge on my side," she explained, trying to press back the wave of sadness thoughts of their marriage always brought. "Mommie and Marino told me there was really no other way to stay in Hollywood, support myself and see where this career thing might take me if I didn't do it because his estate had cut me off and Mr. Hughes is paying me peanuts."

Jetty arched a silver brow to accent a suddenly critical stare. "Come on, child, this is ol' Aunt Jetty you're talking to here. Is that really what drove you to a drastic first move like that? The *only* reason?"

"He wasn't fighting for me, Jetty. I don't know. I was just so angry and hurt."

"So you were trying to hurt him back?"

"Just get a reaction out of him, I suppose."

"I suspect the reaction you got wasn't the one you wanted."

"I saw a girl in my living room with him," she admitted.

Jetty's tone remained steady. "She was only a friend there to help him pack up his things. There were two of them there that night, and one of them brought her boyfriend along to help with the heavy boxes. He told me all that himself, said he was grateful to have had the help because he was such an emotional wreck leaving that house."

"The fact remains, Aunt Jetty, I have to be able to support myself until my career takes off."

"What you mean, child, is support yourself, *and* the two of them. Listen, sweetie, you know how much I love your mama. She's as dear to me as if she were my own child. But you can't live your life for her, and she sure as hell has got to stop trying to live hers through you!"

"She just wants the best for me," Harlean softly countered.

"Don't kid yourself. Jean Bello wants the best for Jean Bello. That girl wanted to be an actress more than anything in the world for as long as I can recall. Sake's alive, that's all she talked about when you were little. She was like a dog with a bone."

Jetty slapped her chintz-skirted knee for emphasis.

"I remember how she was, and I know what this career of mine means to her now. It's the most important thing in the world to her."

"Decide what *you* want, not what she wants. It's your turn now."

Another of Jetty's white Persian cats jumped onto Harlean's lap with that, settled in and began to purr, just like the other cat had done when she was here last.

"It seems ol' Tuck here fancies you as much as his brother did. Unless I miss my guess, he'll be here any minute."

Harlean wanted a dozen pets as soon as she could have them. A full menagerie would do nicely she thought as she stroked the cat's sleek fur, and she fully intended one day to have that. She would always be an animal lover and a champion of them.

A moment later, exactly as Jetty had predicted, Nip, slightly smaller and with wider eyes, jumped onto Harlean's lap, competing for space with his brother, their cute names having come from the pages of a children's story.

"Well, now, if that's not a sight. Just like when you were a child, your mama said animals of all kinds were drawn to you," Jetty exclaimed with pleasure. "Look at how smitten those two boys are with you. You certainly haven't lost your touch. Say, I have an idea. You're feeling lonely these days, and I've got these dreadful allergies, all that long hair, it's a frightful battle for me. How would you feel about taking the boys for a while?"

"Oh, I couldn't possibly." The thought of separating anything or anyone these days was the last thing Harlean wanted. Both of them continued to purr on her lap. "They're your beautiful cats and I'm sure you'd miss them too much."

"They'd be right up the road in Beverly Hills and, the way you are with them, I know they'd be happy."

Harlean knew what her aunt was trying to do. No one understood the heartache of a broken marriage like someone else who had suffered through one. Jetty was trying to give her another focus for her love and attention for now, and for that she was grateful. She stroked each of them, their lovely soft fur. It would be nice to have more pets around, to grow her little animal family to keep her company.

"Are you sure you wouldn't mind?"

"I think it's a terrific idea. But I reserve the right to come and visit them often." Then she leaned forward in her chair. "And think about what I said, will you, sweetie? Make a divorce *your* choice if you go through with it, not your mother's choice. I know full well this isn't easy for you, the being alone now when you've been loved. Nobody wanted me to have that, either. I listened to them for a while, then I got my dander up. If he hadn't gone and died on me, I'd still be his." Jetty let out a heavy sigh and lay her head back against the chair. "All that wasted time…"

The last four words especially lay like a stone on her heart on the long drive back to the city. Everything Jetty had said struck Harlean in such a powerful way. She had gone out there for sympathy, and she had come away disturbed by events she felt she had no control over.

But didn't she really?

Yes, mother had instigated and encouraged this divorce but, in the end, it was her life, her decision. She knew it was time she took responsibility for that fact.

Harlean was relieved more than glad to find that Mother and Marino had gone out. She so badly needed the quiet just now to think and process everything. She was trying hard to grow up, and grow into the woman she knew she was meant to be, but life was certainly not making it easy for her. She understood more clearly at this moment than ever before what a monumental decision lay ahead for her life.

She set Nip and Tuck down and Oscar immediately came to investigate. Harlean watched them for a moment, then went to her room and sank onto the edge of her bed in complete emotional exhaustion. Just as she kicked off her shoes, the phone rang.

"Hello?" she cautiously said, almost afraid these days, with creditors hounding her and the divorce looming, to hear who might be on the other end of the line.

Chapter Twenty

"Hello, Daddy."

While they spoke a few times a year, they corresponded by letter most often. Harlean hadn't expected at all to hear his voice today.

"I'm sorry, sweetheart, that I haven't phoned often enough. But I do miss you so."

She gripped the receiver more tightly, not wanting him to hear the disappointment she long had felt that their relationship wasn't a closer one. Her mother had seen to the distance between them initially after their divorce but, as with Chuck now, the reality was that Mont Carpenter hadn't fought hard enough through the years to keep them close.

"I know, Daddy. Don't worry about it."

"You're dreadfully angry with me, aren't you?"

"It's not you, I promise."

She had far too much on her mind just now to dredge up old disappointments and longings for a father. At this point in her life, she would take what he had to give because she didn't like the idea of losing anyone else whom she held dear.

"If you're sure... Say, how'd the picture turn out? You said in your last letter you had wrapped up filming."

"I won't know for a few weeks. It's in editing now. I had some problems with the director, so I really hope they like me in it when it's done."

"I'm sure you will be marvelous. The world will finally see what I always have." There was a strange tension between them since they both knew he hadn't physically seen his daughter for such a long time. "So I wanted you to hear it from me, sweetheart. The thing is, I'm...getting married again."

Not today, of all days when she was this blue, she thought, after the feelings her intense conversation with Aunt Jetty had dredged up.

"I'm really happy for you, Daddy, that's great. Congratulations."

"Oh, sweetheart, you don't know how good it is to hear that from my best girl. Her name is Maude. She's such a wonderful woman and I just know you two will get along like a house on fire."

She closed her eyes for a moment, willing an even more sincere tone into her voice because she did love him and she would always hope for a better, richer relationship between them one day. "I'm sure we will, Daddy. I look forward to it—not just writing letters with you and talking on the phone here and there." That had never been enough to fill the void her father left in her life. "Hopefully I can get back there real soon."

"So they're calling you the Platinum Blonde now, I see. Maude read that in the newspaper back here the other day while she was at the beauty parlor."

"That's Mr. Hughes's publicity machine at work."

"I don't mind telling you it's still odd hearing my Harlean called Jean Harlow."

"Mommie is happy about it."

"Oh, I have no doubt," he said, and she could hear the slight edge returned to his voice, in spite of what a mild-mannered gentleman he usually was.

"Mr. Hughes calls her Mother Jean, so now everyone has started calling her that," Harlean explained with a small snicker. But her father did not laugh in return.

"Well, listen, I'd better go. Maude has made a reservation for us over at the country club for dinner."

"Yes, sure, you need to go. And, Daddy…"

"Yes, sweetheart? Listen, Baby, are you okay? I know your life must be a whirlwind right now between your career and the divorce and everything."

"I'm happy for you, I mean that, Daddy, I really do."

He deserved her support, and she meant to give it to him, just as she had given it when she hadn't felt it the day Mother married Marino Bello.

Harlean had always known how deeply her mother had hurt her father by leaving. Recalling that now, she was a little ashamed of herself for not being more enthusiastic about Maude when she'd heard about her initially. She would be better on their next phone conversation, she promised herself that.

Oscar jumped onto her lap and Harlean stroked his downy-soft little head as Nip and Tuck followed suit. The little trio were such a comfort to her already, and she needed the nearness of something she cared about just now as she hung up the phone receiver and felt the utter emptiness around her.

While *Hell's Angels* was still in postproduction, Howard Hughes had begun the massive task of staging the movie's premiere. He boasted all over town that it was going to be a spectacle unlike any other, and he had the money to back up his vision.

After Christmas, 1930, Howard Hughes enlisted the help of Sid Grauman, whose Chinese theater was strategically located right in the center of Hollywood Boulevard. Hughes planned to take over the entire street for the evening in May when the movie was set to premiere.

Exciting as the prospect of such an event seemed, Harlean grew more restless in the interim. While he had done that one favor for Paul Bern, now Hughes refused to loan her out to another studio until all of the editing on the film was complete, so she consoled herself with photo shoots and visits to watch postproduction. Harlean still loved learning all she could about the business of movie making so there was some consolation in that.

Finally, she was invited by the noted art director George Holl to come in and see some of the pieces he was creating as part of the advertising campaign for the movie.

Even imagining herself depicted in movie posters was a thrill.

After she and Rosalie had finished lunch at a restaurant on Hollywood Boulevard they walked toward his studio, which was right across the street from the theater. Harlean could not help but sigh with nostalgia as she glanced over at the place that signified so *many* of her girlhood dreams. It was still unfathomable to her that someone as renowned in the movie business as Holl was painting a poster bearing her name and likeness, one that would soon grace the forecourt of Grauman's Chinese Theatre. For any girl even the idea of such a thing was a dream come true.

"Are *you* the Platinum Blonde?" The eager female voice behind her was tentative and young. "You're Jean Harlow, right?"

Rosalie shot Harlean a glance as they both turned around to see a freckle-faced, redheaded teenage girl. She was wearing a navy blue school uniform, and a hopeful smile, and she was carrying an oversize book bag over her shoulder. It looked to her like the one Harlean always took with her into the studio.

"Yes, that's me." She smiled brightly.

She was struck by how much the girl reminded her of herself only a few short years ago. Since Harlean was wearing unstructured beige-colored slacks, a tennis-style sweater with a button up shirt underneath and no makeup, it surprised her that she had been recognized by anyone at all. "What's your name?"

"I'm Susan. I have that picture of you with Clara Bow on my bed at home. Gosh, I wish I could get you to autograph it. You're in *Hell's Angels,* that movie everyone is talking about, aren't you? With that dreamy Ben Lyon?"

She was chattering nervously in the way Harlean herself had often done when she was first starting out in the business, so her heart softened even more.

"I am, in fact. Everyone is talking about it, are they?"

"Oh, yes! School is full of gossip about it. You're in it. My friends are never going to believe this!"

"Where do you go to school, Susan?" Rosalie casually asked.

"Hollywood School for Girls."

Harlean couldn't help but laugh. It was yet another coincidence. "Why, is that a fact! I was a student there myself once."

"No!" Susan squealed with delight, and the sound of it lifted Harlean's mood.

"I absolutely was!" Harlean said with the same delight as the girl. "Tell you what—my friend Rosalie here and I were just about to go up and have a look at a poster they're doing for the picture. How 'bout you come up with us and maybe Mr. Holl will have something lying around that I can sign for you?"

Susan's lips parted in genuine surprise. "Do you mean it, Miss Harlow?"

"Come on," Harlean declared, never losing her own genuine smile. It was what she would have hoped if, as a teenager, she had ever actually gotten to meet Pola Negri.

Harlean happily introduced herself to the receptionist as she put a casual hand on the teen's shoulder. A moment later, the trio was shown down the corridor to Holl's studio. Harlean could see her likeness from the doorway, propped on an easel. The poster, with a painted image of her face, was crowned at the top with a single glaring word: *Sex!*

Seeing it, she felt the blood leave her face. The uncanny likeness to her, and the word, so inextricably linked, was absolutely horrifying. In spite of how aggressively they were promoting her as the Platinum Blonde, this was the last thing Harlean had expected, or wanted for her career. There were already so many hills to climb over it as it was. Rosalie sent her a withering look of sympathy that only made her feel worse.

"Wow," the teenager exclaimed, looking from Harlean to the poster, and back again with her own stunned expression. "You look so...voluptuous."

"Why, shit damn and howdy," Rosalie exclaimed in her Texas drawl as Holl rose from his art table and came forward.

"Miss Harlow," he said with a genial smile. "Think we'll sell a lot of theater tickets with these?"

Around the prominently placed poster was a collection of others. Words and phrases like *thrilling, air spectacle* or *multimillion dollar!* were used on different designs to promote the film. But one element was consistent—her face and her name dominated all of them. In every case, Jean Harlow was either the only name painted, or it had been placed far more prominently than Ben Lyon or James Hall. She couldn't imagine that her two costars would be happy about that.

"So, what do you think?" he asked her with hands now expectantly poised on his hips. "If these don't make you famous, nothing will," he proudly declared of his work.

"Or they'll make her *infamous*," Rosalie quipped in a low tone. "She's not wearing a stitch of clothing in the poster for the front of Grauman's."

"It's a rendering…" Holl defended as his smile began to fade in the face of the collective shocked reaction "…a stylized image of the character, to sell movie tickets."

"But that's Jean's name up there, not the character. They're gonna think she's as slutty as Helen."

"It's all right," Harlean intervened, but only because arguing the point further in front of this young impressionable girl felt unsavory to her. "Mr. Holl, my friend Susan here would like my autograph but I'm afraid I haven't anything to sign for her. Could I trouble you for a slip of paper and a pen?"

Susan's eyes brightened at the request, and seeing that again in this tense moment renewed Harlean's spirit for the fight. She did not like at all how Hughes's team was using her in promoting the film. She felt more tawdry than she ever had in her life. But if she expected to pursue the kind of films Paul Bern envisioned for her, Harlean knew that first she must pay her dues, and do it in a smart, professional way. When she had the success she fully intended to have, then she could put her foot down. Like it or not, for now the world would have to think of Jean Harlow as a loose woman. With this kind of promotion there was no avoiding it and it would be a challenge to change that perception, but now she was ready for the fight.

"I think I can do better than a piece of paper," Holl said, grabbing a photograph from his table.

It was a still from the movie, a shot he had used in the design of one of the publicity posters. The image was of Harlean and Ben locked in a passionate embrace.

"Will this do?" he asked, handing it to Harlean, along with the pen.

Susan's eager, pimply smile broadened as she glanced down at the image of the handsome young actor. "I'll be the envy of the whole school. I'll never let it out of my sight, Miss Harlow!"

"Then it'll be my pleasure," Harlean said with a sweet expression that she forced herself to keep as she took the time to autographed it thoughtfully.

"Do you want to come over to the house for a drink? You look like you could use one, under the circumstances," Rosalie asked her as they drove down Hollywood Boulevard, back toward Beverly Hills afterward.

"I assumed they would be provocative," Harlean sighed as she tried to concentrate on the road. "Just not quite *that* provocative."

"Well, they did look sexy."

"They looked tacky. People are gonna think I'm like Helen, just the way you said, and God knows how long it will take me to live that down."

"Mr. Hughes is trying to use what he can to market the picture. After all, that's Hollywood. Nobody in this town is quite what they seem. Look at you—you're nineteen and you look twenty-eight. And I have it on good authority that not just James Cagney but Charlie Chaplin wears lifts in his shoes, and Mary Pickford wears false eyelashes regularly to get her eyes so big. You really can't take any of this to heart, honey. Personally, I'd kill to be in your shoes right now with a part like that in a picture that's a hit before it premieres. Racy or not, you're about to become a star, Harlean McGrew," she exclaimed. "Oh, my stars, I've got to stop calling you that now, don't I, *Miss Harlow*?"

Harlean thanked her for the invitation but declined it when

she dropped Rosalie off a few minutes later. She wanted to be alone for a while. Marino and her mother had driven up the coast to Santa Barbara for a couple of days so she had the house all to herself.

Oscar met her at the door with an excited little yelp while the cats lounged together on the sofa, less impressed by her return. As she bent down to scoop the dog up into her arms, the phone rang. For a moment, Harlean considered not answering it. She did not want to speak to anyone just now with her mind still reeling, and she wasn't sure for the moment she could handle any more surprises. But as it continued its loud, persistent jingle, she relented.

"Hello?"

Now the voice on the other end really was the last she expected to hear.

"Hey, doll. It's Chuck, do you think we could talk?"

Chapter Twenty-One

Harlean sank onto the sofa beside the phone. She could hear how his voice quivered. There was a fragile quality to it that reminded her of so many precious moments between them that she had been trying to forget.

"How are you?" he asked.

She wanted to snap back and ask him why he wanted to know that now, after all these months, and with their divorce nearly final.

She drew in a breath and exhaled instead. This was what she had wanted, after all—just the two of them with time alone to sort things out.

They had seen each other only once, two months ago from a safe distance in court. It had been a gut-wrenching experience since both of them had hurled accusations at each other and, through it, Chuck had refused even to look at her.

"I'm good," she replied cautiously. "How are you?"

In spite of everything, she truly did want to know.

"Pretty damn miserable without you, to tell you the truth."

A silence fell between them as Harlean tried to hear what

he was really saying. There had been so much bitterness and acrimony. "Where are you, Chuck?"

"I'm back in Chicago at my grandfather's place. He took me in for a while." There was another stiff silence before he added, "So the picture will premiere soon, I guess. I've been reading about it everywhere. That Howard Hughes must be quite the showman."

"He's a character, all right."

"Did he give you any trouble?" She heard Chuck's tone harden with the question, and she remembered how quickly his voice could change, just as he could.

"Not how you mean. He's just difficult, and a little peculiar."

"I'm excited for you, honestly I am. It's gonna be a big hit, doll."

"You hated every minute of me having a career."

"I was an idiot, a big, dumb, jealous idiot," he said.

"I kiss a man in the picture, Chuck, two of them, in fact." She could not keep the warning tone from her voice, nor did she want to any longer. She was still hurt, still wary of him and his temper, and she had become a stronger woman since their separation. She could feel that strength now girding her heart.

"Actors act. I get that now."

"Do you?"

"Jesus, Harlean, I want my wife back." She heard the desperation climbing into his voice. She knew how difficult it was for him to be vulnerable like this.

"It's too late for that, Chuck."

"We have time before the divorce is final. It's only too late if we let it be—us and your mother."

"I'm not letting you start in on her again," she warned, feeling as defensive as she was confused. "This was never about her."

"The hell it wasn't."

The doorbell rang at that moment and the sudden sound made her jump for how focused she had been on Chuck's voice. With her heart already racing, and emotion crushing her so that she couldn't think, Harlean glanced across the room. Outside the living room window, she saw Paul Bern's car parked in front of the house. She had completely forgotten she had agreed to let him take her to dinner.

"Look, Chuck, I have to go."

"I'm not giving up on you, Harlean. Not till we hash this all out."

"Well, for now, I have to go."

"I'm calling you back tomorrow. I'll call at the same time so you'll know who it is, if you have to grab the phone before Jean or Marino. Just please tell me you'll answer and we can talk again."

Why did he always do this to her every time she thought she had let go?

Paul rang the bell again.

She glanced over at the door. She was gripping the phone receiver tightly. "I have to go," she repeated.

"Tomorrow, doll. Answer when I call, please?"

As promised, he phoned her every day for three days after that while the Bellos were away, and they spoke. While they were both cautious, there was even careful laughter between them a time or two.

Chuck said he would come back to Hollywood. They had things to discuss in person, and Harlean found herself wanting that—not wanting things as they once were, but wanting closure. At the very least, she wanted to end things on a better note than with the memory of those terrible fights or with a day in court. Nostalgia held a heavy pull, but she knew she was viewing things through rose-colored glasses.

Then suddenly, after the third day following the Bellos' return from their trip up the coast, the calls ceased. Harlean waited in the living room at the agreed-to time, yet the phone did not ring again. It was two days before the *Hell's Angels* premiere and while she had begun to think of asking Chuck to escort her if he did return to California, his sudden silence brought confusion.

On the subject of Chuck, her mother and Marino were the last two people she could ask for advice. "Why not ask Paul Bern to escort you?" Rosalie suggested as they walked together along a quiet stretch of Santa Monica beach late one afternoon. "He seems a nice enough fella. He sure does like you."

"It's not like that between us. We talk about books and poetry. He's never even tried to lay a hand on me."

"Then that's perfect."

"I just don't understand why Chuck stopped calling, Rosie. We were talking, and it felt good to sort out all of those lingering issues. I want us both to be able to move on with no regrets."

The beach breeze was cold and Harlean pulled her scarf more tightly around her neck as a seagull soared over the water beside them. The waves crashed and the sea foam rushed in, swirling around their bare feet.

"Maybe there is a logical explanation. You could call *him*?"

"I just can't," she said, and even Harlean could hear the ache in her own voice.

She could feel her old defenses flaring in the echo of that declaration. Her love for him made her feel far too vulnerable. Harlean could not abide the sensation any longer while she was trying so hard to become independent and strong in a business that absolutely required it.

"I'll think about asking Paul," she said. "Hopefully, he'll be free."

"Oh, he'll be free, honey, don't you worry 'bout that. No matter how he acts for now, that man's got a thing for you!"

Marino thrust the newspaper at Harlean the moment she arrived at the breakfast table. Her mother sat beside him in her dressing gown and slippers. Both of them were wearing irritatingly eager expressions.

"It's absolutely perfect for us, Baby! Read the ad. Marino is going to speak to the real estate agent first thing this morning. Just look at that house. It's fit for a king—or in our case, a rising young movie star."

Harlean opened the newspaper warily. Marino had dog-eared the page.

Our Masterpiece Overlooking Los Angeles Country Club
Magnificent ten-room English stone–trim house. Perpetual view of country club, city, sea and mountains. No details have been overlooked to make this the perfect home. Large rooms, finest hard wood…4 bedrooms, 3 beautiful baths, den.

"Whoa, wait a minute you two. We're not anywhere near ready for something like this!" she exclaimed as she looked back at them. They looked like children on Christmas morning. She knew them only too well. This had already been decided.

"Oh, nonsense," her mother chirped. "Don't be so uninspired, Baby. You know what Marino always says!"

Harlean rolled her eyes in response. How could she not know what Marino always said? Quoting Oscar Wilde liberally was a favorite pastime, an irritating hobby.

"'Anyone who lives within their means suffers from lack of imagination,'" Marino said unnecessarily.

She desperately wanted to quote Wilde herself at that moment that "quotation is a serviceable substitute for wit." However, she held her tongue.

"Darling girl, now that you are about to be a star, you need to live like one. Remember, appearance is reality!"

"Mommie, Mr. Hughes is only paying me $150 a week."

"For now. But once the picture is released you'll be in the driver's seat, and that will be chump change."

"Well said, my dear," Marino chimed as he drank his coffee with a nonchalance that suddenly made her want to slap him.

She was the one working, worrying, fretting—and allowing herself to be transformed. Not him. Not either of them.

"I drove by the house yesterday afternoon and I can tell you ladies both that it is truly magnificent. It looks rather like an English manor."

Marino had always believed himself destined for life as lord of a manor somewhere so the comparison did not surprise her. At this particular moment it irritated her more than ever.

"I can't believe you two would decide something like this on your own." She was suddenly angry with both of them and, for now, unwilling to stifle it. It had been a few days with one challenge too many.

"Nothing has been decided yet," Marino said calmly.

"That's not true, and you know it! You mean to get that house, I see it in both of your faces."

"Baby!" Her mother gasped indignantly. "Is that any way to speak to your stepfather?"

"Actually, I was speaking to you."

"What in heaven's name has gotten into you?" Jean huffed with escalating anger that she could clearly hear.

"That spirit you push me to show doesn't always just go

where you want it to," Harlean shot back, surprising herself with the warning tone in her voice. "Sometimes I actually get angry, too!"

She wasn't totally sure where it was coming from but a growing sense of inner confidence prevented her from reining it in right then. Her mother definitely wouldn't like it. That much she knew as her mother's face began to turn crimson and her expression hardened to one of anger.

"You might feel like the toast of Hollywood right now, young lady, but don't you *dare* be disrespectful to me!" she growled furiously.

As frustrated as she was at their assumptions, and how they took advantage of her, Harlean simply could not have her mother angry and raging at her—which was the next thing that always followed an expression of indignation like this one.

That was a dark storm she knew well enough to avoid at all costs. And right now, without Chuck in her life, she felt as if her mother was the only anchor she had.

"I'm just saying that in the future I'd like to be made aware of important things like that before you and Marino decide them."

"It seems to me, my dear, that your mother and I were doing just that by telling you about the house," Marino interjected as Jean lit a cigarette as a way to calm herself.

His tone was irritatingly even, with the usual note of condescension.

He and Mother were not going to take no for an answer about their house now that there was the slightest hint of her success in the air. Perhaps she hadn't fully won this round but she had made a first stand—she had spoken up at last, and Harlean was proud of herself for that. She was continuing to work toward that confident woman she wanted to become, and she had made great strides since she arrived back in Hollywood. Today was another step forward, but it was just a step.

If she survived the movie premiere, now so close at hand, the three of them would soon be moving to Club View Drive and on their way to living like royalty, even if they were destined to do it for now on a servant's paltry wages.

On the twenty-seventh of May, five months after filming finally concluded and she had turned nineteen—and six months after Harlean first sued Chuck for divorce—*Hell's Angels* was at last set to premiere.

Ahead of time, the Caddo publicity team had told her how everything would go. True to his promise, Howard Hughes had arranged such a spectacle, and promoted it so widely, that the frenzied, cheering crowd wound for blocks down Hollywood Boulevard just to gain a glimpse of the monumental event. Blinding searchlights lit the night sky, highlighting a squadron of military planes as they flew overhead, to mirror those in the film, and a carpet was rolled up to the theater where the coterie of stars would appear and wave to the adoring crowds.

As Harlean, Paul Bern, Jean and Marino waited for the long, black limousine provided by the studio, she tried very hard not to think of the night ahead. She didn't like crowds, and even the thought of public speaking made her uneasy. She was a virtual unknown, starring in the biggest, most heavily promoted picture in years, and Quarberg had informed her that she would be required to step before the assembled masses to say a few words.

She had also been told that all of Hollywood's biggest stars would attend a night where the focus would be on her, the Platinum Blonde. Her mind spun at the list of names she had been given: Gloria Swanson, Buster Keaton, Mary Pickford,

Cecil B. DeMille, Charlie Chaplin. All of them had confirmed that they would attend.

There was not a person on the list she had not idolized for years.

Paul touched her arm as she stood in the living room, wearing a stunning snow-white silk gown which Caddo had provided, along with an extravagant white fox-fur wrap. Her lovely white-blond hair matched the shade of her ensemble exactly.

"You really do look exquisite, my dear," Marino said.

"He's right about that," Paul agreed with the compliment and he looked at her in a way that felt calming.

In the several evenings they had spent together over these past few weeks, Paul had never seemed to have anything but a professional interest in her and yet, she found it strangely appealing, in spite of his being a forty-year-old, potbellied man.

"Oh, with all the fuss going on, I almost forgot," Marino said as he dashed into the kitchen himself, leaving the two of them alone for a moment.

"Are you all right?"

"I'm terrified, actually."

"You will be spectacular. You'll see. And I will be right there beside you," he reassured her just as Marino returned bearing a long flower box.

"This came for you earlier, my dear. I assumed it was flowers, so I popped it in the icebox."

Harlean removed the ribbon and the box top and the sight of a large, exquisite orchid corsage inside was a surprise.

Only one person in the world would have sent it to her.

"That thing certainly won't be missed if you wear it!" Marino said dryly. "It's huge."

"I think it's lovely. Is it from Mr. Hughes?" Paul asked.

Harlean did a perfunctory search for a card, yet there was no need to find one. She knew then that something had prevented Chuck from continuing to phone. Though she was loath to admit it, Harlean realized that her well-meaning mother must have had a hand in it.

Though she was outraged at that, for now she wanted to wear the corsage, and she would do just that.

She would deal with her mother tomorrow.

They could hear the roar of the massive crowd and voices on the loudspeaker as they sat in a long line of limousines, all approaching the theater at a crawl. Searchlights lit the night sky, highlighted by the extraordinary promised aerial display which they could see through the car windows.

When they arrived and she emerged from the limousine, Harlean was quickly encircled by a mob. Paul gave her hand an encouraging little squeeze before he, her mother and Marino melted into the crowd that surged forward around her car. At the same time, a group of policemen moved in to protect her and spirit her up a flight of stairs to an office to prepare before she was to go before the microphone, the fans and the camera.

The office into which she was ushered was small and dimly lit but for a cluttered makeup table adorned with lights. A young female publicity assistant drew off Harlean's wrap for her and tossed it aside as her colleague, a wiry young man with a beak-like nose looked on.

The girl was pretty, with wide brown eyes and lovely chestnut-colored hair. "I'm Kay Mulvey, from Lincoln Quarberg's team, Miss Harlow. I'll be working with you from now on, going with you on press events. It's nice to meet you."

Harlean was grateful for the female companionship, especially since they seemed to be of a similar age, and she had such a warm and genuine smile. "I'm sure we'll get along great and please call me Jean," Harlean said, trying to steady her nerves in the face of so much commotion and noise just beyond the walls.

When the young man on the publicity team tossed her wrap onto a chair, the corsage came loose and tumbled to the floor. Harlean saw it fall and stood to retrieve it just as a silver-haired man, wearing a natty herringbone jacket and crisp necktie, came in and approached her.

"Thank you for coming, Mr. Factor," Kay Mulvey said as she shook his hand. "Mr. Hughes considers this an honor as well as a personal favor."

He studied Harlean with an almost clinical intensity from behind round, horn-rimmed glasses, before he let a very small grin soften his expression. "My pleasure. She really is a lovely girl. Fabulous skin."

Harlean struggled not to gasp or gape at him. Max Factor was nearly as famous as his cosmetics were, and for his reputation for enhancing the beauty of countless celebrities. She sat silently with one eye on the fallen corsage as he personally enhanced her eyebrows, sharpening their shape, then he changed the shade of her lipstick amid the deafening roar of the crowd beyond the office wall.

"Hey, you can't come in here!" Kay Mulvey called out as she charged toward the door.

It was Chuck standing there, a little awkwardly in a stiff navy blue suit and necktie, having somehow pushed past the phalanx of police and guards around the theater or cajoled his way inside. Perhaps a story about being her husband had worked.

Stunned, Harlean rose very slowly from the makeup chair.

"My dear, would you like the boy ejected?" Factor carefully queried as his gaze slid from one of them to the other.

"Could we have a moment?" she managed to ask.

Chuck took a step forward into the scene. Seeing the corsage lying on the floor, he bent down, picked it up and handed it back to her. Harlean could hear Mary Pickford being introduced beyond the walls and the crowd roared at the sound of her name. Her heart was racing—for so many reasons.

"I wasn't sure they'd give it to you," Chuck said as Max Factor and the two assistants went to stand near the office door offering them a paltry moment of privacy.

"You didn't include a card."

"I was pretty sure they wouldn't give it to you if they knew it was from me, doll, or want me involved on your big night."

She felt her walls against him go up again as they stood facing one another. She was still drawn to him and she probably always would be, but so much had happened. "What are you doing here, then?"

"In spite of our differences, I wanted to be here for you tonight. I remember how you hate crowds."

He picked up her wrap, then eased it around her shoulders, coming near enough to her that she could smell the familiar musky scent of his skin. Could they ever find their way back to each other?

Should they even try?

He brushed a finger along her jaw and looked for a moment like he might kiss her, before he gently repinned the delicate corsage onto her wrap.

"I went to Hughes's office yesterday," he softly confessed.

"You did?"

"I demanded to know where you were since your phone number was changed and I was out of my mind with worry. I kind of acted like an idiot."

"Not you?" she exclaimed, managing the hint of a twisted, teasing smile. "I had no idea the number was changed, honestly. I've been so busy with promotion for tonight. I should have guessed, though. My mother probably thinks she did it for my own good."

"She answered the phone last week and told me to stop bothering you. I should have told her to go to hell but I know how much you love her."

He ran a hand behind his neck. The door opened again. Lincoln Quarberg and the young, blonde assistant now carrying a clipboard, were with Harlean's agent, Arthur. Max Factor and Kay moved forward with them until it felt like they were crowding her and she could not breathe. None seemed to care for the fragile moment they had come upon or how they were about to extinguish it.

"It's time, Jean. Gee, there are at least a half-million people out there. They're lined up for miles!" Kay announced.

"I'm sorry I've been so blind, Harlean," Chuck said haltingly as he glanced at the door, then back at her, refusing to let go of the moment that had taken five months to happen, even though they could both see that it was fleeting. "I know how much this life means to you and I want you to know that I support you going after it with all your heart."

"You won't believe it. Hughes has life-size war planes dangling from buildings and real planes buzzing the night sky. You are about to be big business!" Arthur exclaimed.

"He's right." Chuck smiled. "You are about to be something big."

"Come on, Jean," Arthur urged. "Like Howard Hughes always says, it's time to dazzle them!"

As he and the publicity team led her to the door, Harlean stopped and turned back. "He comes with me," she said, surprising even herself with her declaration.

"Impossible!" Lincoln Quarberg barked. "Mr. Hughes expects you to make a star's entrance. This is the most pivotal night of your life, and I am not about to let you do it with some nobody. Besides, Bern is waiting, and he, at least, is wearing a tuxedo."

"Go ahead, doll," Chuck returned with tender assurance. "I'll be waiting when it's over."

"They won't like me, Chuck. The director said I was awful. There will be boos all around."

"Not a chance." He offered an encouraging smile then, but he did not move nearer to her. She knew he was trying to let her leave. "Go on ahead, and meet your public. It's what you've wanted, and worked so hard for. You deserve this moment."

"Are you sure?"

"Yes, go ahead now. We'll talk later. Your fans are calling. You can't keep them waiting."

After two years of trying and failing, Jean Harlow was suddenly what the papers termed an "overnight success." In spite of some cruel reviews, calling her performance "awful," the public loved her and the movie itself was a hit.

Arthur Landau brought the newspapers and trade papers to the house the next morning as the phone rang off the hook. Each time she heard it, Harlean perked up in bed, calling out, "Who is it, Marino? Is that one for me?"

But none of the calls were from Chuck.

"Look at the review in *Variety*, Baby!" her mother exclaimed as she plopped down onto the bed beside her and proudly read aloud, "'...This girl is the most sensuous figure to get in front of a camera in some time.' Now, what do you think of that?"

"Is that *all* they said?" Harlean asked, knowing of her mother's well-meaning penchant for hiding the more negative aspects of Hollywood in order to keep her daughter cheerfully ambitious.

"Let me see it," she said, grabbing the paper from Jean's hand so quickly that she hadn't time to hold on to it. Then she read aloud herself as Arthur, Marino and her new publicity assistant, Kay, stood loitering awkwardly just inside the doorway to her bedroom.

"They say that you might always have to play those kinds of roles but then the writer adds that no one ever starved possessing what you've got."

She lowered the paper and surveyed their collective expressions.

"But I don't want to play those kind of roles," she firmly announced. "I can do more, I know I can. People will start believing I'm like Helen, some man-eating femme fatale if this is all I do."

Her mother laughed. "Oh, don't be silly. This is all wonderful news!"

"Why did you do it, Mommie?" She asked the question and her tone suddenly was low, vulnerable. "Why did you change the phone number without telling me?"

She had chosen this moment to confront her mother. Harlean still wasn't good yet at confrontation, she couldn't make it seamless, but she knew she had to try standing up for herself. Jean shot Marino a stern look and, in response, he and Arthur took Kay and retreated from the room.

"Really, Harlean? You want to talk about that *now*?" She only ever used her daughter's given name when she was perturbed. "Last night you became a star. You need to get this divorce behind you, not cloud the issue by listening to his whining."

"That was never your choice to make!"

"Stop being so naive, it doesn't work that way. You needed help, I helped you."

"We are working it out on our own, whatever ends up happening."

"Over my dead body. An impulsive child named Harlean

Carpenter married that silly boy. You are Jean Harlow now. I am not about to ever let you forget that."

Their conversation was interrupted by a commotion out at the front door. A honey-warm voice, yet one that sounded like a whirlwind, suddenly filled the house. Harlean let out a weak smile, knowing it was none other than Aunt Jetty.

Jean Bello sprang from the bed and bolted from the room as Harlean scrambled to find her bathrobe.

"Where is our Baby, the big star?" Jetty loudly asked in her telltale warm voice. "I need to hug that child while she still remembers who I am!"

Harlean knotted the tie on her bathrobe as she stepped into the living room just in time to see silver-haired Jetty scoop up both cats, Nip and Tuck, kiss each of their heads, then set them back down onto the sofa.

"There you are, fresh from your amazing evening. I listened on the radio to every minute of you all arriving. How exciting that must have been!" she exclaimed with zeal and her usual dramatic flourish as she enveloped Harlean in a great embrace while Arthur, mother, Kay and Marino looked on.

"Chuck asked me to come, so the cavalry has arrived. You know, dear, that I am always in your corner until you two, and you two alone, figure it all out," Jetty whispered to her privately as she held on to her. "He told me what's been going on... Marino, be a dear, would you, and fetch me a cup of coffee?" she asked in a louder voice as she then turned to Arthur.

She placed her hands on her hips. No one else would ever know she had come into Beverly Hills for anything other than to offer her congratulations. Harlean knew that Jetty reveled in being an enigma. It was one of the many things she adored about her aunt.

"And who might this young man be?"

"Arthur is my agent, Aunt Jetty, and this is my new publicity assistant. Kay Mulvey, Arthur Landau, meet Miss Jetta Belle Chadsey."

"Look at you, with a team around you. Soon you'll be too grand for ol' Aunt Jetty."

"Never," Harlean replied. She could feel herself absolutely beaming at the unexpected visit. Jetty always liked to say that one of the gifts of her older age was having gained the ability to mother differently than a real mother. As much as she loved her mother, Harlean craved that difference, especially now that she was trying to learn how to deal in a better, and more healthy, way with her.

"Go get dressed, why don't you, Baby? Your mama and I will go into the kitchen and see what Marino got up to with my cup of coffee. Come on, Jean."

Under the circumstances, Harlean felt compelled to eavesdrop. After all, it was her life hanging in the balance. She moved to the doorway beside the kitchen then slipped around the corner close enough to hear.

"All right, then," she heard Jetty say in a far more terse tone than the one she'd heard only moments before. "What is all this nasty business about you trying to keep those two young lovebirds apart? Honestly, Jean, where's that romantic young girl I so well remember?"

"She died the day I married Mont Clair Carpenter," Jean snapped back, and Harlean could just picture her mother's posture; rigid, unmovable, her expression as cold as her words. "Chuck McGrew isn't any more capable of giving Harlean what she needs than Mont Clair was of me, and I'll be damned if I'm going to let him try."

"Be reasonable, honey. Those kids love each other."

"He doesn't love her, Jetty. For God's sake, he cut her off without a penny so that we had to sue him and that despicable family of his."

"I've talked to him myself and he's just not willing to give you and Marino any money if you won't even let them see each other. You changed the phone number on him, Jean, just when they were getting somewhere."

Harlean marveled at her mother's silence following the comment. Jetty was the one person her mother couldn't intimidate with her blustering and indignation.

"I did what I had to do to protect my baby," Jean replied in a tone that had softened considerably. "If she goes back to that lout, it'll be the end of her career. He's as bad as her father in every respect! He has no dreams for her and certainly no vision."

She rounded the corner and moved into the kitchen with tear-brightened eyes. "You're wrong. Yes, he has his problems, but Chuck isn't all bad. You can hate him all you want, but I don't and I never will! And I don't hate my father even though you worked so hard to keep me from him, too. There's nobody I hate in this world. I love you with all of my heart, Mommie, but to tell you the truth, I'm not very fond of you at the moment!"

As the last words left her lips, the enormity and futility of this entire situation, on three hours of sleep, descended on Harlean. She felt something inside her snap like a twig, something as fragile as her innocence once had been. She turned away and as she did, she heard the last vestiges of their harsh exchange.

"Chuck has made her absolutely crazy. God, Jetty, I can't handle her when she's like this!" Jean raged.

"My dear girl, I love you like a daughter, but you can be as cruel as a she-devil when you want to be. Harlean is a grown woman now, not a baby, no matter what we call her. She needs love in her life besides yours. She needs her husband."

"You have no idea what she needs. No one else does. I was

there when she was so sick as a little girl that everyone swore she would die. But not me, I wouldn't let that happen! She's always been fragile since then, always needed me to worry after her and care for her! That image of her so desperately sick will never leave my mind, nor will my resolve to protect her—her heart and her health! It was me who brought her this far, me alone! Not you, not her father and certainly *not* Chuck McGrew. Right now, until she gets her head straightened out, the love and advice of her mother is all she needs and all she will get!"

Harlean watched her mother come storming out of the kitchen after that, and then troop toward her own bedroom to dress. By instinct, Harlean followed, but Jean slammed the door on her daughter as well as on any further discussion of the matter.

It was still an odd sensation being angry with her mother for the devotion she so long had felt for her. But it had been a blind kind of devotion. These past months, as Harlean had steadily begun to come into her own, she saw some of the controlling, horrifying things Jean had done for what they were. Forcing her to terminate her pregnancy, purposely leaving the Hesser photographs for Chuck to see in order to create a problem, and then secretly changing their telephone number, had all been designed to secure Jean's place in Hollywood. Harlean was the conduit. Letting her daughter make any major decisions threatened that, and thus threatened Jean.

Harlean walked Aunt Jetty to the front door after that and, as they embraced, Harlean whispered to her. "Do you know where he is?"

"He's at my house, sweetie. I told him he could stay as long as he needs to for the two of you to figure out what's next."

"The studio has my day all planned out but tell him I'll come tonight."

Harlean knew that, after dinner, her mother and Marino would retire to their bedroom, giving her the freedom to sneak out and make the drive to Long Beach. She had no idea what would happen between them when she got there; she only knew she owed it to her heart, and her new sense of self, to find out.

"I have several interviews set up for you this morning, then a meeting with Max Factor about a potential endorsement, and a photo shoot over at the studio at two o'clock. Mr. Hughes wants to see you in his office after that." Kay gripped her pen and clipboard as she dutifully detailed Harlean's schedule. "We really should be going, Miss Harlow."

"When we are alone like this if it's not Jean, then it's Mrs. McGrew, please," Harlean snapped, not meaning to sound harsh but unable lately to help it.

She was stubbornly holding on to that part of herself, and would until the very end, if it came, even as Jean Harlow loomed over her more and more with each day.

Last night before finally surrendering to her bed in exhaustion, Harlean had gone to the jewelry box that sat on top of her carved walnut dresser. She had taken out the small, gold wedding band Chuck had once slipped onto her finger. Replacing it on her own hand, putting it back where it once was meant to be, softened her heart and it gave her the feeling of a small measure of control. She would keep it there, she decided, until the final moment of their marriage.

More determined than ever to decide on her own what she truly wanted, she dressed, feeling the many parts of herself beginning to converge. For a few hours, Harlean McGrew would need to remain a shadow behind Jean Harlow. The public wanted to meet the new star and hear what she had to say, and she intended to give them what they wanted.

★ ★ ★

The heady sensation of being in the spotlight had quickly been tempered by the realization that the press believed she and her image were one and the same. Platinum Blonde now preceded her wherever she went. While she had understood all along that her unique beauty had opened doors, she was well aware that it would not be enough to keep them open for long.

Harlean tried calmly to tell them that people were confusing her with her character. She kept each interview as upbeat as possible, explaining with her sunny smile that in her next picture she hoped to portray a woman with more depth, or take on a comedy role.

While she knew she shouldn't have been, she was shocked by the brazen questions she was consistently asked about her personal life even after her patient explanations. All of it only reinforced her determination to be taken seriously as an actress. They would not triumph in the end, she would.

When the last photo shoot of the day was over, she could not get to Howard Hughes's office fast enough. While he had called the meeting, Harlean had her own agenda. She needed to disassociate herself from Jean Harlow, at least for a few days, so she could dash out to Long Beach and see if she still had a marriage to fight for, or at least to gently close this important chapter of her life.

At first, Hughes's secretary said she was late for their appointment and that now he wasn't in, but then his voice from behind the closed door became too loud and animated to be denied. He was standing up behind his desk gazing out the window and arguing with Louis B. Mayer when Harlean pushed past the secretary and into the cluttered office.

"I'll call you back, Louis," he finally turned around and said. "Congratulations, Miss Harlow. This morning you woke up officially a movie star. How does it feel?"

Steeling herself, she moved forward so that only his cluttered desk was a barrier between them. She gripped the edge of it and leaned nearer. "Mr. Hughes, I need you to give me a few days off to see one last time if I can fix my marriage."

It startled her that his response was a burst of laughter. "They said you had a sense of humor, kid, but that's hilarious."

"I'm dead serious, sir."

"Then you're mad as a hatter," he volleyed with an incredulous sneer.

"But you don't understand."

"No, *you* don't understand." He shook his head. "Don't go soft on me now, Harlow, after all I've invested in you. This is the big time, not some two-reeler. You and I are going to promote the hell out of this picture. Like it or not, you're a star now and that comes with a wagonload of obligation."

She fought to maintain her composure, and her conviction. After all, she had gotten Hal Roach to listen to reason. She wasn't about to let this one go easily, either.

"I'm sorry, I'm just trying so hard to have this career and figure out my marriage, too. My husband is a good man, Mr. Hughes, and I know the timing is rotten but Chuck and I just need some time to talk things through."

Something in her tone seemed to soften him more. She could feel her eyes fill. He walked around his desk, touched her shoulder and indicated with a nod that, for the first time in his office, she should take a seat. He drew a handkerchief from the breast pocket of his suit coat and handed it to her just as the tears began to fall.

"Life is full of choices, Harlow. It is for all of us."

"I'm discovering that," she said, dabbing her tears.

"Look, tell you what, kid, go for the two week press tour we've already organized. The dates are set, people are waiting. Use that time to really consider what you want. If you still want to save your marriage when you get back, I'll pay for your hotel suite myself."

"Deal," she said because she knew there was really no other choice.

Decisions. Choices. They were like the reflection from mirrors in a fun house, not always what they seemed to be. Harlean was trying to meet the challenges of sudden fame and to be Jean Harlow, but the gentle girl inside of her, daughter and wife, still pushed forward wanting to be acknowledged and heard.

That night when she returned to Maple Drive she found the house in disarray. Her mother, Marino and an overwhelmed-looking Kay were loading boxes and placing them in the center of the living room. She was afraid to ask what was going on after the day she'd had.

"We're so excited about the move that your mother and I wanted to get a head start with the packing," Marino said as she set down her handbag and kicked off her heels beside the front door to the clatter of dishes in the kitchen nearby. "Your mother has enlisted a friend of yours to help since you'll be leaving soon. Jean actually has a whole list of things for her to do."

Harlean was struck by the revelation as she padded barefoot into the kitchen and saw her girlhood friend. Bobbe Brown glanced up as she held a stack of plates in her hands. She had grown into a pretty, honey-haired young woman with a slim shape, pencil-thin eyebrows, full cheeks and an endearing gap-toothed smile.

"What are you doing here?" Harlean smiled as she set down the dishes and they drew one another into a hardy embrace. "I haven't seen you in ages!"

"I tried to phone you a few times—see if we might get together, but you've always been busy, especially these past few months."

The girls had spoken here and there but they hadn't seen one another since that first lunch date after her first trip to the casting office. "I know, and I'm sorry about that," Harlean replied, meaning it. "But you're here now."

"The studio has already been receiving more fan mail for you than you have time to answer. They don't want your image to suffer if you don't respond while you're out promoting the picture, so I've been hired to help," she happily explained.

"Well, that's great… Gosh, it's good to see you here. I really can use my friends around me right now."

There seemed an increasing number of things her mother had recently neglected to tell her. Nevertheless, she chose not to confront her now. She was gaining strength at choosing her battles, and at selecting the timing but there was too much else going on right now. Instead, Harlean planted a kiss on her mother's cheek, appreciating the attempt to uncomplicate her life by bringing in reinforcements—today most of all.

She didn't always like what it was that drove her mother, but she understood her motivation only too well. First and foremost, she wanted stardom for her—and lately Harlean had begun to want that more and more, too.

Harlean took an apple from a bowl near the sink, then leaned back against the kitchen counter. "Mommie, how did you know Mr. Hughes would have me traveling as soon as tomorrow? He only just told me about it this afternoon."

"Oh, he and I spoke this morning," Jean said blithely as she grabbed two frying pans and searched for an open box to pack them.

"Mr. Hughes phoned you?"

"Actually, Marino and I went into his office to see him when you were at that first interview with Kay."

Harlean knew well enough how her mother's mind worked, and to what lengths she was willing to go to turn her own dreams for her only child into reality, yet this stunned her. There was nothing Mother Jean would not do to thwart a reconciliation with Chuck.

Had Aunt Jetty betrayed her plan to go to Long Beach? Harlean couldn't bear even to contemplate it. Besides that would have been impossible.

She thought now how little surprise Hughes had shown at her request for time off, as if he had been warned. Everything made sense now.

Her decision, moments ago, not to confront her mother was eclipsed by a new sense of ire.

"What did you have to speak to my boss about without me knowing?"

Her mother stopped and set down the pans as she shot Harlean a cold stare. It was one with which she was all too familiar. Jean could change so swiftly like that. Ironically, it was the one thing Jean and Chuck had in common. Her heart fluttered with anticipation of a coming storm.

"Are you questioning my actions on your behalf?" Jean asked in a tone of indignation.

Bobbe gave Harlean a wary sidelong glance, then silently she slipped from the kitchen.

When her question went unanswered, Jean exhaled an exaggerated sigh and pressed her lips into a thin line of disapproval before she continued. "You know perfectly well we have yet to hire you a manager, so in the interim, Marino and I are still having to take on work on your behalf. We went to see Mr. Hughes in our capacity as your management team."

"What about Mr. Landau?"

"Now, Baby, Arthur is an agent, which is an entirely different thing," she replied, and her voice suddenly dripped with condescension. It held the thought that Harlean had no ability to distinguish between the two without her mother's guidance. She could see more clearly now that was the primary way she had kept the upper hand all this time.

"It's just that, last night, Mr. Hughes didn't say a word about me going so suddenly on a press tour," she said suspiciously.

"I'm sure he had a few other things on his mind about that mammoth premiere without worrying about what he did or didn't tell you. Whatever Howard Hughes sees fit to schedule for you, Baby, we all need to be grateful for it. There is good money to be had from a press tour. And think of the exposure!"

"I just thought I'd have a few days."

Jean widened her gaze. Her blond eyebrows rose to sharp peaks. "A few days to do what exactly?"

As usual, Jean always seemed one step ahead of Harlean.

"I don't know, to rest, I suppose. I haven't really had time to catch my breath."

Jean sighed. "Do you suppose Miss Clara Bow or Miss Mary Pickford whine or complain like that? They are stars, consummate professionals, and now you will need to be one, as well." Her eyes blazed with new conviction. "We have been given a chance here millions of girls would kill for, so we are going to seize it together for all it's worth."

Harlean put the unbitten apple back in the bowl. She wasn't hungry anymore.

"All right, well, anyway, Mr. Hughes said this one is only for two weeks. I suppose I can manage that."

Her mother's laugh was harsh. "My baby girl, this is only the beginning. The studio is putting together a three-month tour of theater houses and vaudeville stages all across the country to promote the picture after that. Mr. Hughes is very excited about getting you out there as the face of *Hell's Angels*, and stirring up the crowds as it premieres in different cities. You are who everyone is dying to see. It's all so terribly exciting."

Harlean clenched her hands until she could feel her fingernails gouging her palms. The thought that it would always be a strenuous challenge like this to go up against her mother moved again as a shadow at the back of her mind. The reality of that was never far off.

But fame brought star power with it, and money could bring independence. She needed to keep that in mind, a murmuring voice inside of her said. She needed to earn money to pay the new exorbitant rent at the Club View Drive house that the Bellos wanted. Eventually, it just might allow her to gain enough of an upper hand to decide for herself, once and for all, what she did and didn't want in her life.

She must keep playing the game to get there, and she knew it.

As her mother went back to packing, and Bobbe cautiously returned to the kitchen, Harlean slipped into the hallway to phone Aunt Jetty's house. Right now it was imperative that Chuck know what was going on. More misunderstandings seemed intolerable at such a critical crossroads for them.

The dial slipping back and forth after each number made a telltale sound. Harlean held her breath until she realized there had never been a dial tone.

Marino came up behind her.

"Sorry about that, Baby. They cut our phone service earlier this afternoon."

Harlean lowered the receiver into the cradle and looked back at him. "I gave Mommie the money yesterday to pay it."

"With everything going on about the premiere, she needed a new pair of shoes for her dress. You understand."

"She spent the phone money on shoes?"

"You know your mother. I'll take care of it myself first thing in the morning. If you can spot me a few dollars, that is."

Desperation clawed at her. "But I'm leaving first thing in the morning! We won't have a phone tonight!"

"It's only one night, my dear. Surely you can do without it until you are on the road," he said with that slickness that always made her slightly uneasy.

With no phone, she'd have to get the message to Chuck in person. She dashed toward the front door, grabbing her handbag and her shoes on the way.

"Where the devil do you think you're going at this hour?" Jean said as she barreled toward her daughter.

"I need some fresh air!"

"You need to pack."

"You don't understand!"

Jean's face took on a malevolent expression. "I understand perfectly well, and I also know what's best for you. Haven't I always? Now," she said more evenly, "go in and start packing."

She might as well have said, *I'm barring the door, and locking you in to keep you from Chuck McGrew.* Harlean knew at that moment the result would have been the same, no matter what words she used.

Rosalie rode along the next morning to see Harlean, Kay and Mother Jean off at the train station. The air in the car was thick with tension. It not only came from mother and daughter, but Jean and Marino had not been getting along. The daily bickering between them had escalated to such a fever pitch in the past two days that her mother had volunteered herself as chaperone for this trip, in spite of what Harlean knew was her desire to decorate the vast new rented house on the hill before they all moved in.

She thought her mother also meant to be her unspoken jailer on this whirlwind swing through New York, Philadelphia and Chicago. In spite of her newfound celebrity, Harlean still believed herself to be the property of others, a circumstance from which she longed to break free. But that would not change overnight. There were few things worse in her mind than her mother's wrath. That, coupled with the flicker of disappointment in Mother Jean's eyes that Harlean saw when she challenged her, often felt worse than going up against her. She was working hard now to work within the framework of her mother's consummate skill at manipulation without making things more tumultuous. Howard Hughes's professional claim over her only sealed Harlean's seeming compliance to the will of others. It was difficult to find her way back to Chuck through the tangle of all that.

Rosalie nearly swooned when she looked across the platform in front of the great shiny train, the *Sante Fe Chief*, and saw the tall, dark-haired Hughes and his strikingly pretty girlfriend Billie Dove talking to an elegantly dressed James Cagney, as the trio waited to board the car.

"Mr. Hughes sure is handsome in person, don't you think?" she drawled.

Harlean watched her friend's face flush as a porter lifted her traveling trunk up the train steps. "I suppose so. If you like domineering, power-hungry men with a phobia about germs."

Rosalie gasped. "No kidding?"

"He never touches anyone. Not to shake hands or anything."

"That must make romance a bit of a challenge," Rosalie quipped as they both looked over at smartly dressed Billie Dove, who wore delicate white gloves, along with a beige suit and heels.

"Golly, I'm gonna miss you, Harlean, even if it's just for two weeks. I feel like we've been through so much together."

Harlean felt that, too. "I need you to do me a favor."

"Sure, honey, anything."

"I need you to telephone my aunt Jetty in Long Beach. Jetta Belle Chadsey. Tell her about this sudden trip, and that I might not be able to telephone her myself. Chuck is staying with her. I trust her, she'll get him the message."

"Land sakes, Harlean, your mama isn't gonna let you telephone your husband, and you a big movie star now?"

"You know both of them. I think they mean to fight to the death over me."

"That must be plain awful, being in the middle of all that between them."

"You don't know the half of it," Harlean sighed as the train whistle blew.

When at last they arrived in Chicago, there was a throng of young women all waving magazines and squealing. Harlean was glad Howard Hughes stepped onto the platform first and led the way into the crowd. He was, after all, a celebrity in his own right. But the crowd ignored him and began screaming more loudly. Accustomed to the attentions of women, Cagney descended next with a jaunty smile but, to her surprise, they ignored him, as well.

"Well, I'll be," Jean murmured with a broadening, pleased smile. "It's you they want, Baby."

"That can't be. The picture only just premiered."

"True. But Mr. Hughes's whole publicity team has been working overtime for weeks cultivating your image for this exact moment. You're already a household name."

Harlean was instantly enveloped by the crowd when she stepped off the train and they saw her. Very quickly the group of girls became a mob, all squealing and shoving their magazines at her to sign.

In the midst of the melee, Howard Hughes himself became an impromptu bodyguard as he and James Cagney ushered her toward the waiting car.

"They just kept saying, 'We love your hair. How do you get it that shade?'" Harlean said breathlessly as she felt herself melt against the back of the car seat, and her heart throbbed with the exhilaration.

The next stop was the same, and the next after that.

It was a blur of interviews, radio appearances and cheering crowds.

Yesterday, few had even known who she was. Today she had a millionaire bodyguard, a police detail and a bevy of clamoring fans everywhere she went. It was a great deal for a girl from Missouri to take in.

Slowly yet steadily on this trip, and much to her surprise, the young, uncertain teenager was slipping back behind this new, stronger version of herself and Harlean felt herself becoming Jean Harlow. But she would only tolerate this blonde vamp persona for so long, that much she had absolutely decided. She had far more bubbling up inside her now—ambition, vision and her own dreams—and her newfound desire to unleash it on her own terms was growing each day. Every move she made from here on out must be deliberate, not just in public but in her personal life, as well.

CHAPTER TWENTY-TWO

The two-week tour was an exciting, if slightly blinding, blur of accolades and interest in everything about her. Exhilarating as that was, Harlean was glad now at last to be returning home. She had managed secretly to mail a single letter to Chuck, reiterating what she hoped Rosalie had told Aunt Jetty by phone. She had given her missive very quickly to the concierge at the hotel in New York before she was whisked away by her entourage to a newspaper photo shoot with a group of local "meet the movie star" contest winners.

After they dropped off Kay and were headed back to the bungalow on Maple Drive, Jean glanced over at her daughter. "Baby, I wanted you to know that I've done a lot of thinking on this trip and Chuck McGrew isn't the only deadbeat husband who needs to be gotten rid of."

Harlean looked across at her mother, whose expression was one of resolve.

"I'm going to divorce Marino."

Her mother's penchant for catching her off guard never ceased to amaze her. "But I thought you loved him."

"Passion is not love. You and I both have confused the two for far too long."

With her thumb, Harlean spun her own wedding ring that was hidden at the moment by the tight clutch of her other hand. She and Chuck were nothing like Mother and Marino. "I honestly don't know what to say."

"Say you're happy for me. I know now that I should have done it a long time ago."

The driver pulled the limousine up to the curb, turned off the engine, opened Harlean's door and went around to retrieve their luggage. Jean covered Harlean's hand with her own.

"We will move to the new house, just the two of us. Make a fresh start of things, hmm? And after your divorce is final, you'll be free to see that dear Mr. Bern more often."

"I don't love Paul Bern, and I'm certainly not attracted to him. He's incredibly nice, thoughtful and smart, but—"

"Well, that's a beginning. Good, stable marriages have been built on far less than that."

"Mommie, I *am* married. I still *feel* married."

"A temporary state of insanity for which I am convinced there is a treatment, I assure you."

As they withdrew from the car beneath a starry night sky, Harlean caught a glimpse of a car at the end of the block with its headlamps dimmed. The car was distinctively green in color.

"Come on, let's get you inside. You have another big day tomorrow; an interview, a photo shoot and that party up at the Pickfair estate. Perhaps, you should take me as your date, two lovely single blonde ladies, who knows who we would meet," her mother mused as they neared the front door. An invitation to the Pickfair, the Beverly Hills mansion of silent-screen stars Mary Pickford and her husband, Douglas Fairbanks, was the most coveted one in town.

Harlean considered arguing about the marital status of each of them, but decided she was simply too weary at the moment even to try. She turned around one last time to look down the street but the area had already been submerged in the black of night.

Marino met them at the door wearing a black velvet smoking jacket, crisp black trousers and burgundy-and-gold monogrammed slippers. Harlean thought he still looked more like a gangster than a movie star—although she was well aware that the latter was the look he sought.

Jean let him kiss her cheek before she pushed past him, and Oscar welcomed Harlean home by barking and nipping at her heels to be picked up. Tuck sidled against her calf as she reached down to scoop Oscar into her arms as Nip approached. She was always so happy to be reunited with her pets.

"Do be a dear and make us a couple of stiff drinks, then it's off to bed for both of us," Jean directed her husband. "The Baby and I have another hectic day of publicity rounds tomorrow."

Harlean could see that his wife's tone had surprised Marino. "I assumed you'd want to see the progress up at the Club View Drive house, dear. The decorators are nearly finished, and they have done a splendid job."

As Jean ignored him and headed toward the master bedroom, Harlean could only offer a sheepish shrug. Then she went to her own bedroom on the opposite side of the house and closed the door, grateful for a bit of solitude at last. As she sat down on the bed, her eyes found the framed photograph of her and Chuck from their honeymoon cruise still set out on the bureau. God, how she missed that moment when their naivety and love had made the fairy tale of forever actually seem possible.

Could that have been only two short years ago? It felt like a lifetime.

She fell into a dreamless sleep after that and it seemed she had only just closed her eyes when she woke to clattering noises. She squinted at the bedside clock and saw that it was half past four just as her bedroom door swung open, crashing back on its hinges and hitting the wall. As she struggled to sit up, Chuck staggered toward her, wild-eyed and very drunk.

"I've had it with waiting, do you hear me? Time to take the bull by the horns myself, doll!"

He stood swaying inside a cone of light and shadows cast from the hallway behind him. His ginger-colored hair was tousled, and his face was unshaven. The prominent coppery stubble on his chin surprised her most. She had never seen him so unkempt.

"What the hell are you doing here, Chuck?"

"Once and for all, Harlean, will you come away with me and let me take care of you like a proper wife?"

His eyes blazed red with desperation and his words were slurred. Harlean sprung from the bed and dashed toward him.

"Shhh, Chuck, for heaven's sake, it's the middle of the night!"

"I need you, Harlean… I've waited and I've been patient. God knows I have, and we've played our games with each other, but I need my wife back! I need things the way they used to be!"

"The way they used to be, Chuck, was tumultuous and drunken. That doesn't seem to have changed," she declared. A hint of bitterness she could not fight crept into her whispered tone.

"Well, I'm *not* letting you go this time," he continued, slurring. "One way or another, you will remain my wife!"

"You're threatening me?" she asked as incredulity tumbled

over her anger, and her heart began to sink again beneath the weight of a thousand disappointments in him that had come before this one.

"Two hours from now I'll be on a plane back to Chicago, with or without my wife. You will never find me to serve your final divorce papers on me if you allow that to happen."

Love between them, such a fragile thing, shattered inside of her then. "Get out of here before they hear you, Chuck! Go sleep it off," she grumbled as she slipped on a silk dressing gown and tied it at her waist.

He reached out and drew her against him, but Harlean pushed herself away.

"Stop it, Chuck."

"You're my wife, I have rights!"

Harlean slapped him hard, hoping to startle him. Her voice shook with anger. "I don't want you. God, you make me sick when you're like this!"

"You bitch!" he growled like a wounded animal, gripping his jaw.

The word hit her as sharply as if he had struck her in return.

Chuck's expression fell very swiftly then from anger to contrition. He collapsed onto the end of her bed and surrendered his face to his hands, utterly inconsolable. She heard a small sound, an attempt to make an excuse, leave his lips but he stopped himself.

"Jesus, I'm sorry," he murmured.

"Everything all right in here?"

Harlean hadn't heard Marino approach, but suddenly he was standing in the doorway, his black dressing gown tightly knotted at his stout waist. "Come on, son," he said with a surprising tone of calm. "I'll put a pot of coffee on. Let's go wait for it and then have a cup while we let her dress."

Harlean was instantly suspicious about the sudden gesture,

especially when she saw that all of the lights in the house were already on. Harlean had no idea how much they had heard, but Mother was curiously absent from the scene and the house was small.

As Marino scooped fresh coffee grounds into the pot, Harlean leaned against the kitchen doorway arch and crossed her arms over her chest. As she watched him sit there like a scolded boy, she felt the passion she had loyally held for Chuck all this time slip further and further away now, with each beat of her wounded heart. Why, she wondered, had he needed to come here like this and chase away the last vestiges of her compassion?

It was Jean who answered the front door a moment later and ushered in their silver-haired attorney. He was dressed sharply in suit and tie, which seemed odd for this hour of the still-dark morning. Harlean's heart skipped a beat when he set down a valise that he was already unzipping.

"Good morning, Mr. McGrew," he said.

His clipped tone of voice was all business as he set a stack of documents onto the kitchen table directly beside Chuck's coffee cup. He loomed over the table until Chuck pulled his head from his hands and picked them up.

"What the hell are these?"

"Your divorce papers, Mr. McGrew, citing your violent nature, to which, since I could hear you all the way out on the street, I can now attest personally with the judge. You've been served. In spite of your clever attempt at evasion, there is no avoiding the inevitable now."

"I'm not signing them!"

"Doesn't matter, son, you've been formally served."

The suddenness of the declaration rocked even Harlean and, for a moment, she could not move, nor find her voice. A week ago, perhaps even hours earlier, she would have come to

Chuck's defense but amid the maelstrom, the fight had simply followed the passion out of her, even though her mother once again was involved.

Mother must have seen the car as she had when they returned, and summoned the attorney, and then Marino had kept Chuck there cooling his heels until he arrived. Mother had wanted their divorce all along, and finally a moment had arrived for her to prevail and she had taken it. Chuck jumped from the chair, toppling it behind himself in reaction.

"Really, Charles, can't we all behave like civil adults?" Jean asked in a tone of calculated calm that Harlean knew all too well.

"You're not a civil adult! You are a pariah, a cold and ruthless human being!"

"It's not all her fault, Chuck, we've had our problems."

He shot her a look. His eyes were blazing. "Why the *hell* doesn't that surprised me that you would take her side? I've never had a chance with you, Harlean, not against her! Evil witch wants you all to herself, so now she has you," he growled and bolted for the kitchen door.

Harlean was absolutely frozen.

"To the devil with both of you...*both Jean Harlows!*"

He shook his head in disgust, then turned back to her. "Damn, how I love you, Harlean Carpenter McGrew. God help me, but I always will."

She heard the front door slam after that. By the time she reached the window in the living room, Chuck was already in his car parked on the street, behind her own. She heard the engine roar, watched the headlamps flare.

"Baby, *finally*—let him go," her mother urged in a honeyed tone as she came up, like a shadow, behind her.

Completely devoid now of self-control, Harlean reeled

around and shot her mother a menacing stare. "Mommie, please, just this once, shut up!"

With the words barely off her lips, she watched helplessly as Chuck drove his car into the bumper of hers. How like a metaphor it seemed then, in this strange hour just as dawn began to break Chuck destroying the last vestiges of the life two wild teenagers had tried to build on a foundation that never could have supported them.

She put her hands to the window glass, her wedding band glinting in the deepening sunlight, as he rammed her car once, twice, three times, damaging it—as they forever were. Then, at last when she could bear it no longer, she forced herself to slip the ring from her finger and look away.

Harlean had gone back to her bedroom, curled up at the foot of the bed and wept herself back to a dreamless sleep after Chuck left. Once again now she awoke with a start, this time to the sound of arguing. Yet again, she wasn't certain, for a moment, what was happening.

"I promise you, if you try to divorce me, I'll have no hesitation sending the unpublished Hesser photographs directly to Chuck's attorney!" Marino declared loudly. "Things aren't settled yet and that would certainly tip the balance in the boy's favor."

"You wouldn't dare," Jean growled.

"Would you care to try me, my dear?"

"You'd do that to our girl?"

"I would do that to *you*."

Harlean knew that Marino referred to the photographs Edwin Bower Hesser had taken in which she had become relaxed enough to remove the scarf and pose entirely in the nude. In the moment, her mother had encouraged it, and Harlean hadn't seen the harm in complying since he was such a noted photographer.

But it was bad enough that, to forestall the divorce, Chuck's attorney had used the published Hesser photographs to infer that Harlean deceived him and had posed indecently. If the McGrew camp was given the nude photographs from that shoot, they would have the power, not just to hurt her personally, but to damage her career. At this new pivotal juncture, a wounded Chuck just might strike back at her like that if he received them now when the wound was so raw.

Harlean walked warily into the kitchen where Jean and Marino stood facing each other like combatants in a private war. Mother's arms were crossed over her chest, her face was crimson, ablaze with her signature indignation. Marino's lips were pursed and turned up slightly signaling his belief that he had won. For a moment, the two of them were at a standstill.

"Where are they, Marino?" her mother asked.

"As if I would actually tell you... Darling, think clearly. You honestly believe you can get rid of me now when we are just about to cash in on her?" he asked with the calm affectation of a man who saw himself as being far above his means. He cast a quick glance at Harlean, but was unfazed by her presence. Then he looked back at his wife. "I'm not to be tossed aside like that foolish boy you just chased away."

"You wouldn't dare send them," Jean brayed.

"I'd do it in a heartbeat. If I'm going down, you're both going with me."

The die was cast. Harlean would no longer have Chuck in her life, but Marino Bello was here to stay. Today, the cost of fame seemed incredibly high to her, and it was growing higher. She only hoped that in the end, it would be worth the price she was so dearly paying.

Chapter Twenty-Three

Soon after the *Hell's Angels* premiere, "Platinum Blonde Clubs" began cropping up all across the country as girls tried to look like Jean Harlow and copy her exact shade of silvery blond they saw in magazines.

She had become a phenomenon.

In the face of such opportunity, publicist Lincoln Quarberg devised a brilliant campaign to capitalize on the growing momentum surrounding her. He arranged a nationwide contest challenging anyone to exactly match Jean Harlow's distinctive hair color. The whirlwind in which Harlean was living kicked into high gear as the contest caught on.

After Chuck returned to Chicago, Harlean plunged even more fully into work, preparing for the next publicity tour. She was glad for the distraction yet she quickly found it difficult to walk down the street without being stared at or asked for an autograph. Now everyone knew who she was. Steadily, her studio-funded wardrobe grew more elegant. Leather pumps and high-heeled Italian sandals replaced her favorite socks and white sneakers in public. She commonly wore fur coats and jewelry as accessories. Even though she preferred the simpler garments, she reminded herself that looking like a star for the public was a part of the deal.

Young girls followed her home. Consistently now, she required Kay or Bobbe—some person at least—by her side for protection lest she be mobbed. If she was making a public appearance, there were policemen and guards.

One afternoon, after she had posed for the well-known photographer William H. Mortensen, she and Bobbe walked out of his studio and back into the midday sunlight. Like Hesser, Mortensen had photographed some of the most glamorous girls in Hollywood and she was excited to have posed for him even though he had assured her, with a surprisingly nervous stutter, that the honor was all his.

"Gosh, Harlean, if you'd have told me when we were both at school that one day you'd be a star like this, I'd probably have laughed right in your face—although you always were the prettiest of us, hands down," Bobbe teased.

"That's Jean Harlow to you, now," Harlean giggled, sounding, she knew, more like a teenager than a movie star, but it felt so good to be able to laugh again with a friend she knew she could trust. There were likely to be fewer of those in her future and more need than ever to rely on family and friends.

A group of adolescent girls Harlean had caught a glimpse of waiting near the door were still there when they came out. Seeing her, they surged forward, excitedly shoving copies of her various publicity photos at her.

"Please, Miss Harlow, will you sign this?" one asked in a high-pitched squeal.

"You're my idol," cried another. "Golly, your hair looks just like a cloud!"

"How lovely of you to say," Harlean brightly exclaimed, bending down and giggling right along with them, in her French silk suit with a fox-fur collar and dyed-to-match heels.

After she signed each of their magazine covers with thoughtful inscriptions, she glanced at Bobbe. "I don't know about you, but I'm starved. Would you girls like to join us for a hot dog? My favorite stand is just around the corner."

She watched their expressions go swiftly from shock to sheer delight. "*You* eat hot dogs, Miss Harlow?"

"Sure," she said with a sunny smile. "They're my favorite food. Come on!"

After that, they all trooped around the corner to the yellow hot dog stand with the cheery pink-and-red awning. The girls gaped at her as Harlean bought lunch for all of them and ate her own hot dog with unabashed delight. She asked each of them their names and what they wanted to be when they grew up as a black Cadillac pulled to the curb beside them. Her mother sprang from the car, trailed closely by Arthur Landau who, it was clear, had followed her.

"What on earth do you think you're doing?"

"What does it look like? We're having lunch, of course." Harlean answered her mother lightly, but the girls' expressions all turned guilty in the face of what sounded like a reprimand.

"You can't just go off with random teenage girls like this anymore, for heaven's sake. You're Jean Harlow," Arthur charged.

"Well, 'Jean Harlow' was famished," she quipped, even as he wrapped a protective arm over her shoulder and shepherded her toward the open car door.

"Wait just a minute now!" Harlean commanded as she stopped in her tracks and pivoted back away from him.

Then she opened her handbag and withdrew four theater tickets for a weekend showing of *Hell's Angels* which had been meant for Rosalie, Ivor and two of their friends, but she would get others. This suddenly felt too important to her right now.

"Here, girls," she said, handing them over. "Enjoy the picture, with my compliments."

Clutching at them greedily, each of them swooned and cried out their thanks and proclaimed their utter devotion to their new idol as Harlean was led toward the car.

"Clearly she needs someone more commanding with her now, a personal assistant who can handle the growing challenges of her fame."

Arthur was speaking to Jean, who sat with him in the front seat. It was as if Harlean and Bobbe weren't inches away behind them as he steered the car back into traffic.

"I have to agree with you, Arthur," said her mother.

"As it happens, I've had a letter, a rather insistent one in fact, from a candidate who has quite an impressive résumé. She has followed your daughter's notoriety and, as she is between jobs, she thought perhaps she could be a helpful guide. I have meetings all day tomorrow, I'm afraid, but should I send her up to the new house for an interview?"

"Sure, that'll work," Harlean answered as she leaned forward, gripping the back of the front seat in an attempt to be heard.

This was her life, after all. She was beginning to believe that, at last. Within that realization was a level of pure moxie she hadn't known before and she definitely liked the way it felt.

"I'll let you both know what I think."

"*We* will decide," Jean Bello added without turning around.

"What's her name?" Harlean asked.

"Blanche Williams," Arthur said.

"I'm going to like her. I've already decided that," Harlean could not resist adding in order to get the last word.

The impressive, two-story Tudor-style house on Club View Drive sat alone on a steep rise, far up from the street, so that it gave the appearance of nearly touching the sky. The fact that it was accessible only by climbing a long, steep flight of flagstone steps, made it appear almost majestic. Marino had fought for the house almost more for himself than he had for Harlean. Nothing less than a mansion would do, and he had made that clear in the dealings with his wife over the Hesser photographs.

It still did not matter to him, or to Jean, that Harlean's income from her contract with Howard Hughes remained a frighteningly paltry sum for the lifestyle they had adopted. Things would improve, they both said. All they must do was believe it.

In response, Harlean had gone to Hughes several times since the premiere of *Hell's Angels*, pleading for either another movie role, or to be released from her contract. She desperately needed to earn more money, but she was denied both requests. He alone had made her a star, he stubbornly continued to declare. He alone meant to capitalize on it.

She tried to shake the feeling, but Harlean steadily grew to despise him for the control he insisted on keeping over her.

Since Paul Bern had not found her an appropriate picture, either, Harlean had been forced to grudgingly agree to yet another multicity publicity tour to promote the picture as it opened progressively around the country. Since she was still uncomfortable speaking in front of crowds, the prospect was made more excruciating, but there was no other choice. The McGrew fortune was no longer accessible. She could only rely on herself to pay the bills, and she meant to find a way to do it.

Harlean descended the carpet-softened mahogany staircase the next morning to meet her new assistant. At the moment, she had too much on her mind to have anything more than a passing interest in interviewing the woman Arthur had arranged for her to meet. Besides, she was probably a dour old maid who, whether Harlean liked it or not, would be assigned to monitor her when her mother was not available.

The large wood-paneled living room, with its impressively beamed ceiling, lay ahead. She made her entrance in a white silk dressing gown with white fur lapel and fur-topped high-heeled slippers that clicked across the hardwood floor as Harlean entered the room. To her surprise, Blanche Williams was not old, or dour, at all. The chocolate-skinned woman, with the tight ebony curls, had the most incredibly warm and wise eyes. The connection Harlean felt before she spoke a word was stunning to her. Harlean was someone trying to beat the odds in a world marked by challenges. So was Blanche Williams. She had not come here as a servant, but as someone with goals and determination. The pride in her expression, as she extended her hand and Mother Jean looked on, was something Harlean instantly admired.

"It's a pleasure to meet you, Miss Harlow."

"You as well, Miss Williams."

"You need an assistant and I need a job. I'm quite capable of handling the busy world you're living in just now. I've done it before, I can do it again, for you."

Her tone was direct, not pleading. She did not pander, which Harlean welcomed.

"I've taken the liberty of reading all about you, and speaking to Mr. Landau so that I am up to speed, should you decide to hire me."

"Miss Williams's references are impeccable. Everything checks out," her mother said as she gestured to the paper-filled folder that lay on the coffee table between them.

"When can you start?" Harlean asked.

Blanche's eyes widened slightly but she did not smile. "Why, right now, if you'd like."

"Shouldn't you at least ask her a few questions?"

"I don't need to. I have a good feeling, and I told you I was gonna like her."

"Forgive me for saying so, but your hair truly is the most extraordinary shade," Blanche said.

"Actually, so is yours. We'll look like salt and pepper together," Harlean chuckled.

"Baby, you can't go saying things like that!" her mother gasped.

Only an instant of awkward silence followed before Blanche finally smiled, then began to laugh, too. "I hope she does," Blanche said. "It will make working here so much more comfortable."

"Would you like to come up and give me a hand with the outfits for my publicity tour?"

"Sure, if you'd like."

"I'm in a sorry state, trying to decide on my own from the collection the studio sent over, and I leave tomorrow. *We* leave, actually. I believe that's the arrangement."

Blanche and Jean Bello exchanged a glance. Her mother was suddenly more wary. "Are you certain, Baby? The two of you are bound to get looks."

"I'm growing quite used to that now," said Harlean, still smiling at Blanche as if they were already the best of friends. "Come on up. I haven't a moment to waste."

A combination of trains and terrifyingly small prop airplanes took Jean Harlow across the Midwest so that she could greet the crowds of her fans. Blanche Williams accompanied her everywhere, carried her date book and pressed her determinedly through throngs of autograph seekers with a firm hand. By the time they arrived in Chicago, they had become true friends.

They were late to board the train because a local radio executive who had been squiring them around town had run out of gasoline. Mother Jean was not happy they had been reduced to hailing a cab.

Harlean mounted the train steps in her own foul humor, after listening to her mother's tirade about it. But it was more than that. This was the exact platform where she and Chuck had waited to embark on their honeymoon, culminating in the cruise with his grandparents. She loathed how fragile the memory still made her feel after everything. That chapter was over, she reminded herself. She was a star now—or nearly so.

In spite of how busy the Caddo publicity machine had kept her these past few days, memories of Chuck seemed still to loom, moving in and out from the shadows of her mind, where they lingered. They were divorced. She wanted to forget him—she needed to forget him. It was time to move on. But putting her plan into action was still difficult.

Ever allowing herself to love again seemed absolutely impossible.

"If it isn't Sunshine, right here in the flesh!"

The familiar voice was a welcome sound so far from home. Once she reached the top train step, she glanced up and met the kind, cherubic smile of Oliver Hardy.

"Babe!" Harlean cried, and flung herself into his arms. There could not have been a better time in her life to see an old friend than now. "Oh, my gosh, what are you doing in Chicago?"

"On my way home to Georgia for a little R & R. I just stopped off here. And will ya look at you! If you're not the cat's meow," he exclaimed. As he did his signature comedic move, fluttering fingers over his heart, with a sweeping gaze he took in her tailor-made tweed traveling suit, kid leather gloves and matching hat.

"Expensive looks good on you, Sunshine, you wear it well."

"They're only clothes, Babe, bought for this tour by the studio."

"But still, fit for a star."

They sat down together in the first-class compartment after that and Harlean couldn't get over how happy she was to see him. Her mother and Blanche sat facing them as more passengers filed in past them down the aisle. Both women seemed uninterested in their reunion, as each opened a book and began to read so that Harlean felt an all-too-rare moment of privacy.

"I always told you you'd be a star. Remember?"

"Of course I remember, Babe. I think you were my first real friend in Hollywood."

His round cheeks colored at the compliment. "Our final picture with you in it turned out to be quite a success at the box office. Although Stan wasn't as happy with it as I was."

"Neither was my grandfather. *Double Whoopee* made him angry, but *Bacon Grabbers* sent him over the edge."

He had stopped sending her money after he'd seen her first Laurel and Hardy picture, and he had never softened about it, but she didn't see a reason to add that to the conversation now. No one really cared about what people privately struggled through. Everyone—even stars—had their problems. Besides, she was certain most everyone in Hollywood assumed that *Hell's Angels* had made her wealthy as well as famous, and Harlean had no desire to whine and complain, particularly not to a man who had worked so hard for his own success. The only thing that was going to grow her bank account was ingenuity and dogged hard work, and she was now fully and quite stubbornly committed to summoning both.

If Hughes wasn't going to find another film role for her, Paul and her mother would have to gang up to have to persuade him to loan her out to another studio. There would be no other way to keep up with her mother and Marino's increasingly lavish lifestyle.

"So, how are things with that young fella of yours?" Babe asked her with that rich sincerity she so loved about him.

"We're divorced, I'm afraid. Or we will be by the time I get back to Los Angeles."

"Oh, Sunshine, I'm so sorry. You seemed so in love with him."

"I probably always will be, Babe. But some stories just aren't meant to have a happy ending."

"Speaking of stories," he said, seemingly glad to change the subject. "Are you still writing that novel you were always musing with us about on set?"

Harlean felt herself smile and the sudden feeling of tension ease. "I am actually, trying to, anyway. I don't know yet if it's any good, though. I haven't gotten very far with it, but it's such fun to lose myself in another world."

"A world *you* have total control over."

"Exactly."

As she settled into her seat, she caught a glimpse then of the dark-haired, mustachioed man in an expensive pin-striped gray suit and fedora who had just taken the seat across the aisle from them. Harlean stifled a gasp when she realized that it was the handsome actor, William Powell, who she'd seen at the Brown Derby, before she'd ever even gotten so much as a walk-on role.

She wondered with the delight of a die-hard fan if Powell had any idea who she was now. She could not stop staring at him, shamelessly hoping to draw his gaze. Blanche and her mother were still reading their books and didn't seem to notice. Babe however did.

"Don't even think about Bill Powell, Sunshine. He's madly

in love with Carole Lombard. They might even be engaged by now. Haven't you been reading your magazines?"

Her heart sank. Lombard was the stunning blonde actress who, as luck would have it, Harlean often thought she resembled. But of course she knew she flattered herself. Lombard's performances always had that wonderful spark of comedy which Harlean could only dream of having one day.

"I was just about to ask you to introduce us," she said bravely.

"Sorry. Ol' Babe here doesn't know him personally."

"I'm sure he knows you. Everyone knows Laurel and Hardy."

"Let's just say Bill Powell and I don't run in the same circles. He's a leading man who women swoon over, and I'm a fat man who makes my living doing odd faces and pratfalls," he said with a self-deprecating chuckle.

"Have it your own way. No introduction," Harlean relented with an expression that was half pout, half clever smile, as she opened a novel by Willa Cather she was halfway through.

But even as she said it, she knew she would meet William Powell one day, whether he was married to Miss Lombard or not. After all, a girl could dream—and hadn't her dreams gotten her this far already?

The anticipation of getting to the last stop on her tour had been on her mind since the day she had embarked on it. Her final appearance would be in Kansas City, and she had agreed to have dinner with her father and his new wife while she was there.

As glad as she was that her father had finally found happiness, Harlean had never actually had to share his love and devotion with anyone else before. Because there had been the physical distance between them, their relationship had taken on a mythical status in her mind. Because they hadn't seen one another since she was a child, he had remained the handsome man in brown-and-white photographs she cherished. Although she desperately wanted this reunion, the prospect of having to meet this woman at the same time she saw her father for the first time in many years brought with it a spark of jealousy.

Jean chose to remain at the hotel and make phone calls while Harlean took a car and driver to the Italian restaurant on a quiet tree-lined street on the outskirts of the city. Blanche had offered to join her for moral support, but this was something Harlean knew she needed to do alone no matter how awkward it was.

The driver would remain outside while they dined and could whisk her away at a moment's notice if there were any problems—with either fans or the unknown Mrs. Mont Clair Carpenter.

Harlean was wearing a sedate navy blue suit with pearl buttons, sleek pumps and an oversize hat, in an attempt to draw attention away from her increasingly recognizable face and hair.

She entered the crowded, candlelit restaurant and glanced around to take it in. The ceilings were low and the walls were a rich red. The tables were covered with red-and-white-checkered cloths and topped with flickering candles, which cast the entire place in a deep crimson glow and gave it an inviting feel.

She was shown by a host to a table near the back of the restaurant where her father and a woman were already seated. Her heart was racing. Harlean could see them sitting closely and talking as she approached. The moment Mont Clair glanced up and saw her he sprang to his feet and a broad, happy smile took over his face.

"Ah, here she is!"

His hair was spotted with early gray now, Harlean thought with surprise, and he was wearing round spectacles with thick lenses. He wasn't at all the young, handsome father of her girlhood memories, but an ordinary-looking middle-aged man.

"Here's my girl, at last," he exclaimed and drew her into a tight embrace.

The moment was more awkward than she wanted it to be because, in spite of her fantasy about her father, he was still a man she hardly knew.

"It's so good to see you, Daddy."

As she finally stepped back, her gaze landed on the petite woman with dark, tightly curled hair who had remained seated, but who looked up at her now with a tentative pencil-thin smile and warm, hazel eyes.

"Baby, this is Maude, my wife," he said proudly.

Maude Carpenter extended her hand. "It's a pleasure to finally meet you. Mont talks about you nonstop. Do you prefer to be called Jean or Harlean?"

"Anything you like, really. These days, I'm not entirely sure who I am, to tell you the truth," she replied as her father held out her chair for her, then pushed it in.

Harlean tried not to stare, but Maude looked so entirely different from her mother that it was difficult not to be taken a little aback. Maude had sallow skin, slightly sunken eyes and there was gray in the temples of her hair, like her father's. She looked much older than Jean Bello, Harlean thought.

"Gosh, what a beauty my baby has turned into. You're much prettier than any of your pictures in those magazines," Mont Clair said proudly as his wife smiled and nodded in agreement.

They sat in awkward silence for a moment after that as waiters dashed past with loaded plates of spaghetti and aromatic platters of roasted meat.

"So, Maude, are you enjoying married life?" Harlean forced herself to ask in a bright tone she summoned up.

"Oh, yes indeed! Your father is a wonderful husband."

"I'm so happy for you both," she said, and to her surprise, she found she suddenly meant it. Seeing him happy was so nice after how badly she knew her mother had treated him.

Harlean also knew now what it took to make a happy marriage—and to lose it.

"I was sorry to hear about things with you and Chuck," Mont Clair said as he fingered his water glass. "He always seemed such a nice young fella."

"He still is, Daddy."

Maude dotted her mouth with her white linen napkin then and stood. Her husband rose in response and dutifully drew back her chair. "Would you two excuse me for a moment while I go powder my nose?"

Harlean was still smiling as her father sat back down, then leaned forward and took both of her hands, linking them with his own on the tabletop. He squeezed them tightly.

"I think she wanted to give us a moment alone. My Maude is a real terrific gal. I gave up thinking I'd ever find someone again," he said, and there was what sounded like a note of apology in his tone.

"You look good, Daddy, different from the photos you sent, but real good."

"Well, I'm sure happy, I can say that much."

"You always knew I hoped you and my mother would reconcile. But I know now that those were just foolish dreams."

"They were dreams you and I shared for a long time, Baby, believe me—a lot longer than I should have had them. How *is* your mother?" he asked, and she saw the sadness in his eyes.

"Same as always. Ruling Hollywood like she owns the place."

"So long as she's not ruling you. I *do* remember how she can be, after all."

"She loves me, Daddy, and a lot of my success is due to her refusing to let me give up. I really do owe her everything."

"And that's just the way she likes it."

Harlean was happy at that moment to have Maude return to the table with freshly brightened lipstick and an engaging smile. There would be no further talk of her mother now, she felt quite certain, as Maude settled back in their midst.

"How lovely it is to see the two of you together," she exclaimed. "This means so much to him that you could meet us for dinner like this."

"I only wish it could be for a longer visit. But my train leaves tonight."

"Oh, dear. Tonight? Won't that be rather late?" Maude asked.

"It's a sleeper car. I need to get back to Hollywood."

"I'm sure the studio is keeping you mighty busy these days," her father said.

"I'd like to be a lot busier but Mr. Hughes doesn't seem too keen on letting me make a new picture just now. I think he wants to get his money's worth out of this one first. I'd love to do a comedy next, though, something where I can really stretch myself. Did you see *Safety in Numbers*?"

"The Buddy Rogers picture, why sure." Maude smiled. "That's the kind of thing you want to make?"

"I'd give my eyeteeth to play a part like Carole Lombard did in that one," Harlean crooned. "And I'm gonna get the chance, you just wait and see if I don't!"

"I just believe you will," Maude said.

The evening was over before she knew it, gone in a whirl of reminiscing and too much food. Just past ten o'clock, Mont

Clair pulled his daughter close against his chest out on the sidewalk beside her waiting car.

"Be happy, Baby," he said in a tender tone. "There's more to life than work, you know. Do you have a new fella to keep that pretty smile of yours bright?"

"Not really like you mean. There's someone I keep company with now and then, but we're just friends. He works for MGM and he's trying to get me that comedy role to play," she said of Paul Bern.

"Romance can grow even from an unlikely friendship if you have enough in common. Just ask my Maude," he said proudly.

She thought right then how her father seemed like the happiest man in the world. She hadn't expected to like Maude but she did. She'd had no idea how content that would actually make her but when she boarded the train that night, Harlean was smiling. It had been such a healing dinner, important for them all.

Chapter Twenty-Four

A week after she returned from the publicity tour, Howard Hughes relented to the tag team pressure of Jean Bello and then Paul Bern, who were urging him to loan Harlean to MGM Studios for *The Secret Six*, a film about the underworld.

Harlean would play the femme fatale role.

While the Bellos were irritatingly persistent in their phone calls and appearances at Hughes's office on Harlean's behalf, it was Paul who had been savvy enough to show him how the film was the perfect vehicle for her. It would continue the momentum that had begun for his studio-crafted image for her, without more major investment on his part. There was nothing to risk and everything to gain, but a comedy role would have to wait.

"It's just not right, his loaning her to MGM for thousands of dollars a week, and still only paying her pennies," Jean raged, and the cocktail in her hand sloshed onto the living room carpet.

Even now, in spite of her daughter's growing success, Jean had that way of talking to Marino about Harlean at times as if she weren't even in the room. While tension between Marino and Jean flared from time to time after their nasty divorce confrontation, for the most part it had blown over, and the rancor ceased. More often than not, they found common ground and a united front pushing Harlean ever closer toward that massive stardom that seemed nearer than ever to them all.

Tonight in response, Harlean took a sip of her own strong gin and tonic as Marino tried to calm the situation his wife seemed intent on making worse. It was the night before filming was to begin and tension at home was the last thing she wanted. During these last challenging months, she knew alcohol had become far more of a friend than it should, especially in light of what had happened with Chuck because of it, but for now it was the only thing that quieted the frustration and eased the loneliness.

"I've been telling you all along that Landau character is absolutely useless for the Baby. She needs a sharp agent, someone who will be an absolute shark for her."

"Someone like you, my dear," Marino said from his place on the sofa as he took a long drag on his cigarette.

He crossed his legs as his wife paced back and forth.

Harlean cast a glance at Paul, who seemed at the moment exceedingly uncomfortable in the midst of their conversation. In the past few weeks, Harlean's heart had softened toward him, thanks to his growing devotion to her and her career.

He seemed to take seriously everything she said and did, which only served to cement her own belief in herself. She still did not feel the faintest physical attraction to him, but as she sat there silently, listening to her mother rage on, she thought how perhaps now, with the wound on her heart from Chuck still not fully healed, that a platonic male friend—a dear one—was for the best.

"It's still a man's world, and a man's business," Paul quietly observed, drawing Harlean's attention back to him. "But perhaps the two of you together might think of taking on the task permanently rather than hiring someone when you know her best of all."

Jean and Marino looked at him as if he had uttered words in a foreign language. Then Harlean saw the familiar spark of ambition brightly light her mother's eyes. A smile broke across Marino's face a moment later.

"Well, I suppose we could," said her mother, as if it had never crossed her mind.

But everything crossed her mind.

"Hughes won't like it," Marino warned.

"Since when has anyone's opinion ever stopped her?" Harlean asked, and everyone began to laugh because they all knew that it was true.

Harlean continued to loathe the image of Jean Harlow as a vamp, but it had taken on a powerful life of its own so swiftly that there seemed no doing battle with it. Even when she intentionally wore wide leg trousers, bobby socks and lace-up shoes onto the set the next day, she was received with catcalls and whistles. Few cared that she had a generous heart, was well-read and incredibly smart about the business she had been studying since the first day. But they would not be able to underestimate Jean Harlow forever.

"Don't mind that," Blanche told her as they walked together, casting scowls at the crew. "Like my friend Mae West said a couple of years ago, 'There is no such thing as bad publicity.' You remember that."

"I didn't know you knew Mae West."

"I worked for her for a while. There are a lot of things like that you don't know about me," Blanche said as she gave just a hint of a smile.

"One of the many reasons I like you," Harlean chuckled.

"You don't let people know everything about you right at first. You make them earn that. It's just how I am, too."

As she approached her place on set, there were three chairs. One was for the director, George Hill, and the two beside it were marked for Jean Harlow and someone named Clark Gable. Another chair for the star of the film, Wallace Beery, was separated from the others off to the side.

"I wonder who the heck this Gable character is. Paul didn't tell me much about him, other than he's some New York stage actor trying to make it in Hollywood now, and that he has quite a reputation with the ladies."

These past two years she'd met enough handsome young actors to be fairly certain she wasn't going to like this one any more than she had liked them. With the exception of Ben and Jimmy, who she loved, most were far too vapid and egocentric for her taste. Even gorgeous William Powell had seemed a bit sullen on that train ride they had shared.

Since Wallace Beery's reputation for belligerent behavior with his female costars was well-known, Harlean decided to meet this Gable fellow before she decided not to like him.

The business had already taught her that an ally could come in handy.

Just then, the tall, strikingly handsome actor, with a wide, genuine smile and massive hazel eyes, approached her and introduced himself. Clearly, she thought, he was aware of the effect his smile had on women, but his swarthy good looks did not have the same effect on her.

"I've got to say, you're not at all like the kind of girl I'd imagined you were," he said sheepishly after they had conversed for a few minutes.

"Well, join the club. It's growing bigger by the day. You can be the president, if you'd like."

"You're quite funny, Miss Harlow."

She softened, but still only slightly. "Call me Jean."

It wasn't what she wanted to say. Everyone called her the Baby but with trust so important to her, that offering was far off.

"Jean, it is. And my friends call me Gabe."

"By the way, every girl on the set has been eyeing you. I'm obviously the last to know you are kind of a big thing, Gabe."

"I've played enough third-rate theaters and road companies never to take myself all that seriously," he said warmly, and his eyes crinkled at the corners.

That way he had about himself, in addition to being so good-looking, was likely what drew Hollywood.

"I don't take Jean Harlow all that seriously, either," she responded with a genuine laugh.

Clearly, they had surprised each other. They weren't friends yet, but Harlean found herself already thinking that could change one day and they actually could be.

In spite of her initial optimism, by noon Harlean was at her wit's end. Beery was as rude and abrasive as she'd expected, but she forced herself to hold her tongue. It felt like *Hell's Angels* all over again. Then her mother waltzed onto the set to have lunch with her. Much to Harlean's surprise, she came with newly coiffed hair, dyed just that morning, the exact platinum shade as her daughter.

"Who did your hair for you?" she asked.

Harlean could hear the gossipy murmurs around them about it. Rosalie had been in Toluca Lake Park working on a picture so Harlean knew she hadn't done it.

"After looking positively everywhere in town, I finally found this lovely man who said he would kill to be the one doing your color, so I auditioned him for you," she explained with a pleased smile. "Since you and I look so much alike I thought, why not? The results are impressive, wouldn't you agree?"

It honestly struck Harlean as desperate, and even a little sad, but she could not let that show. If her mother wanted to dye her hair to match hers, Harlean decided to appear duly flattered by the compliment, at least outwardly. The age difference between thirty-nine and almost twenty notwithstanding, Harlean was still devoted to her mother's zest for life. She knew there were those, like Chuck, who didn't understand her or who questioned her motives. Harlean now accepted that there would always be those people. But there was still no one like her mother for her absolute unfailing belief in her daughter's destiny—a destiny that had come true, she believed, in large part because of Jean Harlow Bello. In spite of her manipulating and her obsessive need for control, she still owed her mother everything.

The next day of filming felt longer to her and more intense even than the first. In spite of Harlean knowing all of her lines, Beery seemed to want to vent his frustrations on her, and he took every opportunity to do so. With neither of them highly experienced, she and Gable became fast friends amid the tumult Beery created on the set.

"Gosh, I was nervous. How'd I do?" she anxiously asked him after she'd finished shooting a scene.

"Gee, kid, I'm no expert, but you do shine," Gable exclaimed as the crew began to set up the next scene.

She smiled at him with heartfelt gratitude and, while she decided to accept the compliment, she went on to ask him the same question several more times. In return, he asked her about his own performance since Beery intimidated them both.

"So, what's a nice dame like you doing in a business like this, anyway?" Gable asked that afternoon.

The two of them were playing a game of cards while the director conferred with the formidable cigar-smoking Louis B. Mayer, who had taken this occasion to come onto the set.

Gable wore a black tuxedo and Harlean's costume was a flowing evening gown with which she wore dangling rhinestone earrings. They both found the portly, bespectacled Mayer a commanding presence even though Harlean had gone to school with his daughter, and they had shared that good-natured challenge that had launched her career. Irene Mayer's father was such a force in Hollywood that nothing could soften that.

She and Gable kept playing until they saw Mayer and his male assistant approaching the card table.

"Oh, damn, we're both done for," Gable quipped beneath his breath and kept his head down. "Well, it was nice knowin' ya, kid."

Harlean stifled a nervous giggle that faded quickly as Gable shot to his feet. She set down her fanned hand of cards and stood up beside him, both of them looking more like guilty children about to be reprimanded than two rising stars in a Hollywood picture.

"Harlow, Gable, I've just had a look at the dailies from yesterday and the two of you've got chemistry. I'm pleased. Keep up the good work," Mayer announced in a gruff, no-nonsense tone.

He chomped down on his cigar.

"Thank you, sir," Gable said as he raked back his dark, oiled hair, then shoved his hands into the pockets of his tuxedo trousers.

"How old are you, Harlow?"

"Nineteen, Mr. Mayer, but I'll be twenty in March."

"My daughter's age. You look much older than she does."

"I went to school with Irene, sir. My name was Harlean Carpenter back then."

His eyes lit with recognition. "Your mother was the divorced woman."

"She's remarried now. The two of them manage my career."

He wrinkled his nose as if he smelled something foul beyond the odor of his own cigar smoke. "The Bellos."

He rolled his eyes before he walked away.

"Your mother must be somethin' else," Gable said after Mayer had left the set.

"Oh, she's a force, all right," Harlean quipped. "I'm just happy she's in my corner!"

But the set for *The Secret Six* did not always lend itself to levity. Beery continued to bluster and rage much of the time, lashing out at the cast and crew at will. Even though she had endured similar behavior from the director James Whale, Harlean did what she could to stay out of Beery's way—until late one afternoon, when she delivered a line incorrectly.

"Dammit to hell, can I ever be in a picture with one dame in it who has bigger brains than tits?" he crudely growled.

Harlean felt the blood drain from her face. "I'm sorry, Mr. Beery, but it was just one line."

"One line that means we have to film the whole damn scene over again at this hour!"

She felt the powerful press of tears at the backs of her eyes but this time she stubbornly refused to cry them. No, not this time. She had come too far to give a bully the satisfaction.

"I said I'm sorry."

"Well, I am *not* losing my dinner reservation for some blonde bimbo!"

Suddenly, it felt like someone had turned a switch in her mind. She'd had enough. "Listen, there is no reason to be nasty. I'm sorry, and I'll get it right the next time!"

Harlean could hear whispers from the shadowy sidelines where the director and the assistant director sat watching the exchange. She tipped her chin up, trying to rise above the moment.

"You damn well better, toots, because I'm in no mood for amateurs today."

She felt Gable approach behind her in support but before he could intercede, she took a step forward toward Beery. She stiffened her spine, along with her resolve, and met his angry stare straight on.

"All right, listen, mister, I didn't like it very much yesterday when *you* made us all wait because you were late getting back from lunch and then *you* flubbed your line, and you did it more than once. Yes, we all noticed. But no one bullied *you* because even we *amateurs* know about respect for fellow actors! And don't *ever* call me toots again."

She came close to poking a finger in his chest. But less is more, she thought, remembering that sage advice Hal Roach had once given her.

"Fair point," Beery finally conceded after the charged silence that followed. The sharp lines of his expression softened. Then he said, "Let's take it from the top, gang."

The suggestion was uttered as amenably as if he was everyone's friend.

The great Wallace Beery had backed down.

Harlean tried very hard not to show a victorious smile as everyone gradually returned to their places, but the pride she felt in that moment was exhilarating.

As everyone packed up after the day of shooting, Gable approached her. He was still wearing that smoldering grin that Harlean was sure had seduced more than a few women.

"Say, kid, what about hitting the Cocoanut Grove tonight

with me?" Gable asked as she slipped her arms into the sleeves of her gray coat.

"For starters, I hear you're married."

"You gonna hold that against me when I'm just asking for a few drinks and a little dancing to relax after a long day at the office?" he asked with a charming smile that, quite against her will, made her knees weak. Oh, he was trouble, all right.

But Harlean arched an eyebrow and smiled back at him, knowing full well that she could give as good as she got in the clever repartee department.

"That's *all* you want?"

"So bring a date if you're that concerned. I'll bring a friend. Come on, what do you say, kid?"

Harlean had agreed to see Paul that evening but, even though she was smart enough to avoid Gable romantically, she had come to really enjoy his company, too. They understood one another and they shared the same sense of humor. There was also something about the similar place they both were in their careers that made her feel a deepening connection with him. Even after a couple of days she knew he would be a big star—if his wife, or a jealous husband, didn't kill him first.

The Cocoanut Grove was in full swing by the time she and Paul arrived to join Gable. He was sitting at a prominent table in the center of the room, as if he were holding court, and there were two very pretty, scantily clad girls standing next to his chair and giggling in open flirtation. She watched him revel in their attentions, hardly noticing her approach.

"Hello, Hal," Paul said to Gable's companion, a man with a prominent forehead and dark hair that was combed straight back matching a thick, neatly trimmed mustache. He was a burly man, but not stout, attractive, but not handsome.

He stood to shake Paul's hand as Gable gradually turned his attention back to the table.

"Jean, this is Hal Rosson. He's one of our best cinematographers at MGM."

"Miss Harlow," Rosson said with a sedate nod.

He had the most lovely eyes, she thought, gentle and a little mysterious. She could see already that he had a reserved, gentlemanly manner about him that was intriguing.

"Always a wise move to make friends with the guys who can make you look good," Gable said through that winning smile that eclipsed everyone around him. "But seriously, Hal's a real peach. And he can drink me under the table any day, which earned him my respect right out of the gate. Hello, Jean. My, don't you clean up swell."

"Where's your wife tonight, Gabe?" Paul asked as they sat down at the table covered in white linen, amid the upbeat jazz tune.

"She's a society dame. She doesn't go for this sort of thing," Gable replied easily as they all picked up their menus and began to peruse them.

Harlean thought Paul was needling the actor, knowing perfectly well that his wife did not live in Hollywood and that Gable spent most of his social time with Joan Crawford.

They'd only just ordered when the table full of men beside them began to laugh and heckle.

"It absolutely *is* her, it's that tramp from the picture, I tell ya. I'd know that rack of hers anywhere," one of them cackled.

The others quickly joined him. Harlean felt a hot rush of embarrassment flush her cheeks. She knew perfectly well it was what the world thought of her.

"Ask her to dance, Phil. I bet she dances real fine."

His tone assured her it had not been a compliment. Again, a chorus of guffaws rose above the rousing orchestra tune.

"Easy, fellas," Gable intervened. His smile disappeared and his eyebrows knit together in a frown. Harlean could hear him try to maintain an affable tone in his warning. "We are with a lady right here. Let's keep things clean, shall we?"

Again the trio snickered.

"She's a starlet, not a lady," one of them said loudly enough to be heard by everyone.

"Do you want to leave?" Paul asked her.

Hal stood. Something about him reminded her of a prize-fighter. "You two aren't leaving, they are," he firmly announced.

"All right, easy there now, boys. Nobody wants any trouble here," one of them said in a far more conciliatory tone as their laughter quickly faded away. Standing and tensed, Hal seemed more intimidating than she had at first imagined him to be.

"Then apologize to the lady or we'll have you tossed out," Gable added in support of Rosson's credible threat.

Harlean watched with appreciation as Clark and Hal defended her, and Paul stood ready to whisk her away if need be.

"Sorry, Miss Harlow," one of them finally said. The other two grumbled out similar, short grudging words of contrition as Gable and Rosson eased back into their chairs.

"People are gonna keep thinking I'm like that, especially when this new picture is finished. I need to do a comedy soon, to change people's minds," she said.

While she spoke to them all, she had intended the comment for Paul, who had the power at MGM to find her the right comedy role and to stand up to Howard Hughes in order to get it for her. She knew he was working on it but she was determined to keep the notion at the forefront of his mind. In response, Paul gave her hand a pat.

An elegantly dressed couple was shown to the table beside them then. It took her attention from the trio of men who now were subdued and seemed to fade into the background of music and clinking glasses. The man wore a black tuxedo

draped with a white silk neck scarf, and he had his arm around
the striking blonde with him.

"Be still my heart," Gable exclaimed as he clutched his
chest dramatically but in a low tone of voice. "An angel has
just walked in the door and sat down beside me."

"That's one you can't have, Gabe. Gossip is Carole Lombard
is taken," Paul quietly informed him. "Mr. Mayer told me at a
dinner party last night that she and Bill Powell are engaged. It
was really just a matter of time, so tuck your charms back in."

"Never say never," Gable mused as the man seated his date
and when he turned, Harlean saw that it was indeed the dashing actor from the train and the Brown Derby and every fantasy she'd ever had.

In this crowded room, filled with laughter, music and the
buzz of activity, William Powell's chair was close enough to
smell the spicy musk of his cologne. For a moment, she was
too starstruck even to move.

"Let's congratulate the happy couple, shall we?" Gable said
with a devilish grin. "I've always wanted to meet an angel."

"Evening, Hal," William Powell said, affably nodding to
Hal Rosson before introductions were needed. "And Paul,
nice to see you here, too."

"Bill, do you know Clark Gable?" Paul asked.

"Haven't had the pleasure, I'm afraid, but I've heard a lot
about you. Doug Fairbanks and his wife sing your praises.
And this is my gal, Carole," Powell said.

As Harlean heard the proud tone in his voice, her heart
sank a little. Carole Lombard may be gorgeous, but she was
lucky to have such a debonair man look at her as devotedly
as he did, and speak as though he were delivering lines from
Shakespeare.

"Bill and Carole, this is Jean Harlow," Gable added. "We're
working on a picture together right now with Wallace Beery."

"My sympathies to you both," Powell joked as his gaze finally met Harlean's. *Those eyes*, she thought. *I could drown in them.* "Of course. You're the girl from *Hell's Angels*. Loved that, didn't we, honey?" he asked Lombard, who acknowledged Harlean with a polite nod. "You were just terrific in it."

"Thank you," she finally replied, although she was quite certain the sound of her voice was more like a croak. Even after all the movie stars she'd seen, he was still that appealing to her.

Film stars, movie industry moguls...she couldn't quite believe the company she was keeping these days. It was still striking to her how far a girl from Missouri had come, and she hoped never to take any of it for granted.

After that, she danced with Gable, and then once with Hal, as Paul looked on. Hal was nice, she thought, but so reserved. As they danced on the crowded floor she bumped into someone behind them. As if the evening already wasn't unbelievable enough, when she turned around, Harlean came face-to-face with Pola Negri's smoldering kohl-darkened gaze. For a moment, she couldn't speak, or even think. The actress, who she so long had adored, looked just like she did in the pictures and magazines. She knew that she was staring, but she couldn't help herself. Negri was so elegant and delicate looking. All of her girlhood dreams of life in the motion picture business came rushing back at her in that instant.

"Say, you're Jean Harlow, aren't you?" Negri asked in a surprisingly thick Polish accent Harlean had never envisioned her having.

Ah, the benefits of silent films to actresses like her and Clara Bow.

"I am," she managed to mutter as her mouth went dry.

"Gee, you're even lovelier in person than in the magazines. I'm sure you know my friend, Charlie," Negri said, introducing her dancing partner, Charlie Chaplin.

For Harlean it was almost too much—her idol *and* a movie industry powerhouse both smiling at her, knowing who she was. It was a shining moment, one she would never forget, made that much sweeter since Pola Negri was as nice as Harlean once prayed she might be.

This moment redoubled Harlean's intention to do the same thing, now that her own turn in the spotlight was growing brighter.

"We'll have to get together for lunch one of these days," Negri said.

"Sure, any time, Miss Negri, that'd be swell," she exclaimed over the loud music as they all began to dance again.

Her idol's dark eyes flashed as her smile broadened. "Oh, come now. I'm Pola, especially to my friends. Isn't that right, Charlie?"

"Absolutely," Chaplin concurred as he took her in his arms again in time to the music.

Pola Negri tossed Harlean one last glance over her shoulder before they whirled back into the crushing crowd of dancers. "I'll give you a call real soon, okay?"

Chapter Twenty-Five

Now that Jean and Marino were officially handling Harlean's management, they took it on with a vengeance. Jean's resolve was as firm and clear as it had always been. She intended to wake up the studio heads to her daughter's soaring popularity, and thus garner a better deal than the one to which Howard Hughes was firmly holding her. Even now, he was charging $2,500 a week unapologetically, and still paying her a paltry $150 from it.

Hughes still balked at giving Harlean a comedy role, or even something meaty. Instead, he wanted to keep capitalizing on her sexy image, so he loaned her out for a film at Universal Studios where her part was similar to the gun moll she had last played, and not that far from the trampy Helen in *Hell's Angels*. Harlean felt increasingly trapped.

Once shooting had wrapped, the Bellos organized another publicity tour where Harlean would sign autographs and meet more of her fans, particularly members of the Platinum Blonde Clubs. At least there would be good money coming in from that.

Harlean overslept on the day they were to leave Los Angeles but it was just as well, she thought. It was rare nowadays to get much sleep or solitude with her mother commanding the house with the precision of a military base. She propped herself up on her elbow as Oscar stood squealing near the door to be let outside. She called for Blanche but there was no answer.

The huge house was silent.

"I guess it's up to me, hmm, little man?" She smiled at the dog as he yipped excitedly in response and began to wag his tail, knowing what lay ahead.

Harlean drew on an ivory silk dressing gown and matching slippers, then fluffed her hair as she shuffled toward the staircase, rushing after Oscar, who was down the stairs and now barking at the front door. No sooner did she turn the handle and draw it back, than Oscar dashed out and down the steep steps toward the street.

"Hey, wait a second!" she called out, still half-asleep, and tried not to trip on the many stone steps ahead as she chased after him.

In front of the house across the street, a menacing sable-colored German shepherd with coal-black eyes snapped and barked in warning. "Oscar, no!" she cried as she dashed after him.

"Rinty, heel!"

She heard the sharp command in a male voice rise above the barking of one dog and the warning growl of the other. In response the shepherd froze, then sat back on his haunches compliantly. He was silent and motionless as Harlean reached Oscar, who, less than half the shepherd's size, still yipped and barked directly beneath the bigger dog's nose.

"Oscar, that's enough, for heaven's sake!" she said, scooping him up into her arms. "Gee, I'm sorry," she said breathlessly to the tall man in a gray dressing gown over pajama bottoms, holding his newspaper as he stood beside the dog.

"No harm done. Rinty is well trained. I take it you're the new neighbor," he said affably.

"Jean Harlow," she said, extending her free hand to shake his, and feeling slightly embarrassed that her own dog was far less disciplined.

"Lee Duncan. And this is my boy. Around town they call him Rin Tin Tin."

"Of course, the dog from the pictures!" Harlean said in recognition.

He was, in fact, the most famous dog in the world. Everyone knew their story. As an American soldier during the war, Duncan had rescued Rinty from the battlefield in France and brought him home. She had read the famous canine had nearly won the Academy Award in 1929 for best actor until they had decided to award the prize to a human. "I didn't know you guys lived across the street."

"We like to keep a low profile around here. Rinty works a lot," he said with a smile. "I'm betting you feel the same way these days."

Duncan had a friendly manner that quickly set her at ease. "I'm traveling quite a lot to promote my last picture."

"Why don't you set him down, see how they get along?" Duncan suggested. "Rinty will behave."

"Are you sure? He's awful big. He could probably eat Oscar in one bite."

"He prefers filet mignon to little dogs," Duncan chuckled. "He could use a friend in the neighborhood. We both could. Especially one who isn't looking for anything from us."

Harlean nodded in understanding. "The price of fame."

"I've met your mother and her husband. How 'bout you all come to dinner here when you get back from your trip? I'm a fair chef, as it happens. I'll whip you all up a home cooked meal, and we'll let Rinty and Oscar get better acquainted."

"I'd like that," she said. "We both would."

Harlean was making new friends, building a life for herself and beginning to do some of it on her own terms. She had begun to like this feeling of growing up and taking the world by storm. Well, at least *Jean Harlow* did.

The response to her appearances on the next publicity tour across the country to keep promoting her image and earn extra income exceeded the last one, and Harlean was not only overwhelmed but humbled by it. Squealing hordes of adoring girls waited in line, carrying bouquets of flowers and photographs, now along with devoted male fans, and she refused to disappoint them in spite of her lingering stage fright.

As Jean and Marino waited, usually in the wings with Blanche and Kay, she posed endlessly for pictures with all of them and patiently signed autographs until her hand cramped. And each day she began to feel a little more like Jean Harlow—the glamorous star in costly ivory-colored, fur-trimmed silk suits—and less like Harlean Carpenter, the bookish, Midwestern teenager.

When they arrived in Sante Fe, the last stop on the tour, Harlean was exhausted. In spite of the genuine smiles she was able to conjure with her fans, she needed a rest.

She went to the final press conference and autograph signing in what felt like a daze. All she wanted was to go home, see Oscar, Nip and Tuck, and sleep for a week.

Sitting at a long table in a smart beige suit with a fox-fur collar, and a fur-trimmed hat with the city's mayor, dignitaries and the Platinum Blonde Sante Fe Fan Club president, she gazed out past the bright lights. She ignored the flashing bulbs, and tried to answer this new round of questions in ways that sounded fresh and sincere.

When it was over, her fans lined up to have their photographs and magazines autographed. Kay stood behind her, instructing the more zealous fans to keep moving. Blanche was over on the side of the room, holding Harlean's handbag and her date book.

Halfway through the signing, Harlean looked up into the face of an adolescent girl with short blond hair and wide bright blue eyes. As the girl offered up a publicity still of Jean Harlow, her hands trembled.

"What's your name, sweetie?" Harlean asked as she poised the pen over the publicity photograph of herself.

"Lula, after my grandma."

"Oh, I love that name. I've only ever heard that one other time," Harlean exclaimed and as she did, she noticed the older woman standing behind the girl with hands on her shoulders. It was the kind face she remembered from her very first role as an extra.

"It's lovely to see you again, Harlean."

"You've met Miss Harlow before?" the girl said in wide-eyed awe.

"Just once, a few years ago, honey."

"Come along, keep the line moving," Kay interjected from behind Harlean.

"It's all right, Kay." She held up her hand. "Give us a moment. Mrs. Hanford and I are old friends. What on earth are you doing in Santa Fe, Lula?"

"Things worked out all right for me, after all. I live with my daughter and her family now. My lovely little granddaughter here is the light of my life."

Harlean felt a genuine burst of delight renew her spirit. "You're a beautiful young girl."

"I wanna be an actress just like you when I grow up, Miss Harlow, and my grandma, of course. She was in pictures, too!"

"Yes, I know. We were in one together, actually. Your

grandmother was the first person to be kind to me when I got to Hollywood."

The girl's face showed the awe that she remembered feeling herself as a girl when she had first seen Pola Negri. Harlean felt the power of amazement then at how things went around and came back around.

"Please now, we really need to keep things moving," Kay repeated.

"If you ever get to Hollywood gimme a call," Harlean said to the girl with stars in her eyes as she wrote.

To Lula, a lucky girl to share a name with someone you love. I know the feeling!
Best wishes, Jean Harlow

"I see you took my advice about expensive hats," Lula Hanford said.

"I took all of your advice actually."

"It's really good to see you again, my dear."

They shared a smile. "And you, Lula. I'm glad to know things turned out okay for you."

"I was just about to say the same thing to you," she said.

By the spring of 1932, Jean Harlow had worked for every major Hollywood studio, making films for Columbia, MGM, Universal and Fox Films, though the roles were largely the same: gun molls and sexy sirens. But even Constance Bennett, Joan Crawford and Greta Garbo had dyed their hair a similar shade of platinum blond. While imitation was, as they said, the sincerest form of flattery, Harlean would not sit back on her laurels. She was committed to continue learning and growing as an actress.

She took acting classes and voice lessons. She stumbled and then she tried again.

Even though her reviews often suffered, her popularity did not. Finally, Paul had prevailed and convinced MGM to buy out her contract from Howard Hughes. At last, she was living the life she wanted. She had grown up and into the role of a star, and she lived now in the manner the name Jean Harlow provoked around the world.

Then finally, it was time to break ground on a dream that was all of her own. The home they rented at Club View Drive had been someone else's idea of success. The house at South Beverly Glen, where she long ago had bought a vacant lot, would be all hers.

Freshly blonde, late one Sunday afternoon as the sun began to set shimmering and crimson, she sat in the driver's seat of her Sport Phaeton atop the steep hill and gazed at the first bit of framing the construction crew had erected just that Friday. She looked down at the open blueprints in her hands again, then folded them and tucked them in between the seats. It would be a magnificent place. All white, the walls, the carpets and the furniture.

Like the color of hair that had won her fame.

This place would mark a new beginning. This home she was building would represent the success she had worked so hard these past years to achieve.

A black taxi cab pulled up beside her car then, churning up a cloud of dust.

She glanced over as he got out and paid the driver. The years slipped away as the memories tumbled forward. The sweet ones pushed ahead of the bad and brought a small smile to her lips.

He looked good, she thought. A bit heavier, perhaps, but with that same boyish face, lightly dusted with freckles. His tousled copper hair was now tamed into short waves. It felt like such a long time to her now since they had been together. He slipped into the car next to her, closed the door and the cab pulled away back down the steep driveway.

"Hello, Chuck."

"Hey there, doll," he said with a nostalgic tone. "You look real swell—nothing like Harlean anymore, but still, real swell."

"So do you, Chuck."

"Thanks for agreeing to see me while I'm in town. I always did love the view from up here." He turned away from her to take it all in.

"I'm so sorry about everything," he said with a sigh.

There was a silence before their eyes met again. Harlean saw the sadness there. She knew it was bittersweet to him, too, since this place held their dreams for a future that was no longer meant to be.

"Me, too," she softly said.

"I tried, ya know."

"You did fine, Chuck. But we were awful young."

"How come you wouldn't take the money from our settlement? It was yours, you know."

"That was yours from your parents. I couldn't take that from you. After all, we did love each other once, didn't we?"

He put a hand gently atop hers on her lap and gave it a tender squeeze before he drew away. "Most definitely, doll."

"I always wished you had been able to let me in a little more to share with me about what happened with your mom and dad," she dared to say. "I always thought you would have felt less sad if you did."

"Less angry, you mean."

"Yes, that, too."

He paused before he said, "I just couldn't, you know? To

unravel that always felt like I would be unraveling myself. I really thought the grief was going to kill me. I guess a part of me thought it was my fault that I had lived and they both had died."

"But you know that isn't at all true, don't you?"

"I'm getting there, at last, I think," he said.

"You went through a lot as a kid, Chuck."

"I think we both did. That was how we found each other."

Harlean tried not to let sadness settle over her—a blanket of memories, guilt and things unanswered. It was long over—so were they. But what they'd shared would always matter to her.

"I finally went to the cemetery, and to my parents' graves," he confessed after a small silence. "It was as hard as I thought it would be, but I said goodbye."

"You never did that before?"

"No, I never did. I know you wanted me to, though."

"I just wanted you to be okay," she explained. "It happened when it was meant to."

It took her a moment to gather her thoughts for the cavalcade of things she was feeling, seeing him again, after how they had ended. "So, why did you wanna meet, Chuck?"

She watched his jaw tighten.

"I'm getting married," he announced. "Strange to admit, especially to you."

She felt her heart skip a beat, but she knew that was just nostalgia.

"She's a society gal, real sweet. I just thought I should be the one to tell you since too often in the past we let other people do the talking for us."

"I'm happy for you."

"So, you gonna marry Clark Gable? There are pictures of you two in all the magazines. That fella is a real looker."

A cad and an incorrigible ladies' man, too, she thought with a spark of humor because he'd been her costar twice now and he had also become a dear friend. They had amazing chemistry on-screen, too, but Gabe was always going on about William Powell's new wife, Carole Lombard, ever since that night at the Cocoanut Grove, so he wasn't interested in her like that. Besides, Harlean had decided she was going to marry Paul. His absolute devotion to her had softened her heart these past months and, in her way, she loved him. But she decided not to bring any of that up now, since she had not even accepted Paul's proposal.

"Sake's alive, no. Gabe's got a string of gals to keep him plenty busy. He's like a brother to me."

"I did think all that stuff about you two was just gossip. You deserve the best, doll. You'll be the biggest star in the world soon, I can feel it. No one will ever forget the name Jean Harlow."

Against her will, tears filled her eyes.

"I guess I always knew that would happen. Stupid of me to fight it like I did. I should've known I couldn't win that one." In the silence, Chuck leaned over and very gently pressed a kiss onto her cheek. "For old times' sake, hmm?"

"You brought me to Hollywood, Chuck. You helped me find that fate. No matter what our problems were, I owe you a lot for that."

He again looked out at the vista before them then, and she did, too. "You'll build a real palace here, I'll bet."

"I'm excited to try," she said. "At least all of the ideas will be mine."

It felt so good, and healing, just to be here with him, of all people.

"We're both moving on with our lives, but I want you to know that I'll never forget what we almost had together," he said.

"What we did have, Chuck, we did—it wasn't almost, not at all."

He reached over to embrace her one final time, and she let him. She wanted that so dearly, too. They clung together tightly then before finally letting go—both at the same time.

Chapter Twenty-Six

Harlean, Jean and Marino were invited to dinner across the street at Lee Duncan's house often during May and June, and Rinty and Oscar quickly became the best of friends. On those occasions, as Duncan barbecued and Marino usually mixed the cocktails, the two canines would romp and tussle around Duncan's backyard to everyone's delight. Paul was regularly with them now that Harlean's engagement to him had officially been announced to the press. Today was no exception.

They still hadn't been intimate but she assumed he was waiting for the wedding night—and the old-fashioned gesture charmed her. Paul was kind and gentle with her, and so wise, she felt as if all she wanted to do most of the time was to curl up at his feet and let him educate her about the world, as he saw it. She knew there was so much to learn from him.

She still wasn't *in love* with Paul. What Harlean felt was nothing at all like the turbulent passion she'd had with Chuck, but she did love him, and it would be a good marriage. Yes, she was certain of that. She sat on his lap now, an arm slung behind his neck, as Ivor took two freshly made gin and tonics from Marino, then handed one to Harlean and one to Rosalie.

Harlean had another certifiable box office hit on her hands with her latest picture, *The Beast of the City*, and so they all felt like celebrating. They waited now for Jean to return from a meeting they'd had with Irving Thalberg at MGM.

Harlean still reveled in the review *Time* magazine had given her, stating that her performance was "a shiny refinement of Clara Bow."

Jean came out into the backyard with Blanche who had accompanied her just then and she accepted a kiss on the cheek from Marino, who was at the bar. Then she descended the few steps onto Duncan's patio, along with Irene Mayer and her husband, David O. Selznick. Irene and Paul had long been dear friends and now she and Harlean were, too, which was an odd turn of events, she thought, but not unwelcome. This was a gathering of all the people Harlean loved best in the world, and those who supported her daily—her group.

As Harlean stood, Irene went straight to her and they embraced. "Congratulations on your engagement, kiddo," she said as she kissed each of Harlean's cheeks in the French manner. "I really had no idea you two were serious, to be honest, but it's great that you'll finally tie down this lifelong bachelor."

Harlean knew they were an unlikely couple, with their age difference, among other things, but all of that could not have mattered less to her.

"Thanks, Irene," she said with a genuine smile as David also gave her a congratulatory hug. "We're really happy about it."

When Harlean looked at her, she saw that her mother, in white turban and fur, even in the warmth of summer, was holding an envelope and she was beaming.

"What've you got there, Jean?" Paul asked.

"It's for the Baby, straight from Mr. Thalberg's desk."

Harlean knew, intellectually, that she shouldn't worry at happy moments like these, yet sometimes her nerves still got the best of her. She'd had more than her share of negative reviews and bad news in sealed missives.

"Well, open it already!" Rosalie exclaimed with an eager smile.

"Can't it wait till after we eat? I'm afraid whatever it is might ruin my appetite."

Paul pressed a kiss onto her cheek. "You can handle it. Let's read it together."

Empowered, yet again, by his steadfast belief in her, Harlean slid her thumb beneath the seal as Oscar and Rinty romped through the grass before them.

Paul looked over her shoulder as Harlean read aloud sincere words of praise and surprise for what she was capable of as an actress. It ended with an offer of congratulations on her "truly excellent performance" and was signed, not formally, but simply, Irving.

Stunned, she glanced back up and scanned the faces of everyone who was gathered now around her. He loved her in *The Beast of the City*, and not just for her looks but for her acting. It was everything she had struggled and hoped for so long to attain, all now in one neatly written note from one of the most powerful young men in Hollywood.

"Did you put Mr. Thalberg up to this?" she asked Paul as her brows knitted into a small frown.

"No one ever puts Irv up to anything. He is his own man. It's a compliment, and a big one. You need to take it that way."

"Oh, Baby, that's just marvelous," her mother exclaimed, joining her two hands prayerfully beneath her chin, and Harlean saw that she had tears in her eyes. "See? I knew all along that this would happen if we just stayed the course."

Bobbe and Kay arrived then, rounding out the group of friends Harlean enjoyed being with the most these days. They came together down onto the patio, in casual shorts, sneakers and polo shirts, and each accepted a drink from Marino who stood in front of a table full of gin, tonic water and glasses. Bobbe was holding a stack of publicity photos in her other arm.

"Good luck getting back across the street after dinner," Kay said. "It's crawling with newsmen and photographers now that you two have announced your engagement."

"What've you got there?" Harlean asked her.

"Just a few photos, special ones the studio wants you to personalize."

"Leave those for me, Bobbe. I'll autograph them for her later," Jean directed. "I'll sign as the Baby."

"But, Mrs. Bello—"

Jean held up her hand. "We're one and the same, the Baby and I. I know what she means to say, and besides she's got a wedding to plan and a new picture to get ready for. She can't be bothered with trivial things."

"Thanks, Mommie," Harlean said as she blew her mother a kiss across the patio. "And thanks to all of you! Now, anyone else ready to eat? I'm starved!"

CHAPTER TWENTY-SEVEN

The Brown Derby was bustling by noon when Harlean and Kay arrived for a last-minute bite of lunch. Even though it was September, the summer tourist crowd now in 1933 had yet to fade. Harlean's eager new chauffeur, Herbert Lewis, in black cap and livery, dashed around to the passenger side and opened her door as Kay got out the other side on her own. Harlean sighed at the size of the crowd gathered outside before them. She hesitated for a moment before they walked toward the front door. Kay hadn't had time to make a reservation, so this was bound to take forever with so many people waiting ahead of them.

Harlean pulled the fur collar of her long, belted camel-hair sweater up closer to her throat just as the crowd outside parted, allowing them to pass. Whispers rose up around them. Harlean realized then that these were not patrons but rather fans eager for a glimpse and perhaps an autograph from one of the Hollywood celebrities who regularly dined there during the noonday rush. Coming here would always remind her of Rosalie and that first lunch.

"It's her, that's Jean Harlow!" a girl excitedly squealed as magazines began to flutter around her like autumn leaves, and pens were held aloft. "Ask her! Go on, ask her!"

"Miss Harlow, please!" another bid her as she shoved the latest issue of *Hollywood* magazine at her. She was on so many magazine covers now but seeing them was still a thrill to her.

As Harlean complied and offered up a sweet smile, the click of a camera punctuated the moment, then another, and the bright flash of bulbs followed.

"We love you, Jean!" The eager cry moved through the crowd as Harlean offered back the autographed magazine and pen and then continued on inside the restaurant.

"Miss Harlow," said the maître d' with a huge smile and a deferential nod. "How lovely to see you."

To her surprise, Harlean recognized him immediately as the man calling himself *Francois*, the struggling actor who once had given Rosalie such a challenge here. That had been the day before her entire life had changed forever, she remembered.

A wave of nostalgia hit her as the maître d' took two menus from the top of the host stand. "Right this way, Miss Harlow. Our best table in the house is right over here."

How silly, she thought, that she'd been concerned about her lack of a reservation. Some part of her would always feel like Harlean Carpenter, the uncertain girl from Missouri, even though she was now one of the biggest stars in Hollywood.

She was still learning how to accept the fact that she had *arrived*.

As she bit back a proud smile for how far she had come, and slid into the booth, Gary Cooper passed by the table and nodded to her. Across the aisle, Thelma Todd looked up from a plate of salad, recognized her and offered up a friendly wave. For a moment, Harlean nearly turned around to see if there was someone famous behind her.

"So then it's settled, is it? You're definitely doing another picture with Clark Gable?" Kay asked as she perused the menu, now unfazed by the attention Jean Harlow garnered.

Kay herself looked the part of an actress today, strikingly attractive and in a steel-blue dress and pearls.

"Yep, we sign the contracts tomorrow."

"I'm so happy for you that it all worked out. You two are sensational together on film."

"We understand each other, I suppose. And it's wonderful, finally, not to be hired just for my looks, or because they want me to play a tramp, but because they actually think I can act."

"You sure *have* earned your stripes," Kay laughed. "I don't think anyone could disagree with that."

After another series of interviews and another photo shoot that afternoon, Harlean returned home exhausted. She climbed the stairs toward her bedroom, eager for some time to herself, and a chance to lose herself in the novel she was reading, before another full day tomorrow. Her days were long now but she found them equally wonderful.

At the moment, she felt as if she were on top of the world. Fragile though that place was, forever susceptible to a tumble at the slightest provocation, she was trying to revel in her hard-won success and, most of all, never, even for an instant, to take this incredible ride for granted.

Jean's bedroom light was on so she popped her head in the door to say hello.

"Well, you're late this evening," said her mother who was arranged on her bed like a magnificent blonde queen bee, covered by a pink satin spread, a white fur coverlet, and propped behind with satin pillows.

She closed the magazine she was reading as Harlean climbed onto the bed and curled up beside her like a little girl. "Tonight was great."

"So how was your day?" Jean smiled as she asked and began to tenderly stroke her daughter's hair.

"The morning was absolutely wild. We went to the Brown Derby for lunch. You should've seen the way people cheered."

"I'm sure you're used to that by now."

"I don't know, maybe it was just that place. I haven't been there in a while, and you remember what happened the first time I went there with Rosalie."

"Indeed I do."

"I signed autographs outside afterward today for almost an hour."

"Surely you're joking. Your schedule was planned down to the minute!"

"Well, people wait for me these days," Harlean said softly, but her voice had an edge of steel to it now. "No one gives me a hard time anymore."

"Except me," her mother said knowingly.

"Except you," Harlean concurred.

"You'll need your rest tonight, my darling. Have you forgotten the big ceremony tomorrow?"

Harlean knew there could be no bigger ceremony in her mother's eyes. Of course she hadn't forgotten. It had become the pinnacle of success—the defining event in any star's career. This one would be as much for Jean Harlow Bello as it was for the second Jean Harlow. They had been on this journey together from the start, seen it together and shared the same fantasy long ago of what it might be like.

"Of course I haven't forgotten. I'm putting my prints in cement at Grauman's."

"Yes, you are." Jean smiled. "Right there along with Clara Bow, Mary Pickford and the rest of the greats."

"You knew it would happen one day, didn't you?"

"I never had a single moment of doubt, Baby."

There was silence that fell between them then, a communion of sorts, for how far they had come together. There was still no one in the world whose company Harlean valued more, nor whom she depended upon more greatly.

"Remember that day we saw Pola Negri there at Grauman's when I was just a girl?" Harlean sighed.

"How could I forget? No one could get near her, but she tossed kisses to the crowd."

"I met her once not long ago."

"Did you?" Her mother's sedate tone was filled with equal parts surprise and envy.

"We bumped into one another on the dance floor at the Cocoanut Grove."

"You never told me," Jean said as Harlean nestled against her mother's chest.

Theirs was such a complex relationship, over which lay a blanket of anger and hurt for her mother's many and intense manipulations along the way. Harlean was not a fool, nor was she blind to any of that. Yet underneath, at the core, was still and always would be a great devotion between mother and child. Families were complex things. Her feelings for her father, for Aunt Jetty…each relationship was different, deep, fragile. She knew now that all love was complex—sometimes not easily explainable, like the feelings she would always carry for Chuck as they went forward with their own lives.

"We were supposed to have lunch."

"No!" her mother said with an incredulous gasp.

"She promised to phone, but I heard she went to England not long afterward. Her career really wasn't doing very well by then."

Jean's eyes sparkled with love and triumph as she looked down at her daughter nestled beside her just as she had done since Harlean was a child. "As one star fades, another ascends.

That's the way it is in Hollywood," she said. "One day, a little girl somewhere will probably see you in the movies, like you saw Pola Negri, and you will change her future. And so it will go."

"Oh, I almost forgot," she added, reaching over and taking three copper pennies from her nightstand. She handed them to her daughter. "Tomorrow, press these into the cement along with your prints, for Mommie, would you?"

"Pennies for good luck," Harlean said. "That's certainly what you've brought me all these years."

"What we brought each other. Then it will be like I am immortalized right along with you."

"Jean! Jean! Miss Harlow, over here!"

The flash of the cameras was blinding. She looked into the excited crowd and felt her heart flutter. In response, Harlean gave them her prettiest Harlow smile which brought a rousing chorus of cheers. It wasn't old, this would never get old. She had worked too hard, and come too far, to ever take any moment like this for granted. It was a thrill.

Sacrifice, disappointment and loss, all of it had taken its toll and it had cost her everything she had emotionally just to arrive at this place—the top of her game. The road had been a long one—but she'd made it!

Harlean glanced down at the wet square of cement waiting for her, and in that moment she thought to herself, *This truly is amazing!* Against her elegant black silk dress she held a distinctive white orchid spray. She had insisted on that particular accent. "Touch has a memory. O say, love, say…" Pennies were to honor the one person who had been key to her success, orchids were for the other.

"Are you ready, Jean?" Sid Grauman asked as he stood beside her.

"I think I've been waiting for this moment all of my life," she replied with a beaming smile as she leaned forward then and carefully pressed her hands into the cold cement, to the roar of the crowd behind her.

★ ★ ★ ★ ★

AUTHOR NOTE

Seventy-nine years after her tragic and untimely death at the age of twenty-six, Jean Harlow's legacy endures, nurtured and lovingly cared for by her noted biographers, as well as in the hearts of her legions of devoted fans. I was well aware of that important legacy before I wrote a single word, and therefore of my responsibility to tell this story with the utmost care and respect.

While Harlow remains an icon, what fascinated me more than her image was the true story of the smart, tenderhearted and spirited teenager beneath the famous platinum blond hair. As I began my research, I wondered: Of the thousands of young girls who found their way to Hollywood in 1928, exactly what elements went into separating her and making her into such a legend? For me, beyond that undeniable "sparkle" of hers, a portion of the answer was her relationship to two people; rivals, combatants, yet both essential for her rise to fame. Most obvious was the first Jean Harlow and her fanatical, lifelong devotion to "the Baby." But the other relationship drew me more. While Chuck McGrew is largely eclipsed in the annals of history by her subsequent husbands, Paul Bern and Hal Rosson, then later by her great love affair with William Powell, and even her famous friendship with Clark Gable, it was Chuck and Harlean's story by which I was fascinated; that young, fragile, tumultuous and doomed love story. Yet was it not that very same tumult, which seemed so intolerable, I wondered, that was, in part, a source of her strength to rise above and triumph? If her marriage had succeeded, would the world have the legend of Jean Harlow today?

It seemed the more desperately Chuck tried to hold on to her, the more he pressed her toward her inevitable destiny. For that, perhaps he is owed some small debt of gratitude, and a sense of understanding for the losing battle he waged. Years after their divorce, she is said to have spoken tenderly of Chuck, even tearfully, wondering what her life would have been like if she had remained his wife. As I completed *Platinum Doll* I found myself wondering that, as well.

Although this is a work of fiction, I have taken the greatest care to respectfully recount events as they are known to have occurred. Some private scenes, such as Chuck and Harlean's final farewell, or his appearance at the premiere, must be imagined, yet were based on their statements of one another years later, and on possibility.

For the sake of narrative flow, it was not recounted, but September 29, 1933, was the second time Jean Harlow left her handprints at Grauman's Chinese Theatre. She had done so four days earlier on September 25, but when the cement had dried it had shattered. Also of note, tennis courts had not yet been replaced by the swimming pool when the McGrews first arrived at the Beverly Hills Hotel, but it was added to acknowledge Harlean's love of swimming.

Throughout this work, I have tried faithfully to recount this period of Harlean's brief, shining life, consulted experts, walked in her footsteps, watched her films, read her novel, and it was my distinct privilege to do so.

I hope I have honored her truly extraordinary spirit.

One special note: true to Jean Bello's prediction, someone in the future did come to revere Jean Harlow. A little girl named Norma Jeane Baker grew up wanting to be just like her... Before she became Marilyn Monroe.

ACKNOWLEDGMENTS

Several Jean Harlow biographies were consulted for this project, particularly, but not exclusively: *Bombshell* by David Stenn; *Jean Harlow, Tarnished Angel* by David Bret; and *Harlow in Hollywood* by Darrell Rooney and Mark A. Vieira. Other works include: *The Story of Hollywood* by Gregory Paul Williams; *Adventures of a Hollywood Secretary: Her Private Letters from Inside the Studios of the 1920s*, edited by Cari Beauchamp; *Early Beverly Hills* by Marc Wanamaker; *Historic Hotels of Los Angeles and Hollywood* by Ruth Wallach; and *Movie Studios of Culver City* by Julie Lugo Cerra and Marc Wanamaker.

I also wish most sincerely to acknowledge and thank: Harlow aficionado extraordinaire, and digital artist, Victor Mascaro (@hollywood_stars_in_color), for his support for and knowledge of this project; Elisa Jordan of L.A. Woman Tours for leading me, with such amazing detail, through the steps of Harlow's Hollywood; the Max Factor Museum for allowing me access to their wonderful Harlow memorabilia collection; and the Hollywood Chamber of Commerce.

My continued respect and admiration for the fabulous Irene

Goodman, a literary agent and friend, unparalleled in support and encouragement of her authors.

Once again, and as always, my deepest thanks go to my unfailingly supportive family and an awesome group of friends who keep me wanting to tell these wonderful true stories from history: Ken, Elizabeth and Alex Haeger, Kelly Stevens, Karen Thorne Isé, Sarah Galluppi, Rebecca Seltzner, and Marie Mazzuca. Your love and encouragement are my greatest sources of inspiration.

PLATINUM
DOLL

ANNE GIRARD

Reader's Guide

MIRA®

1. Shortly after their arrival in Hollywood, Harlean declares that she has no interest in becoming an actress. Do you think she actually believed that of herself at that point?

2. When Harlean agrees to pose for Edwin Bower Hesser, she decides not to tell Chuck about it, despite the likelihood that the photographs will one day be published. Did you attribute that decision exclusively to her youth, or did you feel that some part of her was hoping the photographs might force an issue between them? What might have happened if Chuck had been accepting of that photo session rather than angry?

3. Mother Jean and Harlean have a complex relationship throughout the novel, as they really did during her short life. Did you find yourself understanding Harlean's inability to stand up to her mother, or was that relationship difficult to read about? How did their use of the terms "Mommie" and "Baby" for each other strike you?

4. In the scenes recounting actual events, like the "underdress" mishap, or the San Francisco trip, was

Harlean's naïveté understandable to you given her age, or was it difficult to relate to when faced with the mindset of today's wiser teens?

5. Toward the end of her life, Harlean sorrowfully acknowledged the loss of the child she had conceived during her marriage to Chuck. Did her youth, and her misgivings about Chuck's drinking and propensity toward violence, make her decision somewhat understandable to you? If not, why not?

6. Chuck and Harlean had a tumultuous, short-lived marriage. For its demise, did you find yourself blaming their youth or Mother Jean's influence more? Could anything have changed what happened?

7. While we don't see the marriage between Harlean and Paul Bern take place, that, too, was of a short duration. Knowing what you do of Harlean's spirit and ambition vs. her desire to be loved, if Bern had not died suddenly, do you think they would have remained married?

Why did you choose Jean Harlow as the subject for this novel? What about her life—and in particular, the part of her life recounted in *Platinum Doll*—were you initially drawn to?

While Harlow was a major star in the 1930s, and she has achieved icon status since then, there also seems to be a whole generation who knows nothing about her, the impact she had on Hollywood—or the influence she had on a young Marilyn Monroe. That was a huge draw for me creatively. I was fascinated by her coming-of-age story, her infectious spirit and how she triumphed in such a competitive business. Her marriage to Chuck has been eclipsed through the years and I also felt a duty to share a part of his story for how important he was at the time to her.

In the course of your research, what was the most interesting and surprising thing you learned about Jean Harlow?

I loved learning that she was well-educated, that she loved reading and writing, and that she once described herself as a bookworm. The book she begins writing in the novel, Today Is Tonight, was published after her death. I was also particularly drawn to her love of animals. Learning about the many facets of her life, was a wonderful reminder that one shouldn't judge a book by its cover. There was so much depth beneath that stunning platinum hair.

What was the most challenging part of writing *Platinum Doll*? The most rewarding?

Based on the research of her biographers, I accepted the premise that abortion was the likely cause of the loss of her child. It was a challenging sequence to write, particularly because, later, Harlow was quoted as saying that one of her greatest regrets was the loss of that same child. Trying to take on Harlean's mindset, theorizing about why she allowed it to happen, and yet making that sensitive and highly personal decision understandable and palatable for readers was probably what challenged me the most. I hope I succeeded.

I think the most rewarding part occurred during my research as I discovered what a huge legion of wonderful, devoted experts and fans Jean Harlow maintains to this day. I was privileged to get to know many of them during the process, to visit many of the places Harlow knew, and to benefit from their broad knowledge of her life. I was thrilled to be able to add many of those details to the novel.

In your previous book, *Madame Picasso*, you explored the art world of Paris. In *Platinum Doll*, you wrote about film in America. What is it about the cultural arts of the early twentieth century that you find most inspiring as a writer?

The period from the turn of the century all the way through the 1930s was a time of such dynamic and explosive creativity, and new thought, which is so exciting to contemplate and to imagine having been a part of, whether in art, literature or film. sure to those who lived it, it felt like anything was possible. own career, I continue to be inspired by the idea of crossing creative boundaries and the possibility of being part of something totally new, just as Pablo Picasso and Jean Harlow both were.

Can you describe your writing process? Do you outline first or dive right in? Do you write scenes consecutively or jump around? Do you have a writing schedule or routine? A lucky charm?

I begin by reading everything I can get my hands on about my subject, as well as the times in which they lived—history, politics, fashion—so that I have a framework established in my mind. I do make a general outline of where I think the story will go, but then I dive in. I write scenes consecutively, but oftentimes the story veers completely away from the outline I intended it to follow as I get to know the characters and allow them to tell their story through me. That really is the best part of the process. My schedule is fairly strict. First coffee, and then I write at least something every day, almost always mornings so that I don't lose the flow of the story. My lucky charm is a coin, a 1551 douzain from the French Renaissance I found on my first research trip. I keep it on my desk to remind me that the people I write about were once as real as that coin, and so I have a duty to be respectful with the stories I have been entrusted to tell.